Sorrow's Requiem

ALAN NASH

authorHOUSE®

AuthorHouse™ UK Ltd.
1663 Liberty Drive
Bloomington, IN 47403 USA
www.authorhouse.co.uk
Phone: 0800.197.4150

© 2014 Alan Nash. All rights reserved.

*No part of this book may be reproduced, stored in
a retrieval system, or transmitted by any means
without the written permission of the author.*

Published by AuthorHouse 01/14/2014

ISBN: 978-1-4918-8875-9 (sc)
ISBN: 978-1-4918-8876-6 (e)

*Any people depicted in stock imagery provided by Thinkstock are models,
and such images are being used for illustrative purposes only.
Certain stock imagery © Thinkstock.*

*Because of the dynamic nature of the Internet, any web addresses or
links contained in this book may have changed since publication and
may no longer be valid. The views expressed in this work are solely those
of the author and do not necessarily reflect the views of the publisher,
and the publisher hereby disclaims any responsibility for them.*

In memory of Nick-Nick.

To the real Steph,
I'll always be here.

Prologue

DECEMBER 1989

The suburb sat quietly on the outskirts of the city, unrecognised as being a place of any real money yet, equally, none of the residents would describe themselves as being in any financial hardship. All of the homes had gardens that were maintained religiously, all of the driveways contained at least one family car and everyone was known to each other, if only by their first names in some cases. It was a picturesque scene, the likes of which wouldn't be out of place if it were to adorn the front of a festive greeting card, especially on a night like this as the snow fell lazily through the still air, slowly adding to the thick blanket of white that covered anything that wasn't moving.

All along the street, curtains were closed to the darkness as families enjoyed their night together, playing games or watching the seasonal programming on their televisions. Young children lay in their beds, dreaming of the gifts Santa would be bringing them as their parents wrapped the presents before finding a place in which they would be hidden away from youthful investigation.

Plotting a cautious route through the snow, a plain black car made its way slowly along the street, eventually pulling up outside one of the homes. The driver, a young man in his early twenties, cut the engine and turned off the headlights before reaching across to remove a package from the glove box, which he placed on the passenger seat. He then leant forward to take off his treasured leather vest, slipping on a plain, black, hooded top in its place, leaving the hood up in order to fully cover his head.

The man took a moment to study the back of the vest, his sacred Cut, as he'd done so many times over the last couple of months, running his fingers over the patch that was sewn into the leather. The patch was an image of a skull with a solitary tear falling from the right eye socket. Above the skull were emblazoned the words 'SONS OF SORROW' and underneath was the name of the city.

It'd taken him nearly two years of suffering, two years of living as a second-class citizen whilst he served his time as a probationary member but, eventually, they'd voted him in and awarded him his top-rocker. It was the moment he'd been waiting for, the moment at which he'd become a fully-fledged member of the Motorcycle Club and the moment from which he'd finally be able to make a difference. Now, that difference was about to be realised.

"And so it begins" Ruckus muttered under his breath, before carefully folding the Cut and hiding it under the driver's seat.

With a deep breath he picked up the parcel, opened the door and jumped out of the car, stealing a glance up and down the street as he pulled the hood tightly around his face. The snow was getting heavier, he noted, and that was just what he needed as he made his way up the driveway to the front door of the house.

The woman who answered his knock must have been in her late thirties and, despite the baggy jumper and tracksuit bottoms hiding her figure, it was clear that she looked after herself, as did every woman in the neighbourhood, he expected; it wouldn't be done to let your image slip around here, would it?

"Can I help you?" she asked, tentatively.

"I'm so sorry to trouble you" Ruckus answered, politely. "But I need to speak to Malcolm, if he's in?"

Emphasizing a glance at her watch, the woman made no attempt to disguise her feelings towards the imposition. "We weren't expecting to have any visitors" she said, sharply.

Nodding, Ruckus made sure to display contriteness by keeping his head lowered. "I appreciate that" he replied, "and I wouldn't intrude on your evening if it wasn't urgent. I really need to see him."

"What about?" the woman asked. "And who are you?"

"Of course, I should have introduced myself. I'm Mike. I work with Malcolm and I need to get this package to him before our meeting in the morning."

"He hasn't mentioned any meeting."

"That's why I need to speak with him."

"Couldn't you have telephoned?"

"I wanted to" he said, "but the snow's knocked out my phone line and he really needs to know about what's happening tomorrow morning. That's why I drove all the way out here."

The woman hesitated, glancing back inside the house as the concept of someone going to such lengths began to work its way through her initial frostiness. "OK" she finally agreed, stepping aside to allow him in from the cold. "He's in the study."

Thanking her, Ruckus stepped in through the door, making a big gesture of his attempt to wipe all of the snow from his boots. "Would you like me to take these off?" he asked, as the woman closed the door behind him.

"Oh, don't worry about it" the woman replied, finally smiling at him. "It's just wood and tiles from here to there; it'll only take a moment to mop up any footprints. Would you like a hot drink? You must be freezing?"

"No thank you" Ruckus smiled in reply. "I should only be a few minutes and then I'll leave you all in peace."

The woman nodded and led him through the house, knocking on the study door as they entered.

"Mike's here to see you about a meeting at work tomorrow" she announced.

A momentary look of confusion flashed across Malcolm's face as he looked up and saw the man standing in the doorway. "How the devil are you, Mike?" he asked, chirpily. "And what are you doing, bothering me at this time of night? Don't you ever stop working?"

"You know how it is. Live to work, and all that" Ruckus chuckled in reply.

Malcolm rose from his desk and stepped across the room to shake his hand before gently ushering his wife out and closing the door.

"What the hell are you doing here?" he hissed, when he was sure they couldn't be heard.

Despite the man's size, Ruckus wasn't intimidated in the slightest. "You owe us money" he replied, calmly stepping past and taking a seat at the desk, placing the package in front of him as he leant back and put his feet up on the impeccably varnished mahogany. "It's time for you to settle the debt."

"And Billy sent you, did he?" Malcolm questioned angrily, as he walked around the desk and returned to his seat. "Billy told you to come to my house in the middle of the night and collect money I've already told him I don't have?"

Reaching into his pocket, Ruckus pulled out a pack of cigarettes, without offering them to Malcolm as he took one for himself.

"We don't smoke in this house" Malcolm pointed out, but his words fell on deaf ears as Ruckus shrugged his shoulders and lit up anyway.

"And this is a very nice house" he replied, blowing smoke directly across the desk.

Silence fell between them, as Malcolm wafted the smoke away from his face, and then a slow smile began to spread across his lips. "What the hell do you think you're doing?" he asked. "Since when does Billy use strong-arm tactics like this?

Ruckus didn't respond, so Malcolm continued.

"You're new to this, aren't you? Well, you've got a lot to learn about how this works. You see, me and Billy go a long way back and he knows he'll get the money."

Again, there was no response forthcoming as Ruckus took another drag on his cigarette and sent more smoke billowing across the desk.

"My wife will smell that" Malcolm stated, again wafting his hands across his face, "and that'll bring her in here."

"Why would I give a fuck about that?" Ruckus asked in reply. "Bring her in; I'm sure she'd be interested to know how you spend your evenings."

"There are no secrets between me and her." Malcolm lied.

"So she knows you gamble your money away on a regular basis, does she? She knows that you come into our Casino when you're supposed to be working and risk everythin' on the flip of a card?"

"I'd hardly say that I'm risking everything. I've never exceeded my limit."

"It's got fuck all to do with your limit" Ruckus answered. "The only limit you need to worry about is the limit of our generosity and, at the last count, it seems that line was reached and breached, my friend."

"I'll let Billy be the judge of that, and we're not friends."

Ruckus shook his head as he leant forward to take the mug that was sitting on a coaster. "Well, Billy's judged" he said, tapping the excess ash from his cigarette into the drink.

"You expect me to believe Billy's decided that without telling me?" Malcolm asked, ignoring the disrespect.

"No," Ruckus replied, "I expect you to pay the fuck up."

Silence again fell between them, as Malcolm considered the statement. "And how do you expect me to do that, at this late hour?" he asked.

Ruckus took a long, sweeping look around the room before answering. "Like I said," he eventually answered, "this is a real nice house. It's the kind of house I'd expect would have a safe secreted somewhere in a real nice study, such as this one we're sitting in right now. In fact, I'd suggest it'd be the kind of safe that someone put a tidy sum of money in this afternoon."

Now Malcolm's expression changed, just slightly, as the confidence he'd carried started to waver.

"What are you talking about?" he asked, a little unsteadily.

"I'm talking about you openly stuffing cash into the thing, without checking for any bastards who were watching from your garden as you did."

"You've been spying on me?"

"I wouldn't call it spying" Ruckus argued, as he finished his cigarette and dropped the butt into the mug, finally taking his feet from the desk and sitting forward in his chair. "It was more like keepin' a close eye on our investments."

"Your investments?" Malcolm asked.

"Yeah, our investments" Ruckus smiled. "We're applyin' twenty percent interest to cover the debt."

Shaking his head, Malcolm began to smile again. "I get it" he announced, now sitting back himself. "You're new and you're trying to impress your boss, is that right? You're trying to show him you're worth keeping around?"

Ruckus only maintained his smiled in response.

"You think that, by coming in here and taking my money, Billy will be pleased with you?" Malcolm continued. "Well, now it's time for you to listen up, boy. As I've told Billy before, you'll get your money when I'm good and ready to hand it over and, until then, you'll just carry on my line of credit as you've always done. I don't really know what's brought about this pathetic attempt to hustle me but, quite frankly, I'm disappointed to see it."

Ruckus continued to smile.

"Are you even listening to me?" Malcolm asked. "Are you even hearing what I'm saying? Let me help you out, in case I'm being a little too subtle for your tiny mind to comprehend. It's time for you to leave."

The last sentence was drawn out slowly, each word emphasized and dripping with distain, yet Ruckus' smile didn't falter for a second as he rose from his seat and picked up the package. "Ah well" he sighed, "It was worth a try."

Now laughing, Malcolm also rose to his feet. "You boys might know how to run an illegal casino" he chuckled, "but you sure as hell know nothing about anything else. You've always been small-time and that's not going to change any time soon."

"You've got me there" Ruckus replied, as he allowed himself to be guided towards the door. "We have always been small-time and people like you know that. I guess that's why you know you can take advantage of our good nature?"

"I wouldn't call it taking advantage of you; it's more like utilising your generosity."

Ruckus nodded his appreciation of the sentiment. "That's really well put" he replied. "The thing is, it turns out that I'm not in the least bit generous."

With that, he ripped open the package and pulled out the Silenced Colt M1911 pistol he'd procured on the way there, slamming the butt of the gun into the side of Malcolm's head. The man staggered backwards and Ruckus quickly prevented any retribution by aiming the barrel of the gun directly between the man's eyes. "You see" he said, calmly. "I 'ain't like Billy, or the rest of them brow-beaten pussies who call themselves a Motorcycle Club. I'm not gonna stand by and watch as arrogant mother-fuckers like you take the piss out of us, just because we're worried about having to fend off a bit of heat. Times are changin' and you should feel proud that I've chosen you to be the beginning of the revolution. Now, open the fuckin' safe or I'll open up a hole in your fuckin' face."

Dazed from both the blow to his head and the sudden shift in the meeting, Malcolm struggled to find an answer as he stood, rooted to the spot.

"I said" Ruckus continued, ensuring that his words were filled with disdain, "open the fuckin' safe."

Malcolm shook his head. "I can't do that" he replied, as his orientation began to return. "That money isn't for you."

"It won't matter who it's for" Ruckus responded. "Not when your skull's dripping down the wall."

"Let me ring Billy" Malcolm asked, his voice now starting to shake with panic. "I can sort this out with him."

Ruckus looked at him and took a deep breath as he cricked his neck. "Fine" he said, as he opened the door and called out into the kitchen. "Could you pop in here for a moment, Darling? Malcolm's having a bit of a problem with something."

Wide-eyed, Malcolm watched as his wife entered the room. He stood, torn between backing down and jumping to attack, as Mike grabbed her by the throat and pinned her to the wall with the barrel of the gun pushed firmly into her eye socket. "Now" he hissed, "open the fuckin' safe!"

Still Malcolm didn't move, so Ruckus lowered the gun and pulled the trigger, sending a bullet into the woman's foot. Malcolm cried out as the gun was levelled back at the woman's head and her screams were quickly stifled by Ruckus' hand over her mouth. "Do you know why they call me Ruckus?" he asked, with a proud smile. "It's because I can't seem to go anywhere without creating some sort of big, unnecessary commotion."

"OK. Please stop" Malcolm begged. "I'll get you the money."

Tears streamed down the woman's face as the man finally moved over to where the safe was hidden in the floor behind the desk. He opened the door and pulled out a bag, emptying the contents on the desk. "That's all I have" he announced, without taking his eyes from his wife's. "It's not all of it, but I'll get you the rest as soon as I can."

Ruckus considered this for a moment, and then nodded. "That'll do" he said. "We'll consider the rest as being your payment."

"Payment for what?" Malcolm asked.

"For the message that's bein' sent to every other mother-fucker who thinks he can screw us over" Ruckus chuckled, as he pulled the trigger and allowed the woman's body to slump to the floor. Before Malcolm had the chance to react, Ruckus turned the gun towards him and sent a bullet directly through the middle of the man's forehead. "And for that, we thank you" he finished, as silence descended for a last time.

Bending down, Ruckus wiped his hand on the woman's jumper, removing the blood that'd splattered on his skin. He then picked up the discarded bag and re-filled it with the money before leaving the room and making his way to the front door.

As he reached the door, he turned to look back into the house and saw Malcolm's two young children watching him from the top of the stairs, their expressions a blend of confusion and intrigue. Judging by the look of them, they could only have been three or four years old, and they must have come to investigate the strange noises they'd heard downstairs.

"Shit" he mumbled to himself, as he raised his gun.

Chapter 1

JULY 2010

Saturday night in The Skinning Pit could never be described as being particularly busy, not in comparison to other venues. Perhaps it was down its location? Standing alone and proud amidst offices and small businesses, the place was well away from the central hub of nightlife. Then again, maybe it had more to do with the genre of music with which the owners of the bar persisted? For years the Heavy Metal scene had been dying out, gradually being replaced with catchy rock tunes and pop anthems that, at best, would be described as Bubble Gum by the more discerning of listeners. Yet The Skinning Pit stubbornly maintained its dedication to the 'old school'.

Realistically, it was probably a little of both, but that was how the staff and patrons liked it. Although, externally, they may argue they carried a more accepting nature, a more open mind to the alternative than some of the more fashionable members of the public, the truth was that they thrived on the fact that they were considered outcasts by society. They loved the fact that, to most, they were regarded as being weird and more than a little tapped and it was somewhat ironic that, in their attempt to prove themselves as being unique in a world of judgement, they'd created one of the most elite of places in which to relax.

"Heads up, Grizzly. You've got a fan!" Sam whispered, nodding towards the end of the bar as he turned to put the customer's money in the till.

Unable to stop himself, Ben followed his friend's gaze along the sea of faces, until his eyes rested upon the young, very attractive woman at the end of the line. "Don't be ridiculous" he whispered back.

Sam shook his head. "Really?" he asked. "Well, why then, is she sitting with her friends on my side of the room, yet she insists on going to your end of the bar to be served?"

"That'd be because she knows she's actually going to get a drink from my end, as opposed to dying of thirst while she waits for you to stop screwing around" Ben laughed.

"Go fuck yourself!" Sam smiled. "Just because you throw the drinks at people, doesn't mean that you're a better barman. Ok then, so tell me why, given she's in a group of five people, she's the only one who comes to get the drinks? And take a look at her. Take a look at what she's wearing. Are you seriously trying to tell me that a bunch of young girls, all decked to the nines in the height of fashion, are actually closet fans of Thrash and Hardcore Metal? Look at them, they'd all rather be in church than spend any more time in here, yet she's insisting they stay. Why is that?"

Ben hesitated for a second, giving his friend all the encouragement he needed.

"You fucker, you know I'm right!" Sam laughed. "Well?"

"Well what?" Ben asked, somewhat lamely.

"Well are you gonna tap that, or what?"

"Don't go there" Ben replied.

"Don't go where? Up the sweetest valley in here tonight?"

Ben shook his head.

"No, seriously" Sam continued. "She's young, she's hot and she's got an ass you'd find it hard to resist biting a chunk out of."

Again, Ben shook his head in response, but Sam wouldn't let up.

"Dude!" he explained, disappointedly. "A few years ago, you'd have been smashing the youth out of her before we'd even finished closing up. You've gotta snap out of this."

"What are you guys talking about?" Steph interrupted, as she struggled through to the bar with armfuls of empty glasses.

"Nothing" Ben replied sheepishly, taking the glasses from her.

"Bullshit!" Sam laughed, flashing Ben a knowing glance. "I was just pointing out the presence of a stalker to this poor, clueless fool."

"Oh, you mean that pretty, young, hot bit of stuff who can't take her lustful eyes off him?"

"You too?" Ben pleaded, as he loaded the glasses into the washer.

"She was asking about you" Steph continued, revelling in his discomfort. "She wanted to know if you were single."

"Did you tell her he was gagging for it?" Sam asked, thoroughly enjoying his turning of the screw.

"Of course not!" Steph exclaimed. "I told her he was struggling to get over being hurt in a long-term relationship and that what he really needs right now is just for someone to hold him and be there for him, on account of his firm belief in true love!"

"And she fell for that?" Sam asked, laughing as he patted Ben on the shoulder.

"I don't know" Steph laughed in reply. "But all of them had full drinks when she announced she was getting another round in."

"Ah, shit" Ben sighed. "Well, thanks to you two retards, I'm gonna have to find a way of letting her down gently now, aren't I?"

Steph smiled and raised her eyebrow. "Or you could just see where it goes and have a little fun?"

Ben froze as his thoughts desperately scrabbled to find a response, until a loud crash resounded from the back of the room.

"What the hell was that?" Sam asked, getting up on his toes to try and see over the crowd.

"I'll bet it was that group of idiots who've been in here all day" Steph suggested.

Standing at well over six foot tall, Ben was easily able to look over the crowd and see the circle that'd formed around the fight. "For God's sake" he muttered. "Can't we just have one Saturday night when it doesn't kick off?"

"And deprive you of your chance to shine?" Sam asked, lifting the hatch and standing back to allow Ben through.

"Or my chance to get my ass handed to me" Ben replied, looking back from the hatchway.

Sam looked up and down the man's giant frame, taking in the muscles that practically rippled under the strained fabric of his t-shirt. "Like that'll ever happen" he laughed.

Shaking his head, Ben moved out into the crowd, with Sam following closely behind. Regardless of the confidence they had in him, he always worried when things like this happened, he always worried about the possibility that some minor incident or some small fracas could escalate into something that even he wasn't able to handle. In his early days here, it would usually have been just a couple of lads who'd had a few too many beers and allowed a simple argument to descend into something more sinister. Nowadays though, with the rapid rise of gangs and violence on the streets of the city, there was always a chance that it could be an issue which proved to be far more dangerous than a drunken disagreement.

Reaching the source of the commotion, Ben saw that Steph had been right; it was the group who'd been in there since early afternoon and two of them were locked together, rolling around pathetically on the floor as they tried and failed to land any real blows. The rest of them were stood back amongst the crowd, yelling encouragement to neither man in particular, enjoying the fight with seemingly no interest in who might emerge the victor.

Stepping forward, Ben grabbed each of the brawling men by their arm and, with consummate ease, lifted them both to their feet, holding them apart as they continued to swing their fists.

"Are you sure you're ok?" Steph asked, gently running her hand over the back of Ben's head as she checked for any swelling.

The four of them, Steph, Ben, Sam and Andy, the bar's DJ, were sitting at their usual table for closing-time drinks. The room now resounded with the familiar silence that followed the locking of the doors and they could finally relax into their down time after what had proven to be an eventful night.

"I'm sure" Ben replied, trying to hide just how much he was enjoying her delicate touch. "It was only a glancing blow."

Sam snorted his disagreement. "A glancing blow?" he remarked. "Dude, the piece of shit smashed a bottle on your head."

"Ah, he caught me with the weak part of the glass. I'd have been screwed if he'd clocked me with the base."

"Like that would've made a difference" Andy pitched in. "Your head's like a block of concrete, mate."

"Yeah, but his heart's soft as shit" Sam chuckled. "Seriously Dude, you should've smacked the guy into next week."

Steph flashed them both a disapproving glance. "You're laughing about this" she said, "but them idiots could've done some real damage tonight."

"You're kidding, right?" Andy asked. "Did you see the guy's face when Ben turned to look at him and he realised all he'd done was piss him off? I tell you, I could smell the shit from all the way back there in the booth!"

"I do wish I'd have seen that" Steph admitted, allowing her lips to develop into a wry smile as she looked at Ben. "He'll be having nightmares about you for the next week, at least."

"He's not the only one who'll be having dreams about you" laughed Sam. "I'm pretty sure your stalker would've given anything to be in the guy's place when you picked him up and carried him out the doors"

Ben let out a long sigh. "Not this again?"

"Of course this again. The girl couldn't take her eyes off those big, strapping arms of yours and she practically creamed herself when you came back to throw out the other two pricks. When they took one look at you and ran for it, that poor girl had already made up her mind she was going to marry the shit out of you!"

Steph rolled her eyes. "Don't be so disgusting, Sam" she scolded, before smiling as she finished her sentence. "You shouldn't be so crass about how a woman's body reacts when she's in love."

Her last word was drawn out with a wavering, sickly tone to her voice as she playfully nudged her shoulder against Ben's.

"So, who's betting she's waiting outside when we leave?" she continued.

"Who's betting she's already planning the wedding?" Andy laughed.

"And who's calling the ambulance, when I knock you all out?" Ben replied, as a smile spread across his lips.

"Ah, crap" Sam announced, glancing at his watch. "The stud's getting arsey, so I think it's time to call it a night."

Steph looked disappointed. "You're not staying for another drink?" she asked.

"I wish I could, but I'm on strict instructions from her indoors; I'm to be home at a reasonable hour tonight, otherwise I'll have hell to pay in the morning."

"Yeah, I've gotta go too" Andy told them. "You want a lift mate?"

Sam nodded.

"How about you two?" Andy asked.

"I want another drink" Steph replied, looking at Ben. "You up for another one?"

Ben didn't hesitate in agreeing and, as he did, he couldn't fail to spot the sideways glance Sam flashed at him as he rose from the table.

"Well, you two be good" Sam smiled, focussing his attention on Ben in particular. "And watch out for any stray stalkers when you leave."

"Don't worry" Steph smiled, "Ben's got me here to protect him."

"Yeah, that sure fills me with confidence" Sam laughed, before narrowing his eyes slightly and focussing on Ben. "I'll see you tomorrow."

With that, Sam and Andy said their goodbyes, leaving Ben and Steph alone in the dim light of the bar. Ben fetched them both another drink and, when he returned to the table, Steph was staring quizzically at him.

"What?" he asked.

Steph continued to stare.

"You're starting to freak me out" he joked, although he had a strong feeling she was about to broach a subject that caused him no small amount of unease. "Have I got something on my face?"

"I'm just trying to work out what was wrong with her" Steph replied, confirming his fears.

"What was wrong with who?"

"Do I really need to tell you?"

Ben looked at her blankly and took a long swig of his drink as he tried to come up with a response. "I don't know what you're talking about" he finally answered.

Steph sat back in her seat and stared deeply into his eyes. "Ben" she said, quietly. "She was hot, she was sweet and she was clearly into you in a big way. Why wouldn't you want some of that?"

Breaking eye contact, Ben turned his attention to the label on his bottle, of which he was making a good job of ripping off as he again found himself searching desperately for a response the woman would accept. "I'm just not comfortable with the idea of picking up a girl in a bar like that" he finally answered, immediately realising how crap it sounded.

"Picking up a girl like that?" came the instant, and not unsurprising, reply. "You mean talking to someone you're attracted to, getting to know them and then deciding whether you want things to go any further?"

Ben took a breath, unable to respond.

"There's nothing sinister about that" Steph continued. "It's actually quite a normal way of doing things and you know that, which is why I'm guessing there's some other reason for your refusal to even try."

Now Ben could feel his heart racing in his chest as his cheeks began to flush and he reached into his jacket pocket to pull out a pack of cigarettes. He offered one to Steph, without resuming eye contact, and then took one for himself. "I just wasn't that in to her" he replied, after lighting both of their cigarettes and taking a long drag of his own.

Steph shook her head and took a moment to study him before speaking again.

"I don't get it" she said. "Almost every night I work with you, you have women practically throwing themselves across the bar, yet I've never seen you accept any of their advances. It's been what, three years? Why don't you want any of them? Surely you've been attracted to some of them? Even I've been attracted to some of them and I've never been so much as curious in that sense."

Ben shrugged, still floundering for something to say.

"What is it?" Steph asked. "Don't you want to be with anyone? Is it that you want to be on your own? Because I can't believe that spending your time alone in that flat is . . ."

"Please, just leave it" Ben snapped, cutting her short and then instantly regretting it.

Steph looked at him, stunned, as the silence of the room began to weigh down on them.

"I'm sorry" Ben whispered. "I just don't want to talk about it."

The initial shock of his outburst began to edge away from her expression and her features softened as she smiled and took his hand in hers. He looked at her and she gazed deeply into his eyes as she spoke.

"No, I'm sorry" she said. "I know I go on about it and I shouldn't, it's just that you've always been there for me when I've needed you, right from the first time we met and I was trying to deal with all the shit I had in my life back then. I was struggling and it didn't help that every guy I came across had no interest in helping me or talking to me like a normal human being; they all wanted something from me, but you didn't. You were so different to all of them that I knew I could trust you, I knew I could tell you things I've never told anyone and I can't begin to tell you how much that meant to me, both then and now. Ben, I love you in a way I've never loved anyone else in my life and I just want to see you happy."

As his heart tried to burst its way through his chest and his ears were filled with the sound of the blood rushing through his veins, Ben knew exactly what he wanted to say to her, he knew exactly what he wanted to do and, for a second, he thought he might actually succeed. He took a breath as thoughts began to bombard his mind, storming across his brain like a hoard of mercenaries hunting for a kill, bringing with them the inherent knowledge that'd plagued him for so long.

"I know" he replied, once again giving in to the inevitable, "and I appreciate that. I am happy, Steph."

Steph looked at him for a while longer, making no attempt to disguise her doubt. She sighed and then leaned in to kiss him on the cheek. "I hope so" she whispered into his ear, before pulling back and taking a swig of her drink.

Ben waved to Steph as the taxi pulled away from the kerb and zipped up his leather jacket in response to the breeze. It may have been summer and the days were getting hotter, but the early hours of the morning still held an icy chill and, for some reason, he was feeling the cold a little more than usual tonight. Lighting a cigarette, Ben turned to begin his usual walk home as his thoughts drifted to the conversation he and Steph had just shared.

What had she meant by telling him she loved him in a way she'd never loved anyone before? And why had she kissed him on the cheek? They'd always hugged when they said goodbye, but she hadn't kissed him before. Was she trying to imply something? But, if she was, then surely she wouldn't have pushed so hard for him to hook up with that woman, would she? Maybe it was some sort of a test? Maybe she was just trying to see whether he was open to other options?

"Jesus Christ" he muttered to his reflection as he passed The Skinning Pit's blacked-out windows. "What the fuck are you doing?"

He'd been here before, trying to wrap his head around the most innocent of gestures. The fact was that the woman was in a long-term relationship and there'd been no indication that would change any time soon. He and

Steph were close friends, that's all. They were close friends and he was almost hurt tonight, so it was understandable that she'd be a little more emotional than normal. As for the comment that she loved him in a way she'd never loved anyone before, well he'd spent the whole time he'd known her making sure that he was there as a true friend, so why wouldn't she feel closer to him than any of her other friends? He'd positively and deliberately encouraged that very feeling, so why was he now having difficulty understanding it? Why was he making such a big deal out of it?

Taking a deep drag on his cigarette, he inhaled deeply and shook his head as he expelled the smoke into the air. Maybe he should've taken advantage of that woman tonight? She was stunning, he couldn't argue with that, and she'd clearly been making an effort to talk to him. For all the jokes, Sam was right, it wouldn't have taken much to get her number and maybe that was what he needed? For the last three years he'd convinced himself that he wouldn't find anyone he wanted to be with more than he wanted to be with Steph, but how did he know unless he gave someone a chance? It was a question which went unanswered as he passed the alleyway that ran along the side of the bar and the sound of movement came from the shadows.

Startled, Ben's heart raced as he stopped in his tracks and peered into the darkness. He listened intently as silence returned and chastised himself for his unease. It was the middle of the night, so it wasn't going to be anything more than a cat or a fox disturbing the discarded bottles in the bins that he himself had put out there only a couple of hours before. What did he think it was? Burglars trying to break their way into a bar whose takings were modest to say the least? Or did he possibly think that the guys he'd thrown out had waited for hours in the cold, just to try and give him a beating in retribution? Laughing at his own ridiculousness, Ben turned away to continue his walk home, until another noise came from the alley. This time it was louder and he was sure he heard a groan.

"Shit!" he cursed, as his heart picked up the pace once more.

For a moment, all he wanted to do was pretend he hadn't heard anything. He wanted to turn and walk away, to get back to the warmth and safety of his home, but what if someone was in real trouble back there? No matter how much he wanted to deny it, the noise was one of real pain and, deep down, he knew that if he walked away now, then it would always play on his mind.

Another groan carried through in the breeze and he almost choked on the lump that'd formed in his throat.

"Hello" he called out, figuring that he should at least check the situation before trying to call for any help. "Can you hear me?"

The sound of his voice resulted in sudden, seemingly startled movement amongst the bottles and refuse that always lined the floor of the alley, and then silence returned once more.

"Hello" he called again. "I'm not going to hurt you. I just want to check you're ok. I'm coming in, so don't be scared."

This time there was no response, so he took a few steps into the alley and then waited a few seconds for his eyes to adjust to the darkness. Having taken out the empties so many times, he knew the alley like the back of his hand and it was only a matter of moments before he could make out the big, industrial bins against the wall about a hundred yards ahead of him. There was no sign of anyone there but, given the wind had a tendency to whip along the gap in the buildings, he presumed that the person was sheltering in the space between the bins.

As he slowly moved further into the alley, the crunching of broken glass under his feet seemed to become louder within the confines of the walls and he heard more movement ahead of him. He stopped for a second, desperate not to scare whoever was there, and he took a breath to speak again, but his words were halted when he saw the long hair hanging over the side of the bottle bin.

The person wasn't sheltering in between the bins. For some reason, they were lying amongst the broken glass.

The lights were off as Steph walked in and she closed the door behind her before pausing for a moment in the darkness, surprised to hear the shower running. She turned the hallway light on and glanced at her watch, noting that it was past three in the morning. Maybe Rob had just got home from a night out, she thought to herself as she slipped off her jacket and contemplated making a hot chocolate before she took herself to bed, but she was sure he'd said he was staying in tonight.

"Rob, I'm home" she called up the stairs, before walking through to the kitchen and turning the kettle on.

There was no response from Rob, probably because he hadn't heard her over the sound of the water, so she headed up the stairs whilst the water boiled.

"Rob, I'm home" she tried again, next to the bathroom door, and she couldn't help but let out a giggle at the sound of him slipping in the bath; it was nice to know she could still startle him at times.

A second or so later, a somewhat hasty acknowledgement came from behind the door as the water was turned off and she heard him stepping quickly out of the bath. She chuckled again as she walked through to the bedroom to get changed, where the surprise that'd greeted her when she walked into the house turned rapidly into confusion.

The bed had clearly been slept in, as the sheets were balled up on the floor in a way that suggested they were ready to be loaded into the washing machine, with the duvet discarded on the floor. The windows were wide open, allowing a chilling breeze to flow freely into the room, and there was a strange smell in the air, although she couldn't tell exactly what it was. Her first thought was that Rob had probably got drunk and had himself an accident, it wouldn't be the first time that'd happened, but that wasn't what she could smell, was it? It was less of an affront to the senses, more flowery and pleasant...

"You're back early!" Rob exclaimed, cutting off her thoughts as he rushed through the door.

She looked at him, still dripping wet and trying awkwardly to wrap a towel around his waist whilst he practically ran towards her. "What..." she began, but he cut her off in his haste to provide an explanation.

"We need to get a new duvet" he announced, sternly. "I've been sweating buckets under that piece of shit thing tonight. Those sheets are soaked through."

"We've only just bought that one" she mumbled uncertainly, glancing from him to the duvet and then back again, "and it's the thinnest you can get."

"Well it ain't thin enough" he snapped.

Steph's mind tried to work its way through what was happening. "But we were freezing last night" she pointed out, "and tonight isn't exactly any warmer."

Rob looked at her and she noted the anger which flared in his eyes. "Whatever" he eventually stated, pushing past her to get to his dressing gown.

It was obvious that the man wasn't in any mood to talk, so Steph ignored the multitude of questions that ran through her head. "I'm making a hot chocolate" she said, as she walked over to the sheets. "I'll stick these in to wash."

"I'll sort those out" he hastily offered.

Startled, she stopped and turned to face him. "What?" she asked.

His expression had softened considerably. "I'm sorry" he said. "I was just frustrated at not bein' able to sleep. You have a sit down in the living room. I'll stick these on to wash and I'll bring you a hot chocolate."

The sudden and dramatic change in his mood caught Steph off-guard and she stood still for a second or two as she tried to understand what was happening.

"Seriously" he continued, "you're back early, so I figure you've had a shit night. You have a rest and I'll get you your drink."

"But I'm not back early" she answered, somewhat perplexed. "It's gone three in the morning and I'm normally back late when it's been a rough night."

"Is it?" he asked, genuinely surprised. "Shit, it felt as though I'd not got any sleep, but I must've had a couple of hours."

Steph looked at him; this was fast becoming bizarre. "It's ok" she said, turning away and walking downstairs to the kitchen, "I'll make it."

He hurried after her and, as she re-boiled the kettle, he threw the sheets into the machine and quickly positioned himself right next to her at the counter. His proximity caused her to take a step to the side as she reached for a mug.

"Do you want one?" she asked.

"Yeah, why not" he replied.

Now she was genuinely perturbed; he never drank hot chocolate. She moved to reach past him and get another mug from the draining board, but he leant across to stop her. "I'll get it for you" he muttered.

As he turned she looked past him and that was when she noticed the two wine glasses amongst the things on the draining board. "Did you use those?" she asked.

"Use what?" he questioned, failing to convince with his attempt to show surprise.

She shook her head. "The glasses" she confirmed.

Rob hesitated for a second. "Oh, those" he said, giving a less than genuine chuckle. "Yeah, Ginge came over with a couple of beers and the nob thought it'd be funny if we drank 'em out of wine glasses; like those ponces in the trendy bars."

"Ponces?" she questioned, as doubt flooded her mind.

"Yeah, you know" he urged. "Those ponces who drink fancy lagers from wine glasses."

"They're not drunk from wine glasses" she replied, the hesitation in her voice clearly portraying her uncertainty. "They're drunk from chalices."

"Well, excuse me" he said. "Whatever they're called, it was still funny."

"I guess you had to be there?" she asked.

Rob nodded. "Yeah, I guess you did. So, how was work?"

The kettle finished boiling, so Steph made their drinks and then took a seat at the kitchen table. "Wild" she answered. "There was another fight."

"Another one?" he asked, taking a seat opposite her. "They're becoming more regular."

"Only at the weekend."

"That's 'cause you only have customers over the weekend."

Steph gave a sarcastic laugh, instead of justifying his statement by arguing.

"Was anyone hurt?" Rob asked, ignoring her sarcasm.

"No, Ben put a stop to it before that happened. You should've seen him, Rob, it was awesome."

"What? Did he get on his knees and beg for them to put aside their differences, before leading them in a verse of Kum Ba Yah?" Rob laughed.

Ignoring his mickey-taking, Steph continued. "If you must know, he picked the two of them up like rag-dolls."

"But the hippy didn't throw a punch?"

"Of course he didn't, and he's not a hippy."

"Don't give me that gentle-giant bullshit. The guy's a purebred pussy."

"Why? Because he chooses not to hurt people?"

"That's exactly why he's a pussy. I'm not sayin' he should be goin' round picking fights, but if someone starts one then he should be able to end it."

"He does end them."

"No, he just moves them outside."

"What do you want him to do? Steam in there and knock everyone out?"

Rob pondered his response for a moment. "D'ya know what I think?" he replied, ignoring the question. "I think that, for all his size, the guy's soft as shit."

"He's not soft" Steph announced. "If you must know, one of the men smashed a bottle over his head and it didn't come close to fazing him."

"Big whoop" Rob laughed. "How can it faze him when there's nothin' in there to damage?"

Steph looked at him in disbelief. "Why are you doing this?" she asked.

"Why am I doin' what?"

"Slamming Ben."

"I'm not slamming him; I'm just having a laugh."

"No, you're not. You always do this whenever I mention him."

"Well, maybe I'm just sick of hearing how amazin' the guy is. If he's so amazin', why's he not got a woman, eh?"

Her silence provided all the encouragement to continue that Rob needed.

"I'll tell you why he doesn't have a woman" he stated. "He doesn't have a woman because he's a fucking homo!"

"I'm not even going to . . ."

"You're not even gonna what?" Rob interrupted, his voice becoming aggressive. "You're not gonna justify that with a response? You're not gonna rise to the bait? Fuck off, Steph. You always do this; you always stand up for that prick."

"That's because he's a good man" Steph calmly replied, "and he doesn't deserve this abuse, whether he's here or not."

"Oh, fuck off!" Rob exclaimed, hurling his mug across the kitchen and jumping up from the table. "If you love him so much, why don't you go and fuck him? Let me guess, the pussy has a needle-dick and, deep down, you know you need a real man to give you a good filling?"

With that, he stormed out of the kitchen, leaving Steph sitting there, stunned and wondering what the hell was going on.

Rushing forward, Ben almost lost his footing as his body involuntarily recoiled at the sight which greeted him when he got to the bin. The person back there wasn't a vagrant, it wasn't a drunk or a druggie; it was a woman and she was naked. All over her body, lacerations painted a morbid spider's web and her skin glistened with moisture that, from the smell and the colour, he could only guess as being a sick combination of blood, urine and, most likely, other bodily fluids.

Ben felt his legs weaken as his mind began to race, a barrage of thoughts fighting for precedence in his head as panic threatened to overcome him. He needed to check that she was still breathing, that much was obvious, but he also needed to keep her safe from any further harm and he needed to call for some help. Secondary to those thoughts, pushing their way in as a dramatic latecomer to the party, was the idea that whoever had done this to her might still be nearby and they might not take too kindly to someone interfering with their sick game.

With a deep breath, he tried to get things into some semblance of order. He hadn't seen anyone around as he walked towards the alley and it was more than likely that anyone leaving someone in this sort of mess wouldn't intend on hanging around to be caught. With that in mind, it was probably safe to presume that he was on his own out here, so that worry could be pushed away until proven wrong. That just left the issue of the girl herself, didn't it?

"Can you hear me?" he asked, as vague recollections of basic first aid training resurrected themselves in his mind. "My name's Ben Trowman and I want to help you."

At the sound of his voice, the woman let out a groan and tried to back away from him, but her movement was severely and painfully hampered by the broken glass in which she lay. It seemed redundant to tell himself that she was likely to be scared of anyone who came near, yet the knowledge of that pushed its way into his thinking anyway. So how was he going to help her if she wouldn't let him approach? He couldn't leave her in the cold like this and he hadn't exactly got a score of blankets and hot water bottles to hand.

Removing his phone and cigarettes from the pockets, he slipped off his jacket and tried to place it over her, but the proximity of his arms just caused more of an attempt to back away from him.

"I'm just trying to cover you up" he tried to tell her, but his voice only seemed to cause further anguish and he could see the pain in her expression increasing with every movement.

He wondered whether he'd be able to lift her out of the bin, but where would he put her then? Covered in shit and broken glass, the floor was probably worse. Maybe he could get her inside the bar? But that would mean leaving her alone whilst he opened the place up again and he worried that the act of moving and carrying her somewhere unknown would only further enhance her fear.

"Fuck!" he cursed, as frustration began to get the better of him.

Why was he being so hesitant? The fact was that this girl needed his help and he, right now, wasn't exactly stepping up to the plate. He needed to do something or she was going to die out here.

"Stop moving" he demanded, deliberately adding an edge to his voice. "If you move, the pain will only get worse as you're lying on broken glass. I'm going to cover you with my jacket and then I'm going to call for an ambulance. I'm not trying to hurt you."

Whether the tone of his voice had succeeded in getting through to her, or whether she was merely co-operating through fear, his words seemed to do the trick and she allowed him to cover her as best he could with his jacket. He then took a step back and punched the number into his phone.

As he awaited the response, Ben prayed that they would make it there in time to save her.

Chapter 2

All was quiet in the room, save for the steady beep of the heart-rate monitor which stood by the bed. Danielle Draper looked on as the girl slept peacefully, her face a picture of calm that somehow belittled the carnage which lay beneath the sheets. In over fifteen years as a fully-fledged doctor she'd dealt with countless cases of sexual assault and each one had left their own indelible stain on her heart, but this was by far and away the worst she'd ever seen.

The external injuries the girl had sustained were bad enough, a plethora of lacerations and bruises that could only have been caused by knives, glass, whips, chains and fists, but it was the internal damage that had left her reeling. The brutality of rape would often result in the tearing of flesh around the vagina and anus, but it'd taken them a long time to remove the splinters of wood and glass that were embedded deeply in both of this girl's orifices. She'd been exposed to a torture that went far beyond extreme and, even though the physical injuries would heal. Dani couldn't begin to fathom the psychological damage that had been done.

Noting the time, Dani filled in the details of her hourly check-up on the chart at the foot of the bed and took one final look at the girl before she left the room. As she closed the door quietly behind her, she was surprised to see her friend, Emily, rushing along the corridor towards her.

"What are you doing here?" Dani asked. "I thought you had the weekend off?"

"I'm covering a shift for Jan" Emily breathlessly replied as she pulled up in front of Dani. "I heard you were heading up the team looking after the girl. How's she doing?"

Dani looked at her, a little confused. "I thought Jan was away this weekend too?"

Emily shook her head and waved her hand dismissively in the air. "Bloody shift changes, don't worry about it" she mumbled. "How's the girl doing?"

"Not too good" Dani replied hesitantly, still a little confused by Emily being there but grateful that she was nonetheless. "But we've got her heavily sedated and we won't know how badly this has damaged her until she wakes up."

"Any idea who she is?"

"No, not yet. She was unconscious and naked when they brought her in, with no possessions and no way of checking her ID."

"What about the guy who found her? Doesn't he know anything?"

Again, Dani was a little taken aback; she didn't think the circumstances had been made public knowledge yet. "How do you know about him?" she asked.

Emily's expression took on the look of someone who was surprised by the question. "It's in the paper" she replied. "It says that the guy works in the bar next to which she was found. Apparently, he came across her when he was leaving work."

Shaking her head, Dani let out a short sigh. "Those vultures don't miss a trick, do they?" she exclaimed.

"What did you expect? They've got their fingers on every pulse in this city and they aren't going to miss something like this, it's liquid gold for their front pages. A local hero saves a poor girl? They've got outrage and heartwarming in equal dosage this time."

Dani glanced at her watch as she shook her head once more. "If they know about it already, then I'd better prepare the statement" she muttered, mainly for her own benefit. "I expect they'll be calling for updates any time soon."

"Forget that for now" Emily suggested. "Have you spoken to the guy who found her yet? I wonder if he might know something that'll help you to deal with her when she wakes up? Have you been given his contact details? You should give him a call."

"I was just on my way to speak to him."

A combination of surprise and intrigue painted themselves across Emily's expression. "He's here?" she exclaimed.

"Yes. He has been all night, he's in the waiting room."

Emily considered this for a moment. "I'll come with you" she said. "I'd like to see this hero for myself."

With a chuckle, Dani accepted the offer and led the way along the corridor. "So, how was the party last night?" she asked. "You don't seem too worse for wear, given it's only just gone seven o'clock."

"I didn't go in the end" Emily replied. "I figured it was better for me to get some sleep if I was going to work today."

"I'll bet your fella wasn't too happy with that?"

"No, he wasn't, but he understands. Besides, any annoyance he had about me not going has been overshadowed by his getting home after two and waking me up as he tried to get into bed through a haze of booze. The way I see it, it's going to take a fair bit of grovelling for me to let him off the hook."

"You are unbelievable" Dani marvelled.

"Why?" Emily asked, through a smile that was nearly as broad as her face.

"The guy plans for ages to take you out for a good time but you let him down and now you have him grovelling for forgiveness?"

"You say that as though it's a bad thing" Emily laughed, as they arrived at the door to the waiting room. "Which one is he?" she asked, peering through the window.

Dani glanced past her and scanned the room for a few seconds before pointing the way. "He's over there, in the corner."

Emily followed her gesture and then let out a slight gasp. "You're kidding me, right?" she mumbled. "I thought he was here to pick up my patient, the biker who lost an argument with a bus. He doesn't look like the kind of man who would wait around this long for a girl he claims not to know."

"Don't be so judgemental" Dani scolded. "What does it matter what he looks like?"

"Maybe it shouldn't matter what he looks like, but when the man is that big you need to be thinking twice about taking him off by yourself."

"Why? What's he likely to do?"

"It's not what he's likely to do, it's what he could do that worries me. Are you telling me that you're happy to take your chances with him?"

"I don't think there's any chance being taken" Dani argued, although her friend was starting to plant a seed of doubt. "The man stopped to help a stranger and has waited to find out whether she is ok. I hardly think that's the action of someone who intends to hurt somebody."

Stepping back from the window, Emily pulled Dani into the middle of the corridor and stared intently into her eyes. "I'm not joking here, Dani" she said, with all traces of humour gone from her voice. "I hope I'm wrong, I really do, but he looks like a biker and you said yourself that it must have been a group of people who did that to the girl."

Dani thought back through her conversation with Emily and didn't recall mentioning anything about the attack. Damn, she inwardly cursed, the media have probably started the speculation already and if they had, then she could be sure that their contact with the hospital would likely become borderline harassment.

"If it was a group of people" Emily continued, distracting Dani from her thoughts, "then there's a good chance it was one of those biker gangs and there's also the chance a man like him is involved with people like that."

"But, if he was" Dani replied, as her mind returned to the conversation, "then why would he have waited here for so long?"

"To make sure that she was dead?" Emily speculated.

"Don't be ridiculous. He was the one who called for the ambulance, so why would he have done that if he wanted her to die?"

Emily shrugged her shoulders, but the intent of her stare was unwavering. "Who's to say that he was the one who called the ambulance? How do you know that he hadn't gone back to check that she'd stopped breathing and came across the man who was actually trying to help her? Who's to say that he didn't kill that man and then take his place in the ambulance when it arrived?"

The premise was so big, so fanciful, that it was almost impossible to believe, yet Dani couldn't stop the seed growing in her mind as doubt began to wash right through her. She looked at her friend, hoping to see some evidence of jest in her eyes, but there was absolutely none. Maybe the woman was going over the top with her speculation and maybe it was unlikely, but how was she to know for certain? Then again, how could she do her job without some element of trust?

"Look" she said, trying to smile convincingly. "I know you're probably just being over the top with this, but I have to talk to the man. I have to try and find out more if I'm going to be able to help the girl when she wakes up. Just because he's big, doesn't mean he's not the good-natured man his actions paint him out to be."

Emily nodded as the seriousness softened in her expression. "You're probably right" she conceded. "I was just a bit shocked when you pointed to him."

Dani nodded her understanding of that as Emily glanced at her watch.

"I've got to go and check on my own biker" Emily smiled. "But you promise me that you'll be careful with that guy."

"I promise" Dani smiled back. "And I'll look forward to telling you how wrong you were."

After raising her eyebrow in acknowledgement, Emily turned and walked quickly along the corridor, leaving Dani alone to look again through the window and to take a deep breath before stepping through the door.

The voice cut into his doze, causing him to flinch in surprise as full consciousness suddenly returned.

"Mr Trowman?" Dani repeated, smiling kindly as he looked up at her.

"Yes" was all Ben could say in reply as his senses took their time in returning. "I'm sorry, I closed my eyes for just a second and . . ." he said, his sentence tailing off as a slight embarrassment prevented him from stating the obvious.

"It's not surprising" Dani chuckled kindly, "you've had a long night."

A brief and awkward silence fell as Ben searched desperately for something to say, opting for a slightly uncomfortable half-smile when he realised he had nothing.

"I'm Doctor Draper" Dani continued, eager to save the guy from the anguish that had so clearly painted itself across his expression. "The girl you helped is my patient."

"Has she woken up?" Ben asked, now feeling a little more composed.

Dani shook her head. "I'm afraid not, we've got her heavily sedated for now, until we can establish the full extent of the damage. Would you mind coming with me for a private chat?"

"About what?" he asked, his confusion causing the question to sound unintentionally aggressive.

"Just about the girl" Dani replied, thankfully ignoring the tone in his voice.

Ben shook his head. "I can't really tell you anything you don't already know" he said, a little more casually.

"We'll see" Dani smiled. "If nothing else, there's some good coffee in my office and the chairs are a lot more comfortable than out here."

Quickly rising to his feet, Ben towered above her and Dani involuntarily took a step back as she took in his full size. "That sounds good to me" he said a little nervously, as he realised he might have intimidated the woman. It wouldn't be the first time that'd happened and he inwardly cursed himself for forgetting that. "I can barely fit one of my cheeks on these small seats" he joked, in the hope that acknowledgement might help her recognise he meant no harm.

Dani smiled a little uneasily in response before leading him out of the waiting room. They walked along what seemed to Ben as being a labyrinth of corridors, until they reached her office and she opened the door to allow him in.

"Please, take a seat" she said, gesturing towards her desk as she made sure the door would remain wide open and walked across to the coffee machine. "How do you take your coffee?"

"White, with one sugar please" Ben replied, as he sat down.

Having made the drinks, Dani took to her own seat on the other side of the desk and waited a few moments whilst he took a sip of his drink. "You look as though you needed that" she smiled, before taking a sip of hers.

Ben nodded. "More than I realised" he replied. "How's the girl?"

Dani shook her head. "Physically, her wounds will heal, but not without leaving a few scars. It's her mental state that I'm worried about and that's why I wanted to talk to you."

"I'm really not sure I can be of much help" Ben apologised.

"You'd be surprised. Sometimes what seems like the smallest of details can end up being the most significant. I understand that you don't personally know the girl?"

Ben shook his head.

"You work in the bar, don't you? Had she been in there last night?" Dani asked.

"Not that I can recall. It was hard to see her face in the dark and the injuries were so bad . . ." Ben answered, his reply drifting away as visions of her lying in the bin returned to his mind.

Dani noticed his discomfort and was a little surprised by the moisture that seemed to be forming in his eyes. For all that she'd argued the guy couldn't have been involved, Emily's words of warning must have stuck in her mind and she scolded herself for letting the man's size dictate her presumption that he might be as tough inside as he clearly was out.

"So how did you find her?" she asked, keen to move him through this as quickly as she could.

Ben took a couple of seconds to compose himself. "I was walking home after finishing work and as I walked past the alley I heard her."

"You heard her?"

"Yeah, I heard a groan."

"A groan?"

"Well, it was sort of a cross between a groan and a moan, if you know what I mean? It's hard to describe, but it sounded as though someone was in pain."

"So you went in to check?"

"Yeah, of course I did" Ben replied, having noted the trace of surprise in her voice.

Dani shook her head slightly. "I'm sorry" she said. "I guess I've become used to people ignoring everyone else. Most people would have walked on and pretended that they hadn't heard anything."

"Don't get me wrong" Ben confirmed. "I did think of that. We sometimes get the homeless sheltering back there and, initially, I presumed it was one of them, or possibly someone drunk or on drugs, but I couldn't leave them, not when they were making that sound."

"Well, I'm glad you didn't" Dani said, after a momentary pause, in which she found herself becoming a little intrigued by the man in front of her. "You've saved the girl's life."

Ben's cheeks flushed slightly, another response that caught Dani a little off-guard.

"When they brought her in, they said that she'd been found in a bin full of glass?" Dani asked.

"Yeah, it was the one we use for the empty bottles and the broken glasses. It all goes for recycling, so we don't tend to take much care when throwing the stuff in there."

"Is it likely that there would be anything else in there? Needles or general waste?"

"I couldn't say. The bin doesn't have a lid, so it's possible that people could throw other stuff in there. Why? She's not been infected with anything, has she?"

"I can't say, I'm afraid" Dani apologised. "For one thing, we're still running tests and for another, it's confidential information."

Ben nodded his understanding. "Do you have any idea who she is?" he asked. "Has she got any family or friends coming here to be with her?"

"No, unfortunately not. We're going to have to wait for her to wake up before we can establish any details."

Shaking his head, Ben let out a sigh. "It's not right that she should be alone" he said, almost to himself.

After seeing the emotion he felt when he pictured the girl and then his blush when she'd told him he'd saved her life, this was a third moment that left Dani somewhat taken aback.

"That's why you've stayed here, isn't it?" she asked.

Ben looked at her, a little quizzically.

"I'd been wondering why you were still here, given that you didn't know the girl" she explained. "It seemed odd that you would wait around after being told that she was stable."

Unsure of how to reply, Ben nodded.

"You're a unique individual, Mr Trowman" she said.

"Please, call me Ben" he asked.

"Well, then. You're a unique individual, Ben" she smiled. "Look, we're not expecting her to come out of sedation for a good while yet. Why don't you head home and get some rest?"

"Will I be able to come back?" Ben asked. "Given that I'm not family and I don't even know her name."

Dani reached into her drawer and took out a card. She wrote a number on the back of it and handed it to him. "This is my personal number" she said. "I'm not supposed to give you any information regarding a stranger but, as far as I'm concerned, you've more than earned the right to know how she's doing. Give me a call when you've had some sleep."

Ben took the card gratefully. "But what if something happens in the meantime?" he asked. "Would you mind giving me a call?"

Passing him a pen and paper to jot down his number, she smiled and nodded. "Of course, I'll be glad to."

Albert looked up at the early morning sun, soaking in the slight mist that hung in the air as his thoughts drifted to dreams of spending a beautiful day like this enjoying a round of golf, a spot of fishing or even just a long walk in the countryside, hand in hand with the woman he loved. It was a dream which, only a few short years ago, would never have found a foothold in his mind. It was a vision that would never have been able to push past his desire for the hustle and bustle of life. Back then the daily grind was all that mattered to him, it was all that dominated his desire and nothing, not even his beloved wife, had been able to find even the smallest of niches in his plans.

His lust for business, for the pressure and worry of office life, success and money were paramount to him. Each day had become a pursuit for more, a chase for the impossible, regardless as to how much he'd already obtained. Holidays, weekends and even just evenings had ceased to exist for him, with each passing moment he was away from the office causing more anxiety than any amount of pressure or deadlines could ever hope to achieve. It was his entire existence and it'd been cruelly ripped from him when he turned sixty-five.

Compulsory retirement they'd called it, but he'd known the real meaning behind the words. It was for his health, they'd insisted, but he'd known they were merely telling him they thought he could no longer do his job. They'd even thrown him a wake, or a party as they insisted on calling it, to celebrate his passing from the land of the living into the purgatory of old-age. But he'd shown them, the naysayers and doomsday merchants, hadn't he?

The letter had referred to it as a retirement package and they'd speculated that he could use it to live out his dreams, to savour the fruits of his labour. To them, it was a substantial amount with which he could spend what remained of his life slipping into a coma of inactivity but, to him, it was a means by which he could prove them all wrong. Mary had been furious when he'd told her his grand plan, making no attempt to hide her anger as he outlined what he was going to do, and he actually thought he might have lost her at one point. But that was what he did, he'd made a life out of convincing others that they should follow his lead, and she'd eventually come round to the idea, even becoming somewhat enamoured by the concept.

It wouldn't be work, he'd explained, it wouldn't be the cut and thrust of business that she feared. They were financially set for the rest of their lives and all the coffee shop was, was an opportunity for them to become a valued and integral part of the community. He'd painted a picture of lazy afternoons, chatting and laughing with the customers in their safe haven from stress and worry. He'd manipulated her dreams to the point at which she longed for the opportunity that was being presented and she'd fallen in love with the concept, truly and totally in love.

He'd watched with absolute delight as she'd immersed herself in the project, helping to choose the location, the décor and the drinks that they'd be serving. He'd even been able to stand back as she cut deals with suppliers and drove forward their advertising campaign as though she'd been doing this all of her life. It was majestic, the way she worked, and their grand opening was more than he could ever have hoped it would be.

When the doors opened, the place became packed and, over just a short space of time, she knew their regulars as if they were family. The place was a success and the best of it, he realised when he looked back at those days, was that they spent each day together. Every hour that passed, they were able to enjoy each other's company in a way he'd forsaken for so long and, every day, he was reminded of exactly why he'd married her. But then it had all changed.

Whether it'd happened immediately or whether it'd taken time, he honestly didn't know. He knew that it must have been a slow process but, in his mind, it'd been so fast that he hadn't been able to take it all in. The few offices that'd provided their surroundings ceased to be places of business as companies farmed out their work and cut costs at every corner, the stores which provided their weekend custom moved with the development of the new city centre, taking with them the business on which they survived and all they were left with was the occasionally lost shopper and a handful of their loyal regulars. In what seemed to be an instant their idyllic lifestyle was drained to nothing and now, where once they thrived on their hopes and dreams, their days were filled with worry and anguish.

As it had all started to collapse, Mary had begged him to cut their losses, she'd implored him to finally take a step back and enjoy what remained of their lives but, once again, his defiance had taken a hold. Their tender caresses and sweet words were replaced by arguments and aggression as he insisted what they were suffering was merely a temporary set-back and that he would find a way to bring back their happiness. His belief that he would be able to survive had become almost tangible in its fierceness, yet he hadn't been able to do it, had he? For all his drive and desire to keep things going, he was walking into the face of an unstoppable storm and, as he set up the chairs outside, he looked through the window and saw Mary sitting in her usual position next to the counter, reading the paper as she did every morning.

They'd been married for nearly fifty years, sweethearts since school. Not a day went by when he didn't look at her and feel honoured that a woman of such beauty and passion had chosen him out of all the boys, even when his glances in her direction were met with the launching of a cup, a plate or any other heavy object she could lay her hands on. He knew that his stubborn ambition drove her mad and he longed for her to truly see things through his eyes, to see why he needed to persist with work and why he persisted with a place that seemed to do nothing but hurt them, but she never would.

Mary had long ago lost the desire to fight, to battle through these hard times and, whilst he would do almost anything to succeed, the one thing he wasn't able to do was to watch as his darling wife lost her ability to enjoy life. That was why he was looking into selling up, that was why he now felt comfortable with the idea of giving up. Whatever he'd hoped to achieve with this coffee shop, whatever dreams he'd hoped to fulfil, nothing was worth jeopardising the happiness that his life with her would continue to bring. His only hope now was that he hadn't left it too late.

With the final chair in place, Albert flicked over the sign on the door to show the place was open and stepped inside to await the underwhelming trade that Sunday morning would inevitably deliver. Mary glanced up from her paper as he entered and he could tell from her expression that something had troubled her.

"What is it, Honey?" he asked, hoping that it would be something she'd read and not something he'd done.

Mary continued to read for a few seconds before looking up at him and he saw the distress in her eyes as she spoke. "It says here that a girl was attacked last night and that she was found in the alley by The Skinning Pit. Apparently the man who found her worked in the bar; do you think that might have been Ben or Sam? I'm sure they said they were both working last night when they were in here yesterday afternoon."

"Yes, they were" Albert replied, starting to become a little concerned himself. "Does the paper say who the girl was?"

"No, it just says that the man found her on his way home from his shift."

Albert let out a sigh. "That's a relief, for a second I thought the girl might have been Steph; she was working last night too."

"How do you know it wasn't?" Mary asked, as her own worry increased at the thought.

"Because it says that the man found her after his shift which means that it can't have been Steph as neither of the boys would ever allow her to leave on her own."

"You're right, of course they wouldn't." she answered, relaxing a little. "They're such nice boys; they always have time for a chat when they come in and they're always so polite. I hope they're ok."

"Why wouldn't they be?" asked Albert.

"Well, it worries me, them working in a rough place like that. I wish they would get themselves better jobs, especially with Sam having just had his daughter."

Albert had the ominous feeling that she was about to broach one of her more favoured complaints about the place and he acted quickly to try and divert her away from it. "Now, Mary." he replied. "You know that the bar seems rougher than it is; that's the thing about the type of music they play, its bark is definitely worse than its bite. They make sure the place is free from the real trouble makers. I'm sure the location of the attack is just a coincidence."

"You might be right about that, but that's what I've been telling you about this area; it's getting worse" Mary answered, immediately seizing on the opportunity and causing Albert to groan inwardly. Damn, he thought to himself, this was what he'd hoped to avoid. "There never used to be all these types of goings on but now we've got graffiti, vandals and girls being attacked. What's next; arson and murder?"

With a shake of his head Albert walked through to the back room knowing that, once she started on this, there would be no stopping her.

Was it the bright sunlight shining through the flimsy curtains that had woken him, or was it the intoxicating aroma of bacon frying in the pan that'd filtered into his nostrils? Had the birds, singing their morning call outside the window, gently coaxed him into consciousness, or had his body rested well enough and woken him naturally from his slumber? Maybe his body had sensed that he was now alone in bed and begun to crave the tender closeness of a lifelong soul mate, without whom he found it difficult to sleep?

"Sam, you lazy bastard!" Karen screamed from somewhere in the vicinity of their kitchen. "Get your worthless, good for nothing ass out of bed!"

No, he realised with a sigh, it was probably the loud, ominous crash that'd put a dramatic end to his dreams. He wondered whether he could get away with pretending that he'd slept through it all, whether he could actually manage to get just a few more minutes of kip before he had to face whatever nightmare lay on the other side of the bedroom door.

"Did you hear me?" she screamed again, almost in answer to his question. "I said get up!"

Kicking back the covers and swinging his legs out of the bed, he sat upright and rubbed the sleep from his eyes. Penny's cries were now resonating around the flat, seeming to add their own weight to the strife he was in and it felt as though she was following her mother's lead in blaming him for something. That was the problem, wasn't it? There was far too much oestrogen in this flat to make life fair for him now. Maybe next time he'd impregnate her whilst standing on a strip of tinfoil and wearing a fireman's hat, or whatever it was claimed you had to do, in order to ensure that you gave birth to a boy?

"Sam!" came another scream, this one seeming to vibrate the walls of the building.

A mild sense of dread swept through him as he pulled on yesterday's t-shirt and slipped into a pair of tracksuit bottoms. As he opened the door to the hallway, for a second, he considered turning left instead of right and making a break for it through the front door. Who knew? If he ran until his legs could run no more, maybe he would actually escape? Then again, he figured, when Karen was pissed off, there was nothing that'd stop her from catching him; even carrying a baby in her arms, she would still get to him.

Readying himself to make the apology that would be needed, whether he'd done something wrong or not, he turned right and walked to the kitchen doorway. As he got there, the mouth-watering smell of Karen's cooked breakfast was tempered a little by the sight of her kneeling on the floor, surrounded by the contents of the cupboard that'd somehow flung itself off the wall.

"Good morning, my little Sunbeam" he said, casually catching the tin of fruit that she launched towards his head. "Had a little accident, have we?"

A second tin arced through the air and he easily caught that one too but the third, thrown in quick succession, hadn't been anticipated and he barely managed to duck out of the way as it sailed past his head and thudded into the wall behind him. "The only accident here is you, you useless git!" she shouted. "I thought you'd fixed this bloody thing ages ago."

Sam placed the cans on the table and walked over to where his five month old daughter, Penny, was crying in her cot. "I had fixed it" he answered, lifting her up and checking that the source of her angst was down to the loud crash, rather than a need for her nappy to be changed. "You watched me do it."

"I watched you do something that you thought would fix it" she replied, looking up at him as he walked towards her with Penny in his arms. "But, like everything you do in this place, you've screwed it up."

"I clearly didn't" Sam smiled, unable to resist the opportunity to crack a joke, even when his girlfriend was on the verge of killing him. "Otherwise it would've stayed up."

Karen fixed him with an icy stare and, for a second, he wondered whether he might just have made light of one too many bad situations but, gradually, her grimace softened into a smile as she shook her head and sighed. "For once, just for once, I'd like to be able to stay mad at you for longer than a few minutes."

"Ah, you're too besotted by my irresistible good looks to stay mad at me" Sam laughed.

"You mean I'm just too amused by your stupid face" Karen laughed back, standing up as she cleared up the last bit of the debris from the floor.

"That's better" said Sam, leaning forward to kiss her on the cheek. "I much prefer waking up to a smiling girlfriend, rather than the antichrist. It's not like you to act so harshly when something goes wrong in this place, what's really wrong?"

"I don't know" she answered. "I'm sorry, I've just had a bit of a shit morning; Penny's been restless, I had to deal with an annoying religious nut at the door, the cupboard collapsed and, to top it all off, this was in the paper."

Sam handed Penny to Karen and picked the paper up off the table. He could feel her gaze on him as he read and his heart sank as the story unfolded. "Why didn't you wake me up to tell me about this?" she asked when he'd finished.

"I didn't know about it" he answered, somewhat taken aback by what he'd read. "Andy gave me a lift home; it must've been Ben who found her, he stayed behind for another drink with Steph."

"Well?" Karen asked, raising her eyebrows expectantly.

"Well, what?" Sam replied.

Karen rolled her eyes before speaking again, clearly disappointed that she'd have to point out the obvious. "Well what are you waiting for? Go and call him."

"It's too early to do that" answered Sam. "It says here that he found her in the early hours of the morning, so I'm guessing he's probably catching up on his sleep. I'll call him later."

"But don't you want to know that he's ok?"

"Look, he found the girl; he wasn't the one who was attacked. I'm sure he'll be fine; he would've called me if there was anything wrong."

"Would he though?" Karen asked, as her expression became one of exasperation. "Would he call you if there was a problem? Look, we both know that he wouldn't want to disturb anyone, even if he was in trouble. He'd suffer it until he knew he wasn't going to be a burden."

She was right, of course. Ben never called unless he knew it was ok to do so and, whilst there was no doubting the guy could look after himself, he did sometimes need a nudge before he'd consider sharing his problems. Then again, he figured, knowing him and Steph, he knew they'd probably stayed much later at the bar and there was no way he'd have got home until a couple of hours ago. He also knew that, when he called him, Karen would be on his shoulder and she wouldn't let up until she'd found out everything, but the bloke would need to sleep, so he had to find a way of delaying the phone call.

"I tell you what" he said. "How about we have some breakfast and then I'll call him before I head out to work?"

Karen regarded him with a quiet contemplation before scowling a little as she passed Penny back to him, who'd now stopped crying and almost seemed to be mirroring her mother's look of frustration. "Ok" She answered. "But just make sure that you do. Now, you put Penny in her chair and I'll serve up the food."

"It's a deal" he replied, whilst he silently offered up an apology to his friend; Buddy, he thought to himself, you're about to wake up to a Karen special grilling

---

Lee stared at his reflection in the mirror, running his hand over his bald head and tracing his fingers across the scar which ran around the side of his skull. Did it make him look more dangerous, or possibly even sexier? Maybe it was a little bit of both? Either way, it was going to take some getting used to, given that this was the first time he'd been without long hair since his early teens. As for the scar, well, he didn't really care about that and they'd said it would eventually fade anyway.

"Don't worry, you look positively dashing" Emily stated from the doorway.

Spinning on his heels, Lee immediately felt embarrassed about being caught admiring himself. "It feels fucked up" he mumbled in reply as he reached for his new leather vest.

Emily smiled, knowingly. "You're dressed already?" she pointed out. "Anyone would think that you can't wait to get out of here. What's the matter? Have you not enjoyed the company? Just because I'm your doctor, doesn't mean that my feelings can't be hurt."

"You're ok" Lee smiled back, "but this place is a shithole."

"I'll take that as a compliment" Emily laughed, understanding his point of view as she pushed the wheelchair into the room. "That's a bit of a swanky new vest."

"Thanks, but it's called a Cut" Lee replied, still struggling to get comfortable in the new leather.

"Well, that's a swanky new Cut then. What do the words on the back mean?"

Lee looked at her, a little disappointed that she didn't know. "Abyssus Tutela?" he said. "It's Latin for Hell's Guardians. It's the name of our club."

"You're in a biker gang?" Emily exclaimed, appearing shocked by the news.

"Not a gang" Lee corrected her. "We're a Motorcycle Club and would you have treated me different if you'd have known?"

Emily floundered for a moment whilst she tried to find a reply. "No, of course not" she eventually stammered. "You just seem too nice to be involved with those types of people."

"Those types of people?" Lee asked, raising his eyebrow at the prejudice.

Now Emily's cheeks began to flush and she opened her mouth several times in an attempt to reply, until Lee's laughter saved her the trouble.

"I know what you meant" he chuckled, "and no, we're not outlaw like those vicious fuckers you read about in the paper. Honestly, we're a legitimate club."

"You don't go round beating up women and selling drugs?"

"Of course not" Lee replied.

"So what do you do?" Emily asked, now genuinely intrigued. "What do you mean by legitimate?"

"I mean that we're a bunch of guys who like riding bikes and being part of something, that's all."

Nodding, Emily seemed to be understanding. "So, what do you do for money, if you don't mind me asking?"

"A few of the boys work day jobs as mechanics and bouncers, but we also own a strip club in town."

"I thought you were legitimate?" Emily asked.

"Hey, it might not be to everyone's taste" Lee replied, smiling at her shocked reaction. "But watching tits and pussy is a legal pastime, which makes us legitimate even if it's not the type of thing you're in to."

Again, Emily's cheeks began to burn red. "I'm not a prude" she proclaimed. "I just . . ."

"I'm glad you don't think you're a prude" Lee laughed, cutting her off in a bid to increase her embarrassment. "In fact, with a body like yours, we could use a sexy nurse if you feel like proving it? What d'ya think? Fancy shaking your ass up a pole some time?"

"I don't think the hospital would appreciate me doing that" Emily answered, wondering just how much jest had been in his question.

"Ah, that's a shame" Lee chuckled. "I'd bet your tits would look fucking great on a stage!"

"Get in the chair!" Emily demanded, laughing.

"I can walk" Lee insisted.

"Not until you've got out the doors, I'm afraid. It's hospital policy."

Reluctantly, Lee sat himself in the chair and Emily pushed him out of the room. They navigated the corridors on the way to the entrance and, on the way, Emily noticed Dani standing against the wall, staring at the door to her office.

"Kev" Emily called out to a passing orderly. "Would you mind helping this patient out please?"

The orderly readily agreed as Lee looked up to Emily for an explanation.

"I'm sorry, Lee" she said hurriedly, as she started rushing towards Dani, "but I think my friend's in trouble. I'll see you again when you're in for your check-up."

"What's happened?" Emily exclaimed as, for a second time that morning, she ran along the corridor towards Dani.

At the sound of her voice, Dani turned to face her and Emily immediately saw the concern in her expression.

"I told you taking him somewhere private was a bad idea" she continued. "What did he do?"

"He didn't do anything" Dani replied, turning her attention back to the door.

Following her gaze, Emily waited silently for a few moments, until it was apparent that her friend wasn't intending to elaborate on the statement.

"So what's going on? Why are you stood out here?" she asked, as the muffled sound of raised voices filtered into the corridor. "And who's in there?"

"Ben's in there" Dani replied, the increasing anger in her voice becoming blatantly obvious, "with two Detectives who decided to turn up, unannounced."

After briefly glancing back towards the door, Emily looked back at Dani. "So why are you so mad about this? I take it they're investigating the girl?"

Dani gave a silent nod of confirmation.

"So isn't it right that they talk to the guy who found her?"

Again, Dani nodded.

"Then why are you so mad about it?" Emily repeated.

"Listen to them" Dani muttered, without taking her eyes off the door. "They're not talking to him in there, they're yelling at him."

"Well, maybe he's not answering their questions?"

"Or maybe they're just clutching at straws?"

Both the comment and the venom with which it was laced caught Emily by surprise. "What's going on?" she asked. "You're starting to worry me."

"There's something wrong with them" Dani answered, still focussing her attention on the door. "This isn't right."

"What isn't right?"

"The way they're going about this."

Reaching out to take a hold of her arm, Emily turned Dani to finally face her. "Talk to me" she urged. "Tell me what's happening."

Slowly, Dani's expression calmed a little and she took a deep breath before she spoke. "I spoke to Ben" she said, "and he's a genuinely nice guy. He's stayed here all night because he didn't want the girl waking up and being by herself."

"Well that's nice of him" Emily muttered, unsure of anything else to say.

"We finished talking" Dani continued, "and as we were walking back to the entrance, I saw the two detectives storming along the corridor."

A look of confusion began to spread across Emily's expression. "They were back here?"

Dani nodded. "Yes, and they were looking for me."

"But, shouldn't they have been waiting for you to go to them?"

"Exactly" Dani exclaimed. "But they decided they were too good for that."

Emily's confusion increased. "Is the girl awake then?"

"No, she isn't" Dani replied, as the anger found its way back into her voice. "And when I told them that, they decided to drag Ben in there and slam the door in my face."

"Well, isn't it right that they talk to him?"

Dani glanced back at the door and, when she looked back to Emily, her eyes were burning with rage. "I hadn't told them who he was" she snapped. "He could've been anyone, but they wouldn't listen to me."

"Maybe they'd spoken to him last night?" Emily suggested.

"It's not likely" Dani replied. "They didn't even know his name."

Silence descended as they looked at each other, neither of them quite knowing what to say next. They both knew that the situation wasn't right and that the actions of the detectives should be reported, but they also knew there was little point in complaining to a police department which, at best, held hospital staff in minimal regard.

"So, tell me more about him" Emily insisted, as curiosity won the battle in her mind. "Ben, is it?"

Finally, Dani smiled as she realised she should have known the woman wouldn't be able to resist asking. "Like I said" she replied. "He's a really sweet guy."

"That's something you'd say about your granddad!" Emily laughed. "I want the real story."

Dani chuckled as she shrugged her shoulders. "I don't know much about him" she answered, "other than he's genuinely concerned about the girl."

Disappointment practically exploded across Emily's expression. "You are useless" she scolded. "You get a guy like that, alone in your office, and all you can tell me is that he's concerned for someone?"

"What did you want me to do? Pounce on him the moment I shut the door?"

Emily sighed. "You could at least have found out more about him. How old is he? What's he in to? Where does he live?" she asked, before pausing as a mischievous grin spread across her lips. "Is he single?"

The last question had been so obviously coming, right from the moment Emily had started talking, that Dani shook her head as she replied. "That's a little inappropriate" she said, with a smile.

"There's no inappropriate when a guy looks that good!" Emily exclaimed.

The statement was clearly made to wind her up but, given the regularity of Emily's insistence that she should find herself a man, Dani wondered just how much genuine intent lay behind the words. She opened her mouth to provide a reply, but was halted by the sound of Ben's voice ringing out from behind her office door.

"For the last fucking time, I didn't do this to her!"

Without hesitation, both of them rushed forward and Dani threw open the door. The older of the two detectives, Crowther, was sitting in her chair whilst the other, Wishall, was standing next to him, leaning forward with his hands on the desk. Ben had clearly been sat in the chair he'd occupied whilst talking to her but he was now also standing and leaning forward over the desk, face to face with Wishall.

"What's wrong, Mr Trowman?" Crowther asked, ignoring the interruption. "Have we touched a nerve?"

"Carry on with this bullshit and I'll fucking touch something!" Ben hissed, without taking his eyes off Wishall as his hand clenched into a fist.

Dani noticed the action and her heart sank with the realisation of what Ben was likely about to do. "That's enough!" she exclaimed, stepping across the room and placing her hand on Ben's shoulder.

At the feel of her touch, Ben turned to face her and she looked up at his eyes in which, where there had previously been nothing but a genuine kindness, there was now only pure rage. It was a dramatic contrast that caused her to take a step back and, for a second, she couldn't tell if it was fear or disappointment which was making her heart race.

"Doctor Draper, I don't believe we gave you permission to come in?" Crowther sneered.

"No, you didn't" she replied, finally managing to compose herself, "but I will not have this kind of nonsense here. This is my office, not an interview room at the police station."

"For the purposes of our investigation, we'll use any room we like" Wishall stated, arrogantly.

His voice seemed to re-ignite the anger in Ben and he spun round to face him. "This isn't a fucking investigation!" he once more hissed, his voice low and guttural as his muscles tensed involuntarily. "This is a fucking witch-hunt!"

"For someone who's so adamant that he's innocent, I'm a little intrigued by your over-reaction to our simple questions, Mr Trowman" Crowther said, slowly and with obvious intent. "I'm starting to think that there might be something you're not telling us?"

"The only thing I haven't told you is what I want to do to your fucking smug face!" Ben spat, leaning back over the desk, towards the detective.

"Ok" Emily announced, moving across the room and positioning herself next to Ben. As she gently manoeuvred her arm across his chest in a bid to hold him from doing anything stupid, she flashed both of the detectives a scolding glance. "I think this has gone far enough. Do you have any evidence with which to charge this man?"

After a few moments, and a returned glance of concern, Crowther shook his head.

"Well then," she continued. "I suggest that this interview is over. I take it you've got his contact details? Well maybe, when the girl wakes and gives you some real evidence, you might want to contact him then?"

They all looked at her without speaking and she, in turn, looked at Dani.

"I'll escort the two detectives to the exit" Emily said, leading them without any argument towards the door, before subtly nodding in Ben's direction. "I'll leave you to finish things up with Ben."

Dani's first reaction was one of panic, as she thought about being left with the man who, only a few seconds ago, looked as though he was ready to kill someone. As they left the room she nervously turned towards Ben and her fear immediately drained away when she realised why Emily had left them alone. He was still standing, although the shivers that now racked his body threatened to put an end to that, and his eyes, which had been so filled with anger, were now showing a deep sadness that seemed to cut right through her.

Grabbing the chair, she slid it behind him just before his legs gave way and, having collapsed on to it, he bent forward to cover his face with his hands.

"Ben" she whispered, wrapping her arm around his shoulders as she squatted down next to him, "it's over."

Slowly, he rubbed his eyes with the palms of his hands, before sitting upright and looking at her. "I'm sorry" he barely muttered, as he so obviously fought against the tears that were threatening to fall.

"It's ok" she replied, with a warm smile. "I defy anyone to keep their anger in check when they're dealing with those two."

Ben shook his head. "I've never reacted like that before" he said, as he began to regain a hold of himself. "I don't know where that came from."

"Maybe you've never been accused of raping a girl before?" Dani suggested, honestly.

Again, Ben shook his head. "They didn't even ask about the girl" he told her. "They just kept repeating that I was there by myself and asking why I called for an ambulance, instead of leaving the scene."

Now it was Dani's turn to shake her head, and she wished it was through disbelief rather than a confirmation of her expectations. "Look" she said, making sure to catch Ben's eye as she spoke. "Unfortunately, it seems that the case has been given to two detectives who are more concerned with a speedy result than the correct one. You've got nothing to worry about. Just don't drop yourself in it by swinging your fists at them; that's what they were looking for."

"I don't swing my fists" Ben told her, finally managing a half-smile. "I've never done that before and I don't know why I wanted to then. I think I'm just tired and they managed to get under my skin."

"Well, why don't you get yourself home and have some sleep" Dani suggested, rising to her feet. "I'll call you when the girl wakes up."

"Thanks" Ben replied, also standing.

They both looked at each other for a moment, as each of them wondered if there was anything more that needed to be said. With a warm smile, Dani turned to lead him out of the office, but she was halted as the sound of running footsteps echoed along the corridor, followed immediately by the sight of the crash cart being rushed past the open door.

"What's going on?" Ben asked, as the shrill beep of Dani's pager caused them both to flinch in surprise.

Grabbing her pager, Dani pressed the button to halt the sound and looked at the screen. "I don't understand this" she muttered. "There's no one on this ward who was in any danger of suffering a heart attack."

Before Ben could reply, Emily rushed back into the office. "Come quick" she exclaimed, breathlessly, "it's the girl!"

Chapter 3

"So, that's where you're hiding!" Steph exclaimed, as she walked into the kitchen. "What are you doing in here?"

Ben had been lost in his thoughts, staring out of the window whilst he smoked a cigarette. He turned round at the sound of her voice and managed a half-smile. "I just needed a minute or two to myself" he replied.

Steph returned his smile and joined him at the window. "Have you got one of those for me?" she asked, nodding towards his cigarette.

He passed her the pack and his lighter, stubbing out his finished butt and absent-mindedly lighting a new one once she'd taken one for herself.

"Chain smoking?" she smiled.

Ben looked at her, a little perplexed, until he realised what she meant; he hadn't actually intended to smoke another in quick succession, it was just an automatic action. "Shit" he mumbled. "I didn't even realise I was doing that."

She watched as he continued to smoke it anyway, noting just how tired he looked, and she kind of regretted throwing this barbeque. It'd seemed a good idea, what with The Skinning Pit being closed whilst the police investigated the girl, and Sam, Karen, Andy and the rest of their friends were having a good time in the late afternoon sun. She'd also thought it would be good for Ben to be around people after what he'd been through during the night but, now she was realising just how much it'd taken out of him, she wondered whether it would've been better if she'd just gone round to his.

"Did you manage to get any sleep when you got home?" she asked.

He shook his head. "No" he answered. "I tried, but there was just too much going on in my mind."

"Well, if you want to get your head down for a bit, you're welcome to use my bed. I'm sure no one would mind if you disappeared for a couple of hours."

"Thanks" he muttered, "but I don't think it'd work. Every time I close my eyes, I see her lying in the bin."

Steph reached out and placed her hand on his arm.

"She was so young, Steph" he continued, "and she'd been so messed up."

Not knowing what to say, Steph remained silent next to him.

"And then she died" he said, his voice becoming tainted with traces of anger. "That was the last thing she knew; some fucking animals destroying her and then leaving her to suffer."

A tear rolled down his cheek and he quickly wiped it away, apologising for being stupid as he did. Whether it was the tear, the apology or both, Steph wasn't sure, but she felt her heart sink as the magnitude of the situation truly hit home. She'd never seen him like this and she desperately wanted to help him, but she had no idea where to start.

"Why are you apologising?" she asked. "You've nothing to be ashamed about."

"I didn't even know her" he answered. "I didn't know her name or where she was from, so why should I be so upset by this? If I'd done what most people would've done and gone home when the ambulance got there, then I wouldn't have even known she hadn't made it."

"But that's the point" Steph said, turning him round so she could look directly into his eyes. "You're not like most people, Ben. You're more kind, caring and loving than anyone I've ever met. You're unique and you're a special human being. That's why you stopped when everyone else would have walked on. That's why you stayed with her until the end and that's why, thanks to you, the last moments of her life weren't filled with pain and she wasn't alone."

More tears fell from his eyes as he looked at her and she reached up to gently brush them from his cheeks.

"You're hurting because you care" she continued, "and that's fine, but I'd be willing to bet that, if she could, the girl would thank you. She'd tell you that, even though she's gone, you still saved her life. You made sure she went with dignity and you should be proud of what you've done."

Ben nodded, but didn't seem able to talk. Throwing her arms around him, Steph pulled him into a tight hug.

"I'm so proud of you" she whispered, "and I love you so much."

She leaned back slightly, looking up to see if he was ok. She looked deeply into his eyes and the seconds seemed to slow as she felt herself being drawn in, becoming immersed in their warmth. A voice in her head told her she needed to look away, to pull back from the embrace, but she fought against it, not wanting the moment to end. Her mind began to spin with confusion and, when she saw his pupils flick briefly down to her lips and back, she was surprised to find that the thought he might be about to kiss her was far more than just a welcome idea.

"The women want more meat inside them!" Sam childishly exclaimed, as he bowled in through the door.

Steph quickly pulled away from Ben and turned towards the window.

"What's going on?" Sam asked, flashing Ben a look which spoke volumes. "Why are you two buried away in here?"

"I was just telling our boy how special he is for what he did last night" Steph mumbled, her voice noticeably wobbling a little as she spoke.

"Oh, he's special alright" Sam chuckled as he opened the fridge, seeming not to notice either her faltering voice or Ben wiping his eyes. "So, where's Rob tonight?"

"He's out with friends" Steph answered, her voice finally returning to normal as she turned back to face him.

"Has he found himself a job yet?" Sam asked.

"Not really. He does the odd bit of work when it comes along, sort of handyman kind of stuff."

Sam closed the fridge and carried the food to the counter, where he began unwrapping the meat. "I probably should've got him to put our cupboards up. I made a right cock and balls job of it and Karen's still pissed at me for it."

"Yeah, I heard" Steph laughed. "She couldn't wait to tell me the moment she got here. I doubt that useless prick would've done any better though."

"Not too much faith in him making a career of it then?" Sam asked, raising his eyebrows slightly at the trace of bitterness in her voice.

"The only thing I have faith in, is the fact he'll come home in the early hours of the morning, drunk and penniless."

An awkward silence fell in the room, as both Sam and Ben realised there was more to her comment than she'd intended to let on. Sam looked at Ben and picked up the plate he'd loaded with sausages, burgers and steaks.

"Well, I'll be outside cremating the shit out of this stuff" he smiled. "You'd better come and join us soon or there'll be nothing left. Those women can't get enough of my sausage!"

With that, Sam hurried out of the kitchen, pausing to close the door behind him. Ben looked at Steph and held out his pack of cigarettes.

"Are you ok?" he asked, as the realisation something might be wrong with Steph overtook his sorrow for what had happened to the girl.

"I'm fine" she replied uncertainly, gratefully accepting his offer.

They both lit up and then stood without speaking for a few moments.

"You know I'm not going to believe that" Ben eventually told her, when he was sure she wouldn't say anything more without being prompted.

Steph looked at him for a second and it was clear she was trying to decide whether to tell him what was wrong.

"Honestly, I'm fine" she eventually said, with the most false of smiles. "It's just some stupid stuff, that's all."

"Stupid stuff, like what?" he asked.

"Stupid stuff that's nowhere near as important as what you've been through" she answered.

Ben shook his head. "What I've been through doesn't matter" he said. "It doesn't mean anything that might be happening with you is any less important. What's wrong?"

Taking a long drag of her cigarette, Steph pondered that for a second. "I think Rob might be cheating on me" she admitted.

All thoughts seemed to drain from Ben's mind and his heart practically jumped out of his chest. "What?" he exclaimed.

"Like I said, it's probably nothing" Steph continued. "But when I got back here last night, our bed had been slept in and Rob was in the shower. He said it was because he was too hot to sleep and he was trying to cool himself down but..."

"But you don't believe that?" Ben asked, finishing her sentence when she struggled to do so herself.

She shrugged her shoulders. "I don't know" she answered, hesitantly. "The bedroom window was open and I was sure there was a trace of perfume in the air."

"Well, has there been anything else to make you think that might be happening?"

Again, Steph shrugged. "Not directly" she replied, "but things haven't been right between us for a long time."

"What do you mean, things haven't been right?"

"We just don't seem to talk anymore and he keeps going out."

"Where does he go?"

"I don't know. It's always with his friends, like tonight."

"Have you asked whether you can go too?"

Steph shook her head. "No" she stated, firmly. "That's the thing. I don't really want to."

Ben struggled to find something to say as his mind raced and he felt a little ashamed at just how much he wanted an affair to be true. He desperately wanted to tell her that the guy was no good for her and she should leave him, but he couldn't do that, could he? If he did, then he'd be doing so for purely selfish reasons and he might as well have tried to screw the girl the first time he'd met her; there would've been no point to his actions over the last three years.

"Why? Do you not like his friends?" he asked.

"I've never met them" Steph answered.

"Well maybe that's the problem? Maybe that's become something ingrained and breaking the habit might help to bring you closer together? When was the last time you did anything, just the two of you?"

"I can't remember, but that's not the problem. The thought of spending any time with him just doesn't interest me."

He looked at her, noticing the lack of emotion in her eyes. He hadn't expected anything overt, like tears or rage, but he was surprised to find that there was nothing as she spoke. "How do you feel about him?" he asked, before adding "Honestly".

She pondered the question for a few moments, stubbing out her cigarette before she answered. "I think I still love him" she replied. "But, lately, I'm just not sure why."

"Well maybe you need to figure that out before anything else will make sense?" he suggested, beginning to hate himself for what he was doing.

"But what if I find that I do love him, but he is cheating and has stopped loving me?"

"Then that's something we'll have to deal with" Ben smiled. "But there's no point in trying to fix something when you don't know what's broken."

Steph nodded. "Jesus" she sighed. "I told you this was stupid."

"It isn't stupid" Ben stated, wanting desperately to pull her into another hug but feeling, for some reason, that this wasn't the time. "And don't worry. One way or another, we'll get you through this."

She looked at him, gazing deeply into his eyes, and he was filled with the certainty that there was more she wanted to say but, if there was, she quickly confirmed it would have to wait for another day.

"Thanks, Ben" was all she said, with a smile.

From the outside, the old office building was worn and broken, a shell of a place that blended in perfectly with its surroundings. Many years ago it'd been a hive of activity, right at the epicentre of the city's business district, but following the onset of redevelopment that'd seen the city shift almost in its entirety, it'd been one of the first locations to be deemed surplus to requirements and listed for destruction.

The same was true for its neighbouring premises and people had long ago stopped speculating as to whether the local government either couldn't afford the cost of demolition, or just simply weren't inclined to spend the money. To most, the area had become a forgotten land, an area of the city that was only experienced during journeys which had strayed off course or short-cuts to a more idyllic location. But to a few, it was the only place they wanted to be, a last haven of hope in the financial desperation their lives had become or a home for their addiction to living on the edge.

Ethan leant on the balcony and looked over the plush interior that was such a stark contrast to the view from the street. With a smile, he watched the punters as they put more and more cash on cards and roulette wheels, as though they were completely unaware that they were designed to fall in their favour only just enough to keep them coming back for more. He hadn't been involved in either the renovation of the place, or in the web of payments, deceit and fear which ensured that neither demolition nor the law would interfere with their business, but he loved it none the less.

It was a nest-egg, his father had told him when he'd turned eighteen and was sworn in as a fully-patched member of the club, a retirement plan for when he could no longer lead The Sons of Sorrow. Had he known that Ethan would work his way up to become his father's Vice President, he wondered. When he'd said that to him, had he expected it would be him to whom he was handing over the leadership? Maybe, or maybe not but, either way, he doubted whether Ruckus was aware there was no chance that he would be allowed to retain these ever-increasing profits when his patch was retired.

His thoughts were distracted as his gaze shifted to the sight of Jimmy and Ray entering the casino. "About fucking time" he muttered under his breath, as they quickly climbed the stairs to join him at the entrance to the office. "Where, the fuck, have you two been?

"Sorry Ethan" Jimmy replied, a little breathlessly. "There was a bit of a problem. The girl . . ."

Ethan's glare put an immediate stop to the man's sentence and he turned, without response, to lead them into the office. Ray closed the door behind them and the two of them stood idiotically in the centre of the room as Ethan took a seat on the edge of the desk.

"When you say problem," Ethan began, "are you referring to the fact the bitch was found alive, or the fact the story is on the front page of every fuckin' paper in the city?"

The anger in his voice caused both Jimmy and Ray to flinch.

"It's ok" Ray, somewhat pathetically, protested. "We've sorted it."

"Oh, you've sorted it?" Ethan replied, immediately. "So, the simple plan for Crowther and Wishall to find a dead body and label it as a being just another attack on the homeless has turned into a live woman with witnesses and people demanding a full investigation, but you've sorted it?"

"Yeah" Ray insisted, "We found out the girl had been taken to the hospital and the guy who found her was there, so Crowther and Wishall went to the hospital this morning and made sure the bitch was dead."

"What?" Ethan exclaimed, barely able to believe what he was hearing. "They killed her in the hospital?"

"Don't worry" Jimmy argued. "It was made to look like she'd had a heart-attack, before she could talk to anyone."

Ethan vigorously rubbed his face, foolishly hoping that this was a bad dream. "How the fuck is that sorting it?"

Ray opened his mouth to speak, but was cut off as Ethan quickly continued.

"She was a young, relatively healthy woman and she suffered a heart-attack whilst in hospital" he stated slowly, in the hope that they would actually take in what he was saying, "and you don't think that'll lead to a bigger fuckin' investigation?"

"We know that" Jimmy answered, "That's why Crowther and Wishall are pinning it on the twat who found her."

"So they arrested him?" Ethan asked, hopefully.

Jimmy and Ray looked at each other, before slowly looking back at Ethan.

"Not exactly" Ray replied. "They were pushin' him and close to getting' him to take a swing at 'em, but some bitch fuckin' doctor steamed in and fucked it all up."

Ethan stared at them. "So, what you're actually telling me is that Crowther and Wishall have got fuck all and there's nothing to stop a full investigation being done? That's fuckin' sorted, is it?"

No reply was forthcoming.

"Fuck!" Ethan exclaimed, slamming his fist on the desk.

"What d'you want us to do now?" Jimmy asked, as silence began to return.

Ethan was about to tell them to fuck off out of his sight, but was stopped by a knock on the door before two Prospective Members dragged a man in and forced him to his knees.

"What the fuck is this?" Ethan asked, as the man stared up at him.

"He's reached his credit limit and can't pay" one of the Prospects informed him.

Shaking his head, Ethan looked at the man. "You've picked a fuck of a bad day for this" he said, before looking at Jimmy. "Take this cunt out the back, cut his fucking dick off and choke him with it. And don't fuck this one up, or you'll wind up sucking on your own cock."

"No" the man pleaded, as Jimmy and Ray stepped towards him. "I can get you the money!"

Jimmy and Ray stopped as Ethan held up his hands. "It's a lot of fuckin' money" Ethan replied. "D'you wanna shed some light on where the fuck you're gonna get it from?"

"My girlfriend" the man stammered, as tears began to spill freely from his eyes. "Her parents died when she was just a kid and she inherited a lot of money. She's still got a load of it left, and I can get it out of that, with interest, I promise!"

Noticing that Ethan seemed to be considering the proposal, Jimmy shot him a look of concern.

"The rules don't allow for this" he said. "Ruckus won't be happy if we let this son of a bitch go."

"Fuck the rules" Ethan replied, before again focussing on the man. "Fifty percent interest" he smiled, "payable within twenty-four hours."

The man nodded immediately. "I can pay that" he answered, quickly, "but it'll take me a bit of time to get it."

Ethan stepped forward and took the man's wallet from his pocket. He opened it and removed the driver's licence before throwing the wallet back at him. "Well, Robert" he said, after studying the licence for a few seconds. "You've got five days and the interest rate has just increased to a hundred percent."

"Thank you" Rob muttered.

"If you're not back here in that time," Ethan continued, "then we'll come for you and, trust me on this, your girlfriend, your family and everyone you've ever known will wish to whatever fuckin' god they believe in that you'd kept your word."

Rob scrabbled to his feet and muttered another thank you as he left the office. Ethan watched as he left and then looked at the probationary members. "Show him out the back way and make sure he remembers his promise" he said to them. "And then call round the boys, we're sitting at the table first thing tomorrow."

Lee practically dropped on to the settee as each and every muscle in his body screamed out in agony. His head felt as though his brain was kicking its way out of his skull and all he wanted to do was sleep for a week. The food may have been shit and the place fucking depressing, but at least the hospital bed was comfy and, right at that moment, the longing to be back there was at the very forefront of his desire. Closing his eyes for a second, he hoped no one would notice him taking a nap for a few minutes, maybe half an hour at the most but, predictably, even that minor pleasure would be denied him.

"You fuckin' lightweight" Dom laughed, slumping on to the settee next to him. "You call yourself a Vice President and you can't handle a small party like this?"

"Fuck off, Dom" Lee sighed, without opening his eyes.

"I'm just saying" Dom continued, ignoring the lack of subtlety in Lee's response, "it's only just gone ten o'clock and you're partied out, so maybe it's time you thought about retiring that patch and getting yourself into an old bastard's home?"

"I would" Lee smiled, still keeping his eyes firmly shut, "if it wasn't for the fact that you fuckers would still come and piss me off in there."

"Three set meals, daytime TV and all the biscuits you can eat?" Dom exclaimed enthusiastically, his voice raising just enough octaves to really pierce their way into the very centre of Lee's brain. "We'd fuckin' move in with ya! Here, I got you a beer!"

Now Lee opened his eyes and he turned his head just enough to see Dom's annoyingly chirpy expression. "Are you backwards?" he asked, only half joking. "I'm on so many fuckin' drugs at the moment, that one swig of that shit'd put me right the fuck back in the coma ward."

Dom's eyes lit up. "Shit!" he exclaimed. "You are a fuckin' legend dude! Not even out of the hospital for a full day and you've fuckin' scored already!"

Lee shook his head and closed his eyes again. "Medicine, Dom" he sighed. "I'm on fucking medicine."

The lack of a reply was all Lee needed to confirm that Dom was trying to work his head around the concept and, without having to look, he knew a combination of confusion and concentration would be creasing up the man's expression.

"Stop thinking about it and just go find yourself some pussy" Lee chuckled.

"Right you are, boss" Dom answered. "I think Michael wants a word with you anyway.

Opening his eyes and sitting up, Lee watched Dom make himself scarce as Michael took his place on the settee.

"How you doing?" Michael asked, his friendly tone somewhat contradicting the stern look on his face.

"Like shit" Lee answered, honestly.

Michael nodded his acknowledgement and then took a long, sweeping look around the room. "We could've used you being here" he stated, without looking back towards Lee.

"I'd rather have been here" Lee replied, somewhat sharply.

Now Michael looked directly at him. "Well, maybe you should've considered that?" he asked, "before you decided to fuck off on your own."

"What happened was an accident" Lee replied.

"Not from where I'm sitting."

"And where exactly is it that you're sitting? The bus pulled out on me and that could've happened anywhere."

"It wouldn't have happened if you'd followed my orders."

"I was following your orders!" Lee hissed, struggling to keep his voice low despite the loud music. "You wanted us to bring in more cash, so that's what I was doing."

"I told you to stop with the stealing cars."

"And how else were we going to get money quickly?"

Michael didn't answer, but it was obvious to Lee where his mind was going.

"We're not gettin' into that bullshit!" Lee exclaimed.

"That's not your decision to make" Michael replied, calmly.

"And it's not yours either" Lee replied. "We all voted against it, so it's not happening."

After taking another long and sweeping look around the room, Michael fixed Lee with a firm stare. "D'you think these fuckwits know what's best for our club?" he asked. "D'you think they have any idea of what it'll take for us to grow? I do, and that's why I'm the President."

"But we don't need to grow. We're fine as we are."

"That's a matter of opinion."

"Whose fucking opinion? Yours? Because they all seem pretty happy as things are."

"That's because they're too stupid to realise the possibilities that are out there. If they did, d'you think they'd want to carry on like this? Knowing they didn't have to fuck off and do shit jobs for shit pay?"

"That's better than being in jail, or dead."

"It's the same as being in jail."

Lee let out a sigh of exasperation. "Don't be a fucking idiot" he replied, staring directly into Michael's eyes.

Michael looked at him for a few moments, without reply. His expression didn't change and, if he was angry at the comment, he wasn't showing it. "When I chose you as my second" he eventually said, with a calmness that highlighted an undercurrent of threat "I did so because I thought you were the only one who had the brains to see the future. Maybe I was wrong?"

"Yeah" Lee answered, sternly. "Maybe you were."

Chapter 4

Lying deep within the confines of their clubhouse was a room, a sacred place in which, apart from the very rare occasions on which the need arose, only fully-patched members of the club were allowed to set foot. In the middle of the room sat a large, black granite table surrounded by chairs which, once allocated, could only be occupied by the member to which it belonged. It was within this room that rules were set, discussions were had and plans were made. No one, not even the highest ranking members of the club, were more important than the room. It was the very essence of the club and, once the call to the table had been made, only the most extreme of physical restraints would allow for attendance to be missed.

At ten o'clock that morning, the doors were firmly closed to the outside world as The Sons of Sorrow took to their seats. At the head of the table sat Ruckus, their president and their leader. To his left sat their vice president, Ethan, and to his right sat Touchy, his Sergeant at Arms. The rest of the club occupied the remaining seats, descending in rank with each step further from the head of the table until, at Ruckus' demand the moment he'd been installed as their president, was a seat that could only be occupied by a founder member. However, following the subsequent removal of the remaining originals, it was now a chair that would forever be empty.

Sitting back in his chair, Ruckus let out a long sigh as he rubbed his face with his hands before sitting forward and leaning on the table. "How the fuck did this happen?" he asked, focussing his attention on Jimmy and Ray, "I told you to make sure the bitch was dead."

The two men exchanged worried glances, before Jimmy provided a tentative response.

"She was pretty much gone when we left her" he said. "There was no way she was gonna survive out there. If that prick hadn't have found her, then this wouldn't be a problem."

"But it is a fuckin' problem" Ruckus replied, immediately.

"I know," Jimmy admitted, "but it might work out better this way."

"How the fuck is this gonna work out better?" Touchy interjected, viciously. "Crowther and Wishall could've easily covered this if the cunt had of been found dead in the alley, but killin' her in the hospital means an investigation we won't be able to fuckin' control."

"But it was made to look like a heart-attack" Jimmy argued.

"You fuckin' moron!" Touchy exclaimed. "The bitch wasn't likely to have a heart-attack, so they'll do an autopsy and what d'ya think they'll find? D'ya think they'll figure she woke up and decided to inject herself with something? Un-fuckin'-likely! Whatever was put into the cunt to kill her off will show up when they look! They'll know it wasn't a heart-attack and then we're fucked!"

Jimmy and Ray again looked at each other as silence fell in the room.

"We can fix this" Ethan confirmed, deciding that he'd given both of the men enough chance to recover the situation themselves.

All eyes turned to Ethan as he explained himself.

"Yes, there may be a call for an inquiry" he continued, "but that'll go as part of the main investigation which'll still be done by Crowther and Wishall. They can bury any evidence, but if anyone does push 'em on it, then the guy who found the bitch was there all night and it'll be easy for them to point the finger towards him."

"But he was in with the doctor when this happened" Jimmy pointed out.

"So she's the only one who can fuck this up" Ethan replied. "If she does, then Crowther and Wishall link her to this and that's all that's needed to fuck up her reputation. If she's got any sense, she'll leave it all alone, unless she wants the black mark on her record."

Ruckus considered the suggestion for a few moments, before turning towards Ethan. "Fine" he agreed. "We'll go along with that for now, but you'd better keep an eye on Crowther and Wishall. I don't trust those pricks to do this right."

Ethan nodded his understanding, before providing Jimmy and Ray with a glare that left them in no doubt that he'd expect a return for saving their asses.

"Right" Ruckus continued. "Can anyone give me some good fuckin' news?"

"Satan's Minions are all but fucked" the member known as Knuckle spoke up. "That last raid on 'em pretty much wiped the cunts out and word's out there that anyone thinking of putting on their Cut is gonna get the same treatment."

"What about Jason?" Ruckus asked. "Their President's a resourceful mother-fucker."

Knuckle smiled in response. "That prick's run for cover" he chuckled. "We won't see him around again."

"Well make sure of it" Ruckus demanded. "Like I said, he's resourceful. What about the rest of the clubs? Anyone we should be paying attention to?"

"Nothing to really bother us" Knuckle replied, with a nonchalant shrug of his shoulders. "There is a new club though, calling themselves Abyssus Tutela. I dunno much about them fuckers."

"I've already looked into them" Jimmy stated, seeing an opportunity to redeem himself a little. "They 'ain't outlaw and, from what I can tell, they've no intention to be. They run the strip club in town and, apart from that, most of 'em have day jobs."

Ruckus nodded. "Keep your eye on 'em anyway" he said, addressing everyone at the table. "The last thing we need is for some jumped-up little fucks getting greedy on us. Now, I've got some bad news for you. Bernie passed away last night."

The statement caused a groan to resonate around the room, as The Sons voiced their anguish. Bernie had worked with the club for many years and all of them had liked him, but he'd been fighting cancer for a long time, so the news wasn't completely unexpected.

"So that means we need to find ourselves another safe-house" he continued, after pausing for a moment to allow the loss to sink in. "Banjo, Limpy; I want you two to get out there and find me something we can use. Preferably somewhere sympathetic to our needs but, if not, then somewhere we can create that sympathy. Everyone else, keep your fuckin' eyes open."

With that, Ruckus banged the gavel on its block and the meeting was over.

"Should we help him?" Steph asked, with an affectionate grin.

The Skinning Pit had been re-opened but, if it wasn't for the presence of a few regulars, it'd be devoid of customers. Whether that was down to what had happened over the weekend or whether it was just a regular Monday night, neither of them could be sure, but Steph and Ben were behind the bar with nothing to do but watch on as Lobe, one of their usual patrons, continued to lean so far off his stool that he was practically horizontal.

Lobe had been drinking in the bar since before Ben had started, although he only ever turned up on a Monday, Tuesday and Thursday nights. He looked significantly older than they believed him to be but he never actually spoke, so there was no way of determining his actual age or his real name. They called him Lobe due to a significant chunk of flesh missing from his right ear and they'd often speculated as to how that might've happened, with stories ranging from him being a former soldier, a former policeman and even a former spy. Though the truth was that, given his constantly inebriated condition, they all suspected that there was no way anyone would consider employing him, so he'd probably spent a vast portion of his life as nothing more than a bum.

"How does he do that?" Ben replied, returning the grin.

Steph considered it for a moment, unable to take her eyes off the drunken figure at the end of the bar. "Maybe there's so much alcohol in his system that even the laws of physics don't want to get involved with him now?" she suggested, with a chuckle.

A loud crash signalled the end of their amusement, as gravity finally took hold and Lobe sent the bar stools flying as he hit the floor. With a shake of his head, Ben walked round to help him back up to his feet and then led him towards the door and what would, inevitably, be an interesting journey home.

When he returned to his position behind the bar, he noticed that Steph seemed to have lost herself in some sort of daydream.

"What's up with you?" he asked, cutting into her thoughts.

"It's nothing" she said, absent-mindedly shaking her head and re-focussing on him.

"Oh, yeah?" he replied. "And nothing often causes you to stand there with an idiotic grin on your face, does it?"

Steph's cheeks immediately reddened at the revelation. "I wasn't, was I?" she exclaimed.

"I'm afraid you were" he laughed, "and you looked a right picture!"

"Oh, shit" Steph sighed, with a shake of her head. "I was just thinking about last night."

Ben's heart suddenly began to race as his mind automatically ran straight to the moment he'd been sure they'd shared in her kitchen, although that'd been in the afternoon. "Last night?" he asked, with as much calm as he could muster.

After a moment's pause, Steph again shook her head. "It's nothing" she repeated, "don't worry about it."

"I'm not worried" Ben chuckled. "I'm just intrigued. I haven't seen you with that sort of expression for a long time."

"What sort of expression?" she asked.

"An expression that tells me something good happened" he replied. "So, come on. What's the story?"

She looked at him and, for a second, Ben wondered whether she'd actually tell him. He couldn't stop his heart skipping a beat as hope flooded through him and he could almost hear the blood rushing through his veins as his body involuntarily froze.

"Rob got home last night" she eventually said, immediately crushing Ben's excitement, "and he'd been in a fight."

Ben couldn't find anything to say in response but, fortunately, she'd decided to tell him everything and continued anyway.

"I heard him come in" she explained, mistaking Ben's look for one of intrigue rather than disappointment, "so I went downstairs and found him searching through my handbag for painkillers."

"So the fact that he'd been beaten up and was in pain is what you're happy about?" Ben was unable to prevent himself from asking, a little mischievously.

"No" she chuckled, "of course not! Initially, I was furious that he'd been so stupid, but then he explained what'd happened and it turns out that one of his friends was the one who'd got into a fight and all he'd done was try to defend him."

"So, you're happy that his friends are morons but he's not?" Ben asked, now genuinely confused.

Steph rolled her eyes, as though Ben's lack of understanding was foolish. "No" she replied. "I'm happy because he's realised that they're no good for him."

This time, Ben didn't even bother to say anything as his mind tried and failed to work out why that would have left her daydreaming.

Seeming to finally realise she wasn't being too clear, Steph explained further. "We talked" she said, "and he's admitted that he's been the problem between us over the last couple of months. He told me that he hasn't been sleeping with anyone, although he did admit to considering it, but he's realised that it's the people he's been hanging out with who've twisted his mind on that. Ben, he actually apologised to me and promised that things will be different from now on."

"And you believed that?" Ben asked, bitterly.

"Not at first" she answered, with a smile. "But then he started kissing me and, honestly, it felt like it did the first time we hooked up."

Ben felt as though he'd been hit by a truck and his stomach threatened to expel everything he'd eaten over the last week as his legs momentarily wobbled. He felt the blood drain from his face and he considered looking away, but that'd make it too obvious that something was wrong.

"I won't go into details" Steph continued, seemingly too lost in the memory to notice anything else, "but we had sex for the first time in ages and, honestly, it was better than it's ever been!"

Anger flared in Ben, but it was directed solely towards himself; he should've known this would happen, the moment she'd told him there was a problem yesterday. Why had he allowed his mind to convince itself that something had actually happened between them?

"Well, that's good" he said as honestly as he could, calling on all the experience he'd gained over the years he'd known her. "Hopefully he means it this time."

"I hope so too" she replied, with a satisfied smile. "And I think he does, if last night's anything to go by."

Fortunately, one of the few remaining customers approached the bar, giving Ben the chance to turn away from Steph for a few moments. He served the requested drinks and then decided to grab a cloth and head out to give the tables a clean, much to Steph's surprise.

"Were you wiping the dust off them?" she chucked, when he returned. "God, it's going slow tonight."

"Yeah" Ben agreed, now filled with a desire to get away from the place. "What say, if no one else comes in, we close up early?"

Steph nodded enthusiastically. "Absolutely!" she exclaimed.

They stood there in silence for a few minutes, neither of them having anything in particular to say.

"By the way" Steph eventually said, "what size was your jacket?"

Ben looked at her, slightly surprised by the question. "Why?" he asked.

"Because I've decided I'm going to buy you a new one," she answered, warmly, "to replace the one you lost saving the girl."

"You don't have to do that" Ben replied, quickly.

Steph nodded. "I know," she said, "but I've already decided that I'm going to, so don't bother to argue with me. I would've picked it up today, but I've lost my bloody bank card."

Chapter 5

Lying on an old, piss-stained mattress in the centre of what used to be the living room of his flat, Billy slept fitfully. Surrounded by the residue of many a night such as the last, his dreams were filled with memories of his past, images of his actions over the years, that caused his body to jerk under the filthy sheet, scattering the empty bottles and cans across the floor. With a scream, he sat bolt upright, his wide eyes staring straight ahead, before a violent lurch in his stomach sent him rolling to the side as a jet of vomit ejected itself from his mouth and splattered across both the mattress and the floor.

Groaning, he lay back and stared straight up at the ceiling, too scared to close his eyes in case the action brought with it another bout of nausea. From the brightness of the light which filled the room, he figured it must be late morning, or even early afternoon, not that it mattered much to him, for time had long ago ceased to carry any meaning.

There was a point at which he'd lost track of it all, at which his days had become nothing more than an endless journey through purgatory, but he had no real recollection of when that was. For now, the only thing he cared about was that he'd be able to sell enough drugs during the day to ensure that his nightly struggle to reach oblivion would be successful. Who knew? Maybe one of these days his body would finally give up and take the hint, instead of merely punishing him further with its constant failure to die?

Slowly, he pushed himself up again, pausing for a moment in the expectation that his head would begin to spin with the movement. When the dizziness failed to materialise, he continued his attempt at standing up and then looked down at himself, recoiling when he saw the vomit that covered the front of his t-shirt and the gradually drying wetness that stemmed from the crotch of his jeans.

"Fuckin' hell" he mumbled, his throat feeling as though it'd been wrapped in barbed wire.

He bent down and picked up an almost empty bottle of Vodka that lay discarded on the floor. There was barely a mouthful of its contents remaining, but he was grateful for the warmth the liquid provided as he swallowed it down and threw the bottle into the corner of the room. He then stripped off his clothing and threw them into the same corner, before stumbling out of the room and into the bathroom.

Turning on the taps, he stepped into the cold water of the shower and offered up a silent prayer of thanks that the water company had seen fit to sympathise with his plight for one more day at least, even if the electric company had removed the ability to heat the damn stuff. Once he'd become used to the icy chill he did his best to wash the filth from his skin, whilst he allowed his bladder to relieve itself at the same time, before shutting off the taps and stepping out of the cubicle.

The towel he picked up was hardened with a crust of dirt, so he discarded it and walked back into the living room, where he picked up a semi-clean t-shirt and wiped away the majority of the water on his body. He then dressed in the cleanest clothes he could find and picked up his bag of drugs on the way to the front door.

"Please, God" he whispered, as he stepped out into the sun-drenched street, "let today be the day."

Chapter 6

It was mid-morning and Ben and Sam were the only customers in the coffee shop. In fact, now Mary had popped into the back room, they were the only people in the place.

"How much longer would you give them?" Sam asked, keeping the volume of his voice low, in case Mary walked back in. "It's been like this for months now and they can't be making any money."

Ben looked round and shook his head. "I wouldn't give them long" he replied, mournfully.

They sat in silence for a few minutes as each of them habitually considered ways in which they might be able to help their friends but, as always, they were stumped. In the past, they'd discussed the possibility of linking the place up with The Skinning Pit somehow, but they just hadn't been able to find a way of doing that; it wasn't as though they were overflowing with custom themselves and their weekend crowd just weren't the kind to frequent a quaint coffee shop on a regular basis.

"So, come on then," Sam urged, keen to move on from the subject of the shop's demise, "Are you gonna tell me what I walked in on at the barbeque or not?"

With a shrug of his shoulders and a shake of his head, Ben tried to make out he'd no idea what the man was talking about.

"In the kitchen" Sam prompted. "You and Steph in a bit of a clinch?"

"Oh, that?" Ben replied, casually. "She was just making sure I was ok, you know what she's like."

"It looked a lot more than that to me mate" Sam smiled.

"No," Ben stated, firmly, "it really wasn't"

The frown put a deep crease in Sam's brow as he regarded Ben for a second. "What's happened?" he asked, the joviality dropping from his voice.

Ben gave a slight shake of his head. "Nothing" he answered, resignedly, "but I was sure there was something more when she looked at me. It sort of felt as though she was waiting for me to kiss her, or something."

Sam contemplated that for a moment, before replying. "Dude" he said, "I've walked in on you two hugging before, and I've never felt as though I'd interrupted something. Maybe there was something there? From what she was saying afterwards, it's clear she's not happy with Rob at the moment."

"That's just it" Ben stated. "I thought so too until she told me that, when he'd got home that night, he apologised for the way he's been acting and promised to change. She was adamant that things were going to go back to the way they were when she first met him."

"But you don't believe that?" Sam asked, noticing the cynicism in Ben's voice.

"I don't trust him" Ben sighed. "By all accounts, he's been a proper bastard over the last couple of months, yet he gets into a fight and when he gets home everything's changed?"

"He got into a fight?" Sam exclaimed.

"Yeah. Apparently his mates got into some trouble and left him alone to deal with it, so now he's realised they're no good and wants to dedicate himself to Steph, or something."

Confusion painted itself across Sam's expression. "But I thought him and his mates were tight?" he asked, somewhat rhetorically. "It doesn't make sense that they'd leave him hanging like that."

"Exactly" Ben replied. "But apparently they did and apparently, as Steph so eloquently put it, it resulted in the sex they had that night being better than it's ever been."

"Fucking hell," Sam sighed, sitting back in his chair, "I'll bet you enjoyed hearing about that?"

With a half-smile, Ben nodded. "Oh, it was awesome" he answered. "Just what I wanted to hear."

"So, how are you with all this, really?" Sam asked.

Ben shook his head. "It's fucking me over" he admitted. "I don't know if I can do this for much longer."

It was a reply Sam had expected, in fact, his only surprise was that his friend hadn't confirmed it a lot sooner. "You've gotta move on from this" he said, honestly. "I know you love her, but you can't spend the rest of your life putting yourself through all this."

"But that's the problem" Ben replied. "How can I move on when I love her this much? She's the first thing I think about when I wake up and the last thing I think about before I go to sleep. When I'm with her it's like nothing else matters and whatever I'm doing it's always better when she's there with me. I've tried thinking about other women, I've tried finding someone else, but the fact is that, unless I find someone I love more than Steph, then I'm fucked."

Sam rubbed his eyes and let out a long sigh. "It worries me to hear you say that, Dude" he said, staring into Ben's eyes.

"It worries me too" Ben replied, honestly. "But short of moving away completely, there's nothing I can do and I'm not doing that. At least this way I get to spend time with her occasionally and, unless she suddenly realises that I'm the guy for her, I'm just gonna have to suck it up."

Their conversation was halted by the ringing of the small bell above the door and they looked over as two men entered. Both of them were big, dressed in plain black from head to toe, and neither appeared the type to crave a morning cup of coffee and a cake. Ben and Sam watched as they walked through the room, appearing to scrutinise every nook and cranny in the place as they made their way to a table in the far corner, as far away from the windows as they could physically get.

Summoned by the sound of the bell, Mary came through from the back room and flinched a little in surprise when she saw who'd entered. She tried to conceal her taking of a deep breath, but her nervousness was obvious as she approached the two men and, when they sent her away without ordering, Ben and Sam flashed each other a mutual look of concern.

"How are you boys doing?" Mary asked with a wavering smile, as she walked over to their table.

"We're fine, thanks" Ben replied, making his glance in the direction of the men as obvious as he could to her. "Are you ok?"

Having realised that Ben had recognised her concern, Mary seemed to relax a little when she answered. "I'm ok, thanks" she said, with a cursory glance around the room. "I'm just a little tired of all this. The place isn't what it used to be, that's for sure."

"I'm sure it'll pick up" Sam suggested, unconvincingly.

"It's not just the shop" Mary sighed. "It's the whole place, the whole city. Every day I read about more violence and the vandalism's just getting worse. And then there's what happened to the girl you found, Ben. Honestly, I just want to sell up and move away from here but this is Albert's dream and I hate to see him fail like this."

The two men stood up, before Ben or Sam had the chance to reply. Silently, they walked towards the door, staring at Ben as they passed.

"What the hell was all that about?" Sam asked rhetorically, as the door closed behind them.

Dani stood alone in her office, staring out of the window without actually paying any attention to the world outside. If her mind wasn't so far away, she'd have seen visitors drawing on the last few drags of a cigarette before heading in to see their loved ones, she'd have seen the hospital's orderlies running about with beds and wheelchairs and she'd have seen her colleagues racing between wards or catching a quick break themselves. As it was, all her thoughts were focussed on the telephone call she'd taken almost an hour before.

"So, you decided not to bother meeting me for lunch then" Emily stated as she entered the room, breaking Dani's trance.

"Huh?" Dani muttered, turning round quickly.

"Lunch" Emily stated. "You were supposed to meet me in the canteen?"

"Damn!" Dani exclaimed, with a shake of her head. "I'm sorry. I got side-tracked and completely forgot."

Closing the door behind her, Emily walked fully into the office. "What's going on?" she asked.

"They've finished the autopsy on the girl," Dani replied, taking a seat at her desk, "and they found a puncture wound in her foot."

Emily looked a little confused as she also sat down. "Drugs?" she suggested.

"Not that they could find" Dani answered. "But her levels were significantly unbalanced which, at her age, is a little strange."

"Has the pathologist offered any suggestions?"

"The only thing he can think of, is that someone must have injected her with potassium."

"Potassium?" Emily muttered, almost to herself. "But that would have brought on the heart-attack straight away, which means someone must have given it to her here, in the hospital."

Dani nodded.

"Why would they do that?" Emily continued. "Unless they'd made a mistake?"

"That's unlikely" Dani replied. "There was no one on the ward who would have needed potassium, as far as I know."

"So, what are you suggesting?" Emily asked. "That someone gave it to her intentionally?"

Dani didn't reply, providing all the answer Emily needed.

"You can't be serious?" she exclaimed. "There's no reason for anyone to do that."

Sorrow's Requiem

"There is if they didn't want her to talk."

A whiteness washed over Emily's face as the blood drained from her cheeks. "You think someone murdered her?" she asked.

For a moment Dani looked at her in silence, as the concept worked its way back through her mind. "I know it seems ridiculous," she said, "but I can't see any other reason. Dosing her with potassium was the only way to ensure that she didn't survive, without leaving any hard evidence, and it makes sense that the people who did this didn't expect her to be found, let alone to be able to tell the police exactly what happened."

Now it was Emily's turn to fall into silence, as she thought about Dani's allegation. "Have you reported this?" she finally asked.

"No" Dani answered. "Not yet."

"Well, what about the pathologist? Has he put it in his report?"

"He's mentioned the puncture wound and the high levels of potassium, but he hasn't speculated as to what might have happened."

Emily took a deep breath. "Good" she replied, with a relieved nod of her head.

"Good?" Dani asked. "Why is that good?"

"It's good, because I don't want to see you becoming wrapped up in all this" Emily answered, frankly. "Dani, there's no evidence that this actually happened" she continued. "It's all just speculation."

"But there needs to be an investigation" Dani argued. "If someone within the hospital is connected to this, then they need to be found."

"But who could it be?" Emily pointed out. "Have you any idea who could be involved with this?"

Dani shook her head.

"Then all you'd be doing is labelling everyone as a potential murderer, based on the thinnest of evidence. You know how this place is. People won't understand that there are legitimate concerns, all they'll see is that you're making wild allegations against them and that won't do anything but damage you."

"I can't just let this lie" Dani replied. "That poor girl was murdered."

With a sigh, Emily looked fixedly at Dani. "You don't know that for certain" she said, through a half-smile. "If the pathologist could state that's what happened, then I'd back you all the way, but even he can't say for definite that something hadn't caused the high levels before she was brought in. Maybe it was a hereditary problem that has nothing to do with the puncture wound?"

"So, how did she get the puncture wound?" Dani asked.

"Who knows" Emily answered. "Maybe whoever it was that attacked her tried to dose her up with something but she kicked out of it? Maybe that's why they beat her so badly?"

The idea began to filter through to Dani's mind, pushing its way through her doubt. "Maybe you're right?" she muttered, hesitantly.

"Look" Emily said, firmly but not unkindly. "The report will go to the police and they'll review it. If they feel there's something there that needs investigating, then they'll investigate it. If that happens, then I'll help you in whatever way you need but, until it does, I'm just asking that you don't put yourself in the firing line."

Dani thought about that for a few seconds, before nodding her agreement. "Maybe you're right" she said.

"I'm always right" Emily laughed.

Almost as though she'd been directly connected to the music, the girl swayed and moved in perfect time to the rhythm of the song. Each carefully rehearsed movement appeared completely natural, unplanned and improvised as her body painted a visualisation of the music that entranced and enthralled the watching eyes. Slowly and deliberately, she traced the fingertips of her right hand around from her hip to her back and then continued up the length of her spine, stopping only to unhook the clasp of her bra as she held it in place with her left arm. She fixed her gaze on one watcher in particular, her eyes burning with a lust that seemed to drive itself directly into the man's heart and suddenly, as the tune reached its crescendo, with one swift and almost unperceivable motion she exposed herself to the expectant crowd.

From his stool at the end of the bar Lee couldn't see the man's face, but he didn't need to. It was obvious from the way he hastily plunged his hand into his pocket and pulled out a bunch of notes that the guy had just fallen in love and, honestly, he couldn't blame him. As the next tune kicked in, an all-together heavier track with a riff that almost dripped with filthy intent, the arousal of the girl's routine moved up more than a couple of levels. Practically making love to the pole, she writhed around the stage, sending the on looking crowd into frenzy until the breathtaking finale, in which her full nudity was presented in more than just a little glory.

"Jesus" Lee whispered to himself, as he turned back towards the bar and looked at the barmaid.

"Speaking as your girlfriend," Sarah said, with a sly wink, "should I be worried by that expression on your face?"

"Speaking as my girlfriend," Lee smiled in reply, "you should be inviting her into our bed."

Sarah let out a snigger of derision. "Babe" she said in good humour. "You can barely handle me on my own."

Lee laughed in agreement. "You got that right" he chuckled. "Who is she?"

"Her stage name's Elixir" Sarah answered, with a quick glance towards the stage, from which the dancer was leaving to rapturous applause. "She came in about a week ago, looking for a job. Alex agreed to give her a shot, so tonight's her trial. I'm guessing you approve?"

"Approve?" Lee exclaimed. "It was all I could do to stop myself from throwing cash on to the stage."

"Ah, that's just because you haven't had any pussy for nearly a month. Your judgement's impaired by desperation."

"Impaired judgement or not, just don't take it personally if I get her number."

"And don't take it personally when I give you a matching scar on the other side of your skull!" Sarah chuckled, with a hint of promise in her voice as she threateningly waived an empty bottle in the air.

Laughing, Lee backed away in mock fear. "Where is Alex?" he asked. "I need to have a word with him."

"I think he went into the office," Sarah replied, before narrowing her eyes threateningly, "but after that performance, he's probably already in the changing room, waiting to drool all over Elixir."

"Oh, good" Lee smiled, taking delight from the predictability of his reply. "Then I can kill two birds with one stone. Can you pass me a pen and some paper? She'll need something to write her number on."

Sarah shook her head and turned to the back counter of the bar. When she turned back round to face him, she was brandishing the knife they used to cut the lemons. "Here" she smiled, "you can give her this. She can carve the number into your bald head."

Placing his hand over his heart as he jumped off the stool, Lee mimed offence at the response. "So cruel" he gasped, before walking away.

Alex was in the office with Elixir, who was still to get dressed after her performance, looking up and down her naked body.

"What d'you think?" he asked, as Lee walked in. "Should we sign her up?"

Lee looked at her and noticed that, whereas even strippers could often feel a little uncomfortable having their bodies scrutinised in this manner, she seemed perfectly comfortable on display in the bright light. "That was good" he said to her, doing his best to appear as nonchalant as he could. "I'm guessing you've danced before?"

Elixir nodded. "A few places" she replied. "But I like to move around and now I've ended up here, so figured it was time to get some work."

"So you're planning on sticking around for a bit?" Alex asked.

"A lot depends on how much you're going to pay me" she answered, honestly.

"Don't you mean it depends on whether we offer you a job?" Alex suggested.

"You saw my show" Elixir smiled in reply. "I mean it depends on how much you're going to pay me."

With a chuckle, Lee looked at Alex and then back to Elixir. "When can you start?" he asked.

"Hang on!" Alex exclaimed, undoing his belt and dropping his jeans. "First you've got to earn your position!"

Looking down, Elixir shook her head. "No" she firmly stated. "I'm not sucking you off."

"Why? Because you're not that kind of girl?" Alex asked.

"No" she answered, flashing Lee a wink. "Because I couldn't even use that tiny thing to floss my teeth" she laughed.

Whilst Alex gingerly pulled up his jeans, Lee joined her in laughing at him. "Welcome to the club" he said to her. "Why don't you go and get yourself dressed and then we'll sort out the paperwork?"

Nodding, Elixir walked towards the door, reaching down to pat Lee's groin as she passed by him. "Now you," she whispered, "I might consider."

"Why the fuck do you do that?" Lee asked Alex, as Elixir closed the door behind her. "And don't give me bullshit about wanting to check their integrity."

"You know I couldn't give a shit about integrity" Alex replied, with a smile. "I just want my cock sucked."

Lee shrugged in response. "I can't argue with that" he smiled. "Look, I need to talk to you."

Slightly surprised by the seriousness that'd crept into his voice, Alex looked at him for a second. "What's up?" he asked, taking a seat on the edge of the desk.

"I'm not sure" Lee answered. "Hopefully nothing, but I don't think I'm that lucky."

"This sounds like it might be bad" Alex suggested.

"It could be" Lee replied. "Has anything been going on while I was away?"

"Like what?"

"Like Michael acting strangely?"

Alex thought about it for a moment and then shook his head. "Not that I can think" he said, somewhat hesitantly. "But he hasn't really been around much."

"D'you know where he's been?"

"No, but I didn't think too much about it. I just figured he had stuff to do."

"Fuck" Lee muttered.

"What's the problem?" Alex asked.

"I'm probably just being paranoid" Lee replied. "But do me a favour? Don't mention this conversation to anyone."

Chapter 7

As the sound of laughter emanated from the corner of the room, Ben looked over and couldn't help the wry smile that spread across his lips. It'd taken him a couple of years to realise what was going on, initially thinking nothing of the phenomenon until, gradually, he'd begun to recognise a few more of the faces than just the couple of regulars who were involved. Every six months, always the last Friday of the month, the lunchtime rush would slowly clear, leaving the same set of between fifteen and twenty people remaining, firmly ensconced in their corner until well into the night.

He watched as Steph attempted to collect some of the empty glasses from their table and let out a quiet chuckle as one of the group stood up and began to gesticulate wildly. From that distance, he couldn't hear exactly what was being said but, from the gestures being acted out and his previous knowledge of the man demonstrating them, he guessed it would be hugely inappropriate yet highly amusing.

Eventually, the man's friends managed to wrestle him back into his seat and Steph made her way back towards the bar, smiling warmly as she looked at Ben and rolled her eyes.

"What was all that?" Ben asked her, keen to hear what the guy had come out with this time.

Chuckling, Steph shook her head as she passed the glasses to him over the bar. "I have absolutely no idea" she replied. "He wanted to know if I'd ever tried some sort of sexual position that seemed to involve dislocating at least four of my joints and would probably end up with me in a coma."

Ben laughed. "Well," he smiled, "have you?"

"Not yet" she answered. "But if I can find myself some peanut butter and a strap-on, apparently I should give it a go tonight."

"Rob will be pleased" Ben suggested.

Now Steph laughed. "Based on what he's supposed to be doing in all this, he's more likely to be crippled than pleased!" she exclaimed, as she made her way behind the bar.

One of the group walked towards them with a clear look of embarrassment on his face. "I'm so sorry about that" he said to Steph. "He doesn't mean any offence by what he does."

"It's fine" Steph smiled. "He's funny."

"Well, let me get you a drink" the man replied.

Steph shook her head. "Honestly, there's no need" she said. "What can I get you?"

The man gave her his order and took the drinks back to the table, after refusing to accept his change. "I insist" he smiled, as he walked away.

"They're a good bunch" Steph muttered, dropping the change in a glass and placing it on the counter behind her.

Ben looked at her for a few seconds. "You're in a strangely good mood" he pointed out.

Steph contemplated that for a moment or two before nodding in response. "I really am" she practically sighed.

"Any particular reason?" he asked, despite having more than a suspicion as to the cause.

"No, not really" she answered, somewhat hesitantly.

Ben's raised eyebrows were enough to demonstrate he knew she wasn't being entirely honest.

"Ok" she admitted. "Rob took me out on a date last night."

"He took you out on a date?"

"Yeah. He came home and announced that he thought we should do something romantic, you know, to show our relationship is starting again."

A non-committal nod was all Ben could manage in acknowledgement, as he felt his heart sink.

"He took me out to a little restaurant in the country" she continued, excitedly. "Then we went for a walk along the river, but we didn't get very far. He pulled me into the first secluded spot we came across and I'll leave what happened to your imagination."

Again, all Ben could manage was a nod of his head and the weakest of smiles.

"And he paid for the whole thing!" Steph exclaimed.

"He paid?" Ben asked, surprise overcoming his disappointment.

"Yep! He's even got himself a job! It's only a couple of days a week, but it's cash in hand and he's looking for something permanent."

"That's good" Ben muttered, failing in his bid to portray sincerity.

Fortunately, Steph was too wrapped up in her own enthusiasm to notice. "Ben" she said almost dreamily, as her eyes all but glazed over. "He's really trying this time."

Ben's mind raced and his heart felt as though it'd been smashed into a million pieces. Their last conversation had pretty much put paid to any fleeting hopes that something might finally be developing between them, but hearing about Rob changing like this was basically the final nail in that particular dream's coffin. He wanted her to be happy, of course he did, and somewhere deep in his brain he was pleased to see the smile that lit up her expression, it was just going to take a little bit of time for that pleasure to overcome his heartache.

"I'm glad to hear it" he said, finally managing to pull himself together enough to appear genuine.

Steph nodded, her eyes narrowing with intent as she stared at him. "Now we've just got to sort you out, haven't we?"

"Steph . . ." he began, before she cut in.

"I know" she smiled. "You're happy and all that, but I'm not going to believe that and I'm not giving up whether you like it or not."

The sound of the doors opening brought a welcome distraction from the conversation, but Ben felt his heart sink even further when he saw Detectives Crowther and Wishall stride in.

Steph watched silently as the two detectives walked out of the office. They'd been in there for over half an hour and the raised voices that'd emanated from the room had only increased her concern. They bid her a cheerfully sarcastic farewell as they left, but she ignored them as she focussed her attention on Ben, whose face was ghostly white.

"What's going on?" she asked, noticing that he was shaking. "Are you ok?"

Ben didn't reply immediately, he simply stared at the doors as they closed behind the two men.

"Ben?" she tried, reaching out to take a hold of his arm.

The touch pulled him out of his daze and he slowly looked at her. "They're determined to prove it was me" he muttered in reply, almost to himself.

"What?" Steph exclaimed. "They're determined to prove what was you?"

"That it was me who attacked and killed the girl" he answered, his voice wobbling a little as he spoke.

"But that's ridiculous" she said, struggling to make sense of what he was saying.

Ben shook his head. "They don't believe that" he replied. "To them, it makes perfect sense."

"But, surely, they'll need evidence and there's no way they'll find any?"

"That's what I thought" Ben stated, before taking a deep breath to steady himself. "But I don't think that matters to them. All they want to do is find a way of pinning it on me and I don't think they'll stop until they manage it."

Steph had no idea of what to say, so she grabbed two glasses and poured them both a large measure of Vodka. "Here" she whispered, "you look as though you need this."

Ben looked at the glass as she handed it to him and then looked at her. "Thanks" he said, finally appearing to pull himself together.

They both knocked back the drinks, before Steph poured them another. "I tell you what" she said, smiling broadly. "We finish here in an hour or so, so how about we hit the town? Just you and me?"

Without the need for any consideration, Ben readily agreed.

"Yeah!" Steph exclaimed, handing him his drink. "Let's get wasted!"

"I'm tellin' ya, man" Touchy sighed. "That gash did shit that'd make a whore blush! The back seat of her car looked like a fuckin' slaughterhouse when I'd done with her!"

Ethan shook his head as he laughed. "You're fuckin' sick in the head" he chuckled in reply. "What about her man? Where was he when you were doing that?"

Touchy gave a cheeky wink as he answered. "That prick was still strapped to the bonnet!" he laughed. "Seriously, the sick bastard watched the whole thing through the window and I swear he shot his bolt when the bitch gagged on my cock!"

Again, Ethan shook his head as his amusement increased.

"He wasn't so fuckin' excited when I drove off with him still there though!" Touchy continued. "He fuckin' shit himself, the pussy! And I mean he actually shit himself, all over the front of the car!"

"Then what d'you do with 'em?" Ethan asked, almost scared to hear the answer.

Touchy smiled. "I let 'em go with a warning" he replied. "And you can bet they won't be using my fuckin' parking space again, that's for sure."

"You could've just asked 'em to move the car" Ethan pointed out.

"Where's the fun in that?" Touchy asked, as a knock on the door signalled the end of their conversation.

Touchy opened it and one of the club's probationary members dragged Rob into the office, followed timidly by a young woman.

"I've got your money" Rob blurted out, as the door was closed and he and the woman stood nervously in the centre of the room.

Ethan looked at him for a few seconds, taking in the remnants of bruising around the man's eye. He then nodded towards the woman. "Is that your rich bitch?" he asked.

Rob quickly shook his head. "No" he stammered, as Touchy walked towards her.

She closed her eyes as Touchy reached up with his hand and began to stroke the back of it from her cheek to her neck. He continued the journey down her now visibly shaking body, pausing for a second to squeeze her breast, before tracing his fingers along her stomach until she let out a whimper as he forcibly planted his palm between her legs. "Then why's she here?" Touchy questioned. "Did you bring her to us as a present?"

"No" Rob again stammered. "She helped me get the money."

"Well, maybe I'll take her anyway?" Touchy sniggered, now firmly rubbing his hand over the woman's crotch. "Unless you wanna try and stop me?"

"Please" Rob muttered, as he now started to shake. "I just want to give you the money and then we'll leave."

"You'll leave when we say you can leave" Touchy hissed aggressively in reply, as tears started to cascade freely from the woman's eyes.

"Let me see it then" Ethan stated, gesturing for Touchy to back away from her.

Quickly, Rob stepped forward and emptied a bag of cash on to the desk, before moving back to stand protectively next to the woman. Ethan sifted through the small bundles of notes and gave a slight chuckle as he looked back at Rob.

"I've got to admit," he smiled, "I really didn't think you'd come through with this. Let me guess, your girlfriend doesn't know you've taken it?"

Rob shook his head.

"And, judging by the fact the two of you are carrying rather large bags," Ethan continued, "I'm guessing you're intending to be long gone before she finds out?"

Somewhat reluctantly, Rob nodded.

Ethan slowly shook his head as he scrutinised the pair of them. "You fuckin' gutless piece of shit" he said, with some venom in his voice. "I'm bettin' that, if you'd have explained the situation to your girlfriend then she probably would've been glad to help, but I'm also guessing you've been screwin' this bitch behind her back, haven't you?"

No reply was forthcoming, as Rob seemed to wilt under Ethan's intense glare.

"Get the fuck outta here!" Ethan snapped, the sudden rise in volume causing both Rob and the woman to flinch.

Hastily, Rob ushered the woman out of the room and, as the door was closed behind them, Touchy gave Ethan a wry smile.

"Ruckus won't be happy you let that prick go" he said.

"Fuck it" Ethan replied. "We've just rinsed him for a serious amount of cash."

Touchy slowly shook his head. "What're you doing?" he asked. "I know he's your dad, but that won't stop him if he thinks you're challenging him."

"This isn't about challenging him" Ethan answered. "It's about being cleverer in the way we do things, that's all. If I'd have done what Ruckus wants, then we'd have got nothing from that twat and he wouldn't be back to give us more."

"It isn't about the money though" Touchy stated. "It's about keeping up our reputation. What if he goes out now, and tells everyone we let him off?"

"We didn't exactly let him off" Ethan replied, looking at the door. "And I doubt that cunt will say anythin' to anyone after this."

"You can't be sure of that."

Ethan nodded. "I know" he agreed. "But if he does say anythin', then we'll fuckin' destroy him and stick his head on a spike. That'll fuckin' spread the word, don't you worry."

Uncertainty was evident in Touchy's expression.

"Don't you fuckin' say anything to Ruckus about this either" Ethan warned. "He doesn't need to know."

"So, where do you fancy going?" Steph asked, as they wandered almost aimlessly along the street.

Finally feeling more relaxed following the afternoon's encounter with the detectives, Ben gave her a cheeky smile. "How about we grab some peanut butter and a strap on?" he chuckled.

They both laughed as they continued to amble past the various bars and clubs which ran along the length of the city's main street. It was rare that they'd consider drinking anywhere other than The Skinning Pit but, after what had happened earlier on, the idea of staying in there all night hadn't been too appealing.

"We could try the new place that's opened?" Steph suggested, gesturing further along the road. "I've heard it's ok."

"It's completely up to you" Ben replied. "After all, you think you're paying for all this."

"What do you mean, I think I'm paying?" Steph asked, stopping in her tracks and fixing him with concerned stare.

Ben smiled in reply. "Look," he said, "I appreciate the offer, but there's no way I'm letting you pay all night"

"You don't have a choice" Steph insisted. "I'm not letting you anywhere near the bars and if I see your hand go anywhere near your pocket for anything other than smokes, I'm going to rip it off."

"We'll see" he laughed. "When you're too drunk to speak, you won't be in any state to stop me."

Steph winked at him. "Foolish boy" she chuckled. "You're gonna be smashed out of your brain well before me. Remember, I'm the one who's gonna be sorting the drinks."

"Oh, really?" Ben laughed, as they started walking again. "That's a bold statement."

"It's not a statement, it's a promise!" Steph exclaimed, giving him a playful nudge with her shoulder. "Hang on a minute, I've just got to get some cash out otherwise it's going to be a dry night."

"So, you found your bank card?" Ben asked.

"Yeah" Steph replied, as they approached the cash machine. "Rob found it this morning. It was with all the bills, so I must've forgotten to put it back in my purse when I'd finished paying them."

Ben pondered that for a second, whilst Steph inserted the card into the slot. "That's not like you" he said.

"A lot's not been like me, lately" she agreed, punching in her pin number. "But things are starting to get back to normal now."

A few seconds passed, whilst the machine accessed her information, and then she requested the option to check her balance.

"That's not right" she muttered, when the figures appeared.

"What's not right?" Ben asked, immediately concerned by the change in her demeanour.

There was no answer as Steph continued to stare at the screen.

"What's up?" Ben tried.

Slowly, Steph turned to look at him and the worry was evident in her eyes. "There's a load of money gone from my account" she said, her voice wobbling slightly.

"Maybe your bills took longer to come out?" Ben half-heartedly suggested, despite knowing it was an idiotic thought.

Steph shook her head. "No" she answered. "There's thousands missing."

Ben had no idea what to say, and could only look at her blankly whilst she ran through it in her mind.

"I'm sorry, Ben" she said, clearly trying to fight back the tears as she removed her card. "I've got to go home."

Chapter 8

An uneasy quiet fell on the room as Ruckus strode in, leaving Banjo to close the door behind him. The members took to their seats around the table and looked towards him for the meeting to begin.

"What's the situation with the girl?" he asked, getting straight to the point as he turned towards Ethan.

Ethan resignedly shook his head. "It's not good" he admitted. "Crowther and Wishall have got fuck all on the guy and, by the sounds of it, they're not gettin' anywhere fast."

"So, what the fuck have they been doing?" Touchy hastily joined in.

Again, Ethan shook his head. "Fuck all, it seems" he answered. "They interviewed him in the hospital and then at the bar, but he's not given 'em anythin' they can use yet."

Ruckus released a long sigh of exasperation. "This was all supposed to be simple" he muttered, glancing at Ethan.

"Well, it would've been, if Fucknut and Pisswipe over there had done what they were fuckin' supposed to" Touchy announced, glaring across the table at Jimmy and Ray.

Jimmy held his hands up in defence. "It was half two in the morning and the bar was fuckin' closed" he argued. "She was practically dead when we left her."

"Haven't you heard of checking for a fuckin' pulse, you fuckin' dick?" Touchy mocked, aggressively.

"They'll be fuckin' checking you for a pulse, if you carry on" Jimmy exclaimed, angrily.

Laughing sarcastically, Touchy rose from his chair and held his arms out. "Please, bring it the fuck on!" he begged.

"Alright!" Ethan shouted, before Jimmy had the chance to react. "Calm the fuck down, the pair of you."

Without taking his eyes off Jimmy, Touchy slowly sat back down as Ethan continued.

"The situation got fucked up" he said, calmly. "But it's not past saving."

"With those two pricks leading the investigation, I wouldn't fuckin' bank on it" Touchy replied, still angry but managing to keep control of himself.

"Not by themselves" Ethan agreed. "But we can give 'em some pointers."

Jimmy, along with the other members of the club, looked at him with some intrigue. "Like what?" he asked, voicing their thoughts. "If we get too involved, then we're asking for trouble."

"Not if we do this right" Ethan answered. "The problem is there's nothing to tie the guy to the girl and there's no past record Crowther and Wishall can use to trap him. All we need to do is provide them with something that'll give reasonable doubt and they'll be able to do the rest."

"What d'you mean, reasonable doubt?" Ray asked, as intrigue overcame his desire to avoid putting himself in Touchy's firing line.

"Like another body" Ethan replied, with a smile. "But this time, we make sure the bitch can be tied to the guy."

Ruckus, who'd been quietly watching the exchange, finally spoke up. "I don't like this" he announced, with a shake of his head. "Not whilst there's still a loose end to be tied up. There's too much risk. Crowther and Wishall managed to destroy the DNA evidence, didn't they?"

Ethan confirmed it, with a nod.

"Then I say we back away and let it pan out" Ruckus continued. "There's nothin' to link us to the girl, is there?"

"Not whilst Crowther and Wishall are handling the case, no" Ethan replied. "But they need to come up with something or they run the risk of being taken off it and, if it goes to anyone else, then the bitch's identity could cause us some problems."

"Why?" Ruckus asked.

"Because she worked in the casino" Ray admitted, reluctantly.

"What?" Touchy exclaimed, slamming his hand on the table. "You brought her to the party without telling us she worked there?"

"I thought you knew" Ray argued, somewhat pathetically.

Pulling a gun from his Cut, Touchy aimed it directly at Ray's face. "I should fuckin' shoot you right here!" he exclaimed. "You fuckin' prick!"

Ray backed away from the table, as Ruckus calmly reached out and lowered Touchy's arm.

"No one's shootin' anyone" he said, glaring at Ray. "At least, not yet."

"So what the fuck are we gonna do?" Touchy asked.

Slowly, Ruckus turned to Ethan. "You think you can handle it?"

Ethan nodded, before looking at Jimmy. "We've got this."

"Ok" Ruckus reluctantly agreed, before turning his attention to Banjo and Limpy. "Have you two found us another safe house?"

"The perfect place" Limpy answered. "It's a small coffee shop, on the outskirts of the city."

Ruckus was a little hesitant in his reply. "A coffee shop?" he asked.

"I know it's different to what we've used before" Limpy continued. "But, from what we can tell, it's owned by an old couple who're thinking of selling up 'cause the place is strugglin' for business. It's quiet, it's off the radar, the cops wouldn't consider the place and we can disguise the drugs and guns as deliveries of coffee so, if anyone does wanna snoop, then it'll all seem legit. On top of that, it's mainly cash payments, so money can go through the place without any questions being asked."

A low murmur rose around the table, before Ruckus spoke again.

"D'you think they'll be agreeable to our proposals?" he questioned.

"Fuck it, it don't matter" Limpy replied with a shrug, before flashing both Jimmy and Ray a sarcastic smile. "Neither of 'em are getting' any younger and the pressure of a strugglin' business has gotta be weighing down on them so, if they aren't agreeable, then a heart-attack wouldn't raise any eyebrows."

"Then it's settled" Ruckus announced, with a chuckle. "You two, me and Touchy will pay 'em a little visit."

Night was drawing in as Ben pulled his old Matchless motorcycle to the kerb and looked up at the house, which showed no sign that anyone was home. He'd tried to call her several times throughout the day, leaving a number of messages, and the longer it went with no reply, the more enhanced became the ominous feeling in the pit of his stomach. Maybe he was jumping to conclusions, letting his dislike of Rob guide his thoughts, but his certainty that the man was behind the disappearance of her money was unshakeable and he had to ensure that Steph was ok.

Slowly, he alighted from his bike without taking his eyes off the house and, as he walked up the driveway, his mind ran amok with thoughts of where she might have gone if she wasn't there. To his knowledge, she didn't have any family and they shared the same, close-knit group of friends. Sam had already confirmed that neither he nor Karen had heard from her and it was unlikely she would've been in touch with Andy, so there wasn't really anywhere else he could think she would be.

When his knock on the door went unanswered, Ben tried to look in through the front window but the curtains were drawn. He moved over to the kitchen window, through which he knew there would be a gap in the blinds, but he could see nothing but darkness behind the glass. Taking his phone from the pocket of his jeans, he tried her number again, and his heart rate increased when the line rang through to voicemail.

"Steph, please give me a call" he said, with a trace of panic as he hammered once more on the door.

Returning the phone to his pocket, he stepped back from the house and, inexplicably, looked up to the bedroom windows above. He knew there would be nothing to see in them, but he was running out of ideas and, deep down, he hoped there might be a movement of the curtains or some other sign that she was there. Predictably, there was nothing and he began to realise that he was out of options. If she was there, then she clearly didn't want to see anyone and, if she wasn't, then he had no idea where else to look. With one, final throw of the dice, he tried her number again but, as the line once more went to voicemail, he heard the sound of the latch being unlocked.

"You don't give up, do you?" Steph muttered, through a tired smile as she opened the door.

For a second, Ben struggled to find a response as he took in the sight of her. Her hair was dishevelled, her eyes were red and puffy from crying and her dressing gown seemed to be the only clothing she was wearing.

"If you had of held out for just a couple more minutes, I was about to" he finally smiled in reply.

"Damn" she half-heartedly joked. "Well, you might as well come in."

As she turned away, Ben followed her into the darkness, closing the door behind him.

"Why haven't you returned any of my calls?" he asked, as he joined her in the living room.

"I didn't want to talk to anyone" she answered, bluntly.

"Not even me?"

"Especially not you" she stated, firmly but without animosity.

The words seemed to puncture his heart, almost ripping through his soul, and he felt his legs wobble as he stood in the doorway. "Why not me?" he muttered, his voice shaking as little as his mind raced.

Steph looked away from him as she replied. "Because I feel stupid" she whispered.

There were so many things running through his head that he wasn't able to make much in the way of sense out of them but, at the very forefront of his thoughts, was the moment the two of them had shared in her kitchen. Was all this something to do with that, he wondered; did she want to avoid him because he'd, somehow, caused all of this? And, if that was the case, was stupid really the way the thought of something happening between them made her feel?

Unsteadily, he moved into the room and sat down next to her on the settee. "Why do you feel stupid?" he asked, as time seemed to stand still whilst he awaited the answer.

"Because I crowed so much about how Rob was changing" she practically cried, as she buried her head in her hands. "I was busy telling you how wonderful he was being but, all the time, it was just a load of bullshit I should've seen coming."

Relief swept through him and, for a moment or two, he had to fight back the urge let out a cry of his own. "But how could you have seen it coming?" he whispered, quickly regaining a foothold in his thoughts. "He did everything to make you think he'd changed and you can't be blamed for falling foul of that."

"That's exactly why I should've seen it coming" she said, finally looking at him again. "After all the shit, all the crap he put me through, I should've questioned what was going on, instead of just acting like a love-struck schoolgirl."

Ben knew she was right, that his own questioning of the man's intent had been born from exactly the same reasoning, but he couldn't tell her that, not whilst she was beating herself up like this. "So, what's happened?" he asked, hoping that getting her to talk through it might help her past the self-examination that was clearly hurting her.

"He took it" she answered. "He took the money."

"He's admitted it?"

Steph shook her head. "I haven't seen him" she replied. "When I got back here last night, all of his things were gone. I rang the bank this morning and they told me that, apparently, I went in there with a guy a couple of days ago and withdrew it."

The look of confusion on Ben's face was obvious, so Steph continued.

"Apparently, I went in with my card and some household bills to prove my identity" she said. "And then I even signed the form before they handed over the cash."

"So, that's why he found your card with the bills?" Ben muttered, rhetorically. "He used them so that someone could pretend they were you."

"Probably the slut he was screwing" Steph agreed, with a trace of anger slipping into her voice. "And that's how he managed to pay for our night out."

"Fuckin' hell" Ben sighed. "Are your bank doing anything about it?"

A shrug was all Steph could do in reply, as fresh tears started falling from her eyes. She wiped her cheeks in a futile attempt to dry them, but her tears kept coming. Reaching out, Ben pulled her into a hug and held her tightly.

"What can I do?" he asked, knowing there really wasn't anything.

"Stay here with me" Steph whispered, tightening her grip around him. "I don't want to be alone right now."

Ben kissed the top of her head. "I'm not going anywhere" he replied.

"I fuckin' hate this music and I fuckin' hate this place" Jimmy moaned.

"Shut the fuck up" Ethan hissed in reply. "We wouldn't have to be here, if you and Ray weren't such useless pricks."

Shaking his head, Jimmy decided against responding and instead chose to return his attention to the mass of gyrating bodies on the club's dance floor as Ethan continued to lean casually against the bar.

"You wanna drink?" he eventually asked, as he drained the last dregs from the bottle in his hand.

"We 'ain't here to get wasted" Ethan answered.

"That don't mean we can't enjoy ourselves."

Ethan didn't reply.

"Well, fuck it. I'm gettin' a couple in" he continued, turning to the bar and signalling for the barmaid to come over.

Two more beers were passed over to him and, when Ethan didn't take one, he put the bottle next to him on the bar.

"What about her?" he asked, as the barmaid moved away. "She's fuckin' hot."

"And she'll be used to guys hittin' on her" Ethan stated.

"So?"

"So she 'ain't gonna fall for some bullshit. We need someone a whole lot dumber than that."

"Well this place is full of dumb gash, so just take your pick and get on with it."

"It 'ain't that fuckin' simple."

"It 'ain't?"

"No, it fuckin' 'ain't."

"So, what the fuck you lookin' for? What about them over there?"

Following his gesture, Ethan saw the group of women Jimmy was referring to and shook his head.

"No" he replied. "They 'ain't left each other's side all night."

"Then what about them?" Jimmy questioned, pointing to a couple of the women on the dance floor. "You take one and I'll take the other."

Again Ethan dismissed the suggestion, as his attention was drawn back to a girl who'd been dancing by herself for the last ten minutes.

"She's the one" he stated, moving away from the bar. "You wait here and keep an eye out for anyone who shows an interest."

Without waiting for any acknowledgement, he moved across the dance floor, until he was near to the woman he'd spotted. Slowly, he found the rhythm of the song, matching her movements as he drew closer. When he was right in front of her, he waited for any sign that she wanted to back away and, when there was no indication of rejection, he reached out and placed his hands on her waist. The woman reacted to the contact by reaching up to rest her arms on his shoulders and they danced together for the remainder of the song.

They continued dancing to the next two tracks until, with a shake of her head, the woman told him she needed to get a drink and backed away slightly.

"Let me buy you one" Ethan asked.

The woman looked at him for a couple of seconds as a trace of doubt appeared in her expression and she glanced over to the side of the room.

"Come on" Ethan urged. "Just one drink?"

Once more, the woman glanced over to the side of the room, before looking back to him and smiling.

"Ok" she finally smiled, "but just one and then I've got to get back to my friends."

"It's a deal" Ethan grinned, leading her towards the bar.

Jimmy had been watching all of this unfold from his position at the bar. He followed the woman's gaze towards a group who were sat, regularly looking over at her and, when one of them approached the dance floor as Ethan led his conquest away, he immediately left his position and made a bee-line for the oncoming friend, giving no indication that he knew Ethan as they passed.

Free from any interruption, Ethan and the woman quickly arrived at the bar, where he signalled for the barmaid to serve them.

"What can I get you?" he asked.

The woman shrugged. "Anything" she replied.

Ethan looked at her for a moment, giving a slight shake of his head. "No" he smiled. "You look like the kind of woman who knows what she wants."

"Oh yeah?" she answered. "And what would that be?"

Now Ethan's smile turned into a broad grin. "Why don't we get the drinks sorted first?" he chuckled.

Giggling, the woman told him what she'd like and, once he'd passed her a drink, he leant in a little closer.

"So, who are you here with?" he asked.

"Just some friends" she answered, gesturing across the room.

Without looking to where she was pointing, Ethan continued. "And your boyfriend's not here?"

"I don't have a boyfriend" the woman smiled. "At least, not at the moment."

With a nod of acknowledgement, Ethan returned her smile and leaned in a little closer still. "I thought so" he said, slowly moving his arm around her back and resting his hand on her hip. "If he had you, no man would be happy to let you out by yourself in a place like this."

"Is that so?" she replied, looking deeply into his eyes.

"That's so" he confirmed. "Can I ask your name?"

A nervous giggle escaped her as she continued to look at him. "My name's Catherine"

"Well, Catherine" Ethan grinned. "My name's Ben."

Chapter 9

Within the almost tangible darkness of the room, Billy sat on his mattress with his back against the wall and a bottle clutched firmly in his hands. The streetlight outside the window battled with the grime and filth on the glass, to create the faintest of shadows into which he stared without blinking as he took a swig from the bottle. It may have appeared as though he was fascinated by the waste that'd gathered in the corner, mesmerised by the mould on the wall or the festering pile of clothes that'd been discarded there, but the truth was that a whole different vision was gradually pushing its way into his mind.

The image was hazy, clouded by both time and the regular consumption of alcohol, but he could recall the look of fear in the man's eyes as though he was standing right in front of him at that very moment. As clear as day, he remembered the sight of the man's pupils jumping around the room and the way he stammered when he spoke, as his frayed nerves rendered coherent response practically impossible.

Closing his eyes, Billy tried to keep the memory at bay, but he knew the attempt was futile and that, once started, it couldn't be stopped. Maybe this was his penance? Maybe this was the purgatory he needed to live through, before the pain would come to an end? But was there any guarantee? Who could say whether this nightmare would ever be over? For all he knew, once his body had finally succumbed to the inevitable, the afterlife could be an eternal replay of the mistakes he'd made. For now though, as the memory finally took up full residency in his mind, he guessed he had no choice but to re-live the moment.

He stood with Tommo and Ruckus outside a new shop that'd opened in the city. Tommo, his oldest and most trusted friend, was also the co-founder and Vice President of their motorcycle club, The Sons of Sorrow. All the way up to their arrival there, he'd argued that this wasn't something they should do, yet Billy had dismissed the man's opinion in favour of the points raised by Ruckus, one of the club's newest patched members. Now though, as he prepared to lead them into the shop, he was starting to have second thoughts.

"I'm tellin' ya" Tommo repeated. "This is pointless."

"Shut the fuck up, Tommo" Ruckus sighed, shaking his head in frustration before looking at Billy. "We've gotta do this," he said, "if we're gonna expand."

"But we don't need to expand" Tommo argued. "We're making more than enough from the casino."

"If you think it's enough," Ruckus replied, "then maybe you're the wrong man to be our VP? Billy, if we do this, then this city will be ours for the taking."

Tommo let out a snort of derision. "Ours for the taking?" he mocked. "Who the fuck d'you think you are? The fuckin' Godfather?"

"Enough!" Billy exclaimed, glaring at both of them. "Ruckus, we 'ain't takin' over anything and, Tommo, we need to do this. Keepin' the drugs at our clubhouse is too dangerous, so we need to put them somewhere that can't be linked to us, Ruckus is right on that."

Tommo shook his head. "We haven't had any problem before" he stated.

"No" Billy replied. "But how long will that last? All it needs is for one of the members to be picked up sellin' the shit and the place'll be raided in no time."

Billy took the lack of response to be a reluctant acceptance, and fixed Ruckus with a firm stare. "And you" he said, sternly. "Just let me do the talkin' in there."

Ruckus nodded his agreement and the three of them entered the shop, closing and bolting the door behind them, once they'd ensured no other customers were in there. The sound of the door brought the owner, a young man who sported an enthusiastic grin, through from the back, although, his smile quickly faltered at the sound of the bolt sliding into place.

"Can I help you?" the man asked, somewhat hesitantly as he seemed to struggle on deciding which of the men he should focus on.

"Yes, I think you can" Billy answered with a smile, as they approached the counter. "I have a business proposal for you."

"Ok" the owner replied, tentatively.

"You've a nice little place here," Billy continued, glancing around the shop, "and we'd like to help you whilst you're building up your custom."

"Help me how?" the owner asked, allowing a hint of cynicism to filter into his voice.

"By paying you to look after some things for us" Billy answered.

"What things?" the owner questioned.

"Drugs, guns and money" Ruckus stated.

Both Billy and the owner of the shop looked at him.

"Stop beatin' around the fuckin' bush" Ruckus told Billy, ignoring the look of rage that'd developed on his president's face. "He's either gonna agree, if he knows what's good for 'im, or he's not and we'll have to do somethin' about that."

"I told you I'd do the talking" Billy hissed.

"Well start fuckin' talkin' then" Ruckus exclaimed, before staring at the owner. "Look" he said, firmly. "It's fuckin' simple. Either you agree to look after our drugs and guns while we filter money through your accounts, or I cut your fuckin' throat and leave you to bleed all over this fuckin' place."

Now the owner was visibly shaking, as his eyes darted between all three of them. The sound of a voice from the back room only added to his fear and, when his girlfriend walked through the door, Ruckus grabbed her from behind. In one seamless movement, he'd unsheathed his knife and pressed it firmly against her throat, almost causing the owner's legs to buckle beneath him as his eyes widened in panic.

"Calm it down!" Billy demanded of Ruckus, before forcing the owner to look at him. "All you have to do is agree" he said, as kindly as his anger would allow. "Then this'll all be over and we can leave you alone."

"Why are you doing this?" the owner cried, as tears cascaded down his cheeks. "Please don't hurt her."

"All you have to do," Billy repeated, "is agree to this."

The owner's breathing became shorter as he stammered his reply. "I . . . I . . . I can't" he said. "I don't want to go to prison."

Billy briefly glanced at Tommo, who was staring intently at Ruckus. "You won't go to prison" he stated, portraying a confidence that was ebbing away as quickly as his control over the situation. "No one's gonna find anything amongst your stock."

"But what about the money?" the owner asked, almost breathlessly.

"That goes through as cash payments for goods" Billy answered. "You then pay us, less a small fee, and mark it as the purchase of stock."

As his eyes darted from Billy, to Ruckus, to his girlfriend and then back to Billy, it became obvious that the owner's fear was preventing him from processing the concept in his mind. "Is he . . ." he began, gesturing towards Ruckus as he choked on his words. "Is he" he tried again, after clearing this throat, "going to kill us?"

"No, of course not" Billy answered, despite his own uncertainty.

"Fuck this!" Ruckus exclaimed, as he firmly drew the knife across the woman's throat, sending a torrent of blood cascading down her chest.

Before either Billy or Tommo could realise what was happening, Ruckus threw the woman's body to the floor and stepped forward, driving the point of the knife into the owner's eye socket.

"What the fuck!" Billy exclaimed, as he grabbed Ruckus by the collar and pushed him back against the shelving at the side of the shop. "Why the fuck did you do that?"

Ruckus smiled, his eyes burning with the high of his blood lust. "The man was pointless" he replied, as calmly as though he'd merely spilt a drink. "Even if he'd have agreed, there was no way I'd trust him not to talk, the moment he was asked a question."

"You didn't have to fuckin' kill 'em!" Billy screamed, pulling Ruckus away from the shelving and angrily slamming him back against it.

Now laughing, Ruckus seemed impervious to any pain the impact may have caused. "Of course I did" he stated, calmly. "What? You don't think he'd have been on the phone to the cops, the moment we'd left?"

Again, Billy slammed Ruckus against the shelving, in place of giving a response he didn't have.

"Think about it" Ruckus smiled. "When word of this gets out, the next place we go won't be so fuckin' hesitant in workin' for us."

Billy shook his head. "We're not goin' anywhere else" he hissed.

"That's just your fear talkin'" Ruckus replied. "We still have to find somewhere and you know it. What you didn't figure is that we had to send out a message and this'll do that."

"This isn't the way we do things!" Tommo exclaimed, finally managing to tear his eyes away from the bodies.

Ruckus glanced over at him and smiled. "It is now" he stated, before looking back at Billy. "If you wanna run drugs and you wanna be the President," he said, "then you can't be scared to get your hands dirty."

As the memory slowly faded, Billy looked down at the pattern of scars which weaved themselves across his hands. They were hard to make out in the darkness of the room, but in his mind he saw them clearly, along with the tobacco stains and filth that'd become ingrained into his skin. He took another, long swig from the bottle and then leaned his head back against the wall as he let out a deep sigh. He'd certainly done that, he thought, ruefully.

Chapter 10

For the third time in less than half an hour, the shrill beep of the alarm clock cut viciously into Lee's dreams. He flailed an arm in the general direction of the noise, attempting to find the button without having to open his eyes, as he felt Sarah stir next to him.

"Switch the bloody thing off" she muttered, turning away from him and burying her head in the pillow. "And for god's sake, get up."

Reluctantly giving in, he sat up and looked at the table, at which point the urge to hit the snooze button one last time became overwhelming.

"Don't you dare press it again!" came the mumbled and borderline angry statement that put paid to his hopes of just eight more minutes.

Why the hell was the snooze time eight minutes, he wondered, as he flicked the switch and brought a welcome end to the auditory harassment; who the hell decided that eight minutes was the ideal timescale? Why wasn't it five, or ten? Surely a round number would make more sense than a seemingly random figure that'd been plucked out of thin air?

Reaching behind her, Sarah began to gently push his shoulder. "Get up" she repeated, as her shoves quickly increased in their aggression, rapidly becoming feeble punches to his arm.

"Alright" he grumbled in reply, swinging his legs out of the bed.

His head felt as though someone was drilling concrete inside his skull and, as he reached for the painkillers, he momentarily wondered whether this ache was normal after the surgery he'd been through. They did say he was likely to experience headaches, which was why they'd given him the pills, but he couldn't help but feel a twinge of concern at the pain. Turning slightly on the edge of the bed, he swallowed two tablets and took a second to gaze a little jealously at his girlfriend who, it seemed, hadn't found too much difficulty in falling back to sleep.

Grudgingly, he stood up and dragged himself into the bathroom, where he showered and got ready to head out. Despite the refreshing water, he still felt sluggish as he walked back into the bedroom, but at such an early hour of the morning, that wasn't surprising. He dressed in jeans and a sweater, before taking one last look at Sarah as he pulled on his Cut. She was now lying fully across the bed, spread-eagled as though she knew he'd be tempted to climb back in and was doing all she could to prevent it.

With a rueful shake of his head, he left the room and closed the door as quietly as he could manage. He walked a little way along the corridor, stopping outside Alex's dormitory.

"Time to get up" he called into the room, after opening the door only just enough for his voice to carry, without the need to shout and wake the rest of the club.

"Fuck off!" came the barked, and unsurprising, reply.

"Seriously" Lee insisted. "Get up"

No verbal reply was forthcoming, but the collision of something heavy, probably a boot, against the wall was all Lee needed to confirm his words had been understood. He pulled the door to, and made his way down to the main room of the clubhouse, where he headed straight for the coffee machine at the end of the bar. He glanced up at the clock on the wall and saw it was approaching quarter to eight, so he could afford to give Alex fifteen more minutes before he'd have to go and physically drag the man out of bed.

Switching on the machine, Lee took a seat at the end of the bar and lit up a cigarette whilst he waited for the water to boil. He was so used to the place being full of life, a constant stream of club members and women, that the quiet felt almost alien. With a long, sweeping look around, he couldn't help his mind wandering to various moments and conversations that'd taken place, picturing scenes that'd either played out in front of him or in which he'd been involved. A joke here, an argument there, it was amazing to think that so many things had happened there in such a short space of time and the realisation of how significant the place had become to them weighed a little heavily in this thoughts.

The silence was disturbed by the sound of someone coming down the stairs behind him.

"Fuckin' hell, you've actually got up" he exclaimed sarcastically, clapping his hands together in a mock round of applause as he turned in on his stool, but his childish banter quickly ceased when he saw it was Michael, not Alex, who entered the room.

"What are you doing up?" Michael questioned aggressively, clearly thrown by the sight of Lee sitting there.

"I've got my hospital appointment" Lee muttered in reply, somewhat taken aback by the trace of anger in the man's voice.

Michael stood still for a moment, staring at Lee whilst his mind seemed to process what he'd been told. Eventually, he appeared to pull his thoughts together and gave a shrug as he walked to the coffee machine. "You want one of these?" he asked, grabbing two mugs from the shelf under the bar.

Hesitantly, Lee nodded. "Why are you up this early?" he asked.

Again, Michael shrugged. "I've got stuff to do" he answered, a little guardedly.

"What stuff?"

"Just stuff. Why're you going back to the hospital? Is something wrong with you?"

Lee looked at him for a few seconds, watching him as he set about making the drinks. "No" he finally answered. "It's just a check-up."

Handing him his coffee, Michael tried to present a smile as he spoke. "How're you getting there?" he asked. "After all, you can't ride yet, can you?"

Despite the smile on his lips, there was no disguising the bitterness in the man's voice. "I'm getting a lift off Alex" Lee stated, somewhat curtly. "I'm hoping they'll give me the all-clear to get back on my bike today."

Michael gave a slow nod of his head. "Well, let's hope they do, eh?" he said. "Otherwise we'll have to take a look at things."

"Take a look at what things?"

"Things like your position as my VP" Michael replied, instantly. "After all, if you can't ride, you can't lead. Aren't they the rules you agreed when we formed this club?"

"That's a bit harsh, isn't it?"

With another shrug of his shoulders, Michael's smile finally became genuine. "Rules are rules" he stated, almost chuckling. "The timescale doesn't come into it."

"So" Lee practically mumbled. "You're saying that, if I don't get permission to ride my bike today, then I'm out?"

Once more, Michael shrugged his shoulders.

Lee shook his head. "If I didn't know any better," he said, slowly and deliberately, "I might think me being out was something you're looking for."

"Why would you think that?"

"Maybe for the same reason you're up at this time of the morning?"

Now the smile dropped from Michael's lips. "What the fuck do you mean by that?" he scowled.

"Do I need to spell it out?" Lee asked.

"Maybe you do" Michael immediately replied. "Maybe you need to spell a lot of things out, like why the fuck you felt the need to just fuck off and do what you wanted."

"We're back on that again?"

"We haven't fucking left it!" Michael hissed. "I fucking told you to leave the fucking cars, yet you still fucking went anyway."

Again, Lee shook his head. If he'd been looking for certainty that the man was up to something behind the club's back, then this over the top reaction was practically rubber stamping the fact. He opened his mouth to reply, but was cut off before a word could pass his lips.

"I'm fucking late" Michael growled, slamming his mug on the bar before storming towards the door, leaving Lee to ponder what had just happened as he watched him go.

Gently placing the phone back on its cradle, Albert let out a long sigh as he leant on the counter and bowed his head. He could hear Mary in the kitchen, where she was busy baking the cakes that he'd end up either having to eat or throw away after yet another in the long procession of custom-less days that would only serve to endorse his decision. It was for the best, he knew that, and Mary would be ecstatic when he told her, but even the thought of the smile that would likely light up her face didn't do anything to temper the cold, hollow feeling he felt in the pit of his stomach.

The temptation to re-think what had gone wrong pushed its way to the forefront of his mind, as it had done so many times in recent months, but he knew it wouldn't do any good. He could question his actions over and over again, desperately searching for an answer that wasn't there, but that would just make this even harder than it was. It was happening and that was the end of it so, with a deep breath, he pushed himself upright and walked to the door, where he flipped the open sign for what had now become the first of the last times he'd do that.

After sliding the bolts open, he walked through to the kitchen, where Mary was busy taking the trays out of the oven.

"They smell wonderful" he smiled from the doorway.

"Uh-huh" Mary mumbled, without so much as a glance in his direction.

Albert looked at the two trays that had already been placed on the table. "Do you want me to take them through?" he asked.

"What's the point?" she replied, still without looking at him.

Inwardly, Albert groaned as he realised this was going to be one of those days. He considered telling her about his decision and the phone call he'd just made to put the sale of the place in motion, in the hope that it might lift her spirits, but the fact was that things weren't yet certain and he didn't want to get her hopes up, only to have them dashed if it all fell through. For now, he would have to ride this out, so he quietly picked up the trays and went back to the front of the shop in order to place the cakes in the display cabinet.

Whilst he was emptying the trays, he looked up as he heard the door open and saw the paperboy enter with their daily delivery.

"Morning, Albert" the kid greeted him cheerfully, as he placed the papers on the counter and eyed up the cakes. "How's things?"

The crash of a tray hitting the floor in the kitchen provided more of an answer than Albert could ever manage to achieve. They both looked towards the doorway in expectation that some form of reaction would be forthcoming, but when none materialised, Albert couldn't help the mumbled curse that escaped under his breath.

"Yeah" the kid smiled, awkwardly. "I think I get it."

"This is going to be a long day" Albert replied sardonically, as he passed him one of the cakes. "It might be best to clear the area" he continued, finally managing a smile of his own.

With a nod, the paperboy left quickly and Albert braced himself in readiness for the devastation he knew would be awaiting him in the kitchen. He picked up one of the papers and, with his second long sigh of the morning, he walked towards the door.

He'd known there would be cakes strewn all over the floor, that much was obvious, and it was likely that Mary would be motionless with her head buried in her hands as she stood by the oven. What he hadn't expected to see was the sight of four men standing in the kitchen, one of them firmly holding a knife to his wife's throat.

His heart racing, Albert dropped the paper as his eyes darted around the room. He looked first at Mary, at the tears flowing down her cheeks; he looked at each of the men, their eyes fixed firmly on him as they seemed to be waiting for him to make a move and he saw the back door closed but unlocked, which was clearly the way in which they'd entered the building.

"Please, come in" one of the men stated, drawing Albert's attention back to him as he gestured towards one of the chairs at the table.

Albert could only stare at him, unable to move.

"I said, come in" the man repeated, firmly.

Still Albert was unable to move, until another of the men stepped forward and dragged him to the table, sitting him heavily in the chair before positioning himself behind with his hands on his shoulders in order to keep him in place.

The first man to speak then took a seat opposite him, sitting back in a relaxed manner, as though there were merely two old friends catching up. "D'you know who I am?" the man asked, smiling warmly.

With his mind racing, Albert looked at him and gradually noticed he wore the same style of leather vest as the other three, but his had slightly differing patches sewn into the chest. Each of them had one containing the words SONS OF SORROW on the left, however, the man who sat before him had the word PRESIDENT on the right. In his jumbled thoughts, the name Sons of Sorrow seemed to be one he recognised from somewhere, but he had no idea as to who the man was, so he shook his head in reply.

"Well, allow me to introduce myself" the man chuckled. "My name's Ruckus and my brothers here are Touchy, who's just assisted you in sitting down, Limpy, who's stood just behind me and Banjo, who's the gentleman currently making your wife's acquaintance."

"What do you want from us?" Albert stammered, barely managing to find a voice as his eyes continued to flick between Ruckus and Mary.

Noticing the obvious concern, Ruckus chuckled once more. "Don't worry" he smiled. "We don't wanna hurt you."

"Then why are you holding a knife to my wife's throat?" Albert asked, still stuttering with fear.

"I just wanted to ensure your full attention" Ruckus answered, glancing briefly towards Mary.

"Please let her go" Albert begged.

Now Ruckus gave a deep laugh. "I'd like to," he replied, "but that all depends on you."

"How long's this gonna take?" Alex whined, pacing back and forth in the cubicle.

Lee, who was lying comfortably on the bed, let out a groan. "For fuck's sake," he sighed, "please, stop your moaning."

"I'm not moaning" Alex replied, stubbornly. "All I'm sayin' is that, if they give you an appointment, we shouldn't still be waitin' to be seen nearly half an hour after the time."

"You're just pissed that you had to get up" Lee stated. "You didn't have to bring me. Sarah would've given me a lift."

"After working all night? You must be shitting me?" Alex laughed. "So, what d'you reckon? You think they'll let you ride again?"

"I'm still getting the headaches," Lee answered, "so I've got a feeling they'll tell me to hold off for longer. If they do, then I'm fucked."

"Why?"

Lee sat upright. "Because Michael's gonna use it to force me out" he replied.

Now Alex stopped pacing. "What?" he exclaimed. "He can't do that."

"He's planning on using the 'can't ride, can't lead' rule against me."

"But that's only if you can't ride permanently. Even if you're stopped this time, you'll be back on your bike soon. Are you sure that's what he said?"

"Pretty much. In his words, things will have to be looked at."

"When did he say this?"

"This morning, before you got up."

Alex looked at him, slightly open-mouthed at the news. "He was up this morning?" he said, as the beginnings of confusion creased his brown. "Why was he up?"

Lee shrugged. "He wouldn't tell me. All he said was he had stuff to do and, when I asked him what, he kicked off about the accident again."

Slightly shaking his head, Alex tried to work it through in his head. "Why'd he wanna force you out?" he finally asked, rhetorically. "Does this have somethin' to do with what you were bangin' on about last week?"

"I think it does" Lee replied, without hesitation.

"So, are you gonna tell me what you were worried about?"

"Can't you figure it out? What was he pushing for, before my accident?"

Again, Alex gave a shake of his head as he thought it through, until the realisation dawned on him. "Drugs?" he asked.

"Exactly" Lee replied.

"But we voted against that"

"You think that's gonna stop him? The vote was close, but if he gets rid of me and a couple of the others, then he'll be able to force it through with the rest."

"You think he'd actually do that? I mean, he can't just cut people, they have to be voted out."

"He's already started with me, hasn't he? If he can convince a few of the others that the rule applies, then I'm gone whether I'll be able to ride again or not."

"But you'll still have a vote."

"Not until I'm back on a bike."

Silence fell briefly between them, until a thought struck Alex. "You think that's where he's been goin'? Tryin' to sort out a deal?"

"I'm certain of it" Lee replied.

Alex opened his mouth to say something further, but he was stopped as the curtain swung open and Emily walked into the cubicle. She stood and looked at them for a few seconds, as though she sensed something was wrong.

"Have I just interrupted something?" she asked, with a slightly embarrassed smile.

"No doc" Lee answered. "You're fine."

Emily's eyes flicked between them as she replied. "If you need a few more minutes of privacy, I can go and check on another patient?"

Lee shook his head. "We were just talking about a couple of family issues" he said. "It's nothing."

With a shrug of her shoulders, Emily stepped towards the bed and opened up the file she held in her hands. "So, how have you been?" she asked, turning his head slightly as she closely checked the scar. "You've healed pretty well."

"I'm feeling good" Lee replied, immediately.

Fixing him with a questioning glare, Emily looked directly into his eyes. "No headaches, or other pains?" she asked, cynically enough to show she knew he was lying.

Hesitating for a moment, Lee considered maintaining his stance, but something told him he'd only be showing himself up. "I'm getting headaches" he reluctantly confirmed.

"Uh-huh" Emily replied, without any trace of surprise. "Anything else you're not telling me, in the hope that I'll give you permission to get back on your two-wheeled death trap?"

Letting out a sigh, Lee shook his head. "Sorry Doc" he smiled, "but I had to try."

Now Emily shook her head. "I understand that," she said, without returning the smile. "But even if you weren't having the headaches, I'm afraid you're going to have to wait a little while longer before you're riding again."

Chapter 11

"Is it just me?" Karen asked, looking past Ben's head towards the counter, where Albert was motionless, staring into space. "Or does it seem that something's wrong with Albert this afternoon?"

"Mary's probably been on at him for something" Sam suggested, a little too flippantly for her liking, which she demonstrated with a scowl.

"No" she said, again looking past Ben. "I think it's more than that. I mean, where's Mary today? If he's done something to upset her, she usually makes a point of being here so she can tell everyone about it."

Turning his head slightly, Ben tried to get another glimpse of the man. "Maybe she's not well?" he guessed. "That'd explain why he looks so tired and, if he's had to do the baking, it'd also be the reason there's no cakes in the cabinet today."

With a slow nod of her head, Karen contemplated the idea for a moment, before finally turning her attention to Ben. "So, how's Steph doing?" she asked.

"She's doing alright, actually" he answered. "It took a few days, but I think she's finally getting her head around it all."

"Has there been any word from Rob?" Sam asked.

"Nothing" Ben replied, unable to stop his lips forming the barest of smiles. "And I don't think he'll be back."

Both Sam and Karen looked at him for a few seconds, before Sam finally asked the question that was clearly on both of their minds. "And how are you doing with all this?"

Ben looked at him, slightly confused by the question. "Me?" he replied. "Why would I have a problem with this?"

Sam shook his head as he let out a low chuckle. "Really?" he stated. "Come on, Dude. We know you well enough to know that you'll be feeling something about all this, it's the same whenever she's hurt. Honestly, you're like those blokes who suffer from a phantom pregnancy, just before their missus drops a sprog, only they've got an excuse."

Despite knowing exactly what his friend was getting at, Ben still tried to appear somewhat shocked by the statement. "I'm not that bad" he argued.

"Piss off!" Sam exclaimed, smiling broadly. "Steph might as well be a voodoo doll of you, the way you feel the pain of anything inflicted on her. I swear, if I stuck a pin in her leg, you'd walk in with a limp!"

Both he and Karen started laughing at the comment and, despite his determination not to, Ben couldn't help but join in.

"Fair enough" he agreed. "Maybe I do let things get to me more than they should, but it's different this time."

Now Sam and Karen adopted the same, cynical expression as they looked at him.

"Seriously" Ben continued. "It is different. Me and Steph, we're somehow closer now than we've ever been."

Sam's raised eyebrow forced Ben into continuing his defence.

"I'm tellin' you," he insisted, "things are changing between us, I can feel it. First there was the kiss she gave me on the night I found the girl, then there was the moment we shared at the barbeque and last night was the first in nearly a week that I didn't stay at her's, and that's only because I was working. I daresay I'd have been invited round again today, if she wasn't at work herself this afternoon."

"And where have you slept when you've been round there?" Sam asked, bluntly.

"On the settee" Ben answered.

Sam gave a nod as he replied. "On the settee?" he repeated. "Like you've always done?"

Ben paused for a moment, the comment causing his certainty to waiver a little. "Yeah" he eventually said, defiantly. "But that doesn't mean anything."

"And maybe all the other stuff doesn't mean anything, either?" Sam suggested.

Looking at him, Ben struggled to find a response as he felt the confidence drain from him. As though realising his statement may have been a little harsh, Sam softened his tone as he continued.

"All I'm saying mate," he smiled, "is that you need to be careful about where your head's going with this. Yes, it seems things have changed between you, but you're her best friend and she feels safe with you. Given all the shit she's had to deal with over the last week or so and, by the sounds of it, it's probably been going on for a lot longer than that, maybe she's needed to feel some affection and that's all it is? Maybe, without realising it, she knows that you're not gonna be a twat about anything she does and it's better she looks for it from you, than some random stranger who might fuck her over."

"So, you're saying she's just using me?" Ben asked, bitterly.

Letting out a sigh of frustration, Sam shook his head. "I'm not saying she's using you, Dude" he said. "I'm just saying that, right now, her head's gonna be messed up and she trusts you completely, so it makes sense that she'd look to you to help her through this. There's every chance she doesn't realise what it's doing to you and maybe, if she did, then she'd feel terrible about it."

Feeling his heart deflate, Ben looked down at his drink as his mind raced. Deep down, he knew Sam had a fair point, but he hadn't been there, had he? He hadn't seen the way she acted when they'd stayed back for a drink, he'd only seen the end of the moment in her kitchen and he hadn't been at her's all week. All Sam had to go on was presumption based on the past, and Ben was certain that things were different between them now.

"Maybe you're right," he said, looking once more at Sam, "but, equally, isn't it possible that she's started seeing me in a different light? Who's to say that she hasn't found herself falling in love with her best friend?"

Sam only looked at him, as though he'd run out of argument, so Ben turned his attention to Karen.

"You're a woman" he said.

"You've noticed?" Karen replied, with a smile.

Ignoring the comment, Ben continued. "Can you tell me that doesn't sometimes happen? Can you tell me that people don't sometimes fall in love with their best friend?"

Karen opened her mouth to reply, but Ben's confidence was returning rapidly and he didn't give her the chance to speak before carrying on his argument.

"At the end of the day," he said, "I know her better than anyone. I know her good points and I know her bad points. I know what she likes and what she doesn't. With me there's no need to worry about being herself, she doesn't have to create some sort of bullshit pretence until she gets to know the guy well enough to show him the things he might not like. She knows I love her, regardless, and maybe that's something that's worked its way into her head? Maybe she's realised that she loves me too, but she just needs a bit of time to adjust to the idea of us being more than friends?"

In the periphery of his vision, Ben could see Sam shaking his head, but his attention was focussed only on Karen, who took a deep breath before speaking.

"I'm not going to say it doesn't happen" she smiled, much to Sam's clear disappointment, "but I'm not going to say it is happening either. From what you've said, I'd agree that things have changed between you, but that could merely be that she needs her best friend right now, more than she's done in the past. Without seeing how she is around you, I can't say what's going on."

Again, Ben felt his heart sink a little, but Karen quickly tempered the collapse as she finished telling him her thoughts.

"Why don't we all go out?" she suggested. "Penny's with my mom tonight, so me and Sam were thinking of having a few drinks anyway. We can hit The Pit when Steph's finished her shift and we'll drag her out on the town, whether she wants to or not."

As she finished, her and Ben both looked to Sam for his agreement of the plan.

"What you lookin' at me for?" he asked, with a smile. "You think I'm going to pretend I have a choice in this?"

"How the hell have we ended up here?" Sam asked, raising his voice in order to be heard over the music.

Ben shook his head as he shrugged, "Steph didn't want to stay at The Pit and the pair of 'em wanted to dance."

The two of them were stood on the club's balcony, overlooking the dance floor, where Steph and Karen were more than cutting a little loose.

"Jesus, would you look at them?" Sam exclaimed. "Steph's got a few moves, I'll give her that, but as for Karen? I love her dearly, but she can't dance for shit."

"She's not that bad" Ben lied.

"You only think that because you haven't taken your eyes off Steph since we got here" Sam laughed in reply. "If you can manage it for just a second, take a look at my woman. She looks like an epileptic fish that's flung itself out the tank."

"Why don't you head down there and teach her a few moves?" Ben suggested, with a chuckle.

"Sod that" Sam laughed in response. "No, I prefer to just watch and take it in. That way, when I feel like a bit of peace and quiet at home, I just drop my review into the conversation and boom, she locks herself in the bedroom for a few hours and I get to watch TV!"

"How the hell do you manage to get her to stay with you?" Ben marvelled, as Karen left the dance floor and started walking up the stairs.

Also noticing her approaching, Sam quickly leaned towards him. "It might not be obvious, but I make sure she's always drunk" he whispered, before holding out a drink as Karen approached. "Here you go, Babe," he smiled, flashing a quick wink at Ben, "get this down your neck."

Oblivious to the wink, Karen gratefully took the bottle of beer from him and immediately savoured a long and satisfying swig, causing both of the boys to burst into laughter.

"What?" she asked, uncertainly.

"Nothing, Babe" Sam replied, leaning in to kiss her on the cheek. "I'm goin' for a piss."

Before she had the chance to respond, he left the two of them alone. Karen watched him as he went and then took his place next to Ben, leaning over the balcony.

"She seems to be happier than she's been in a while" Ben pointed out, as he continued to watch Steph dancing.

Karen briefly followed his gaze. "She does" she agreed, looking back at him. "But then, I've not seen her all week, so I can't really tell if there's any difference."

"I don't just mean this week" Ben stated. "I mean she looks happier than she has done in a couple of months."

Almost as though she sensed she was being spoken about, Steph briefly glanced up at them and cheekily stuck her tongue out at him, before slipping back into her own little world.

"It's little things like that which are screwing me up" he muttered, seemingly to himself. "I just can't work out whether it's just a friendly gesture, or whether there's something more. She never used to do things like that when we were out."

"I don't know what to tell you, Ben" Karen admitted. "The only person who can say for sure is Steph."

"I know" Ben agreed. "But if I ask her, then it could very well lead into a conversation I just don't know whether we should have."

"So, what's stopped you from telling her before?"

"You know why" he answered.

"No" she replied. "I know why you didn't tell her when you first met her. But what I want to know is what's stopped you since then?"

"I nearly did, once" he stated, surprising even himself with the confession.

"What?" Karen exclaimed, clearly a little stunned by the reply. "When?"

"It was the night she told me she'd met Rob" he admitted. "I went round there, just for a normal night of drinking and watching TV, but I'd already planned what I was going to say to her. As the night went on, I built myself up to it but, before I got the chance, she told me about Rob."

"So what stopped you? She'd only just met the guy, so it wasn't as though you couldn't tell her and give her the choice."

Involuntarily, Ben let out a sigh. "You should've seen the look on her face when she told me all about him" he confirmed. "It reminded me of how I feel about her, and I couldn't ruin that."

"So, what's changed? If you were going to tell her then, why can't you tell her now?"

"It's only been a week since Rob left. I think she needs more time to get over that before she can think about moving on."

"Well, maybe you've just answered your own question?"

The statement stung Ben a little. He hadn't ever thought about it from that point of view and he gave a slight nod of agreement as he turned back to lean over the balcony, from where he saw Steph subtly moving away from a guy who'd started to dance a little too close to her.

"But what if I leave it too long?" he asked, still watching Steph. "What if she meets someone in the meantime and the same thing happens again?"

Karen joined him in once more leaning over the balcony, also noticing Steph's movement away from the guy. "Look" she said. "Steph's incredibly vulnerable at the moment and it wouldn't be surprising if all she's looking for right now is the affection she's clearly been missing for a while. I can't believe I'm thinking this, but maybe Sam was actually right with what he said earlier? Maybe these little things she's started doing show that, subconsciously, she's aware of the way she's likely to be and she knows she's safe with you?"

He didn't reply straight away, as the words filtered through his mind. "So how long do I leave it?" he asked, eventually.

"Ben" Karen stated, forcing him to look at her. "You know Steph better than anyone else, so the only person who can really tell you that, is you."

"I know" he reluctantly agreed.

She pulled him into a tight hug and whispered into his ear. "You're a good guy, Ben" she whispered. "I know you'll do the right thing, so don't worry so much about it."

"What the hell's going on here?" Sam exclaimed, shattering the moment in his own, unique way as he returned from the toilet. "Karen. I've already told you he's not interested in a threesome, so put him down."

Without even a moment's hesitation, she pulled Ben closer and raised her knee to wrap her leg around his thigh. "He's agreed this time," she smiled, as she began to stroke her hand over his chest, "but only if it's me, him and Steph."

"Ah" Sam replied, acting as though he was completely crestfallen. "Can I at least watch?"

"You can watch it on the internet, like everyone else" Ben laughed, as Karen finally pulled away from him. "I'm off to get drinks," he stated, "same again?"

They both nodded, so he pushed his way through to the bar at the back of the balcony area, where he stood behind a man who was currently being served.

"I'm not sure what to have" the man stated, as he looked along the rows of drinks.

Shaking her head, the barmaid quickly turned to the next customer along.

"Hey" the man exclaimed, angrily. "You were serving me!"

Having taken the next customer's order, the barmaid briefly looked back at him. "You hesitate," she smiled, "and you miss out."

"That's ridiculous" the man grumbled loudly, to anyone who might have been in earshot, but Ben didn't hear him.

All Ben could focus on were the barmaid's words, which had driven themselves deep into his mind. She was absolutely right, he thought to himself, as he quickly turned away from the bar and practically ran back to Karen and Sam.

"I've got to tell her" he announced, causing both of them to spin round from the positions they'd taken, looking over the balcony.

Concern seemed to have plastered itself across each of their expressions, which Ben took to be in reaction to his statement.

"It's ok," he continued, in a bid to alleviate their worry, "I'm not gonna go overboard with it. I just want to make sure she knows."

"That's good, mate" Sam mumbled unconvincingly, as the intensity of his expression increased.

"What?" Ben asked, himself becoming concerned.

Clearing her throat, Karen tried to smile as she looked down at his hands. "Where are the drinks?" she replied. "I'm parched."

Ben hesitated for a moment, as he tried to work out what was going on. "I'll get them in a minute" he muttered. "Where's Steph? I need to talk to her."

"She's still off, dancing" Sam stated flippantly, trying to put himself between Ben and the edge of the balcony.

Easily pushing past him, Ben looked down at the dance floor and felt his heart stop when he saw that the guy, who'd earlier seemed to be causing a nuisance, was now locked in a passionate kiss with Steph.

In the dimmed light of his living room, Ben couldn't settle. One minute he was agitatedly pacing back and forth, his muscles tense and ready to strike at something, and the next he was sitting completely still, staring at nothing whilst unwanted images painted themselves into his mind. His anger flared in an instant, before abating just as quickly, and he felt the need to both cry and scream in equal measure.

The song that played on his stereo wasn't helping either. A dark and emotional track in which the lyrics told of the singer's love for a woman, describing his feelings in detail before revealing that she'd found her love in the arms of someone else. It spoke of how the man knew she'd become a soul mate to his rival, a star in his sky, and it expressed failure to understand why she'd chosen another over him.

In a flash of rage, Ben threw the glass he'd been holding across the room. It shattered into a thousand pieces on the facia of the stereo, yet still the music played on, seemingly taunting him with every word and beat that emanated from the speakers. He jumped to his feet and strode to the shelving, from which he pulled the stereo and sent it crashing to the floor, bringing a sudden and dramatic silence to the room. With a cry of fury, he sank to his knees as the brief and ultimate wave of violent anger subsided, and he buried his head in his hands as the tears that'd threatened for so long, finally escaped and began to roll down his cheeks.

He stayed that way for several minutes, his shoulders jerking erratically as what seemed to be years of emotion flooded out of him. An endless stream of questions raced through his mind, each of them dispersing too quickly for any attempt to find an answer before the next pushed its way into his thoughts, until one eventually managed to take a hold and he had no choice but to give it a voice.

"What am I doing?" he muttered, into his hands.

Taking deliberate and deep breaths, his heart began to slow its relentless pace and he reluctantly raised his head in order to survey the devastation around him.

All she'd done, he contemplated as he gingerly rose to his feet, was to kiss a guy. She'd gone out, as a single woman, and accepted the advances of a man who'd caught her attention. She wasn't owned by anyone and she had no obligation to anyone, least of all Ben, so why had he reacted in this way? Why had he made his excuses and left the club without saying goodbye to her? Why had he stormed home and hit the hard spirits as though they were the first drink he'd had in years? More worrying than all that, why had he just destroyed his own property, purely because of the song that was playing?

There were so many answers that would fit the individual questions, so many reasons for each single action, but only one fact adequately covered them all. He was an idiot, a foolish and selfish idiot with no regard for anyone other than himself. Steph had been left vulnerable by what had happened and she'd reacted in the only way possible, by turning to her closest friend at a time when she needed protection from her fragile emotions.

Scared by how she was feeling, she'd sought solace in having him by her side. She'd chosen him to be there at a time when she could've been forgiven for wanting to be alone, but what had he done with that? Granted, he hadn't cheated on her or physically stolen from her in the same way as Rob, but were his crimes any less vicious? He'd spent years doing all he could to convince her that he was a friend, and then he'd blamed her for not realising how he truly felt. He claimed that he loved her, that her happiness was all that mattered to him, but how could that be the truth when, the very moment she displayed evidence of recovery, he walked away in tears?

Closing his eyes, Ben pictured the scene that was likely to have played out when she returned to the balcony from the dance floor and discovered that he'd gone. He imagined Sam and Karen delivering the excuses he'd made, each of them feeling awkward and uncomfortable as they did so, and he considered the hurt Steph would've felt by his refusal to say goodbye.

He glanced at the clock and realised he'd been home for a good few hours now, which only added to the shame that washed over him. He'd asked their friends to tell Steph that he'd gone because he'd suddenly felt unwell, as lame as that might have sounded, and in that situation he would've expected Steph to ring and check on him, most likely before he'd even managed to make it to his front door. But she hadn't called, had she? There'd been no attempt to contact him, which could only mean she'd recognised the lie and that, in turn, would've left her searching for answers Sam and Karen would've been pressed to provide.

"Fuck!" he cursed, as the magnitude of his pathetic selfishness hit home.

Rubbing his eyes, Ben fought against the urge to phone them all with an apology there and then, despite the obvious fact that disturbing them in the early hours would only compound his stupidity. He knew he'd have to wait until the morning, and even then it all depended on whether they were willing to talk to him, so the rest of the night would be spent agonizing over it all.

Coffee was a good idea, he decided as he stepped over the remains of his stereo and walked towards his kitchen but, before he reached the doorway, he was stopped in his tracks by the ringing of his phone. He raced over to where it'd been discarded in anger a few hours ago and hastily checked the display to see who was calling, and he froze as his heart plummeted to new depths when he saw it was Steph.

Chapter 12

Even though he'd stopped drinking a good few hours before, Ben knew he shouldn't be riding, not with the amount of alcohol that remained in his system, but what choice did he have? Although, technically, Steph's house was within walking distance from his flat, it would've taken the best part of an hour to get there and waiting for a Taxi during the early hours of a Saturday morning was likely to have taken longer still. Some might say that he still should've chosen the safer option but, having heard the hysteria in her voice, there was no way he could've left her any longer than he had to.

He'd deliberately kept to the back streets and side roads in a bid to reduce the risk in his journey and he'd encountered only the occasional car, none of which had been the law and none of which had seemed to pay him any heed. The quiet streets had allowed his mind to wander a little, which only increased the panic he felt, as he tried to work out what Steph had been trying to tell him between her cries. She'd been barely comprehensible, sobbing with fear more than she'd been able to speak, and all he'd been able to grasp was that she was at home and she was in some sort of trouble.

Pulling hard on the throttle of his old Matchless motorcycle, Ben accelerated through a final junction before turning into Steph's road, where his stomach lurched at the sight of a police car parked at the kerb in front of her house. It'd been less than fifteen minutes since the phone call, so the fact they were already there and, by the looks of it, had someone in the back of the car, was nothing short of confirmation that Steph's panic had been more than justified.

From behind, it was impossible to see who was being detained and, as Ben came to a stop at the side of the road, the car pulled away. He watched as it drove along the road and, once it'd turned out of sight, he got off the bike and removed his helmet. He glanced towards the house, noticing that only the kitchen light shone from the windows, before taking a breath to steady his nerves and walking towards the front door.

Even in the dim light provided by the street lights, Ben could clearly see evidence that someone, most likely the person in the back of the police car, had tried to force their way in. There were boot prints and black marks partially concealing cracks that'd formed in both the door and the frame and, judging by the severity of the damage, it was apparent that they'd been perilously close to success in their assault. The only question was whether they'd actually succeeded and, as he reached out to knock on the door, Ben couldn't stop himself from wondering what state he might find Steph to be in.

His knock wasn't answered, bringing further concern as he once more looked down at the damage. Another knock and still there was no answer, but the thought struck him that Steph would be scared and, therefore, unlikely to respond without knowing who was there. He called out her name and moved across to the kitchen window in order to look through the gap in the blinds, where he saw her sitting alone at the table, wearing her dressing gown and with her head buried in her hands.

"Steph" he called again, knocking on the glass.

When he saw her look up at the sound of his voice, Ben moved back to the door, which opened within a matter of seconds.

"Oh, Ben" she cried breathlessly, jumping into his arms.

Dropping his helmet, Ben pulled her tightly against him and they stayed that way for a few minutes, Steph's entire body shaking as her tears fell freely. Gradually, she began to calm down and she slowly eased her grip and pulled away from him. She looked up into his eyes and it appeared that she wanted to say something, but the words seemed to catch in her throat.

"Let's get inside" Ben suggested, picking up his helmet from the ground.

With a nod of her head, Steph backed away from the doorway and Ben followed her through to the kitchen, where she stood in the middle of the floor, as though unable to decide what she should do next. Realising her turmoil, Ben gently guided her back to her seat at the table, before placing his helmet on the side and grabbing a bottle of Vodka from the cupboard. He collected two glasses from the draining board and took the seat opposite her, pouring them both a generous measure.

They drank in silence, Ben refilling their glasses a couple of times, until some semblance of calm began to filter through in her expression.

"What happened?" Ben asked, once he was sure she'd be able to answer.

Taking a deep breath, Steph looked at him for a moment or two, before finally answering. "It was Rob" she whispered. "He tried to kick his way in through the door."

"I saw the damage" Ben replied. "Why was he here?"

Steph gave a shrug of her shoulders. "I don't know" she said. "He was just screaming that I needed to let him into the house and that I was going to pay for what I did to him."

Ben shook his head as he tried to make some sense of what she was saying. "But what does he think you did to him?" he asked.

"I don't know" Steph sighed. "I've been sitting here, trying to work it out, but I can't think of anything."

"Didn't he say anything when he turned up?"

"No. The first I knew of him being here was when the banging woke me up. I came downstairs and tried to talk to him through the door, but that only made him try harder to get in, so I called the police. Then I heard the door crack and . . ."

Her voice trailed off as the recollection became too much for her fragile emotions and her tears again began to fall. Giving her a minute to let it out, Ben topped up their glasses and then reached across the table to take a hold of her hand.

"The door cracked," she eventually continued, looking deeply into his eyes, "and that's when I called you. Ben, I was so scared."

More tears fell and Steph tightened her grip on his hand. Ben leaned across and gently brushed away some of the moisture. "It's ok," he whispered, "I'm here now."

Judging by the early signs of dawn that showed themselves through the gaps at the side of the curtains, Ben figured it must be around five in the morning. They'd been awake all night, talking about anything and everything, ranging from what what'd happened before he'd got there, to reminiscing about good times they'd shared. The Vodka had long ago been finished, as had the remnants of a bottle of wine that'd initially been opened when he was staying there a few nights before, and they were making a good job of finishing off anything remotely alcoholic they could find in the cupboards.

After a while spent in the kitchen, they'd moved to the living room, where the combination of booze and gradually calming nerves had seen Steph decide she wanted to continue the dancing she'd enjoyed several hours ago. At first, Ben had done his best to join in with her, awkwardly swaying and bobbing alongside her in a way that even Karen would've been ashamed of. Eventually though, the self-consciousness had got the better of him and he'd collapsed on to the settee.

"Oh, I love this song!" Steph drunkenly slurred, demonstrating an unwitting sense of irony as the stereo selected the same track which, earlier that night, had sent Ben spiralling into such frenzy.

Closing his eyes for a second, Ben allowed a wry smile to spread across his lips as he pictured the aftermath of his tantrum, but he quickly shook away the thought; that was something he'd have to clear up when he got home, and something that'd never be revealed, not even to Sam. For now though, he didn't need to worry about it as, right there in front of him, was the sight of a stunning woman, dancing in only her night clothes and a dressing gown, lost in a world of pleasure and singing each and every word with all of her heart.

All too quickly for Ben, the lyrics reached their finale, the real crux of the song, and he watched with some perplexity as Steph's movements slowed to the barest of sways. Her singing faded into silence and she looked deeply into his eyes as her expression took on a slightly strange look, almost as though the words were speaking to her the same way in which they'd spoken to him.

Slowly, tentatively, she moved forwards, until she was standing before him. Her gaze remained locked on him as, gently, she pulled on the cord of her dressing gown, which fell partially open to reveal a glimpse of the silk camisole she wore beneath. Taking a deep breath, she reached up and slid the gown from her shoulders, allowing it to fall to the floor as she rested her knee at the side of his thigh. Her other knee followed, resting on the opposite side, and she eased herself on to his lap.

With his mind racing, Ben's heart threatened to burst out of his chest and time seemed to slow as the look in Steph's eyes intensified. A voice in his head screamed disbelief that this was actually happening but, when he noticed her pupils flick down to his lips, a sudden feeling of calmness washed over him.

She leaned forward, hesitantly, and cautiously pressed her lips against his. Ben returned the kiss, placing his hands on her waist as she raised hers to gently caress his face. The passion slowly increased, their lips parting slightly to allow each of their tongues to explore the other's, darting in and out of their mouths as their movements fell perfectly into sync. Steph reached down and grasped a hold of his t-shirt, quickly lifting it up and over his head as she eagerly returned to their kiss, before running her hands over his tight and muscular torso.

Now completely lost in the moment, Ben slowly slid his hands from her waist and round to her back, where his fingers began to trace their way up her spine, lifting the camisole as they travelled higher. Arching her back, Steph pushed her hips against him and let out an involuntary gasp, a moan of pleasure that only increased the pace of Ben's rapidly-beating heart, before she leant forward to kiss him again.

Slowly, her fingers continued to brush over his body and, as she reached down to unfasten his belt, her lips moved around to his neck, where she feathered his skin with kisses so tender that he thought his heart would explode. She pulled open the buttons of his jeans, working her hands underneath the fabric and took a deep breath as she grasped him.

"I want you, Rob" she whispered.

The name drove itself into the very core of his soul, leaving him momentarily fighting for breath as his heart ripped into a thousand pieces. For a few seconds, his head span until, painfully, his thoughts rested on the conversations he'd shared with Sam and Karen and he gently pushed her away from him.

"What is it?" she asked, her eyes swarming with confusion.

Ben looked at her, desperate for his ears to have been playing tricks on him, but the word had been so clear, so precise, that he couldn't escape reality.

"You just called me Rob" he said, almost choking on the words.

As her look of confusion turned quickly to one of horror, Steph shook her head vigorously. "No, I . . ." she began, but she found no conclusion to her sentence as doubt forced its way into her thoughts.

Reluctantly, Ben gave a slow nod of confirmation. "You did" he confirmed.

Again, Steph shook her head. "I didn't mean to" she exclaimed, almost breathless in her panic. "Ben, it was a mistake."

"That's what I'm worried about" Ben replied.

Steph stared at him, as her expression quickly took on a mixture of confusion, hurt and rejection. She hastily backed off him, reaching down to pick up her discarded dressing gown before quickly covering herself.

"Is that how you see this?" she questioned. "You think screwing me would be a mistake?"

Now Ben was gripped with panic as he looked helplessly at her. "No" he stammered. "That's not what I'm saying."

"Then what are you saying?" Steph spat in reply.

Quickly becoming overcome with a feeling of helplessness, Ben struggled to find any explanation for what he was trying to say. "I just think" he began, still stammering as his heart continued to race, "that this isn't what you want."

"How can you say that?" she asked. "Here I am, giving myself to you, and you don't think it's what I want?"

Ben swallowed back the nausea that suddenly washed over him. "You called me Rob" he repeated. "I'm worried that you're just looking for affection, without it mattering who it's from."

Immediately, he realised how the comment must have sounded and, predictably, Steph's anger flared.

"Fuck you!" she hissed, as she backed towards the door.

"Steph, I'm . . ." he began, but his words were cut off.

"Get out!" she spat. "Get out of my fucking house!"

With that, she turned and fled through the doorway, leaving Ben alone in the room. He slumped forward and buried his face into his hands.

"What have I done?" he whispered, into the rapidly descending silence.

Chapter 13

Catherine froze for a second, staring at her reflection in the mirror as the ringing of her doorbell died away. A nervous glance towards the alarm clock on her bedside table informed her that she should still have had a good half an hour to finish getting ready, a fact that was confirmed with a secondary check of her watch, so why had he turned up so early?

With no small amount of panic, she dropped the mascara she'd been in the process of applying, jumped up from her chair and rushed to the window. She leaned against the glass and tried to look down at the front door, but the angle was too acute to allow for a clear view. Backing away, she considered whether she should throw some clothes on or just take the plunge and answer the door in her bath robe.

Taking a deep breath, she decided that staying as she was would be the better of the two options, as at least he'd see that she was in the process of getting ready and not jump to a judgement based on the first things she could grab to cover herself up. With a final, hurried glance at her reflection to check that her make-up looked semi-decent, she left her bedroom and went downstairs to let him in.

"Oh, thank God!" she exclaimed, as she opened the door and saw it was only her friend who stood there.

"What?" Michelle replied, a little taken aback by the greeting.

"I thought it was . . ." Catherine began, her sentence drifting off as she looked up and down the street.

Michelle watched her for a second before speaking. "Are you ok?" she asked.

"Yeah" Catherine absent-mindedly answered, as she stepped back to allow her friend in to the house. "Come in."

After a momentary pause, Michelle accepted the invitation. "You're acting weird" she pointed out. "What's going on?"

As the panic began to dissipate, Catherine was able to steady herself. "I've got a date" she replied, "and I thought he'd turned up early."

"Ah, now I get it" Michelle acknowledged. "Who's the date with?"

"The guy from the club last week"

"Ah, the man you threw yourself at?"

"I didn't throw myself at him!" Catherine protested.

"You didn't exactly play hard to get."

Catherine shook her head. "You saw him" she pointed out. "Would you have?"

Pausing for a moment, Michelle thought about the question, or rather, tried to find an argument to the statement, and when she didn't provide an immediate answer, Catherine chuckled and made her way back up the stairs.

"So, what time's he picking you up?" Michelle asked, as she followed Catherine into her bedroom.

Amidst applying the final touches to her make-up, Catherine glanced at the clock. "In about twenty-five minutes" she answered. "And I can't decide what to wear. I'm definitely going with my new jeans and the shoes I bought last week, but I'm not sure which top will go best."

"Well, where's he taking you?" Michelle questioned, as she grabbed the two garments that'd been laid out on the bed and held them up to compare them.

"I don't know" Catherine replied.

Michelle lowered the tops to look at her friend. "You don't know?"

"No. All he said was it'd be a surprise."

With her expression taking on a trace of concern, Michelle continued to look at her friend's reflection. "Is that a good idea?" she asked.

"Why wouldn't it be?"

"For starters, you don't know the guy."

"What's that got to do with anything?"

"He could be taking you anywhere."

Stopping what she was doing, Catherine turned to face her. "Duh" she mocked. "Isn't that the whole point of it being a surprise?"

"I get that," Michelle replied, "and I'd be impressed if you knew the guy, but you don't. He could be taking you anywhere and do anything to you."

Catherine shook her head. "I hardly think that's going to happen."

"Don't you read the papers?"

"Don't be such a bore" Catherine mocked. "Jeez, I can take care of myself, you know."

"I'm not being a bore" Michelle snapped, now becoming angry at her friend's naivety. "I'm just saying that there's a lot of weirdo's out there and you need to be careful. You might think you can look after yourself, but you don't know what this guy's capable of."

"And you don't know that this guy is one of them" Catherine snapped back. "I've been texting him all week and he's been nothing but a decent guy."

"Anyone can sound decent in a text message."

The unmistakable roar of a motorbike intruded on their conversation, and Michelle walked over to the window. She looked down at the street as the rider pulled up outside the house and made a mental note of his appearance, noting immediately that, whilst his helmet was the type that left his face exposed, he wore shades and covered his mouth with what appeared to be a black Bandana. "I take it this is him?" she asked

Without needing to check, Catherine knew it was and hurriedly picked one of the tops as she dressed. "Yeah" she replied, "what do you think?"

"I can't see him" Michelle answered. "Why's he covering his face?"

Catherine looked out of the window. "That's just a bandana" she replied. "Don't you know anything? It protects his face from the wind when he rides."

Michelle shook her head as an ominous feeling started to creep through her. "Please think about this" she begged. "He can always surprise you on another night."

"No" Catherine insisted, as she applied the finishing touches to her make-up. "Whether you agree or not, I know he's a good guy and I'm going with him."

"Well, can you at least tell me his name?" Michelle asked.

Catherine looked at her disapprovingly for a few moments, before finally answering. "His name's Ben Trowman" she finally, reluctantly, admitted, "and, if it makes you feel any better, he works at a bar in town, that little rocker place called The Skinning Pit."

Because of his height, Ben was an easy spot amongst most crowds, so Andy didn't really need the raised vantage point of his DJ Booth in order to witness the man's drunken staggering around the room. He was already well-inebriated when he'd practically fallen through the doors a couple of hours ago and Ben wasted no time in making straight for the bar to continue what must have been an epic binge, but now he could barely stand upright without needing something sturdy against which he could support himself.

Cueing up the longest track he could find, Andy slipped out of his booth and made his way towards the end of the bar, where Sam was busy serving.

"Have you seen the state of Ben?" he asked, as he grabbed himself a beer from the fridge.

Sam nodded. "Yeah" he answered, taking his customer's money and turning to put it in the till. "I haven't seen him like that for a while."

"What the hell's wrong with him?" Andy continued, standing on tip-toe to try and spot him over the crowd. "I don't think there's a woman in here tonight he hasn't tried it on with."

"Really?" Sam exclaimed. "I hadn't noticed him doing that. It's not surprising though . . ." he began, obviously checking his sentence as though he realised he was about to say far too much.

"After what?" Andy questioned, his interest sparked by the possibility of some gossip.

Shaking his head, Sam tried to dismiss the comment. "Nothing" he replied, taking the next customer's order. "He's just had a few issues at home, that's all."

Andy didn't, for one second, believe that to be true, but he wasn't bothered enough to push the issue. "Well, maybe we should think about getting him home now?" he suggested. "Before he gets himself into real trouble. He's already been slapped a couple of times and I'm sure there's a few guys out there who've considered giving him a smack or two."

"He'll be fine" Sam muttered. "He just needs to let off some steam."

The sound of glass smashing, followed by a raucous cheer, contradicted Sam's comment and he let out a sigh as he gave a slow shake of his head. "Maybe it is time for him to go" he agreed. "I'm snowed here, would you mind sorting him out?"

Nodding, Andy left the bar and hurried back to the booth, where he cued up another track and then quickly pushed his way through the crowd, towards the area from which the commotion had sounded.

When he got there, he saw that Ben was sat on the floor, leaning against the wall with his eyes closed. He was covered in beer, surrounded by broken pieces of the bottle he'd been holding and the glass he must've knocked from the table as he fell, whilst the women who were sat at the table looked at him through expressions that portrayed both contempt and disgust in equal measure.

"Jesus" he sighed, bending down to try and shake Ben awake.

Slowly, Ben opened his eyes and it took a few seconds for him to regain some semblance of focus. He mumbled something incomprehensive and then tried to close his eyes again.

"No you don't" Andy snapped, shaking him again.

More indecipherable words spilled from Ben's mouth.

Grabbing him by the arm, Andy struggled to get him moving but fortunately, once the momentum had been achieved, Ben actually managed to get back up to his feet, although he staggered a little and had to reach out to the wall for support.

"Come on" Andy chuckled, as he started leading him to the doors, but Ben stopped and stared at the table of women.

Clearly appalled by the harassment, the women decided that they'd had enough and quickly left their seats to leave. Ben watched them as they went, until a wry smile spread across his lips.

"I'm goin' wi' 'em" he slurred, pushing Andy away as he staggered after them.

For a moment, Andy considered the fact that leaving Ben to do anything in this state was going to be a bad idea and he knew he should go after the guy and get him into a taxi. On the other hand though, the track he'd selected was reaching its conclusion, so he needed to get back to his booth and, frankly, the thought of dealing with a drunken Ben wasn't something he really wanted to do. He watched on as Ben struggled with the doors and then, once he was sure the man was safely outside, he gave a final shake of his head and returned to his work.

Catherine watched as Ethan walked away from their table, heading to the bar that stood in the corner of the room. They'd been there for a couple of hours now and, although her first sight of the place as they'd pulled up had caused some degree of trepidation, she'd quickly been made to feel welcome by the members of the club and she'd soon relaxed.

Looking around the room, she saw people having a genuinely good time. There were girls dancing without any sign of self-consciousness, the alcohol was flowing freely and the sounds of laughter could be heard clearly over the music. It was such a stark contrast to anything she'd expected when she'd seen the sign on the gates outside, the menacing-looking skull with a single tear falling from its eye. Even the name of the club, The Sons of Sorrow had done little to comfort her, until it'd been explained that it was nothing more than a name and had no sinister meaning behind it.

When he'd said he was going to surprise her, she hadn't dreamed it would be anything like this and, the more she thought about it, the more it made her smile. He'd brought her into his private life, a group of people who clearly meant more to him than anything else, and he'd done it so quickly after meeting her that he must have deeper feelings for her than she'd anticipated. If this wasn't going to be anything more than a casual fling, then surely he wouldn't have opened up his world to her like this?

As Ethan returned from the bar, he placed the drinks on the table and took his seat next to her.

"Are you ok?" he asked.

"Yeah" she answered, a little surprised by the question. "Why?"

"I was worried how you'd react to all this."

"To all of what?"

"To the fact that I'm in a Motorcycle Club" he smiled, nervously. "People tend to think we're bad news and I didn't want you to think the same."

"Oh, Ben" she sighed, gently resting her hand on his knee. "I'd never think that, especially not after meeting everyone and seeing that they're all so nice."

Letting out a long sigh, Ethan placed his hand on top of hers. "I'm so glad" he replied.

Catherine looked at him, at the relief that was so evident in his expression, and she marvelled at the sensitivity he displayed, given how strong and forceful he was to look at. It may have been the unexpected insight, or just the amount of alcohol she'd consumed, but she found herself wanting desperately to kiss him and, when she felt his fingers lightly stroking the back of her hand, she couldn't help but lean towards him as he did the same.

Their lips met and, as he raised his hand to brush his fingers against her cheek, she felt a nervous excitement rush through her. He traced a line around to the nape of her neck, where his light strokes only enhanced her desire for him and, when she involuntarily let out a sigh of contentment, he slowly pulled away from the kiss. For a second, she panicked a little, wondering what he was doing but, as he gazed deeply into her eyes, a joyous realisation dawned on her.

With only the slightest of smiles, he took a hold of her hand and rose from his seat, gently pulling her with him. Cutting a path through all the people in the room, he led her towards a short corridor and she felt her heart-rate quicken with anticipation of what was surely about to happen. She was so lost in the moment, so focussed on their destination, that she barely noticed the few knowing smiles and cheeky winks that were aimed towards her man.

Lying back on the bed, Catherine could only stare up at the ceiling as she fought to regain her breath. Her entire body was tingling with excitement, despite how drained her muscles felt and she was sure that the wide grin that parted her lips would be permanently fixed in place.

As Ethan stubbed out his cigarette, she turned slightly to look at him and was more than a little disappointed when he stood up and walked across the room, without so much as a glance in her direction.

"What are you doing?" she asked, watching him pick up his clothes and dress hurriedly.

He still didn't look at her, let alone answer, as he fastened his jeans and started collecting up her clothing. Her heart sank as she realised what was happening and she expected them to be tossed over to her, accompanied by a somewhat harsh demand for her to leave.

"Why are you being like this?" she asked naively, as she pushed herself upright on the bed and tried to cover herself up.

Again, he didn't answer but, when she saw him ball up her clothes and stuff them into an old rucksack, she quickly stood up.

"Ben" she insisted. "What are you doing?"

"My name's not Ben" Ethan stated, now looking directly into her eyes as a sick smile spread across his lips.

Wracked with confusion, Catherine felt a wave of dizziness as she looked questioningly at him. "What?" she exclaimed.

"My name's Ethan" he laughed, as he zipped up the rucksack and threw it to the corner of the room.

"Why would you . . ." Catherine began, but she was stopped short in her sentence as he drove his fist into her face.

The blow sent her staggering backwards and she fell on to the bed as the taste of blood filled her throat. Tears fell freely from her eyes as Ethan stepped forward and took a firm hold of her hair, pulling her upright and then over to the door.

He dragged her back along the corridor to the main room, where everyone was now standing in a circle, seemingly awaiting her arrival. Despite the mix of pain and confusion that dominated her senses, Catherine could feel the eyes of every one of them staring at her naked body as she was pulled to the centre of the room and forced to her knees.

Slumping forward, she tried to cover herself, but Ethan quickly pulled her back up and held her arms behind her back. The sound of the crowd's laughter filled her ears and she felt the room begin to spin as a woman stepped towards her, handing something to Ethan before taking a firm grasp of Catherine's chin and lifting her head to look at her. Strangely, despite the situation and the cacophony of emotions, it struck her that the woman seemed very different to the rest of the people there. Without any tattoos or unique piercings, she was somehow more formal than the others and that gave Catherine a futile moment of hope.

"Why are you doing this?" Catherine implored, as though the woman might actually consider helping her.

"Because we can" the woman laughed, before spitting in her face and slapping her hard across the cheek, bringing a fresh bout of laughter from the watching crowd.

Catherine felt her wrists being painfully bound behind her back with what could only have been a cable-tie, before Ethan and the woman moved away from her. Desperately, she looked around at the crowd and she now noticed that some of them were brandishing things like rope, chains, baseball bats and glass bottles. It was a scene that sent her emotions into free-fall and, as the people began moving towards her, she was frozen with absolute fear.

Offering up a silent prayer, Catherine firmly closed her eyes and, as a multitude of hands commenced a humiliating examination of her body, her thoughts drifted to Michelle's warning.

Chapter 14

The morgue had never held any fear or revulsion for Dani, dead bodies being an all too familiar sight in such a big hospital, but this visit caused a plethora of emotions for her. It had started when she'd received the call from the Pathologist, David, and now she was actually seeing what he'd described, she felt a little queasy.

"Are you ok?" David asked, having noticed the paleness of her complexion.

Dani nodded, uncertainly. "It's all the same?" she replied.

"Pretty much" David confirmed, as he pulled the sheet back over the girl's body and returned the gurney to the freezer unit. "If anything, it's a little more vicious this time."

Slowly shaking her head, Dani let out an involuntary sigh. "And they found her in the same place?" she asked.

"Uh-huh. I don't have a lot of detail, but the guys who brought her in said they'd had to pull her out of a bin, just like the last one only, this time, she was already gone when she was found."

Again, Dani shook her head. "Did they say who found her?"

"No. From what I can gather, someone called it in. Apparently, it was some sort of an anonymous tip, as clichéd as that sounds."

With her mind racing, Dani struggled to find any reply but, when David offered her a coffee, she gratefully accepted and followed him to his office.

"How old would you say she is?" she finally asked, sitting at the desk whilst the drinks were being made.

"I'd say she was probably around twenty" David replied, "certainly no more than twenty four."

"Christ" Dani muttered, under her breath. "And there's no ID yet?"

"None. Like I said, it's the same as the last girl and I think they'll be relying on dental records, if there's enough teeth to get a match."

"What?" Dani exclaimed.

David sighed, clearly having not meant to deliver that much information. "I'm sorry" he said. "I didn't want to tell you, but whoever did this has smashed out most of her teeth."

Taking a deep breath, Dani accepted the mug that was handed to her and they both drank in silence for a short while.

"Thanks for letting me know about this," Dani eventually said, "you didn't have to."

"I know" David smiled. "But I thought you'd want to hear it, especially after what happened to the last girl."

Dani looked at him for a moment, a little perplexed by the comment. "Why?" she asked.

"Because Emily told me what you were thinking" he answered.

"She told you? When?"

"She came down here after you'd spoken to her and asked what I thought about it all."

"And what did you tell her?"

"The same as I did you" he smiled. "There could have been any number of things that caused the heart-attack and I don't think it's likely that someone in the hospital would have done anything to her. This girl was already dead when they brought her in, which makes me believe that it's only a difference in time-scales, rather than some sort of sinister plot."

"But what about the puncture wound in her foot?" she asked, somewhat frustrated by her friend's lack of confidence. "There must be a reason for that?"

"With all the things that have been done to both of them, there could be any number of explanations for that" David answered. "The sad fact is that these girls have been abused beyond even my wildest imaginations and I can't picture the torture they must've endured. I honestly think you need to let this one go and leave it to the police."

"Like the police are going to do anything" Dani snapped. "They're already looking to brush it under the carpet and I don't doubt they'll do anything more for this poor girl."

Now it was David's turn to look a little perplexed. "What do you mean, they're looking to brush it under the carpet?" he asked. "I gave them enough samples of bodily fluids to get something. Surely they've been able to trace one of the culprits, at least?"

Dani shook her head. "I don't know" she answered, forcing her anger back as she realised she was starting to lose her control. "I haven't heard anything since those two detectives were here. All I know is that they seemed adamant they were going to pin all this on the guy who found the first girl and I doubt they intended to do much in the way of digging."

"But why would they try to pin it on him?" David wondered out loud.

"Because that's the easy solution" Dani replied.

"But, unless his DNA was tied in with the stuff I gave them, then what reason could they have for pointing the finger towards him?"

"That's the point. It strikes me that they took that evidence for appearance and, if they weren't lucky enough for something to pan out from it, then I daresay the case was destined to end up in the unsolved cases file from the very beginning."

"Well, surely they can't dismiss it, now a second girl has turned up?" David suggested.

The previously unconsidered thought drove itself into Dani's mind, bringing with it the realisation that the same two detectives were likely to be assigned to this case as well, and she felt her anger spike once again. "Have they been here yet?" she asked.

"No" David answered. "Not yet, but I'd expect them to be here soon."

"Well, can you let me know when they are? I'd like to be around when they talk to you."

"And why would that be, Doctor Draper?" came a voice from the office doorway.

Dani spun round in her chair and saw Detective Crowther smiling cynically at her, with Wishall, as always, lurking close behind.

"Could it be that you want a clue as to whether we've got anything on your good friend, Mr Trowman?" he continued. "Maybe you're looking to tip him off?"

"What the hell do you mean?" Dani replied, aggressively.

Crowther only chuckled in response, before turning his attention to David. "Where's the stiff?" he callously demanded.

For a moment, David was a little stunned by the comment, shocked by the lack of respect that was being shown, but he quickly remembered Dani's assessment of their approach to the case. "The victim is in there" he replied, nodding past them and into the main room.

"Well, come on then, jump to it" Crowther smiled. "We haven't got all day. We've got people to arrest, you know. Or, should I say, a person to arrest."

His last words were said whilst he looked directly at Dani, causing her heart to skip with the presumption of what he was suggesting.

"Who are you going to arrest?" she asked tentatively, fearing the response.

"Well now" he sneered. "That's none of your business really, is it?"

"I'm just intrigued as to how you've managed to link someone to this, without even knowing who the girl is" Dani replied, ignoring the contempt.

"Who said we don't know who she is?" Crowther smiled, knowingly.

Dani and David exchanged glances. "How on earth could you know that?" David asked.

Crowther's grin widened. "It's called being a good detective" he answered.

Ruckus stared at the man who stood in front of him, his eyes burning with intensity as his gaze seemed to burn right through to the back of the man's skull. Slowly, he shifted his attention to the holdall that'd been placed on the table between them and then, with a drawn-out and deliberate movement, he reached forward to open the bag for a second time, almost as though he was checking that the contents hadn't miraculously changed from his first glance.

"This is it?" he asked, his voice ominously calm under the circumstances. "This is all you've taken?"

The man visibly wilted, clearly struggling to retain his composure in the midst of the club's headquarters, surrounded by several fully-patched members. He'd been concerned about this meeting, panicked even, ever since he'd realised the steady drop in the whorehouse's profits, and the tone in Ruckus' voice delivered nothing that would convince him he'd been wrong in his worry.

"Yes" he barely managed to mumble.

"In two months," Ruckus continued, "this is all the money you've made?"

The man slowly nodded.

Ruckus also gave a slow nod of his head, "So, what is it?" he asked. "Suddenly, all the men in this city have decided they don't like pussy? They've all suddenly developed a conscience and stopped fucking anything that isn't their wives?"

"The sex isn't the problem" the man answered, hoping for some glimmer of salvation. "I've had them bitches working double time."

"Then what the fuck is going on?" Ruckus snapped, finally showing the anger that, until that moment, had lain quietly underneath his calm exterior. "Because the maths don't fuckin' add up!"

Looking down at the floor, the man fought to give his voice enough volume to be heard. "It's the drugs" he admitted. "The punters just haven't been buying them from us."

"So, where the fuck are they buyin' them from?" Ruckus hissed. "And how long has this been goin' on?"

Feeling his legs weakening with every word, the man took several breaths to try and steady himself. He continued to stare at the floor, wishing that it would open up and transport him far away from this place and the scrutiny he was under. "A couple of months" he eventually mumbled.

"I'm sorry" Ruckus stated. "I didn't quite catch that. Did you say this has been goin' on for a couple of months?"

The man again gave a slow nod of confirmation.

"And you didn't think of bringin' this to our attention?" Ruckus questioned. "You didn't think of tellin' us there might be a problem?"

This time, knowing there was nothing he could possibly say that might help him through this, the man didn't respond.

Without taking his eyes off him, Ruckus moved around the table, until he was standing right in front of the man. "Is it too much to hope" he almost whispered, "that you might have at least looked into why this is happenin'?"

Seeing a glimmer of redemption, the man looked up when he answered. "I have" he said. "It seems they're getting their drugs from someone else. I haven't found out who yet, but I'm working on it."

"You're working on it?" Ruckus chuckled, before glancing around at his brothers in the room. "Did you hear that?" he announced. "He's working on it!"

Again, the man bowed his head but, if he hadn't, he might have noticed the slight nod that Ruckus gave to Jimmy, who quietly moved up behind him and then stood ready.

"So" Ruckus surmised. "You found out that someone's trading on our patch, that they're takin' money from our pockets and you didn't think you should let us know? Tell me, how did you think this little meetin' was gonna go down?"

The man wanted to apologise, to beg forgiveness and assure them that he was doing all he could to sort the situation out. He wanted to plead for more time, for help in solving the problem, but he wasn't given the chance to utter a single word before Jimmy forced a clear, plastic bag over his head and pulled it tightly around his neck.

Fighting for breath, the man dropped to his knees, where Ruckus drove his knee into the man's nose, shattering it and filling the bag with blood. With the bag still pulled tight, Ruckus bent over and placed his hand on the back of the man's head, keeping it steady as he repeatedly punched the centre of his face, until all fight had gone and the man became still.

"Get this rid of this prick" he ordered, once he was sure all life had gone from the limp body. "And then get your ass over to the whorehouse; I want to know what the fuck is goin' on over there."

Jimmy nodded his agreement. "D'you want me to stay there and run the place?" he asked, as he tied off the bag to stop any of the blood escaping.

"No" Ruckus answered. "I'll send someone over later. I just want you to get some information from the punters. Find out who's fuckin' us over, and then drop this bag over to Albert at the coffee shop."

Once more, Jimmy nodded his agreement, before picking up the bag and gesturing for a couple of the Prospects to pick up the body.

As the men left, Ruckus signalled for Ethan to follow him into the meeting room and closed the door behind them.

"What's happenin' with the girl?" he asked, taking his seat at the table.

"She was found this mornin' and Crowther and Wishall have interviewed her friends" Ethan replied, as he sat in his own chair.

"And they've confirmed what we wanted?"

"It don't matter. Crowther knows what they need."

"That don't give me any confidence" Ruckus muttered. "He knew what they needed when the first bitch was found. You sure this is water-tight?"

Ethan let out a sigh. "Of course" he answered.

"Don't fuckin' act like that!" Ruckus snapped. "I told you this bullshit was fuckin' risky and it's gonna fuck us over if we 'ain't careful."

"And don't fuckin' doubt me!" Ethan snapped back. "I 'ain't a prick and I know what I'm doin'. They're pickin' the guy up now and they've got enough to fuckin' nail him this time."

Slowly shaking his head, Ruckus stared at his son for a few moments. "This better not get fucked up" he hissed.

"Or what?" Ethan hissed in return.

Ruckus merely continued to stare at him. "It just better not" he finally stated.

Ben slowly opened his eyes, and instantly closed them again as the bright sunlight stabbed into his brain. His head was thudding, genuinely banging and he felt as though his mind had been replaced by barbed wire. He groaned as he tried to push himself upright, instantly regretting the movement as a wave of nausea washed over him and, as the banging intensified, he fell back down again.

He tried to think back over what happened the night before and he could remember ploughing his way through all the booze he had in the flat. He also recalled his decision to go on a quest for more once the alcohol had been drunk dry, but whatever happened after that would need to present itself as horrific flash-backs throughout the day because, try as he might, the rest of the night was nothing but a blank space in his mind. Fortunately though, the banging seemed to have dissipated.

From the position he was in, it was apparent that he'd slept on his settee and, when he moved his legs, his foot made contact with what must have been an empty bottle. Scratch that, he rued, he hadn't slept on the settee, he'd passed out.

Using his arm as a shield, he tried once more to open his eyes, blinking several times in order to help them adjust to the brightness until, finally, he was able to keep them open without too much pain. Then the banging returned with a vengeance, seeming to bounce his brain off the insides of his skull, and he held his head with both hands in a futile attempt to alleviate the turmoil. Surprisingly, that seemed to work for a few seconds, until it came again and he realised the noise didn't stem from his hangover, it came from his front door.

Sluggishly, Ben pushed himself upright once more, trying to ignore the second wave of nausea that threatened to violently evacuate the booze he'd consumed. Very unsteadily, he rose to his feet and staggered towards the door, not exactly keen on seeing who was there, but desperate to bring a halt to the incessant hammering.

"Jesus Christ!" Sam exclaimed chirpily, as the door was opened. "I thought you'd be bad, but you're fucked beyond anything I could've imagined!"

Ben winced at the volume of his friend's voice, knowing it was raised deliberately, and groaned in response.

Taking great pleasure in the pain he was causing, Sam pushed past him and took a sweeping look around the room as Ben closed the door.

"My god" he sighed, as he took in the empty bottles that were scattered over the table and settee. "If you tell me this is down to what happened at the club, I swear I'm gonna punch you square in the face."

"Go fuck yourself" Ben muttered, as he made his way into the kitchen to make a coffee.

"You go fuck yourself!" Sam snapped in reply. "You throw a strop in the club, leave me and Karen to make up some bullshit excuses, you don't take any of my calls and then you stumble into the bar and act like a prick? You need to wind your neck in, my friend because, right now, you're skating on some very thin fucking ice."

"You don't know what you're talking about" Ben stated.

"Oh, don't I?" Sam questioned. "So this isn't all about Steph, no?"

Ben remained silent as the kettle finished boiling and he poured the water into two mugs of coffee.

Sam stared at him, eyebrows raised as he waited for the answer.

"So, what is it then?" he eventually asked, when it became apparent that no explanation would be forthcoming.

Ben passed him a mug as he spoke. "It is about Steph" he admitted, "but it's not what you think."

"Well, d'you wanna enlighten me then?"

Taking a long sip of his drink, Ben deliberated on how to tell him what had happened, until he came to the conclusion that he'd just have to come out with it. "She tried to have sex with me" he said.

"What?" Sam exclaimed, almost spitting out his drink. "When?"

"After the club on Friday."

The look of confusion on Sam's face wasn't surprising, so Ben quickly told him about the phone call he'd received and what had happened when he'd got to Steph's. He then described the moment she'd positioned herself in his lap and went on to reveal that she'd whispered Rob's name into his ear.

"Jesus Christ, mate" Sam muttered, with a shake of his head. "So what did you do?"

Hesitating, Ben thought back through the moment, almost wincing as the memory came flooding back. "I thought back to what you and Karen had said about her needing some affection and, when I told her she'd called me Rob, she said it was a mistake" he finally answered.

"And?" Sam urged.

"And I told her I was concerned that sleeping with each other would be a mistake" Ben answered, with a long sigh. "I said I thought she was looking for something from someone, not necessarily me."

"Jesus Christ" Sam again muttered. "So, what happened then?"

"She threw me out" Ben admitted.

A heavy silence fell momentarily between them, with each man looking to the other for something to be said. Eventually, it was Sam who broke the tension.

"Why did she throw you out?" he asked. "Didn't you explain what you meant to her?"

"I tried" Ben mumbled, almost like a child admitting to misbehaving, "but I was panicking and the words just wouldn't come."

"So, have you tried calling her?"

"I tried several times yesterday, but she wouldn't answer the phone. Then I went round to pick up my bike and knocked on her door, but she didn't answer that."

Sam shook his head in frustration, tinged with just a small amount of pity. "Jesus, mate" he sighed.

They looked at each other for a few seconds, neither knowing what to say next, until Ben finally broke the silence.

"So there you have it" he said. "I've fucked it all up and that's all there is to know."

"I'm sure she'll come round" Sam suggested. "She's probably just embarrassed about it all and, when she's had time to think about it, you'll get the chance to talk to her about what you meant. Who knows? Maybe this is the point when you two realise you need to be together?"

"You didn't see the look in her eyes" Ben pointed out. "I've hurt her, badly."

"But your reasons were genuine and she'll realise that."

Ben wanted to believe him, he wanted to hope that her actions were more than just a drunken need and that she would realise he wasn't rejecting her entirely, but a knock on the door stopped him from thinking any further into it.

Leaving Sam in the kitchen, he went to see who was there and his heart shattered when Detectives Crowther and Wishall practically pushed him backwards as they barged into the flat.

"Had a heavy night, Mr Trowman?" Crowther grinned.

"What are you doing here?" Ben replied, ignoring the comment.

Sam walked back into the room, immediately attracting their attention.

"And who might this be?" Crowther demanded to know. "Is this your partner in crime? Have we struck lucky today?"

Fuelled by his hangover and the intrusion by the last two people he wanted to see right at that moment, Ben's anger flared. "What the hell are you talking about?" he asked.

Crowther's grin widened as he spoke. "And where were the two of you last night?"

Looking between him and Sam, Ben tried to keep himself calm. "I was out" he replied.

Crowther raised his eyebrows. "And what about your friend here?"

"I was at work" Sam answered. "At the Skinning Pit. Ben was there too."

"Oh really?" Wishall interjected, sneering at Ben. "Well isn't that just perfect?"

Alarm bells started to ring for Ben. "What's going on?" he asked. "Why is that perfect?"

"Because more of your handiwork has been found in the alley" Crowther answered, through a broad smile.

It took a couple of moments for Ben to understand what was being said. "Another girl?" he exclaimed, horrified by both the announcement and the callous expressions on the detective's faces.

"Like you didn't know" Wishall sniggered.

Ben was speechless as full realisation dawned on him. "You can't seriously be thinking I had something to do with that?"

"You are Ben Trowman?" Crowther asked. "You do ride a motorcycle and work in The Skinning Pit, right?"

Hesitantly, Ben nodded.

"Then we need you to come with us" Crowther continued.

"Are you arresting him?" Sam exclaimed, as he also began to understand what was happening.

"Well, that's up to Mr Trowman" Crowther smiled. "He can either come with us voluntarily, or we can slap the cuffs on him and drag him out to the car."

Chapter 15

The late-afternoon sun blazed high in the crystal-clear blue sky, radiating it's warmth on everything below as Billy lay back on the grass and closed his eyes for just a second or two, allowing his mind to drift back to yet another memory of his past. This time though, possibly due to the glorious nature of the day or even to the fact that he'd had such a good morning and made more than enough cash to cover the cost of his booze for the next few days, his thoughts brought recollections of which he was actually rather fond.

It was the late seventies and he was seventeen, fresh-faced and full of life as he and his best mate, Tommo, took their bikes out for a spin in the countryside. It was a trip they rarely managed to take, what with their time being so consumed by both chores around the foster home and their desperate search for employment. Honestly, neither of them had any interest in working, especially given the only options likely to be open to them would be manual labour, but they were on the verge of turning eighteen and, once that happened, they'd be out on the street and fending for themselves.

They'd been riding for a while, a good couple of hours at least, and they were a long way out of the city, eating up the miles of country roads that lay in front of them. The trees zipped by, a blur of natural beauty, although neither paid much attention as they pushed their machines faster and faster, trying to outdo each other at every bend. Eventually though, an urge greater than that for speed began to take hold and Billy signalled to Tommo that he was stopping, before slowing and pulling over to the side of the road.

"I thought you were gonna lose it back there, for sure" he laughed, as he stepped off his bike and stretched.

Tommo followed suit, shrugging his shoulders nonchalantly. "Nah" he smiled. "I was just showboating."

Billy looked around. "Showboating?" he exclaimed. "Who the fuck were you tryin' to impress? There's no one here!"

"Come on!" Tommo urged. "You can't tell me you didn't think it was awesome?"

Shaking his head, Billy reached into his jacket and pulled out the small tin he always carried around with him. "Fancy a smoke?" he asked.

"Like you have to ask?" Tommo replied.

They jumped over the rock wall they'd parked up against and sank down with their backs against it.

"I've got another fuckin' interview tomorrow" Tommo mentioned, as he watched Billy preparing a joint.

"Yeah, me too" Billy confirmed. "It fuckin' sucks, the thought of spending our lives in that fuckin' factory."

Tommo nodded in agreement. "But what else are we supposed to do?" he sighed. "We've gotta sort somethin' out, or we're gonna be screwed."

"I ain't workin' for no one" Billy stated, with a smile. "I've got better stuff lined up."

"So, why you goin' to the interview?" Tommo asked. "What you got lined up?"

Billy's smile broadened as he finished the joint and held it up in the air. "This" he stated.

Confused, Tommo looked at the joint and then back to Billy. "That?" he smiled. "So, you're just gonna get stoned?"

"No, you dick" Billy laughed. "I'm gonna sell this shit."

The confusion in Tommo's expression increased. "So, why you goin' to the interview?" he asked again.

"Because I can't exactly tell them what I'm plannin', can I?"

"That's true" Tommo agreed, although he was clearly still struggling with the concept.

Realising the difficulty his mate was having, Billy continued. "I'm goin' to the interview and I'm gonna try and get the job. Then, when they've stopped watching what we're doin', I'm gonna jack that shit in and make some proper cash."

"You think you'll make enough from it?"

"You're shittin' me, right? I can make more than you can dream of, selling this stuff. I've already started rakin' it in, and I ain't even doin' it full-time yet."

"You're sellin' it already?"

"Yeah, course I am."

Again, Tommo struggled with the idea. "Where?" he eventually asked.

"Around the offices in town" Billy answered. "It's fuckin' easy. All I have to do is hang around by the bus stops when the suits are goin' home and they snap it up, especially on a Friday night."

"Well, where the fuck are you gettin' it from?"

"The same place I get my stash from, Filthy Richards over at the retirement home."

"But, I thought he could only get a bit at a time?"

"Nah" Billy smiled. "He's met this guy who's started shippin' the stuff in from some place abroad. Well, he's gettin' it from a guy who's shippin' it in, anyway. And he's told me he wants me to work for him when I've got myself out of the spotlight."

Tommo scowled. "But what if you get caught?" he asked.

"Fuck it" Billy laughed. "That's the beauty of it. The pigs don't give a shit about this stuff, unless you've got a load on you. All I'll ever be carryin', is enough to make a bit of dough so, if they do catch me, they'll think it's just for personal use and confiscate it."

"So, how you gonna make any money off that?"

"That's the thing" Billy answered, as he lit the joint and took a long, deep drag. "I won't be doin' all the sellin'. I've gotta get a bunch of guys to work for this guy, and we all split the profits. You want in?"

Taking the joint from Billy, Tommo nodded eagerly. "Too fuckin' right!" he exclaimed, before he too inhaled a long drag. "But how's this gonna work? Surely the pigs'll wanna know why we're all meetin' up?"

Billy shook his head. "That's why we've gotta put up with shit jobs for a bit" he confirmed. "We work like good boys, but we set up one of them motorcycle clubs while we do it."

"You mean like the Hells Angels?"

"Pretty much. Filthy is sortin' out a house for us to meet at, so we do that for a bit and then, when the pigs stop payin' us any attention, we start movin' the dope. I've just gotta come up with a name."

Passing the joint back over, Tommo now carried an expression of awe as he nodded. "You thought of anythin' yet?" he asked.

"The Men of Pain" Billy proclaimed, proudly.

Tommo burst out laughing. "That sounds like a fuckin' queer film."

"Well, you think of somethin' better then!" Billy replied, tetchily. "And it better sound ominous, like we're not gonna be messed with."

"What about" Tommo began, after a few moments of thought. "The Angels of Agony?"

"That's as shit as my idea!" Billy chuckled. "The Reapers of Fear?"

As the joint was smoked, the suggestions continued to flow, each met with as much derision as the last, until Billy came up with something that stopped the mockery.

"The Sons of Sorrow" he stated, as though he knew it'd be the one they chose.

"The Sons of Sorrow" Tommo repeated, letting the words roll around in his head for a couple of seconds. "I like that" he smiled, "it pretty much says it all."

"Then that's what we'll be" Billy declared. "The Sons of Sorrow, and fuck anyone who gets in our way."

Chapter 16

He should have been happy, relieved to finally be leaving the place but, as Ben picked up the envelope that contained his belongings and he took out his phone, wallet, keys and cigarettes, he felt nothing but emptiness. He didn't want to smile, he didn't want to cry and any anger that may have raged within him overnight had long since dissipated. All in all, he felt like a shell, nothing more than a hollowed-out version of himself that wanted only to sleep.

Tossing back the envelope, he turned towards the exit and strode towards it, without giving as much as a cursory glance in the direction of the officer who sat behind the desk. They didn't warrant any acknowledgement, he figured. Especially not after the way they'd treated him, keeping him locked up without any food or drink. They'd acted as though he was a certified criminal, unremorseful for what he'd done, but he wasn't anything of the sort, was he? He hadn't done anything, yet still they'd stuck him in a cell and, seemingly, left him to rot.

As he pushed open the door, he was forced to shield his eyes from the blazing sun. He'd had some light in the cell, but not much, and the contrast from the florescent strip-lighting in the station caused his tired eyes to take a few seconds to adjust.

"Hallelujah" exclaimed a familiar and welcome voice from behind him.

Turning, Ben saw Sam leaning against the wall of the station, his expression one of obvious concern albeit masked a little by his grin.

"I was beginning to think they'd never let you out" he continued.

"You waited?" Ben asked, his tiredness causing his attempt at displaying happiness to fall a little short.

"Not all night" Sam smiled. "I followed when they brought you in, but they told me you probably wouldn't be released until this morning so, when you still hadn't called me a couple of hours ago, I came back."

"You didn't have to do that" Ben stated, his voice trailing off with the realisation that he was stating the obvious.

Sam shook his head. "I wasn't going to leave you here by yourself, mate."

"Well, thanks" Ben replied, finally managing a smile of his own.

"So what happened?" Sam asked. "Why'd they keep you in there so long?"

Ben shrugged. "I don't know. They just kept going over the fact that someone told them I was the last person the girl was seen with and refusing to accept what you told them, about me being in The Pit on Saturday night."

"But, surely, me telling them that was enough to disprove the statement that's been given?"

"You'd have thought so, but they wouldn't have it. Every time I repeated it, they just waved it off and suggested you might have something to do with this."

As Sam's smile faltered, Ben realised how his comment must have sounded.

"They're not planning to interrogate you" he quickly continued. "They finally agreed to call Andy this morning and, by the sounds of it, he confirmed what we were both saying, so they had to let me go."

"And they couldn't have done that last night?" Sam asked, still clearly perturbed by the thought that he was being implicated.

"Yeah, they could have, but they didn't want to" Ben confirmed. "It was the same as when they grilled me in the hospital. It seems like they wanted me to just break down and admit to murdering the girls."

Struggling to find a response to that, Sam again shook his head. "I just don't understand why they're attacking you with this" he finally said, as Ben took out a much-needed cigarette and drew heavily as he lit it.

"I guess they're just hoping for a simple resolution to the case" Ben suggested, as he blew smoke into the breeze.

"Are they still considering you as a suspect?" Sam asked.

Again, Ben shrugged his shoulders. "I guess so" he answered. "They've warned me that I'm not to leave the city until they confirm otherwise."

"So, what are you gonna do? You can't keep going through this. That's two girls now, what if there's another one found? Will they pick you up again?"

For a moment, Ben couldn't answer him. He hadn't considered that fact and the thought of it made his blood run cold for a second.

"I don't know" he answered, frankly. "What can I do?"

"You could make a complaint."

"Who to? If I start moaning that I'm being victimised, then wouldn't that make it look as though I've got something to hide?"

Sam opened his mouth to reply, but closed it again once he realised there was nothing else he could suggest.

"Have you spoken to Steph at all?" Ben asked, keen to change the subject.

"No" Sam answered. "Honestly, I didn't think about it. Has she tried contacting you?"

Ben reached into his pocket and pulled out his phone, which had been switched off when he handed it over to the police officer. He turned it on and it flashed up with a text message and notification of a few missed calls, causing his heart to skip a little before he was able to open up the details.

"No" he eventually replied, when he saw that one of the calls was from Charlie, the owner of The Skinning Pit, and the others from an unknown number.

Opening the text message, Ben felt his stomach lurch as he read it. "Fuck" he cursed.

"What is it?" Sam asked, craning his neck to see, even though it'd be impossible for him to read the screen.

Ben re-read the message a couple of times, almost hoping that he'd misinterpreted it, but it wasn't exactly cryptic in its wording. "I've been sacked" he sighed.

Looking at him in disbelief, Sam clearly hadn't expected to hear that, so Ben read the message out to him.

"I've tried calling you, but your phone was off, so you must still be with the police. They told me what's happened and I had to close the bar for a second time so I am sorry but I have to let you go. Thank you for all your hard work."

"That's ridiculous!" Sam exclaimed, grabbing the phone to read the message himself. "He can't do this."

"Clearly, he can" Ben replied.

"Well, surely this gives you cause to complain about those detectives now? You haven't been charged with anything, so they shouldn't be fucking up your job."

Again, Ben sighed. "What good would that do?" he asked. "It's not gonna get my job back, is it? Charlie had to close the bar again, so of course he's gonna be pissed, whether I've been charged or not."

"But that's ridiculous" Sam repeated, although he stopped short of saying anything more.

They looked at each other for a few moments, neither of them sure of what to say, until Ben broke the silence by taking back the phone and hitting the button that dialled his voicemail. "I might as well see who's left me a message" he said, as he put the phone to his ear.

Sam watched, a little intrigued, until Ben pressed the call cancel button. "Well?" he asked.

Ben's expression had changed to one of confusion. "That was Doctor Draper" he answered.

Now Sam was confused. "Who's he?"

"It's a she" Ben smiled, "and she was looking after the girl I found."

"Well, what did she want?"

"She wants to meet up with me."

With raised eyebrows, it was clear where Sam's mind had gone.

"I'm sure it's not like that" Ben insisted.

Impossibly, Sam's eyebrows raised further still. "So, what else could it be?" he asked.

Flicking the finished cigarette away, Ben slowly shook his head. "I don't know" he answered.

Dressed in casual clothes, with her hair hanging loosely around her shoulders, Dani looked very different to the figure of authority she'd been in the hospital, but Ben recognised her as soon as he'd stepped through the coffee shop's door. With a smile, she waved across to him and he moved towards her, but found his path blocked by Mary, who'd grabbed a copy of the morning's paper as she'd rushed round from behind the counter.

"Tell me this isn't true!" she demanded sternly, flashing the pages in front of his face.

"Tell you what isn't true?" Ben asked, although the sinking feeling in the pit of his stomach suggested the question may be somewhat redundant.

"Another girl found and you were arrested" Mary continued, switching her gaze between both him and the headline on the page. "It says here that you're the prime suspect in the case and that they had you in for questioning."

Ben took a step back, in an attempt to both give himself a chance to think and to avoid being slashed by the edges of the paper as they swiped perilously close to his nose. He could feel the eyes of the few customers, including Dani, on him and his mind raced as he processed the fact that his name must've been made public.

"Now, Mary" Albert sighed, from his position behind the counter. "The boy's here, isn't he? So it can't be as serious as they are suggesting, otherwise they wouldn't have let him go. That story is probably just the reporters building it all out of proportion, like usual."

Fixing him with a stare, Mary waited for confirmation.

"That's right" Ben nodded, trying to smile. "They did take me in, but that's because I'd found the first girl. Sam and Andy both confirmed that I'd been drunk in The Pit that night, so they realised I couldn't have had anything to do with it and let me go."

Slowly, Mary's expression softened and she lowered the paper. "I'm sorry, Ben" she muttered. "It's just that I read what was in here and panicked, that's all."

"Please can I have a look at that?" Ben asked.

"Of course" Mary agreed, handing him the paper. "Now, come over here and let me get you a drink."

"Thanks, but it's ok" Ben smiled, gesturing towards Dani. "I'm here to meet someone."

Turning to follow his gaze, Mary saw Dani sitting patiently in the corner and, as realisation dawned on her, she quickly turned back to him. "Oh" she exclaimed. "I didn't realise."

Noticing her expression was mimicking the one Sam had displayed upon discovery of the voicemail messages, Ben hastily corrected her. "No" he smiled. "It's not like that."

Again, similarly to Sam, Mary's eyebrows raised cynically, but she didn't say any more as she stepped aside to let him past. Still smiling, Ben walked over to the table, noticing Dani's eyes drift to Mary, who was following closely behind.

"Can I get you both anything?" she asked kindly, before Ben even had the chance to greet Dani.

"Thanks, but I've already got us both a coffee" Dani smiled, turning her attention to Ben. "It was one sugar, wasn't it?"

Ben nodded and they both waited for Mary to move away before taking their seats.

"I've been coming here for years" he explained, when he realised why Dani looked puzzled. "Mary's like the mother I never had."

"You didn't have a mother?" Dani asked, slightly surprised.

"Not in the usual loving, caring sense of the word" Ben replied, with a shrug. "But that's a long story. Thanks for the coffee."

"You're welcome" Dani smiled, before glancing down at the newspaper he'd placed on the table. "I didn't realise they'd printed your name" she said.

Once more, Ben shrugged his shoulders in reply. "It doesn't surprise me" he sighed. "Those two detectives seem hell-bent on proving it was me who attacked those girls and, so far, it strikes me they're not the type to do things by the book. I guess they've given them my name and probably all my other personal details."

"You should complain" Dani suggested, with a slight trace of anger in her voice. "Surely they shouldn't be doing that?"

"That's what Sam said" Ben smiled, resignedly. "But what good would that do? They've already got the information and I've got nothing to hide, so complaining would only give them a reason to think I don't want it out there."

"But what about your reputation? Won't that affect your job if people know you're linked with this?"

For a third time, Ben gave a shrug of his shoulders in response. "I've already lost that" he stated, "so it's not going to make much difference there and, once you've been fired from one of the bars, word quickly spreads to the others."

"They can't fire you for this."

"In the bars, it doesn't take much for them to boot you out. The Pit's been forced to close twice now and, with my name being linked to the murders, I'm not surprised I've been pushed out."

"So, what are you going to do for work?"

"Honestly" Ben smiled. "All I care about at the moment is catching up on my sleep. I'll worry about that tomorrow."

"Oh, I'm sorry" Dani exclaimed. "I didn't think. You should have said something on the phone. I could have met you later, or tomorrow even."

"No, it's fine" Ben smiled. "You sounded worried, what's wrong?"

After checking to make sure no one could overhear her, Dani let out a small sigh and leant towards him so she didn't need to speak any louder than was necessary. "When the detectives came to see the girl's body" she began, before taking a moment to confirm what she was saying in her own mind, "we got into an argument about the fact they intended to arrest you and they hinted that they thought I was somehow involved too."

"But, that's ridiculous" Ben stated, struggling to believe what he was hearing.

"It is, but if they decide they're going to point the finger at me, it could ruin my career, even if it's proven I wasn't involved. I've been up all night, worrying myself silly over it all, and all I could think was to call you, I hope you don't mind."

"Of course not. If it helps, I can tell you they also suggested they were gonna pick Sam up when he started arguing with them, and they didn't mention either of you while they were interrogating me."

"They didn't mention me at all?"

"Nothing" Ben confirmed. "All they kept going over was the fact that one of the girl's friends has apparently told them she went out with me on the night it happened, but

I was busy making a complete fool of myself and I didn't even know her."

"But they still arrested you?" Dani exclaimed.

Giving a fourth shrug, Ben opened his mouth to reply, but he was stopped by the sound of the door opening. Turning in his seat, he saw that the man who entered was large and well built, dressed in jeans, a plain black sweater and carrying a hold-all. He watched as the man walked confidently through the shop, heading to the back room and, when Albert followed him through without a word being uttered between them, he looked towards Mary, who remained behind the counter but stared intently at the door and had gone white as a sheet.

"Can you excuse me for a moment?" he asked, turning back to Dani, who nodded her agreement as she took a sip of her drink.

Ben stood up quickly and walked over to the counter, keeping his gaze locked firmly on the back room.

"Are you ok, Mary?" he asked.

Initially, Mary didn't seem to hear him, so he tried again.

"Yes, I'm fine" she replied hesitantly, finally looking at him.

Switching his focus between her and the door, Ben didn't believe that for a second. "Who's he?"

Again, Mary didn't reply immediately. "Oh, no one" she eventually answered, after seeming to take a little longer than necessary to think about her response. "We're just having some work done and that kind gentleman is helping us out."

Jimmy felt all eyes in the room staring at him as he prepared himself to speak, none more so than those of Ruckus, who's glare left him in no uncertainty that what he was about to say wouldn't be met with any approval.

"It took a bit of doing," he muttered, flexing the stiffness out of his hand, "but I got one of the punters to talk and it 'ain't good."

"Well? What 'ain't good?" Ruckus urged, when Jimmy hesitated for a moment.

"It's true" Jimmy confirmed. "They're gettin' their shit from someone else."

Giving a slow shake of his head, Ruckus continued to stare at the man. "Who they gettin' it from?" he asked.

Again, Jimmy hesitated. "I didn't get a name," he announced, "but, from the description, I figured it could only be our old friend."

"Shit!" Ethan exclaimed. "You sure?"

Reluctantly, Jimmy nodded. "I figured he'd be gettin' the stuff from Filthy, so I went to see 'im and, after a few smacks around his head, he confirmed it."

"Fuck" Ethan sighed, as he glanced at Ruckus, who now sported a satisfied smile.

"Then it's time to purge" Ruckus stated.

"But the guy's a foundin' member" Ethan argued.

"I don't give a fuck if he's the fuckin' president of the fuckin' world" Ruckus snapped. "He knew the rules and he knows better than to shit on our fuckin' doorstep. He's a fuckin' dead man an' that's the end of it."

A low murmur spread around the room, until Ethan spoke up. "We need to vote on this" he stated.

"We 'ain't votin' shit!" Ruckus replied.

Ethan was unmoved by the tone in his voice. "He's a foundin' member and purgin' 'ain't somethin' we do at the drop of a hat."

"It is when a piece of shit like him decides the rules can be broken."

"We gotta get him in. Give him the chance to speak."

"We 'ain't gotta do shit. This is fuckin' happenin' and I want it done tonight."

As Ethan rubbed his eyes in frustration, Ruckus turned to Touchy.

"Take one of the Prospects to do it" he ordered. "That son of a bitch 'ain't worth it bein' done by a patched member an' I want him to fuckin' know it."

Touchy nodded his agreement, as Ethan spoke again.

"This 'ain't a fuckin' joke" he muttered.

"I know it 'ain't a fuckin' joke" Ruckus spat, slamming his hand on the table. "But it's what's happenin' and, until you're sitting in my seat, you 'ain't got a fuckin' say in it, so shut the fuck up."

A heavy silence fell in the room, until Jimmy cleared his throat.

"There's somethin' else you need to know" he cautiously announced, instantly drawing the uncomfortable attention back to him. "Filthy told me there's another player in the city, someone new who's tryin' to do a deal with 'im."

Ruckus stared at him for a few seconds, as though he was trying to work out whether he'd properly heard the statement. "Who?" he asked.

"Filthy didn't know for sure" Jimmy continued. "But he thinks it's another motorcycle club. He's meetin' the guy tomorrow mornin' and he's gonna let me know."

"Fuck that" Ruckus replied. "He 'ain't gonna get anythin' outta the guy, we need to be there, Where's the meetin' bein' held?"

Jimmy shrugged. "Somewhere outside the city."

"No" Ruckus snapped. "It needs to be brought to us. Tell Filthy it's gotta be moved to the coffee shop.

"I'll call 'im" Jimmy agreed.

"Get him here" Ruckus replied. "It'll do him good to remember where his loyalty lies."

Another murmur began to spread, but Ruckus cut it short. "What's happenin' with the investigation into the two women?" he asked, turning back to Ethan.

Still smarting from their argument, Ethan hesitated for a moment before answering. "It's ready to be finished" he said. "The guy's been taken in and his name's all over the papers. All we need to do now is plant the evidence and me and Jimmy are handlin' that tonight. Crowther's gonna be waitin' for our call when it's done and he'll get in there to find it."

"Good" Ruckus replied, without any trace of satisfaction.

Almost groaning as he spoke, Jimmy's reluctance to provide further fuel for an argument was abundantly clear. "The guy's out" he muttered.

In unison, both Ethan and Ruckus turned towards him.

"What?" Ethan exclaimed.

"The guy's out" Jimmy repeated, his voice almost wobbling. "I saw him in the coffee shop this mornin' when I dropped the money off."

"You're fuckin' shittin' me" Ruckus snapped, turning on Ethan. "This shit's gotta be sorted out today."

Doing his best to maintain the impression of calm, Ethan sat back in his chair. "It's probably just that they didn't have enough to charge him straight away" he smiled. "When we've planted the evidence, the guy's fucked."

"He'd fuckin' better be" Ruckus hissed, before he brought the meeting to a conclusion.

Signalling for Touchy to remain seated, Ruckus watched as the members filed through the door and, once they were alone, he leaned in close, despite the privacy that was afforded by the room.

"I 'ain't happy with all this" he muttered.

"With all what?" Touchy questioned.

"With the way this investigation bullshit is bein' handled. We're leavin' too much to chance and that could be risky for us."

With a slow nod of his head, Touchy acknowledged the concern. "Ethan seems to have it under control" he suggested.

"For now he does" Ruckus replied, "but I want you to keep a close eye on it. Let me know if there's any sign of it gettin' fucked up."

"You got it, boss" Touchy agreed.

Chapter 17

Ben woke suddenly, gripped by panic with his heart racing in his chest. The last few days had been a roller-coaster of emotions, spinning him one way and then the other without giving him time to catch his breath. Now though, it seemed that the few hours of sleep he'd managed after getting home from the coffee shop had given his brain the opportunity to work its way through everything and reality was suddenly, devastatingly, clear in his mind.

Jumping out of bed, he paced back and forth as he took deep breaths to try and calm himself down. He tried to focus on just one thing at a time, one problem before the next, but they all seemed so vital, so desperate, that his mind skipped haphazardly between them and he started to feel a little dizzy as he quickly became overwhelmed.

Darkness surrounded him, both visually and mentally, as he stumbled towards the door and out into his living room. He reached for his cigarettes, hastily sparking one and drawing deeply on the smoke, holding it in his lungs for a few seconds to enhance the effect of the nicotine, until he felt his heart finally beginning to relax.

"What the fuck is going on?" he practically cried out. "Why the fuck am I being smashed like this?"

He hadn't done anything wrong, had he? All he'd done was call an ambulance when he found someone in trouble and now his name was being cited as a murderer and a rapist. He'd spent a night in a cell, trapped like a guilty man, and he'd lost his job with little or no chance of working in the city again, at least until his name was cleared and, even then, he would still have to prove his innocence to people.

Reaching for his phone, he checked the screen and his heart sank further still when he noted the absence of any messages. On top of everything, he thought to himself, he'd tried to protect Steph, tried to save her from making what could've been a drunken mistake and, it now seemed, even that had resulted in him being punished. She must've read the papers and seen what had happened, yet still she hadn't tried to contact him.

Overcome by both anger and sorrow, he collapsed on to the settee and held his head in his hands. Uncontrollably, tears began to fall as he felt the solitude of his flat weighing heavily on his shoulders and he stayed that way for a good few minutes until, slowly, his emotions began to steady themselves.

He had to do something, he realised as he wiped at his cheeks with the palm of his hand; he had to make a start on piecing his life back together. Granted, there wasn't anything he could do about the investigation into the girls and he'd have to wait until the morning to speak to Charlie and tell him what was actually happening, in the vain hope it might help to regain his job, but he could do something about Steph, couldn't he?

The clock on his phone had told him it was just approaching half past ten, so The Pit would be closing soon. Sam wanted him to go in for a drink at the end of their shift, so he could go and force her to listen to him, to let him explain himself and to apologise for getting things so badly wrong. Surely, after all these years and everything they'd been through, she'd at least allow him that?

Suddenly, his phone started to ring, startling him enough to bring a flinch of surprise. He looked at the screen to see who was calling and couldn't help a wry smile in appreciation of the irony when he realised it was Sam.

"Oh, for fuck's sake!" Sam exclaimed, as Lobe's coughing fit resulted in a stream of vomit splashing over the bar.

As he slumped forward, his head landed heavily on its side amidst the vile, pungent liquid and Steph recoiled in horror, desperate to avoid being splashed.

"You're the closest!" she laughed, pushing past Sam and forcing him towards the danger zone.

Looking back at her, Sam shook his head in disbelief. "Like that matters" he groaned. "You could've been sitting on his lap and I'd still be the mug who has to wipe him down."

"You've got a baby" she argued, through a broad smile. "So you should be used to cleaning up sick."

"That's not sick though" Sam smiled. "With the amount of booze he's got in him, that's more like pure alcohol. We should bottle it and sell it to the pissheads outside the station."

"Be my guest" Steph chuckled, throwing him a cloth and then standing back to let him through.

Grudgingly, Sam collected the mop and bucket from just inside the door to the office and gave Steph a disapproving shake of his head as he pushed past, playfully shoving her against the counter as he did. He walked round to Lobe and set down the cleaning equipment before reaching out and taking a firm hold of the man's shoulders. Pulling him up, he let out a long, drawn-out moan at the sight of the liquid dripping from his hair, rolling down over the missing part of the ear that'd earned him his nickname.

"Jesus" he muttered, as he grabbed the cloth and tried to wipe some of the filth from the man's skin. "Not even Penny puts me through this."

With Steph laughing in the background, Sam clicked his fingers in an attempt to wake Lobe up but, when that didn't work, he took slight satisfaction from giving the man a quick slap across the cheeks.

Slowly, Lobe opened his eyes, letting out a groan that sent a waft of bad breath into Sam's face.

"I don't get paid enough for this" he complained, before attempting to get the man to his feet and looking over at Steph. "You could at least give me a hand" he suggested.

"No chance" Steph instantly replied, looking horrified at the thought.

Watched on by the few customers in the place, Sam struggled to get Lobe to the door, where he helped him into the street and leant him against the wall. He waited for a few minutes, until the fresh air had finally woken the man's senses enough for Sam to be confident that he would find his way home and then he went back inside, where Steph was finishing up cleaning the bar.

"Thanks" Sam smiled, picking up the mop and bucket.

Steph returned the smile. "I felt a little bit bad, leaving it all to you" she admitted, dropping the cloth into the bucket. "Besides, I didn't want you holding this against me for the rest of the night."

As one of the customers approached they returned to their place behind the bar and Steph served him whilst Sam put the cleaning equipment away.

"Have you spoken to Ben?" Sam asked, once the customer had returned to his seat.

With a momentary flash of panic in her expression, Steph stared at him for a few seconds. "No" she eventually muttered. "Not for a couple of days."

Sam gave a slow nod, having expected the answer. "You know he was arrested, don't you?"

The panic in Steph's expression turned quickly to one of abject shock. "What?" she exclaimed. "Why? When?"

"They picked him up after the second girl was found, claiming that he had something to do with it" Sam replied. "Charlie's sacked him as well."

"What?" Steph exclaimed, again. "Why's he done that? Is Ben ok?"

"I don't know" Sam answered, honestly. "I guess Charlie had enough of the place being closed and the two detectives who're investigating the case must've had a word in his ear about Ben."

"Well, is Ben still in prison?"

"He's got nothing to do with what happened, so they had to release him this morning" Sam replied. "He went home to get some sleep but he can tell you about it himself, I told him to come in tonight."

Once more, a look of panic flashed across Steph's expression. "He's coming in tonight?"

"He'd better" Sam confirmed. "The guy needs a few beers and some serious cheering up, after what he's been through."

Taking a deep breath, Steph fell silent and Sam waited to see if she would say anything more.

"What's wrong?" he asked, when he realised there was nothing coming.

"Nothing" Steph lied.

Shaking his head, Sam let out a long sigh. "I know what happened on Friday" he admitted. "Ben told me, just before they arrested him."

Steph's panic returned, mixed with no small amount of anger. "He told you?" she hissed, wanting to shout, but realising there were people who could hear.

"Of course he did" Sam replied. "Steph, the guy was devastated and he needed to talk to someone."

"That was private!" she snapped, losing a little of her previous caution. "He had no right to tell you anything!"

"Steph, there was no way he could keep something like that to himself, not with everything that's going on at the moment."

"And whose fault is that?"

The question took Sam by surprise and he struggled to find a response. "What are you talking about?" he eventually asked. "He hasn't exactly asked for all this."

"Well, there must be a reason the police arrested him" Steph stated. "They wouldn't have done that if they had nothing against him."

In disbelief at what he was hearing, Sam stared at her. "Will you listen to yourself?" he replied. "After all these years, you know Ben well enough to know he wouldn't do something like that."

"I thought I knew him well enough to know that he'd keep something like what happened between us private, but I guess I was wrong about that as well."

Sam shook his head. "I don't think you mean that" he said. "I get that you're probably embarrassed about what happened, but there's no need to take it out on Ben."

Looking at him, open-mouthed, Steph was clearly struggling to find anything to say.

"Well he'll be here later" Sam continued. "And I don't care how embarrassed or annoyed you are, the two of you care about each other too much to let something like this ruin everything."

"I don't know if I can face him" Steph answered, trying hard to maintain her anger.

"You'd better figure out you can" Sam snapped. "Because I 'ain't having all this bullshit cause a problem."

Having stared at him for a few minutes longer, Steph eventually nodded a reluctant agreement and excused herself from the bar. She rushed to the toilets and, once safe in the privacy of the small room, she stared at her reflection in the mirror before straightening herself up. After taking a deep breath to compose herself, she walked back through to the bar and stopped dead in her tracks when she saw Rob waiting for her.

"What the hell are you doing here?" she demanded, angrily striding across to confront him.

Rob stepped back a pace, raising his hands in an attempt to placate her. "I just want to talk" he pleaded. "I want to apologise for what happened."

"You mean stealing my money?" Steph hissed, bitterly. "Or threatening to kill me while you kicked ten shades of shit out of my door."

"Both" Rob confirmed, taking another step back. "And for everything else."

"Well, I don't want to hear it" Steph snapped. "So why don't you fuck off, right now?"

Bowing his head slightly, Rob again raised his hands. "Please" he begged, "just let me explain."

"Sam, call the police" Steph stated, without taking her eyes off Rob.

"Look" Rob urged, before Sam had the chance to reach for the phone. "Please just give me five minutes and then, if you want, I'll leave."

Hesitating, Sam looked at Steph, who in turn continued to look at Rob.

"You've got five minutes" Steph finally agreed, much to Sam's obvious dismay.

Steph led him away from the bar to a booth at the side of the room, away from the rest of the customers.

"Start talking" she demanded harshly, as soon as they'd sat down on opposite sides of the table.

Hurriedly, Rob explained that he'd taken various drugs on Friday night, which was what led to him turning up at hers. He admitted he wasn't in control of himself and that, whilst locked up by the police, he'd had time to think. All the way through, Steph's expression was one of cynicism, which turned to pure anger when he confessed to the fact that he'd got himself in deep with a biker gang and had no choice but to take the money, which was why he'd disappeared, out of humiliation and shame.

"What about the girl?" Steph asked, once he'd finished talking.

"What girl?" Rob asked in reply.

"The bitch who helped you steal my money" Steph confirmed. "They had you both on camera at the bank."

Rob acted as though he was confused by the question, his expression clearly exaggerated, until he allowed apparent recollection to filter through. "Oh, her?" he exclaimed. "She's just a friend, that's all."

"A friend you were screwing?" Steph spat instantly, in reply.

Again, Rob attempted to appear confused by the question, but Steph moved quickly to stop the pretence. "When I got home from work and you were in the shower" she continued, "I could smell the bitch's perfume in the bedroom and those wine glasses on the draining board just confirmed it."

"I told you" Rob began, determined to maintain his innocence, "they were used by me and . . ."

"Fuck off!" Steph cut in furiously, stopping him mid-sentence. "You expect me to believe that?"

Rob opened his mouth to reply but, again, Steph cut him short.

"This conversation is over" she hissed, emphasizing each word. "I expect you to pay me back the money you took and, until then, I don't want to see you again. If I do, I'll be straight on to the police."

Staring firmly into his eyes, Steph saw right through his attempt to appear hurt as he looked back at her. She watched with absolute contempt as he sat forward in his seat and she felt her skin crawl as he reached out to take hold of her hands. She tried to pull them away, but his grip tightened and she glanced down to see that her skin had turned white under the pressure. Looking back up, intending to say something, she suddenly found herself frozen in her seat when she saw the mask of hatred that'd taken over his expression.

"Shit" Ethan muttered under his breath, as he and Jimmy walked through the doors. "The place is fuckin' empty."

Not wishing to draw any attention to themselves, Ethan quickly swallowed down his disappointment and led Jimmy to a booth in the far corner of the room.

"Get a couple of drinks in" he ordered, nodding towards the bar as he sat down and slipped the rucksack under the table.

"What you havin'?" Jimmy asked.

"I don't give a fuck, just get a couple of beers."

Obediently, Jimmy wandered off to the bar as Ethan looked around the room. He noted the two staff who were working, a man and a woman, and registered they were in some kind of an intense discussion. He also took stock of the customers in the place, cursing the fact there were so few that it would be difficult to do anything without being noticed.

"What they talkin' about?" Ethan asked, as Jimmy returned with the drinks and sat down.

"I didn't catch much" Jimmy replied.

"No matter" Ethan muttered in response.

"So, where we gonna stick the bag?" Jimmy questioned, looking around the room.

Without taking his eyes off the bar staff, Ethan shrugged. "I dunno" he answered. "I hadn't banked on it bein' this dead in here."

"It is ten o'clock on a Monday night" Jimmy unhelpfully pointed out. "And this place 'ain't exactly popular at the best of times."

"But I thought there'd be more people than this. We can't just leave the shit under the table, we need to stash it somewhere it wouldn't be found without looking."

"How about the pisser? I'd bet they 'ain't checked that often."

"Nah" Ethan replied dismissively, continuing to survey the room and watching with interest as the barmaid rushed towards the toilets. "We need to get it somewhere out the back, somewhere the guy might've stashed it himself."

"But how we gonna get it there?"

Before Ethan had the chance to answer, he was distracted by the sound of the door opening and, when he looked over, he suddenly tried to cover his face.

"Fuckin' hide yourself" he hissed, urgently. "Look who's just walked in."

Automatically, Jimmy looked over and quickly followed his Vice President's lead when he saw Rob pass them on his way towards the bar.

Fortunately for them, Rob didn't pay any attention as he walked by, but Ethan made sure to keep them both out of sight as he watched the man speak with the barman. He saw them engage in what seemed to be some kind of low-key argument and, when the barmaid returned, her reaction to Rob spoke volumes.

"What the fuck is all that about?" Jimmy muttered, as the barmaid led Rob to one of the booths on the other side of the room, where Rob sat with his back to them.

Relaxing with the fact that they hadn't been seen, Ethan allowed a wry smile to spread across his lips. "I think that" he stated, "could be our way in."

Jimmy expressed his confusion.

"Did you hear what she said?" Ethan explained. "I think that's the bitch he took our money from."

Slowly, understanding dawned on Jimmy and he joined Ethan in watching the conversation with interest. They saw the barmaid's anger and, whilst they couldn't make out what was being said, it was clear she wasn't happy with the guy.

"What d'you reckon's goin' on?" Jimmy asked, but he was quickly silenced as the barmaid's voice rose and she told Rob exactly what he could do with himself.

"This could be our chance" Ethan quietly pointed out, still maintaining his focus on the developing argument. "She 'ain't gonna want this out in public, so I reckon she'll drag him outside to finish it and then we just need to get rid of that prick from behind the bar for a couple of minutes."

Suddenly, without any real warning, Rob pulled the barmaid across the table, connecting with a head-butt that sent her sprawling to the floor. Instantly, Ethan jumped from his seat and covered the distance between them in a matter of seconds.

The sound of his approach caused Rob to glance over and his expression flicked from fury to fear when he realised who was approaching. He opened his mouth to speak but, before he had the chance to say anything, Ethan slammed his fist firmly into Rob's jaw, sending him staggering backwards.

It took Jimmy a couple of seconds to realise what was happening and, by the time he caught up with Ethan, two more blows had been delivered and Rob collapsed to the floor.

"Get him the fuck out of here!" Ethan ordered.

With a quick nod of agreement, Jimmy passed him and took a firm hold of Rob, clamping his hand over his mouth so he couldn't speak.

As Jimmy dragged Rob to the door, Ethan leaned towards him. "Get rid of him, get Crowther and Wishall here" he whispered, so that no one else could hear, "and get rid of that fuckin' bag."

Again, Jimmy nodded his agreement and, as Rob was removed from the scene, Ethan turned his attention to the barmaid, who was now being helped to her feet by her colleague.

"Shit. Are you ok?" Ethan asked, assisting in getting her back on to the seat from which she'd fallen.

"Thank you" the barman replied, when it became apparent that the woman was still in too much of a state of shock to speak.

"Don't mention it" Ethan smiled, authoritatively checking the bruise that was forming on the barmaid's forehead, as though he knew exactly what he was doing. "We're gonna need some ice for this."

"I'll grab some" the barman readily agreed. "And I'll call the police."

"There's no need" Ethan quickly stated. "My mate's already doin' that. He's gonna call them when he gets that prick outside."

Somewhat dazed by the incident himself, the barman nodded his appreciation and obediently went in search of some ice.

"Are you ok?" Ethan asked the woman again, dropping to his knee in order to be at eye-level for her.

Slowly, her senses began to return and she looked into Ethan's eyes. "I think so" she mumbled.

"Don't worry" Ethan continued, his voice low and soft. "We've got rid of that guy."

The barmaid nodded.

"What's your name?" Ethan asked, gently resting his hand on the woman's arm.

"Steph" she whispered, still struggling a little for words.

"Well, Steph, you're safe now" Ethan smiled, warmly. "My name's Kenny."

"So, what is it we're doing here?" Needle asked, somewhat innocently.

Touchy turned to look at him, the frustration in his expression clearly evident, despite the dark confines of the car. The boy was young, only seventeen years of age, and had been prospecting for less than three months. By choice, he wouldn't have brought the kid along, not for something like this, but Ruckus had been adamant and, frankly, this little shit was the lowest of the low. It'd been less than a week after he'd joined them that he'd earned the nickname, his decision to drunkenly drop his pants and revealing his less than impressive package proving to be a mistake of significantly bigger proportions than the straggler that hung between his legs, and he'd done nothing of any note since then.

"I've fuckin' told you twice" he hissed. "Now shut the fuck up and keep your eyes peeled."

"I just . . ." Needle began, before the anger in Touchy's eyes stopped him short and he quickly looked away.

Silence returned to the car, which they'd parked in a line of vehicles at the side of the road, and Touchy returned to dividing his attention between the street in front and the wing mirror that displayed what was behind.

It was a fuckin' shame, he thought to himself. He'd known the guy since becoming a prospect himself, but the prick was taking from them and he should've known what would happen; he'd been there when the rules were re-written and he hadn't objected to anything that was put in.

Ethan might have been a bit pissed off with the decision, but he knew it was the only thing they could do. Even if he didn't, the little shit needed to start respecting Ruckus' decisions, even if he did think the man was his dad.

"Is this 'im?" Needle asked, breaking Touchy's thoughts as he stared into the wing mirror on his side of the car.

Touchy looked over and then adjusted the rear-view mirror to get a better sight.

"Yeah, this is 'im" he answered, after taking a few moments to study the drunken figure stumbling towards them along the pavement.

Automatically, they both sank down out of view although as the man passed, briefly falling on to the bonnet right in front of their eyes, they realised he was far too wasted to have noticed them, even if they'd have been standing right in front of him. They continued to watch as he crossed the road and then, as he pushed his way into the front door of one of the houses, they quickly stepped out of the car.

Without saying anything, Touchy went to the boot and took out a plastic container and two old rags, tossing them to Needle before reaching back in to remove a couple of lengths of rope.

"Come on and do exactly what I tell you" he whispered, smiling with anticipation as he closed the boot. "Because if you fuck this up, then you'll be the one to tell Ruckus."

Needle hadn't needed the threat to be clarified, but he nodded eagerly and quietly followed Touchy to the house. Reaching for his tools, Touchy gave the door a hopeful push and smiled broadly when he discovered the man had been too drunk to even close the thing properly.

"Fuckin' waster" he muttered to himself, as he cautiously pushed his way in.

Chaos lay behind the door with dusty, mouldy clutter providing a veritable assault on the senses with its pungent, stale smell. Both Touchy and Needle recoiled at the affront and they exchanged repulsed glances as they struggled to find a path through the darkness. Ahead of them, they could see an open doorway, from which emanated the sound of snoring, so they headed towards it, almost dreading what they might find when they got there.

"Jesus fuckin' Christ!" Touchy exclaimed when the room opened up to him, the man's deep sleep enabling him to forget the need for silence.

Behind him, Needle retched as he witnessed the state of the place.

The man had passed out on an old, decrepit chair and, next to it, a single lamp provided just enough light for them to see the mould and filth that saturated everything in the room. Empty bottles and old take-away food containers were scattered across the floor whilst, all around them, there seemed to be a haze of dust and lingering smoke. Kicking debris out of his way, Touchy moved towards the man and slapped him a couple of times in a bid to wake him, but his efforts were to no avail as the man failed to stir.

"Who the hell is this piece of shit?" Needle asked, as Touchy untied the ropes and quickly set to work securing the man to the chair.

Pausing in his task, Touchy turned to look at him. "You need to show some respect" he hissed, much to Needle's surprise. "This man is a founding member of The Sons and, without him, you wouldn't be wearing that Cut."

"That guy is a founding member?" Needle exclaimed, struggling to hide the doubt in his voice.

Touchy merely glared at him.

"I mean" Needle hastily continued, "I just don't understand how he's ended up like this."

"The Club was his life" Touchy pointed out, "and when he left, he was left with fuck all."

"Well, why did he leave?" Needle asked.

"That 'ain't any of your business" Touchy snapped. "Now, soak those rags."

Taking the hint, Needle did what he was told and poured petrol over the rags, whilst Touchy turned his attention back to the man.

"Wake up" he yelled, again slapping the man.

The man let out a groan as he slowly opened his eyes, but it was apparent from his blank stare that his senses were going to take longer to return.

"For fuck's sake" Touchy mumbled, snatching the smaller of the rags from Needle and pulling a silenced pistol from the gun pocket of his Cut.

Unceremoniously, he stuffed the rag into the man's mouth, causing the man to splutter, yet still he wasn't lucid. Aiming the pistol, Touchy sent a bullet into the man's kneecap, filling the room with the man's muffled scream as the pain finally pulled his consciousness into line.

"Welcome back" Touchy smiled, sarcastically.

Whether the man genuinely recognised the face that looked down upon him, or whether he could only register the threat, it wasn't clear. Either way, his eyes widened further as fear found its way through the alcohol to take a firm hold of him.

"Where's the stuff?" Touchy asked, ignoring the continued screams.

The man didn't initially provide any response but, when Touchy sent a bullet through his other kneecap, he quickly gestured towards a set of drawers at the side of the room.

Touchy nodded instruction to Needle, who quickly searched the drawers and pulled out a bag of pills that'd been hidden under an array of filthy and rotten clothes.

"You stupid bastard" Touchy sighed, once more focussing his attention on the man.

Continuing to stare, wide-eyed, the man began to mumble incoherently.

"Shut the fuck up!" Touchy commanded, bringing immediate silence to the room, before he took the larger of the petrol-soaked rags from Needle and firmly tightened it around the man's neck, tying the end of the gag to it, whilst making sure the rest remained jammed in his mouth.

Once he was satisfied that the two pieces of material were secure, he stepped back and handed Needle a lighter.

"Spark it" he ordered.

Needle, who'd turned white as a sheet, only stared at him in disbelief.

"I said, fuckin' spark it!" Touchy hissed.

Now shaking his head in refusal, Needle took a step back. "I can't do this" he pleaded, urging Touchy to take the lighter back.

Aiming the gun directly between the boy's eyes, Touchy remained emotionless as he continued. "Do it or quit the club" he insisted, "but you know the only way out is in a fuckin' box and, believe me, I won't be cryin' myself to sleep if that happens."

Visibly shaking, Needle moved slowly towards the man, fighting to keep his arm steady as he raised the lighter towards him.

"Fuckin' do it!" Touchy spat, growing tired of the delay.

The man's muffled cries again filled the room as Needle looked deeply into his eyes. "I'm so sorry" he whispered, sparking the lighter and jumping backwards as the flames sprang up to engulf Tommo's head.

For some reason, the normality in the appearance of Steph's house took Ben by surprise. He didn't know what he'd expected to find when he got here but, apart from the custom Harley Fat Boy that stood proudly in front of the house, everything seemed normal. For a second, he found himself doubting whether any of it was real, whether the telephone conversation with Sam had actually happened or whether it was merely the imaginings of his over-stretched mind as he'd slept deeply.

Of course it was real, he scolded himself as he cut his engine and stepped off his bike. He'd been fully awake when the phone rang and Sam had even repeated his words when Ben struggled to comprehend the situation. The Fat Boy was evidence enough, matching Sam's description perfectly, right down to the image of the crying skull so delicately painted on the gas tank. The fact was that Steph had been attacked, he confirmed to himself, and he hadn't been there to protect her.

Fighting back the anger that brewed inside him, Ben walked up the path and knocked on the door, taking a deep breath to steady himself as it was slowly opened to him.

"Can I help you?" the man asked bluntly, clearly antagonised by the disturbance.

Ben felt as though he'd been punched in the stomach, as though all the air had been sucked from his lungs. It wasn't that the door had been answered by a man which rocked him, Sam had said the guy who stepped in to save Steph had taken her home, it was the fact he was dressed in nothing but a towel, which had so obviously been wrapped around his waist in a hurry.

"I'm here to see Steph" Ben stammered, hesitantly.

"This late?" the man immediately snapped in reply. "She's asleep and I'm not gonna wake her."

Again, Ben found himself stunned. "But I need to know she's ok" he argued.

The man shook his head. "What?" he asked.

"Sam called me and told me what happened" Ben continued.

Shaking his head, the man stared at him. "Who the hell is Sam and what's any of this got to do with you?"

Struggling for a response, Ben could only stare back at him.

"Look" the man stated. "Steph's had a rough night and I'm not disturbing her, so why don't you fuck off and try calling her tomorrow?"

Torn between the anger that was growing inside and the understanding that Steph would need to sleep, Ben once more struggled to find a reply. "Can you at least tell me if she's ok?" he asked.

"She's fine" the man answered.

"And can you tell her I called round?"

The man shrugged. "And you are?"

"I'm Ben."

"Who?"

Practically feeling his heart break when he realised she hadn't even mentioned him, Ben pathetically repeated his name.

"Fine" the man agreed. "Now, will you please fuck off? I'm going back to bed."

With that, the door was closed and Ben stood alone, dejected and suddenly feeling the chill that carried in the night's breeze.

Chapter 18

The lack of traffic at such an early hour of the morning was making the job of tailing Michael a lot harder than they'd hoped. So far though, through a combination of hanging back as far as he dared and sheer good luck at times, Alex had managed to avoid detection without losing sight of their President.

"Where the hell's he going?" he muttered under his breath, more of a frustrated curse than a genuine question.

"I have no idea" Lee replied, unnecessarily.

They were heading into the centre of the city, where the roads became shorter and the turnings more regular, which caused them both to silently worry that this was where they were going to lose him.

"Did you manage to catch any of his conversation?" Lee asked, without taking his eyes off the motorbike.

Alex, who'd followed the man on his way out of their clubhouse, shook his head. "Yeah" he replied. "But nothing we didn't already know. He checked the meeting was still at half seven, mentioned he wasn't happy about the venue being changed and confirmed he'd be there. Do you seriously think you're right about what's going on?"

"I wouldn't have us doing this if I didn't" Lee pointed out, again, unnecessarily. "But I hope I'm not."

They remained silent for the rest of the journey, neither of them really having anything more to say, as they twisted and turned through the streets. There was a moment of slight panic, when they lost him for a second, but they picked him up again when they caught a glimpse of him on one of the roads that ran parallel to the one they were on.

Eventually, Michael slowed and pulled up at the side of the road.

"He's early" Lee commented, checking his watch as Alex pulled the car to a stop at the kerb, only just close enough to see what was happening.

"So?" Alex questioned.

"So, I'm guessing he's nervous about this."

"Why'd you say that?"

"You said he wasn't happy about the venue being changed, and I don't see why that'd be a problem if the meeting was something straight-forward."

They watched as Michael climbed off his bike, automatically ducking down when he glanced in their direction, and they noticed his seemingly nervous disposition as he looked up and down the street.

"Is that a coffee shop?" Alex asked, when they saw the man tentatively look in through some large, glass windows. "What the hell kind of drug deal happens at a coffee shop? Is the place even open?"

"It doesn't look it" Lee replied, without taking his eyes off their President.

Michael stepped back from the window and looked down at his watch, before reaching into his pocket and pulling out his phone.

Whilst he waited for his call to be answered, Michael cursed under his breath. He knew he was almost half an hour early but, frankly, he wanted to be away from this as soon as possible and he'd hoped Filthy would've been here already.

"Come on" he muttered into the breeze, as he checked the street for a second time.

The road was empty, aside from a few cars parked a long way back, but that didn't do anything to give him peace of mind. Standing out here, at this time of the morning, he felt exposed and the thought kept running through his head that it wouldn't take a genius to figure out something was going on. Not that anyone was likely to pay much attention even if they did see him, not in this day and age, but he was wary nonetheless and the lack of response on the phone only increased that concern.

"Damn it!" he cursed, finally giving up and slipping the phone back into his pocket. "Where the fuck is he?"

Turning round, he looked at his bike and briefly considered giving this one up as a bad job, getting hold of the man later on to re-arrange. After all, he mused, the late change in their plans hadn't exactly filled him with confidence and he couldn't understand why they had to come here to do this when there was nothing wrong with the original plan. Then again, he figured, where would that get them?

Of course he knew none of this would be easy and he was always going to be forced to bend in the wind during these early stages in the negotiations, but when they were established, when they were up and running, it wouldn't take long before they were calling the shots and the money would only increase their standing in this godforsaken shithole of a city.

The click of a latch sounded behind him and he spun round, in time to see the door being opened by a tired-looking, elderly man.

"Take your bike into the alley," the man muttered, "and come in through the back door."

Before Michael had time to respond, the door was closed and the latch clicked back into place. He stood and stared at the glass for a few moments, watching as the man hurried away, and his feeling of unease grew.

Again, the thought of leaving crossed his mind, driven by the way control seemed to have slipped so quickly away from him. Before this, their meetings had been his decision, his choice of location and time, but this sudden shift in power had seemingly come from nowhere and, from what he'd gathered in talking to Filthy up to this point, the change was somewhat out of character for the guy.

Reluctantly, he returned to his bike and free-wheeled it round to the side of the building, into the alley. He positioned the bike, ready for a quick getaway should it be needed, and approached the back door, which was already open.

The room into which he walked seemed to be the kitchen area of the shop and Filthy was sitting at a table in the centre. Immediately, Michael noticed the man was sporting a black eye and it was apparent he'd come out second best in some sort of physical encounter.

"What's going on?" he asked, trying to sound authoritative, despite his feeling of trepidation.

Filthy merely sat still, staring at him as he sat down opposite.

"What's happened to you?" Michael tried, gesturing towards the bruising.

"Just a small disagreement" Filthy finally answered. "It's business."

Michael continued to look at him. "Is that why you changed the plans?" he asked. "Should I be concerned?"

"No" Filthy answered, without emotion. "Everything's fine."

"Then why are we here and who's the guy who told me to come round the back?"

"He's just the owner of this place, it's better that people don't see us together."

"You've never worried about that before."

"Things change" Filthy replied, bluntly.

An awkward silence fell between them, until Filthy eventually broke it. "Shall we have a coffee?" he asked.

Given they were sat in the back of a coffee shop, the question shouldn't have felt as though it was strange, but there was no doubting it increased Michael's sense of foreboding.

"Shall we just get this over with?" he suggested.

"Relax" came the response, in a tone that did nothing to assist the command. "We should have a drink."

Ignoring the look on Michael's face, Filthy called out and the man who opened the door appeared obediently.

"Have you started the water boiling?" Filthy asked him.

"I've just done it" the man answered. "It'll be ready in about five minutes."

Filthy nodded and returned his attention to Michael as the man left them alone once more.

"Are we gonna do this or not?" Michael snapped, becoming increasingly frustrated with how things were going.

"I said relax" Filthy replied. "What's the rush?"

"No" Michael stated, shaking his head as he rose from his seat. "This is bullshit."

A flicker of panic found its way to Filthy's expression. "Ok" he said, forcing a smile on to his lips. "I just thought we could take it easy, that's all. Sit down again and we'll get to it."

Michael remained standing.

"Look" he smiled. "I've checked all I need to check and I know you're not a cop. I wanna do business."

Still Michael hesitated, torn between the desire to leave and the news that they were on for a deal.

"Sit down and we'll talk" Filthy continued.

Slowly, Michael re-took his seat. "Then why all this shit?" he asked. "Why all this cloak and dagger crap?"

"Because this is where it gets serious" Filthy answered. "This is the point at which things need to be done more carefully, or the two of us could end up in the deep end of the shit-pool."

Understanding slowly filtered into Michael's mind. "You mean with the cops?" he checked.

"I mean with a lot of people" Filthy replied. "You think it's just you who wants a piece of this? I've already told you, this is a dangerous business and there'll be some nasty fuckers out to bring you down."

"Like who?"

"Don't be naïve."

"I'm not being naïve. Like I've already told you, if we're gonna do this, then I wanna know who you've been dealing with and who we need to watch for."

Filthy shook his head. "I'm not tellin' you anything about that" he said. "That's not for you to know."

"It is if we're gonna be partners."

"There's no partnership here. All I do is give you the stuff. It's up to you what you do with it."

Michael looked at him for a few moments, trying to gauge whether the subject should be pushed any further. He considered the lack of information and decided, for the time being, it wasn't important enough to hold things up.

"So how does this work?" he asked.

"It works by you telling us why the fuck you think you can push in on our business" came a voice from the back door.

Spinning in his seat, Michael saw three men walking in, all wearing Cuts. His eyes flicked to the patches, to the words sewn into the material, and he froze when he realised who they were.

"I'm sorry" Filthy muttered, rising from his chair to make way for Ruckus.

Too scared to speak, Michael merely looked at him.

"It's such a fuckin' shame" Ruckus smiled, as he sat down. "A promising, up and coming club, ripped apart by their president's mistake. Tell me, what the fuck does Abyssus Tutela mean, anyway?"

"It's Latin for Hell's Guardians" Michael barely managed to stammer.

Shaking his head, Ruckus looked around at his own club's members. "Fancy" he chuckled, leading the mirth. "But why not just call yourselves Hell's Guardians? Why the bullshit?"

Fighting to control himself, Michael took a deep breath. "We thought it was too basic" he replied.

"I'll tell you what's fuckin' basic" Ruckus snapped immediately, all traces of humour how gone from his tone. "Not stepping on our fuckin' toes is basic, my friend."

With that, two of the men took a firm grip under Michael's shoulders and wrenched him up from his chair.

"You know what else isn't basic?" Ruckus continued. "The fuckin' regret you and your boys are about to feel."

"Who the hell is that?" Alex asked out loud, as they watched a black, unmarked van pull up and reverse into the alley next to the Coffee Shop.

"I have no idea" Lee replied, without taking his eyes off the van. "But I've got a bad feeling about this.

"You think it could be the drugs?"

"I doubt it. What's Michael gonna do with them if they are? He can't carry a load that size on his bike and I can't see him leaving it here. Besides, there's no point in picking the stuff up until he's got the boys on board with his plan."

Alex shook his head. "Then who the hell is that?" he asked again.

They watched on in silence for a couple of minutes, each of them keeping a keen lookout for anything that might tell them what was happening but, when nothing materialised, it was Alex who broke the quiet with a thought.

"That van would be big enough to fit the bike in the back, wouldn't it?" he suggested. "Maybe Michael's loading his bike and then taking the stuff somewhere to stash it?"

"But how's he gonna pay for it?" Lee questioned. "He'll need the money from the club and he hasn't mentioned it officially yet."

"Or he could just take it from the safe without telling anyone? That'd help to force the vote through and he did disappear for a bit last night, didn't he?"

The theory took time to resonate in each of their minds and, as it took full form, they exchanged worried glances.

"Shit" they both exclaimed, jumping out of the car.

Cautiously, they edged their way towards the coffee shop, all the time keeping their eyes on the front of the van. They reached the point at which they were about half way between the car and the building when, suddenly, the air was filled with the sound of the van's engine roaring to life and it shot forward, it's wheels screeching on the dry tarmac as it turned away from them and sped along the road.

Immediately, the two of them ran back to the car and Alex gunned the motor but, by the time he'd got the thing started and pulled out from the kerb, the van was long gone.

The thick, black smoke could be seen from a fair distance away, billowing up into the air from somewhere behind the buildings they were passing, bringing with it an ominous feeling in the pit of Lee's stomach.

"Where's that coming from?" he asked, somewhat hesitantly.

Distracted by the question, Alex stopped his search for the van in the alleys and side roads and turned to look where Lee was staring. "I can't tell" he said, further slowing the car and craning his neck to see. "But it looks as though . . ."

His words drifted off as realisation slowly dawned on them.

"Shit!" he cursed, pressing hard on the accelerator to speed up.

With only the slightest of pressure on the brake, he flung the car around the first corner and practically skidded around the next, before pulling to an immediate halt in the middle of the road. Automatically, they both leapt out and sprinted towards the building, although the flames were already dancing through what remained of the front door and all of the windows, the heat preventing them from even getting close to their clubhouse.

Looking at the rows of bikes that remained parked along the front, it took a few moments for Lee to understand what was missing from the picture.

"How many were in there?" Lee mumbled, having realised that no members of the club were stood outside with them.

Alex shook his head and kept his eyes firmly focussed on the building as he replied. "Apart from the few at the strip club last night, everyone was in there" he answered before adding, hopefully "Unless anyone went out early."

As he continued to watch the flames, Lee looked up towards the top of the building and he felt his legs weaken when he saw what was up there, hanging by its neck from one of the front windows.

"What's that, up there?" he asked, needing to pose the question but not wanting to hear the confirmation.

Following his gaze, Alex also looked up and then took a couple of steps forward to try and get a clearer sight of the charred and blackened figure.

"I can't tell from here" he said. "But it looks a lot like . . ."

For a second time in only a few minutes, his sentence ended abruptly but, this time, that was due to the vomit which expelled itself forcibly from his stomach.

The sound of distant sirens began filtering in on the breeze as Lee dropped to his knees. "Michael, you stupid bastard" he muttered.

Chapter 19

"What the fuck was all that about?" Crowther demanded, as he and Wishall burst in through the door of the meeting room with Eddie, one of the new Probationary Members, following quickly behind.

"I'm sorry" Eddie stammered. "I tried to stop 'em but this prick pulled a gun on me."

Crowther spun round, once again drawing his gun and pushing the barrel into the kid's temple. "And I'll fucking pull the trigger next time, you little pissant!" he hissed. "Don't you fucking forget who you're talking to."

Instantly, the room was filled with the sound of multiple guns being cocked as the club members around the table responded in unison, training their own weapons on the Detective.

"And who is he talking to?" Ruckus asked, calmly. "Because, from where I'm sitting, it strikes me that he's addressing two dead men."

"You've got that right!" Crowther replied immediately, without taking his eyes off Eddie. "Thanks to your fucking, know-it-all, cocky-as-shit, Vice President over there."

Standing just inside the doorway, realisation of the danger they were in had painted a mask of terror on Wishall's face. "Let's just calm down, shall we?" he implored, weakly.

As he spoke, half the club shifted their aim to him and he took an involuntary step backwards. Noticing the movement, Crowther finally seemed to realise the same fact as his partner and he slowly re-holstered his gun before turning to look at Ruckus.

"It was simple" he stated, his anger finally falling under some element of control as the members of the club lowered their weapons. "We were supposed to turn up at the bar on an anonymous tip, find the girl's clothes and go pick the guy up. Instead, we get a phone call to tell us where we need to pick up a corpse and, when we get to the bar, we find your Vice President getting nice and cosy with some bitch of a barmaid."

"And the problem is?" Ruckus asked, as though genuinely shocked there was an issue.

"The problem is that we can't keep cleaning up your shit like this, not when you keep changing plans on us." Crowther replied, angrily. "We're already getting enough crap for this investigation, without the need to cover up additional dead bodies."

"While you mention that" Touchy chuckled, "you might wanna get yourselves over to see Tommo. I heard he's not well."

"What?" Crowther asked.

"And it might be worth you looking in to a big fire this morning" Ethan suggested, also chuckling as he spoke. "I hear it was a big one, with almost an entire Motorcycle Club wiped out."

"Yeah" Touchy added. "Apparently, all the bodies were found tied up in one of the rooms and some of them had even been shot. My guess would be it's some sort of ritual suicide pact, especially with one of the cunts decidin' to tie 'imself up and hang 'imself from one of the windows."

The blood drained from Crowther's face and he stood, motionless, as everyone in the room joined in with the laughing.

"It looks as though you might need to get back to work" Ruckus suggested, once the mirth had died down. "I'd hate to think what'd happen to you two if any of this shit found its way back to us."

"You're serious?" Crowther questioned. "All this at once? This is too much."

"Are you sayin' you can't handle it?" Ruckus asked. "Because, if you can't, then you can always back out of the arrangement, but you know how that works."

Unfeasibly, Crowther's face whitened further still. "No" he mumbled. "We can handle it."

"Then why don't the two of you fuck off and do it?" Ruckus replied.

As the detectives sheepishly left the room, Ruckus turned his attention to Ethan.

"You didn't plant the clothes?" he asked.

Casually, Ethan shook his head. "No" he answered. "Somethin' better came up."

"You wanna enlighten me?"

Ethan stared at him for a few seconds, before waving it off. "It's just somethin' that came up, somethin' that gives us a better chance of nailin' it all on the guy."

Returning the hesitation in response, Ruckus shook his head. "I 'ain't happy with this" he snapped. "I told you this shit needed to be deal with."

"It is bein' dealt with" Ethan snapped in reply. "I told you I'm sortin' it, so just fuckin' trust me."

Flashing Touchy a momentary glance, Ruckus let out a sigh. "And what about the body?" he asked.

"Just some left-over business from the casino, don't worry about it."

Ruckus stared at him, as though expecting to hear clarification, but Ethan merely glanced at his watch and rose from his chair.

"I've gotta go" he said, nonchalantly. "Jimmy'll fill you in with the details."

"Sit the fuck down, this meetin' 'ain't finished" Ruckus commanded, as Ethan walked to the door.

Stopping in his tracks, Ethan turned to face his President. He took a breath, as though he was about to reply in kind, but checked himself at the last minute. "I've gotta go" was all he said, before stepping through the door.

As Steph awoke, the first thing she noticed was the numbness. When she'd gone to sleep she'd expected to feel something, be it anger, sadness or even just pain, but there was nothing. It was as though her body had slipped into some kind of autopilot, functioning on only the barest of levels, and it scared her more than anything that had happened in the last couple of weeks.

Maybe that was something, she thought to herself, as she stared up at the ceiling. Maybe the trace of fear was a sign that at least her mind was still working on some level? Maybe it meant that she hadn't completely lost it and there was some way back from this?

Getting herself out of bed, she went to the mirror and stared at her reflection, taking in the bruising that'd begun to show around her eyes. It looked ugly, like a mark of shame that she'd be forced to wear for a few days at least, yet still she felt no emotion. She knew that, if she went out, people would stare at her, passing judgements on their own presumptions of her situation, yet she just didn't care.

Was she in shock, she wondered; was this a normal reaction to being beaten up? She'd always thought shock would come in the form of dizziness and a general feeling of being unwell, but maybe she'd merely put that idea together from films and TV? Maybe this was actually what it felt like and her body needed to calm down before the true effects of the attack began to filter through?

Putting on her dressing gown, Steph moved towards the bedroom door. That was another thing, she realised, as she pulled on the handle and stepped into the hallway. She'd allowed a stranger to stay the night, albeit someone who'd looked after her, but a stranger nonetheless. He could've been anything, especially in this day and age, and the fact he'd saved her from a beating didn't mean he was a decent guy. Yet she'd had no qualms about letting him into her house and then going to bed with him downstairs. He could have done anything to her and, normally, she wouldn't have put herself in that situation but, last night, it seemed the most natural thing to do. Even now, with the cold light of day shining brightly through the windows, she still didn't feel any concern over it.

When she got downstairs, the sheet and pillow she'd willingly handed over were neatly folded on the arm of the settee and the man had gone. On the mantelpiece there was a scrap of paper, on which had been scrawled some sort of a message, so she picked it up and read:

Good morning Steph (or afternoon, depending on what time you've woken up!)

I've had to go out and didn't want to wake you—you needed to sleep. I hope your head's not hurting too much but, just in case, I've left some painkillers next to a glass in the kitchen for you, so wash them down with plenty of water.

I'll be back around lunchtime to check that you're ok and then I'm free all afternoon, if you want me to stick around.

Kenny.
x

Placing the note back on the mantelpiece, Steph glanced at the clock on the wall and saw it was just after half twelve. Had she really slept for that long? Or, then again, was it more a case of passing out than actually sleeping? Either way, she didn't feel particularly refreshed for having such a long rest.

She walked through to the kitchen and picked up the glass, ignoring the painkillers, and filled it with cold water. She drank quickly, swigging back the liquid, before refilling the glass and returning to the living room, where she sat down on the settee and stared blankly at the fireplace in front of her.

For how long she stayed that way, she didn't know, and neither did she really know what thoughts, if anything, were going through her mind. She was empty, well and truly empty, and even the roar of a motorcycle pulling up outside failed to spark any sort of response from her.

A minute or so later, the sound of knocking on the door lead to her automatically standing and going to answer it. She opened it without first checking who was there and went back through to her seat in the living room.

"How you feeling?" Ethan asked, as he closed the door behind him and followed her into the house.

Steph merely shrugged her shoulders in response.

"Well" Ethan continued chirpily, unperturbed by the display of ambivalence, "I figured you probably wouldn't have eaten, so I grabbed something on the way here."

"I'm not hungry" Steph muttered.

Ethan shook his head. "I didn't ask whether you were hungry" he stated, with a smile. "You need to eat, so I'm not taking no for an answer."

Once again, there was a lack of response from Steph.

"Come on" Ethan insisted, playfully reaching for Steph's hand to pull her up.

"Look" Steph snapped, pushing him away and jumping to her feet. "Thank you for what you did last night, but I don't need looking after."

Taking a step back, Ethan raised his hands in a placatory gesture. "I'm sorry" he said, quickly.

After looking at him silently for a few moments, Steph shook her head and walked over to the mantelpiece, from which she picked up her phone. She checked the screen for sign of any missed calls or messages and, when she saw there were none, her heart sank without warning, sending a wave of unexpected emotion that finally brought the tears she needed to cry.

Rushing forwards, Ethan wrapped his arms around her and held her tightly to his chest. "Let it out" he urged, as her body jerked with the outpouring of anguish. "Let it all out."

They remained locked in the embrace for several minutes until, eventually, her sobs began to subside and she gently pulled away from him.

"I'm sorry" she mumbled, wiping the moisture from her cheeks.

"There's no apology needed" Ethan replied, warmly.

Despite the reassurance, Steph still felt a little foolish. "I just hoped Ben might've called" she explained. "But he hasn't."

"Ben?" Ethan asked, as though unsure of the name.

"My friend" Steph continued. "The one I was telling you about last night."

"Maybe he doesn't know what happened?" Ethan suggested.

Steph shook her head. "No" she whispered. "Sam was calling him when we left."

"Well, maybe he hasn't had the chance? Or maybe he's giving you time to sleep and he'll call you later?"

"You don't understand" Steph replied, as fresh tears began to fall. "He would've come straight to me if he knew I was in trouble, at least, he always used to. The problem is that I've fucked it all up and, honestly, I wouldn't be surprised if he hates me."

"What?" Ethan asked. "Why?"

Again, Steph shook her head. "It doesn't matter" she said. "It's my problem."

"No" Ethan smiled. "You've got enough to deal with at the moment. I'm not saying I can help, but at least you can get it off your chest. Come on, let's eat and you can tell me about it."

Somewhat reluctantly, Steph allowed herself to be lead through to the kitchen. They sat at the table and, after a fair amount of cajoling from Ethan, she finally started to talk. She told him about what had happened the night Rob turned up, about what happened between them, which lead to her telling him about the girl Ben rescued from the alley and his subsequent arrest.

Through it all, Ethan listened intently, trying to supress the smile that constantly threatened to spread across his lips. He couldn't believe how convenient this all was and, when she'd finished opening up to him, he tried not to think too much about how perfectly this was all falling into place.

"So, how long have you known him?" he asked.

"A few years" Steph replied.

Ethan sat back in his chair to consider that fact for a few moments. "And, in all that time, nothing's ever happened between you?"

"No."

"I take it he's had other women on the go?"

Steph was a little taken aback by the question. "What do you mean?" she asked.

"I just don't understand why he hasn't tried anything with you" Ethan replied. "It's clear you were close."

"We've always just been friends" Steph stated, still a little confused by where he was headed with this. "But no, he hasn't been with anyone, as far as I know."

"As far as you know?" Ethan asked, further surprising her.

"Yeah" she answered. "What are you getting at?"

Pausing for a moment, as though trying to find the right words, Ethan looked at her. "I'm sorry" he eventually said. "I'm just a bit worried, that's all."

"Worried about what?"

"I'm worried about the fact a guy like that, who's so obviously a catch for the ladies, has been single for so long. It isn't natural."

"But why would that worry you?"

Again, Ethan paused. "It's just that" he began, a little hesitantly, "with the police arresting the guy, I wonder how well you really know him."

Now Steph sat back in her chair, shocked by the statement.

"Don't get me wrong" Ethan hastily continued. "I hope I'm way off the mark here but, from my own experiences, you can't always know what's going on with people."

"What are you saying?" Steph exclaimed. "That Ben might have actually attacked those girls?"

"No" Ethan answered, before hesitating for a few seconds. "I'm just saying you can't always be sure" he concluded.

Steph looked at him for a few seconds, as his words found their way into her mind. "No" she finally replied, "he wouldn't do something like that."

"Just like he wouldn't tell everyone about what happened between you?"

"That's different" Steph argued, unconvincingly.

Chapter 20

Billy stared at the bag, whilst the sounds of the children's cries seemed to echo throughout the whole of the clubhouse. His gaze slowly shifted to Ruckus, who stood proudly over his spoils, and then to Tommo, who shared the same expression of concern.

"D'you wanna tell me that again?" Billy asked, his words pronounced slowly and with deliberation. "I don't think I quite understood what you said."

The cries from the other room seemed to amplify in response.

"The prick was takin' the piss out of us, so I've put an end to him" Ruckus repeated, almost puffing his chest out with pride as he spoke. "And that bitch of a wife too."

Rubbing his eyes, Billy again glanced at Tommo, before returning his attention to Ruckus. "I've known Malcolm for years" he stated, fighting to keep his temper under control. "Why the fuck did you feel you had the right to kill him? Why the fuck did you even feel the need to go there? I didn't authorise that."

"The guy owed us money" Ruckus argued.

"And he would've paid up" Tommo interjected, making no attempt to disguise his own fury.

"When?" Ruckus exclaimed. "Next week? Next Month? Next fuckin' year?"

"When we asked him to" Billy replied, before Tommo had the chance to voice his thoughts. "We've never had a problem before."

Ruckus let out a frustrated sigh. "And that's why they're all takin' the piss out of us" he pointed out. "Malcolm was just one of the fuckers, and you can bet the rest will be thinking twice about holding back their payments, once they hear about what's happened."

"Once they hear about what?" Billy shouted, finally allowing his temper to show. "Once they hear about us voting in a fuckin' psycho?"

"No" Ruckus shouted back. "Once they hear that The Sons of Sorrow aren't to be fucked with!"

"What're you talking about? We don't work like this."

"And that's why we're getting nowhere."

"For the last fuckin' time" Billy hissed. "We're not fuckin' tryin' to get anywhere."

Having reached the crescendo of the argument, silence quickly fell between them, allowing the children's cries to once again filter into the room.

"And what about them?" Billy asked, his voice returning to as calm a level as he could manage. "Is that where you drew the line? You'll happily murder an innocent man and his wife, but you won't hurt the kids?"

"I'm not an animal" Ruckus replied, much to the increased frustration of both Billy and Tommo.

"Oh, I get it" Tommo piped up. "Killing them is a step too far, but making them orphans is an act of kindness?"

"They're not orphans" Ruckus stated, as though it was the two men in front of him who'd lost the plot. "I'm takin' 'em."

"You're takin' 'em where?"

"I'm gonna look after 'em" Ruckus confirmed.

Tommo shook his head. "What?" he asked, astounded by the response. "You're just gonna pretend they're your kids?"

"Why not?" Ruckus stated, defensively. "It's about time that prick, Crowther, started earnin' the money you pay him. He can sort out the investigation and I've got a guy who's gonna sort the paperwork for me."

"Oh, really?" Billy chided. "It's that simple, is it? D'you know how old they are, or d'you even know their names?"

Now it was Ruckus' turn to shake his head in disbelief, genuinely struggling to understand why there was such a problem with the plan. "That don't matter" he sighed. "Their ages will be on the birth certificates I'm havin' made. The boy's name's gonna be Ethan and the girl I'm calling . . ."

As it jettisoned from his stomach, the force of the vomit woke Billy in the midst of the dream and he rolled over quickly as his insides emptied. When the sickness had passed, he lay back on the wetness of the mattress and closed his eyes once again, hoping the returning darkness would bring with it an altogether more pleasant of memories.

Chapter 21

Ben could feel his heart racing in his chest as he repeatedly glanced towards the coffee shop's door. With each beat, his apprehension raised several notches and, the longer it went on, the more he could feel panic's icy grip taking a firmer hold on him.

"Relax" Karen smiled, from across the table.

"Huh?" Ben replied, his attention having been too focussed on the door for him to hear what she'd said.

Chuckling, Karen shook her head. "I said relax" she repeated. "It's Steph we're waiting on, not some sort of psychopath."

With only a nod of his head, Ben confirmed both his understanding and cynicism of that fact.

"Jesus, Dude" Sam chirped up. "What the hell's wrong with you?"

"I just don't think this is such a good idea" Ben stated. "I haven't heard from her in a week, not since she kicked me out of her house."

"Have you tried to call her?" Karen asked.

Ben looked at her for a moment. "No" he confirmed. "When I went round and that Kenny guy answered the door, I asked him to tell her I'd been there. She hasn't called or sent me a text, so I guess she's not interested in hearing from me."

"After all these years, do you honestly think that's true?" Karen replied, again shaking her head. "Do you seriously think she doesn't want to hear from her best friend?"

"I fucked that up, good and proper" Ben argued.

"If that's the case, then why's she agreed to meet up today?"

"Probably for the same reason as me; you didn't give her a choice."

Knowing Steph had also been reluctant for this to happen, Karen didn't reply straight away and that was all Ben needed to push his panic over the edge.

"Fuck it" he exclaimed, rising quickly from his chair. "I can't do this."

The crash of a cup hitting the floor behind the counter rang out and they turned to see Albert standing, staring at the door. All three of them followed his gaze, and saw Steph walking in with Ethan behind her.

"Clumsy bastard" Sam joked automatically, all three of them too caught up in her arrival to note that the colour had drained from the old man's cheeks.

Ben sat down heavily as the two of them approached, deflated by both the missed chance to get out of this and the way in which Steph seemed to have done all she could to avoid any eye contact with him.

"Sorry we're a bit late" she muttered, clearly addressing only Sam and Karen, "but Kenny needed to find somewhere to park his bike."

"Yeah, it's my fault" Ethan smiled, flashing a conspiratorial glance in Steph's direction. "It had nothing to do with Her Highness here, deciding to have a nap in the bath before we left."

"You bastard" Steph giggled, playfully punching him in the arm as they sat at the table.

Ben noticed that she'd chosen the seat farthest away from him and that she made sure her date sat firmly in between them. He also noted the remnants of bruising around her eyes which, despite all that had happened, caused his heart to ache terribly.

"So, you ride a bike?" Sam asked, turning to Ethan.

"Yeah" Ethan shrugged, nonchalantly.

"Don't be like that" Steph exclaimed, briefly glancing at Ben. "It's more than just a bike. Tell them."

Seemingly begrudgingly Ethan continued. "It's a Harley Fat Boy" he admitted.

"A custom Harley Fat Boy" Steph giggled, again glancing briefly at Ben. "And you should see the paint job. It's breath-taking."

Both Sam and Karen nodded their acknowledgement of the revelation, whilst Ben merely sat emotionlessly.

Before anyone had the chance to say anything else, Albert arrived at the table with drinks for Steph and Ethan.

"Thank you very much" Ethan smiled. "How much do I owe you?"

"Don't worry about it, these are on me" Albert smiled awkwardly, before hurrying back to the counter.

All of them looked at each other, bemused for a moment.

"What's wrong with him?" Sam asked, generally. "You reckon Mary's had one of her wobbles?"

"I'll go and sort this out" Ethan stated, rising from his chair and heading after the man.

They watched as he went, all of them a little glad of the distraction, and saw him talking to Albert for a few seconds before handing over the money. When he returned to the table, the awkward silence resumed.

"How are you?" Karen finally asked Steph, through somewhat of a forced smile. "I can see the bruising's gone down a lot. It's barely noticeable now."

"I'm doing ok, now I can leave the house" Steph replied, glancing at Ben for a third time as she patted her hand on Ethan's thigh, "but if it wasn't for Kenny, then I don't know what I'd have done. He really has been a godsend."

"That's good" Karen continued, nodding towards Ben. "He's been worried about you."

"Has he really?" Steph asked, her cynicism made obvious to all.

"I'm going to the toilet" Ben stated, as he jumped up from the chair and rushed towards the sanctity of the rest-room.

Even before the door had closed fully behind him, Ben was at the sink and splashing cold water on his face. He looked at his reflection in the mirror, at the moisture dripping off his skin, and let out a long, frustrated sigh. He'd known that things had gone wrong, that he'd done nothing but damage the relationship with the way in which he'd acted, but he had no idea that it would be this bad.

Reaching for a paper towel, he held it to his face and breathed another sigh as it soaked up the water. The sound of the door opening caused him to look round, just in time to see Ethan walking towards him.

"You alright?" Ethan asked, smiling broadly.

Ben merely looked at him.

"Look" Ethan continued. "Steph's told me what a prick you were to her and, believe me, she doesn't want to be here any more than you."

"What?" Ben exclaimed, stunned by the aggressiveness of the man's comment.

"Yeah" Ethan stated. "She told me how you treated her like a cunt when she needed comfort and I don't blame her for not wanting anythin' to do with you. When I told her you'd come round, she was so angry, she nearly lost it."

Floundering for a response, all Ben could manage was a feeble "She did?"

Ethan's smile turned into a snigger. "I gotta thank you though. From what she told me, if you'd have actually acted like a man, then I'd have missed out on a real trick there. I tell you, after I dealt with that Rob guy, that girl was gaggin' for it. The things she did to me would make a whore blush!"

The statement stung its way into Ben's mind, each word fuelling the rage that was growing inside him.

Shaking his head in wonderment, Ethan quickly maintained the mental onslaught. "I might even keep her around for a couple of weeks" he sighed. "If she carries on the way she has been these last couple of days, I reckon she'll be beggin' me to stick it in every . . ."

The sentence went unfinished as Ben snapped and launched himself forward. Driven only by anger, all control left him as he grabbed Ethan by the throat and slammed him against the wall, immediately forcing the air from his lungs.

Possessed, Ben swung his fist, planting it directly into the side of Ethan's jaw and, when it seemed he would drop from the impact, Ben easily held him in place to deliver two more blows in quick succession before, finally, allowing the man to hit the ground.

Reaching down, Ben pulled Ethan back to his feet, just as the door swung open and Sam rushed in.

"Ben!" Sam exclaimed, grabbing his arm and pulling him back.

Initially, Ben remained unmoved, like a pillar of concrete, but slowly, Sam's voice filtered its way through the anger and he let himself be dragged away.

"Fuck off, Sam!" Ben exclaimed, fighting off the grip.

"What the fuck are you doing?" Sam yelled back.

"I'm fucking going" Ben replied angrily, before pushing his way through the door.

Without having to look, Ben knew all eyes in the room would be on him as he strode across the floor. He glanced briefly towards Steph, shaking his head when he saw the shock in her expression, but then he was out in the sunshine and back on his bike. He gunned the engine and sped away, quickly putting as much distance between him and the coffee shop as he could.

"I just don't understand how he could've done this" Steph sighed, as she handed Ethan a bag of frozen peas from her freezer.

"He's a big guy and he sucker-punched me" Ethan smiled, before wincing as he applied the peas to the bruising on the side of his face. "Otherwise I'd have taken him."

"Don't joke about this" Steph exclaimed, taking a seat opposite him at her kitchen table. "It doesn't make any sense that he'd attack you like that, especially when you didn't say anything to him."

Ethan remained quiet.

"What is it?" Steph asked tentatively, uncertainty suddenly obvious in her voice.

Still, Ethan didn't reply.

"Kenny, what is it?" Steph asked again.

After taking a moment longer to consider his response, Ethan let out a long sigh before he spoke. "I didn't want to say anything, especially in front of your friends" he began, reluctantly, "but I went in there after him because I didn't want him to feel awkward about me being there. I told him there was nothing going on between us."

"And he attacked you for that?" Steph questioned angrily, unable to contain herself.

"No" Ethan replied, shaking his head emphatically. "I also wanted him to know that I was aware of what's happening with the police and that I wasn't going to judge him for anything. That's when he launched at me."

Now it was Steph's turn to fall silent.

"I shouldn't have said anything" Ethan continued, dismissively. "It was my fault."

"How's it your fault?" Steph demanded to know, the anger in her voice still very evident.

"He's under pressure" Ethan replied, calmly. "The last thing he needs is for some stranger to be sticking his nose into it."

"That doesn't excuse him punching you in the head."

Ethan considered the statement for a moment. "But it is a possible explanation" he said. "Otherwise, it could've been . . ."

His words drifted away as he seemed to decide against voicing his opinion.

"It could've been what?" Steph asked, urging him to continue.

"Nothing" Ethan replied. "Forget I said anything."

"No" Steph insisted. "It could've been what?"

"It's just that" Ethan began, before hesitating for a moment. "The reaction was a bit over the top if he's actually innocent in all this. I'm struggling to believe he's not worried about something."

"So, you're saying you think he was involved with those girls?"

With a shrug, Ethan tried to play down his accusation. "Look" he said. "You know him far better than I do. You know what he's capable of and what he isn't."

"I didn't think he was capable of doing this to someone" Steph stated, gesturing to the bruising on Ethan's face. "So, maybe I really don't know him as well as I thought I did?"

Remaining silent, Ethan allowed the thought to linger in her mind.

"I've got something that might make you happy" he eventually stated, standing up and walking towards the door.

Intrigued, Steph tried to follow him, but he gently guided her back to the table and told her to close her eyes before handing her the bag of peas and going outside to his bike. When he returned, he placed a black holdall on the table in front of her.

"What's that?" she asked, as she opened her eyes.

"It's something I was going to give you later" he replied, "but I figured you could do with some cheering up."

Tentatively, she pulled at the zip and opened the bag, recoiling in surprise when she saw the bundles of cash that lay within.

"What's this?" she exclaimed.

"It's yours" Ethan answered.

Steph looked at him. "What d'you mean, it's mine?" she asked, standing and backing away from the money.

Ethan let out a sigh. "Maybe I should explain?" he suggested.

"Maybe you should" came the quick and slightly aggressive response.

"Look, you told me Rob had got into trouble with an illegal casino" he began. "Well, I know a couple of guys who're involved with running a place like that, so I did a bit of asking around and it turns out it was their place he was in trouble with. They told me that they'd charged him double what he owed, as interest because of the way he acted with them. I explained where he'd got the cash from and they agreed to give you back the interest, so it's not all the money you lost, but at least it's something."

Looking at him, it was apparent Steph didn't quite know what to make of the revelation.

"I've also been in touch with Rob," he continued, "and I'll make sure you get the rest."

Slowly, acceptance began to find its way into her mind. "You're serious?" she asked.

"Absolutely" he replied.

"Thank you" she exclaimed, throwing her arms around him and pulling him into a tight hug.

"It's my pleasure" Ethan whispered, returning the embrace. "And I've also made sure that you won't have to deal with Rob, ever again."

Momentarily, Steph's arms tightened around him, before she pulled back slightly and gazed deeply into his eyes.

"You're such a wonderful man" she whispered, as her gaze flicked down to his lips and she pulled his head closer, until their lips connected.

The kiss was gentle, tender and slow and, as they pulled away from each other, Ethan looked deeply into her eyes.

"Can I take you out somewhere tomorrow night?" he asked.

"Where are we going?" Steph replied, eagerly.

"It's a surprise" he smiled.

Chapter 22

Having received no response to his knock on Ben's door, Sam took a step backwards in the hallway, pulled out his phone and tried ringing the man again. He knew it would be pointless, none of his calls had been answered either yesterday or this morning, but he wasn't going to give up easily.

Unsurprisingly, the line went straight to voicemail yet again.

"Ben!" he yelled, stepping forward and hammering on the door. "Your bike's in the parking area, so I know you're there. Open this fucking door!"

Eventually, he heard the lock click and the door swung open. Sam pushed his way inside and noticed, immediately, that there were two bags on the floor, packed and ready to go.

"Taking a trip?" he asked, as Ben walked back towards the bedroom.

Ben didn't reply, so Sam followed him through the flat.

"I take it the police know all about you disappearing?" he questioned, growing tired of the cold shoulder. "And they're happy with that, are they?"

"It's got nothing to do with them!" Ben replied angrily, stopping in his tracks and spinning around to face his friend. "I've done nothing wrong and I've got nothing to feel guilty for."

Expecting the reaction, Sam had kept a good distance between the two of them, yet he still backed away slightly when he saw the expression on Ben's face.

"So why are you running away?" he asked.

"I'm not running away" Ben answered. "There's nothing here for me now. I've got no job, no money and I've lost Steph."

"So, me and Karen don't count for anything then?" Sam replied, with a trace of anger in his own voice. "All the years we've known you mean shit, do they?"

Looking at him, Ben hesitated in his response.

"Well, now I know that" Sam continued, "I guess I'll just fuck off and leave you to it."

He turned towards the front door, expecting Ben to stop him, but nothing came from the man and that merely fuelled Sam's growing rage.

"You know what?" he snapped, turning back towards Ben. "The job thing is temporary and it'll be sorted out just as soon as all this shit blows over, so don't try and play the poor, unfortunate prick on that front. You also know that me and Karen are there for you if you're struggling with money, so that's a load of bullshit. The only reason you're packing your bags and running like a spoilt bastard is because of Steph, and you're the one who's pushed her into the arms of someone else, so why don't you stop being such a pussy and take some responsibility for that."

"What are you talking about?" Ben questioned, visibly rocked by the accusation.

Letting out a frustrated sigh, Sam shook his head. "There was nothing going on between her and that Kenny guy" he said. "She told us that he'd stayed on her settee the night Rob attacked her and that he's been round to see her a couple of times during the week, just to make sure she was ok. But after you played the jealous twat, kicking ten shades of shit out of him when he came to see if you were ok, she was practically all over the man."

"That isn't what he told me" Ben argued.

"By the sounds of it, you didn't give him chance to say anything" Sam replied, instantly.

"No" Ben stated. "He came in and told me that Steph didn't want anything to do with me and didn't want to be there. He told me that, when he mentioned I'd been round to see if she was ok after the attack, she'd been furious."

Sam's frustration turned to confusion. "He said you hadn't been there" he replied, hesitantly.

"What?" Ben asked.

"He said you hadn't tried to contact her at all" Sam confirmed. "And that's why she's angry with you."

"I was there, I told you that" Ben reiterated. "Kenny answered the door in nothing but a towel around his waist."

"But why would he lie about that?" Sam questioned, naively.

Now it was Ben's turn to shake his head in frustration. "He also told me that she thought I'd treated her badly when she needed comfort" he said, "and then he started to tell me about the things they'd done in the bedroom. He made it clear all he wants is to use her in whatever way he can and that was the moment I snapped. That was the moment I lost it and smacked him."

Floundering under the weight of the revelation, Sam couldn't find any response and silence fell between them as each of their minds processed the same thought.

"Something's not right about that guy" Ben eventually stated.

Sam readily nodded his agreement.

"I need to speak to her" Ben confirmed. "Whether she wants to talk to me or not, she has to know what happened yesterday."

"You want me to come with you?" Sam asked.

"No" Ben replied, firmly. "I need to do this alone. I'll call you later."

Using her heel to kick the door closed behind her, Dani hung up her coat and tossed her bag into the corner before making a bee-line for the settee and slumping down, heavily. She let out a long sigh and closed her eyes for a few seconds as her thoughts wandered to poor Mr Turnbull, who'd passed shortly before the end of her shift.

He'd been such a lovely, sweet old man, always carrying a cheerful smile, despite the multitude of illnesses that were destroying his body. Only last week, she recalled sorrowfully, he'd asked his daughter to bring in a big box of chocolates which had been readily shared out amongst the nurses and doctors who'd cared for him. That hadn't been the first time he'd done that, either.

Of course, they'd all known he wouldn't be able to hold out for long, not with the rapid deterioration of his health. But they'd all hoped that his infectious grin would remain in place for just a short while longer and, now, it was gone.

Despite all her years of dealing with this type of loss, Dani still felt it when a cherished patient passed away and, although she would never dream of letting it show in the hospital, she always struggled to hold back the tears when she got home. This time was no different and, as she felt her eyes beginning to moisten, she cursed the fact that Emily had chosen this weekend to take a romantic break with her man. The woman was off, Dani lamented, having fun and relaxing in someone's arms, whilst she was sitting here by herself, with nothing but four walls and a television to keep her company.

If she were here, Emily would tell her that it was all her own fault. She'd say she was driving potential partners away with her stubborn lack of trust, and maybe she would've had a point. Dani didn't allow too many people to get close and she tried to cite her work as being the stumbling block, but she'd seen the hurt that relationships could bring and, frankly, that fact alone was enough to make her happy in being single, for the most part. At times like this though, when it felt as if she were completely alone, she couldn't help but long for a man to be there, to hold her close and tell her it would all be ok.

"Sentimental idiot!" she muttered, chastising herself for her silliness as she wiped her eyes and rose from the settee.

All she was doing was pulling herself into a depressing hole and that needed to be stopped. If she really wanted a man, she thought to herself as she walked through to her kitchen, she could go out there and get one. The fact was that, on the whole, she just didn't want the hassle at the moment.

Flicking the switch on the kettle, she set about making herself a coffee but, as the water boiled, her mind began to wander back into unwelcome territory, starting with what she was going to do with herself that night. She had a day off tomorrow, which should have given her the chance to enjoy herself without worrying about having to get up in the morning, and the urge to go out was clear and present in her mind, especially after the events of the day. But, with Emily away, there was no one to go out with and that thought brought her quickly back to the feeling of loneliness she was trying to avoid.

There must be some decent, single men still out there, she casually considered as she thought about the ones she worked with and all their stories of conquests and one-night stands. Amongst all the pigs and scum, there must surely be a few nice ones left; like Ben, for example. He'd simply been wonderful in the way he'd carried himself and the concern he'd shown. With a body like his, she'd expected him to be full of himself, constantly self-appreciating his muscles and expecting everyone else to do the same, but there hadn't been the slightest suggestion that he thought that way.

He was unique, she figured. A stand-alone guy blessed with both looks and personality, deeply hidden in a world of animals and morons who cared more for themselves than they did for anyone or anything else. To find a guy like that was a dream, wasn't it? After a day like this, having someone like Ben waiting when she got home would be amazing and she could picture it clearly.

She'd walk in and he'd be there, sitting on the settee and watching TV. At the sound of the door opening, he'd turn to greet her with a wide, welcoming smile on his lips, and he'd realise immediately that something was wrong, jumping up and wrapping his big, strong arms around her. He'd pull her into a tight, warm embrace that'd make her feel treasured and then, as he released his grip ever so slightly, he'd lean down and . . .

"Whoa" she mumbled to herself, shaking her head in a bid to push away the thought.

Having only met the guy twice, it was ridiculous to be thinking along those lines. The man was nice, very nice, but she knew where her mind was heading and there was no place for ideas of that nature, especially when she wasn't likely to see him again.

Steph and Kenny were just leaving her house as Ben skidded to a halt. He jumped off the bike at the same time as he removed his helmet, which was tossed back towards the kerb as he strode purposefully towards them.

"What the hell are you doing here?" Ethan demanded, marching to head him off, before he reached Steph. "If you've come for round two, I'm ready for you this time."

"Steph, I have to talk to you" Ben stated, ignoring Ethan as he tried to pass him.

"No you don't" Ethan insisted, finding the strength to push Ben back.

Involuntarily, Ben's hands balled into fists as he faced up to the man in front of him.

"Stop it!" Steph exclaimed, pulling Ethan out of striking distance and facing up to Ben herself.

"You can't trust this man" Ben blurted out, without waiting for an invitation to talk.

"What?" Steph gasped, shaking her head incredulously. "You're the one under investigation by the police and you're the one who tried to beat the hell out of him for mentioning that, yet you're telling me he's the one I can't trust?"

The incredulity spread immediately to Ben, despite his knowledge of the man's lies. "That's not what happened" he stated.

"Then what did happen?" Steph asked, abruptly.

With that question, faced with the prospect of telling her what was said, Ben's confidence immediately drained from him.

"He didn't mention the police" he muttered. "But he did say that the two of you had done things."

"What things?"

"Just, things" Ben mumbled. "Sexual things."

Steph glanced round at Ethan, who demonstrated his own incredulity with a shrug, before turning back towards Ben with a look in her eyes that seemed to be a combination of sorrow and pity.

"Why are you doing this?" she questioned.

"I'm doing this because that man is no good and I don't want to see you get hurt" Ben replied.

"You don't want to see me get hurt?" Steph repeated. "Is that what you were thinking when you pushed me away from you? When I needed you, and you humiliated me by telling everyone about my mistake?"

Ben floundered for a response.

"Is that why you didn't call me when you were arrested?" Steph continued, the anger in her tone increasing with every word. "And why you didn't bother to check if I was ok when Rob attacked me?"

"I came here that night" Ben stated, finally finding a foothold in the conversation. "Kenny answered the door in nothing but a towel and said you were asleep. He said he'd tell you I'd been here."

Steph turned to Ethan, who again shrugged his confusion.

"You weren't here" Steph replied.

"Tell her" Ben implored, looking at Ethan.

"Buddy" Ethan smiled. "I have no idea what you're talking about."

As his sense of panic grew, Ben returned his focus to Steph, but she didn't give him time to speak.

"Kenny slept on the settee that night" she said. "He didn't get undressed, so why would he be wearing only a towel?"

"He was" was all Ben could find in reply.

Slowly, a look of pity spread across Steph's expression. "Ben" she all but whispered. "I know you're going through a hard time, I really do. And I wish I could help, but I can't."

Ben's heart raced as he looked at her.

"I'm sorry things have gone so shit between us" she continued. "But I can't deal with this at the moment. I'm going out with Kenny now and I need time to think."

"Please don't go with him" Ben pleaded.

Shaking her head, Steph looked deeply into his eyes. "I'm going" she confirmed. "I promise, I'll call you tomorrow and we'll talk."

As Ben returned her gaze, Ethan stepped forward and gently pulled her away from him. "Come on" he said. "It's time to go."

Allowing herself to be led towards the bike, Steph continued to look back at Ben.

"Please" Ben repeated.

With a final shake of her head, Steph donned her helmet and climbed on to the bike behind Ethan, who gunned the engine and pulled away from the kerb.

Standing alone in the street, Ben watched as they disappeared along the road, almost crippled by the feeling of dread that grew quickly from deep within his stomach.

Chapter 23

Billy stared at the corpse in the chair, at the blackened, charred mess that was once his friend, and all effects of the alcohol seemed to drain away, bringing a feeling of complete sobriety for the first time in years. He sank to his knees, overwhelmed by the sense of desolation that coursed through him, falling headlong into a depression that sent his emotions into a tailspin.

There was no way he could know for how long Tommo's body had gone undiscovered, or for how long it would have been left to decay. It could have been hours, it could have been days and, if he hadn't decided to come round to see him, if he hadn't have decided upon a need to start putting his life back together, then there was no saying how long it would've been before someone would've discovered this atrocity.

Of course, he knew what had happened and who had done this. They called it purging, his former brothers, they considered it to be penance for betraying them and it was an act that'd been born of a sick and twisted mind. A sick and twisted mind that Billy, whilst not physically bringing it into this world, had unwittingly provided the platform from which it had grown.

As his tears began to fall, he thought back to days gone by, to moments when Tommo had stood alongside him in the face of adversity, until one specific moment took hold and he slumped forward under the weight of the memory.

It was the late 1990's and he sat alone with Tommo in the meeting room of their new clubhouse.

"I can't believe you're actually thinking this is a good idea!" Tommo exclaimed, having listened to Billy's plan.

"What's wrong with it?" Billy asked, genuinely taken aback by the response.

"Attacking Satan's Minions head-on?" Tommo mused. "It's too much of a risk."

"There's no risk" Billy argued. "They're too small to cope with us and, when it's done, the city's practically ours."

"That sounds more like Ruckus talkin'. He's the one who's put you up to this, 'ain't he?"

Billy's expression portrayed the offence he took to the accusation. "You're talkin' shit" he replied.

"Am I?" Tommo questioned.

"Yeah! This is the right move to make, if we wanna keep the money comin' in."

"Since when did it all become about the money?"

"Since the Minions decided to move in on our turf."

"Our turf?" Tommo chided. "Can you hear yourself?"

A little stunned by the reply, Billy didn't respond.

"This whole thing was never about money" Tommo continued. "When we started this club, when you started this club, it was only about being our own masters and not havin' to answer to anyone."

"But if we don't do this, then we'll be answering to the Minions" Billy replied.

"Again, that sounds like Ruckus talkin'."

With another shake of his head, Billy tried to ignore the comment. "Are you sayin' you don't like the fact we've got more money than ever? You don't like the fact the club's got a brand new, purpose-built home instead of the flea-pit we used to have, or that we're five times the size we were and that patch on your back now automatically gives you more respect than you've ever dreamed?"

"I'm sayin' that Ruckus is a fuckin' psychopath and, if you don't do something to calm him down now, you 'ain't gonna be able to control him soon."

"I'm still the President of this club!"

"Then act like it!"

The argument had reached its crescendo and both men fell silent, each of them knowing the importance of the next words that were uttered.

"Look" Tommo eventually sighed. "You know I'm with you, whatever you decide, but I can't keep going along with this forever. If you wanna take on the Minions and you're doin' this because you genuinely think it's the right thing to do, then I'll back you. But if this goes the way I think it's gonna, then I'm not stickin' around after."

Hesitating for a moment, Billy considered his friend's statement. "I get that" he finally acknowledged, with a slight nod of his head. "But this 'ain't gonna go wrong."

Slowly, the memory faded and Billy pushed himself up from where he lay on the floor. He looked again at the corpse of his friend as he wiped the tears from his cheeks. He thought again about the people who'd done this and the way his life had collapsed around him, driven solely by his own determination to die.

"I'm so sorry" he whispered, hoarsely. "I swear to you, my old friend, I'm gonna get my shit together and I'm gonna make the bastards pay for what they've done to you."

Chapter 24

Taking a deep breath, Ben pushed open the door of the coffee shop and walked in, unsure of what reaction to expect after the way he'd behaved two days ago. At the sound of the door opening, Albert looked up from where he was busy preparing for the day and the surprise in his expression was all too apparent.

"Ben" he exclaimed. "What are you doing here?"

"Albert, I'm so sorry for what happened" Ben hurriedly stated, eager to apologise at the earliest opportunity.

"Forget about that" Albert stated, dismissively. "I'm just surprised to see you in here this early. I've only just opened up."

"I couldn't sleep" Ben replied, grateful for the forgiveness, "so I've been out for a ride."

Albert nodded his acknowledgement. "Have you seen Steph?" he asked. "Is she ok?"

Both the question and the haste with which it'd been asked took Ben by surprise. "Why?" he queried in reply.

"Oh, no reason" Albert answered, unconvincingly. "I just wondered if you'd heard from her, that's all. You know, after what happened."

Ben shrugged. "I saw her briefly yesterday" he confirmed, "but she was going out with the guy she came in here with. She's supposed to be calling me today, but I don't know if she will or not."

Again, Albert nodded. "So, you haven't heard from her today?" he asked.

Becoming somewhat confused, Ben shook his head. "No" he stated, glancing at his watch. "It's a bit early for her to be calling me yet, especially seeing as she was out last night."

"Well, why don't you try calling her?" Albert suggested, with barely a moment's hesitation.

Looking at the man for a few seconds, Ben was unsure as to how he should answer. "I think it's a bit too early for that, too" he eventually replied.

"Of course it is" Albert exclaimed, obviously flustered. "I'm sorry. What can I get you?"

"Just my usual, please" Ben muttered, still trying to get his head around the man's eagerness for him to contact Steph.

Without saying anything more, Albert set about making the drink. Ben noticed his hands shaking as he prepared the beverage and, when he handed it across the counter, the cup rattled vigorously on the saucer.

"Are you ok?" Ben asked, as he handed over the money.

"Huh?" Albert replied, before the words could filter into his mind. "Oh yes" he quickly confirmed. "I'm just a bit scatter-brained this morning."

Ben nodded his reluctant acknowledgement of that and made his way to his normal table, where he checked his watch again.

It was too early to be contacting her, he figured. Besides, even though she'd seemed genuine when she'd said it, he still had doubts over whether she would actually call him today, or whether it was nothing more than a way of getting shot of him at the time. Maybe she just didn't want to fight in the street, especially in front of that piece of crap, Kenny? Maybe she had no intention of calling and even if he did try contacting her, then there was no guarantee that she'd actually answer.

Slowly, his mind worked its way through yesterday's conversation, checking for anything that might give him some reason for optimism but, the more he thought about it, the less confident he felt that it would actually happen. Maybe he should give up on it? Maybe now was the time to move on and let her make the mistake she was clearly determined to go through with? Based on her reaction to his attempt at telling her the truth, it was obvious that she wasn't prepared to listen to him anymore, so maybe this was the time to take a step back?

With a sigh, he took another sip of his drink and considered that for a moment or two longer, gradually coming to the realisation that any attempt to let her go would be futile to say the least. Of course he wouldn't leave her alone to go through whatever the man had planned. He'd be there for her, no matter what and he just hoped that, honestly, she still knew that.

Through a combination of pain and anaesthetic, Banjo had finally passed out and his screams, which had seemed to echo through every room in the clubhouse, had now died down to leave a silence that hung in the air like a thick cloud of smoke. The remaining senior members of the club sat at the table, some of them staring at the vacant seat that should have been occupied by Ray.

"He's gone" Ruckus stated coldly, immediately pulling their attention away from the empty chair. "How many others have we lost?"

None of them wanted to address the question, but it was Jimmy who eventually spoke up.

"Obviously there's Ray" he said, fighting back the lump in his throat, "we dunno whether Banjo'll pull through and, other than that, a few of the Prospects who were watching the gates bought it before they could fire a shot off. Everyone else is ok."

Nodding his acknowledgement, Ruckus took a long, deep breath to calm his anger before speaking again. "Does someone wanna tell me how this happened?" he asked, as he swept his gaze around everyone at the table. "Does someone wanna tell me how, when I was told the Minions were fucked, they still had enough about 'em to carry out a fuckin' full-scale assault on our home?"

Whilst it'd been presented generally, his focus fell directly on Knuckle as he asked his second question, causing the man to shift uncomfortably in his seat.

"They were fucked" Knuckle confirmed, somewhat feebly. "They must've got some outside help from someone."

Again, Ruckus nodded, slowly and deliberately. "From who?" he asked, bluntly.

Bowing his head contritely, Knuckle let out a sigh. "I dunno" he admitted, before hastily adding "but I've got Crowther and Wishall lookin' in to it already."

"Do we know any of the bodies?" Ruckus questioned, turning his focus towards Touchy.

"Only two of 'em" Touchy replied. "The rest are strangers and none of their ink puts 'em as members of any other clubs we know of."

Drumming his fingers on the arm of his chair, Ruckus considered the situation for a few moments. "What about their President?" he finally asked. "I take it none of the dead are that mother-fucker, Jason?"

Touchy shook his head.

"Then what the fuck are we all sittin' here for?" he questioned, looking around at each and every face in the room. "Get the fuck out there and find that piece of shit. I want him back here, alive!"

Without waiting for any further instruction, the room rose as one and quickly filtered towards the doors, leaving Ruckus alone with Ethan and Touchy, both of whom he'd gestured to remain where they were.

"What about the bitch?" Ruckus asked, once the doors had been closed.

"She got away during the attack" Ethan admitted. "She took Ray's bike before I could get to her."

"You didn't think of shootin' her when the bullets started flying?" Ruckus questioned.

"I was too busy trying not to get killed. I didn't think she'd get out that fast."

"You 'ain't done much in the way of thinkin' lately" Ruckus hissed, finally showing his anger. "Right from the start, it's been nothin' but a fuck up."

"We'll find her" Ethan answered, ignoring the accusation. "I've got people lookin' for her right now. I'm sure she'll go back to that fucker, Ben and, when she does, we'll know about it."

"And what's your plan if you do find her?"

"When we find her, it plays right into our hands. Trust me, this'll turn out perfect for us."

Ruckus stared at him without speaking for a few moments, before turning to his right. "Touchy" he said.

"Keep an eye on my boy here. He's got until midnight and, when he fucks this up, make sure he don't come back here alive."

By the time he'd reached home, Ben had pretty much convinced himself that he wouldn't hear from Steph that day. He'd actually become pretty certain that he wouldn't hear from her for a while and started to wonder whether moving away wasn't such a bad idea after all. He'd miss Sam and Karen, that's for sure, but making a fresh start might be the best thing for him in the long run and, surprisingly, he was actually starting to look forward to it.

Turning into the parking area of his flat, his mind had wandered to where he might go, when it was suddenly and harshly brought back to the present.

"Shit!" he cried out, as he pulled hard on the brakes, sending his bike dovetailing all over the place in his bid to avoid the motorcycle that'd been left on its side in the entrance. Fighting to keep control, he barely missed slamming straight into the machine and finally managed to wrestle his bike to a stop a few yards inside the parking area.

He took a moment to catch his breath, before lowering the kick-stand and dismounting unsteadily.

"What the fuck?" he cursed angrily under his breath, looking back towards the entrance. "What kind of a prick would leave a bike like that?"

Ben answered his own question as he walked towards the machine; it must have been stolen and then abandoned by the bastards who took it. Someone, somewhere, was probably lamenting the loss of such a magnificent pair of wheels and, he realised as he drew closer to it, this really was a special beast.

It seemed as though every part was custom-built, the exhaust, the stems and even the wheels were as unique as he'd ever seen. It was awe-inspiring, even before he'd noticed the paintwork, and that just completed the picture dramatically; the intricacy in the design on the tank was mind-blowing and depicted a skull against a backdrop of fire. All in all, whoever had paid for this bike to be made had clearly known specifically what they'd been looking for and no expense had been spared in achieving the look they'd wanted.

With all of his strength, Ben managed to wrestle the machine back on to its wheels and he pushed it to the side of the entrance, out of harm's way. Lowering the kick-stand, he took a moment longer to admire the paintwork for one last time before returning to his own bike and parking that up in his space. He then pulled his phone out of his pocket and dialled the police number as he walked towards the stairwell.

The line went to the usual automated message for the emergency services and he was in the process of selecting the option for the police, when he noticed the red hand-print on the stairwell door.

"What the hell?" he exclaimed, as he quickly withdrew his own hand, before it touched the mark.

Looking closely, he examined the door and realised that the red was blood, which was still fresh, and wondered whether it had something to do with the bike being left where it was. Maybe someone took a spill, he guessed. Maybe the bike had been bought by someone in the building and they'd gone back to their flat to clean up, before trying to move the thing?

Cancelling his call before it was answered, Ben figured that it might be a better option to do a bit of asking around before he involved the police. If the bike had been stolen, then a couple of hours delay in the report wouldn't do any harm and it'd be better to make sure he wasn't dropping anyone in the shit unnecessarily.

With that decided, he pushed on a clean part of the door and started his ascent of the stairs, checking for any further blood stains on his way up. If there were any, he figured, then maybe they would stop at a certain floor and, if that were the case, then at least it'd give him somewhere to start when he went to knock on doors. However there was nothing, until he reached his own floor and saw another hand print on the door to his hallway, which caused him to stop in his tracks. He knew all the people on his floor and none of them were the type to even have an interest in bikes, let alone buy one, so why did the trail end there?

Suddenly awash with a deep sense of foreboding, Ben tentatively reached out to push the door open. His heart began to race as the hinges gave their usual squeak and he stepped through but, when he looked along the hallway, all the air escaped from his lungs.

Lying on the floor, leaning against the door of his flat, was Steph and, even from that distance, he could see she was in a bad way. Her clothes were torn and hanging loosely around her body, which was covered in bruises and blood. She was facing towards him and her eyes were closed, one of them through heavy swelling and, for a second, he was certain she wasn't breathing.

Rushing forward, Ben dropped to his knees and scooped her up into his arms, pulling her close and giving thanks when a groan escaped her lips. He spoke her name, and she responded with another groan as he tried to take stock of the injuries, recognising them instantly as being disturbingly similar to the girl in the alley.

"Steph" he tried again, choking a little as tears fell freely from his eyes.

This time, at the sound of his voice, she moved slightly in an attempt to look up at him.

"I'm sorry" was all she managed to whisper, before slipping back into unconsciousness.

The longer the old man stared, the more uncomfortable Dani felt, which must have translated into her expression as he suddenly became a little flustered.

"I'm sorry" Albert blurted out, as his cheeks reddened. "I didn't mean to stare. It's just that I'm sure I've seen you before, but I can't quite place where."

Letting out a slight giggle, more in relief than amusement, Dani nodded. "I was in here a while ago" she answered, smiling warmly, "with Ben, after he'd been arrested."

"Of course!" Albert exclaimed, tapping his finger into his temple as if to underline his next comment. "I'm sorry. This old thing isn't working the way it used to. What can I get you?"

"That's ok" Dani chuckled. "Just a coffee, please."

With a nod, Albert set about making her drink, chatting away as he did. "He's a lovely guy, Ben" he said, almost absent-mindedly. "You can always tell a lot about a man by the way his friends care for him and Sam, Karen and Steph love the guy dearly. They really are a lovely bunch of people and none of them deserve what's happening to them."

"What do you mean?" Dani asked.

Quickly turning round to face her, it was clear Albert realised he might have said a bit too much. "I just mean that" he began, again a little flustered, "all this nonsense with Ben and the police."

"But what's happening to his friends?" Dani questioned.

"Oh, nothing" Albert insisted. "They just care about him and this is hurting all of them, that's all."

The conversation crashed to a halt as Albert finished making her drink but, as he handed it over to her, his expression took on a seriousness she hadn't expected and he nervously glanced around the empty room before speaking in a hushed tone.

"Why don't you give him a call?" he suggested. "He's going to need a friend today."

"What do you mean?" she asked, surprised by both the suggestion and the sudden change in the man's demeanour. "Why?"

"I just" Albert mumbled, before hesitating as he tried to decide on what to say. "I just think he needs a friend. Please help him."

At the seriousness of the request, Dani couldn't help but feel her heart skip a little and her blood, momentarily, seemed to run cold. "What's happening today?" she questioned.

With a shake of his head, Albert made it clear he wasn't going to say anything more on the subject, so Dani gave a noncommittal nod of her head and took her drink to a table in the far corner of the room.

She sat down heavily, her mind racing back over the conversation, and she found herself panicking a little as she questioned why the man had been so desperate for her to contact Ben. Of course, she could understand what was happening to him and she appreciated that he wasn't having the best of times, but why the need to contact him today? Why did he need her help? How could she possibly help him with all this? Glancing back towards the counter, she saw Albert was now doing all he could to avoid her gaze, so she turned her attention back to both her drink and thoughts of Ben.

If she hadn't already realised that the guy was genuine, then the old man's attitude towards him would've been enough to convince her. Like he said, you can judge a lot about a person by the way his friends care for him and, if such a sweet, old man like that, who had no reason to care, could be so concerned about him, then her initial instincts must have been right. The only question was whether she should give him a call today and, based on where her thoughts had previously drifted, she couldn't deny that the idea carried more than a lot of appeal.

Before she had time to consider it any further, the sound of the door opening broke into her thoughts and she looked up to see Emily almost stagger into the shop. The woman was clearly hung-over, wearing dark shades and barely able to walk in a straight line, which was a sight that brought an instant smile to Dani's lips.

"Don't say anything" Emily ordered, practically dropping into the opposite chair.

Dani merely gave a slow shake of her head.

"I can't believe I agreed to meet you this early" Emily continued.

"It's nearly ten o'clock" Dani pointed out, trying not to laugh. "It's hardly early."

"After last night, four o'clock this afternoon would still be too early" Emily replied, bitterly.

"So, it was a good trip?" Dani asked.

Emily shook her head. "No" she stated. "The place was dull, the hotel was awful and the bed was the most uncomfortable thing I've ever had to sleep on. We were supposed to come home last night but, yesterday morning, we decided to give it up as a bad job and come back early. Then, to drown our sorrows, we decided to have what turned into more than a few drinks last night and I woke up with this."

Gingerly, she lifted the hem of her top to reveal a bruise that stretched from her ribs to her hip.

"I have no idea how I did this" she exclaimed.

Now unable to stop herself, Dani openly laughed. "Christ!" she chuckled. "Were you hit by a bus?"

"It feels like it" Emily sighed, lowering her top. "So, how are you? How was work yesterday?"

"I'll tell you in a moment" Dani smiled, feeling the humour drain from her as she thought about the sad news she needed to break. "Let me get you a drink first. Do you want a coffee?"

Emily nodded as Dani rose from her seat and made her way towards the counter.

"Your friend's a little worse for the wear, isn't she?" Albert asked, as she approached.

"Just a bit" Dani replied, rolling her eyes. "Can I get a strong coffee, please?"

"Absolutely" Albert smiled. "And would you like a fresh one yourself?"

Glancing back at the table, Dani considered the question. "Yes please" she agreed.

Albert made the drinks and, when he pushed them across the counter to her, his tone dropped again. "These are on the house" he whispered. "Just, please, don't mention anything I said to your friend. I don't want Ben's problems broadcast."

Dani could understand the request, so she nodded her agreement. "You don't have to give me these for free though" she smiled.

Waving his hands, Albert shook his head. "I insist" he stated, "but please call Ben."

Once more a little shaken by his demeanour, she again nodded her agreement and carried the drinks back to the table.

"Are you ok?" Emily asked, as Dani sat down.

"Yeah, I'm fine" Dani replied, unconvincingly. "That nice man gave us these for free."

Turning in her seat, Emily acknowledged the gesture and returned her attention to Dani. "So" she stated. "You were going to tell me about work yesterday?"

Taking a deep breath, Dani composed herself before speaking. "Mr Turnbull passed away" she said. "Just before I finished my shift."

"Oh, no" Emily sighed. "I really hoped I'd see him again, before he went. Are you sure you're ok?"

"I am now" Dani answered, "but I was a bit lost when I got home."

Emily shook her head. "You should have called me" she smiled. "Please tell me you went out, or did something to take your mind off it."

Dani shrugged. "I had no one to go out with" she lamented, instantly regretting the natural sorrow in her voice.

"And this is why you need a boyfriend" Emily replied, predictably. "This is why I keep telling you to get out there."

"I know" Dani agreed, "but I just don't want to have to sift through the scum that call themselves men."

Now it was Emily's turn to roll her eyes, although the gesture went unnoticed behind the shades. "They're not all bad" she sighed. "What about the guys at the hospital?"

"Are you serious?" Dani asked. "They're worse than the animals in the nightclubs."

Chuckling, Emily agreed. "That's a fair point" she muttered, "but surely you've met someone you're interested in? Like that guy, Ben, for example."

The lack of response provided Emily with all the confirmation she needed.

"I knew it!" she exclaimed, excitedly. "You do like the guy!"

Dani tried to shrug the claim off, but there was no stopping Emily now.

"I bet you haven't called him, have you?" she continued. "He gave you his number and I'll bet you've looked at it a thousand times since, but you haven't had the bottle to actually make contact with him."

Still, Dani didn't answer, leaving Emily to jump to an annoyingly accurate conclusion.

"There's something you're not telling me, isn't there?" she asked.

A loud sigh escaped Dani's lips as she contemplated telling Emily the truth. "I met up with him for a coffee in here" she finally admitted.

The large grin that spread across Emily's lips was all the gesture needed to demonstrate that she wanted to hear more.

"It was a short while ago" Dani explained. "And it was just because I thought he should know about the second girl they found in the alley."

"And how did that go?"

"It was nice. We had a really good talk."

"And you haven't called him since, have you?"

Shaking her head, Dani let out another sigh. "It just doesn't seem appropriate" she pointed out.

"Why?" Emily asked.

"Because of the whole doctor patient thing."

"But he wasn't a patient."

"I know, but it still doesn't feel right."

"It just doesn't feel right because you don't want it to."

A third sigh was all Dani could find in response.

"Why don't you call him?" Emily suggested, in a tone that made it clear the idea wasn't negotiable.

Dani shrugged.

"Call him" Emily insisted. "Call him now and ask him what he's doing today."

"I don't know" Dani replied.

"Give me the phone" Emily demanded. "I'll call him for you."

With a shake of her head, Dani tried to fend off the attack but, no sooner had she started the gesture, she was interrupted by her phone ringing. She reached into her bag and checked the screen, before looking at Emily as her cheeks flushed brightly.

"It's Ben" she muttered, much to her friend's delight.

All was quiet as Sam watched on from where he stood in the bedroom doorway. He looked at Steph, who seemed to be sleeping peacefully, he watched as Ben tenderly brushed a stray hair away from her cheek before turning to face him and the sight of the tears that continued to fall from his friend's eyes shattered his heart.

"I don't . . ." he began to whisper, but Ben gestured for him to remain silent before checking Steph for a final time and then quietly ushering him back out to the living room.

"I don't know what to say" he mumbled, as Ben sat down heavily on the settee and buried his face in his hands.

Taking a deep breath, Ben wiped the tears from his cheeks and looked up. "There's nothing anyone can say" he stated.

Somewhat lost, Sam struggled with how he was going to help them through this, eventually deciding that reason was the only way forward. "Shouldn't she be in the hospital?" he asked.

"No" Ben snapped, before curtailing his anger. "No" he repeated, in a slightly calmer tone. "I'm not leaving her there."

"But those injuries need checking and she needs treatment" Sam argued.

"They're the same injuries as the girl I found in the alley" Ben confirmed. "And I'm betting they're the same as the other girl found, too. I'm not gonna hand her over for her to suffer the same fate as them."

Slowly, the reason Ben wouldn't allow her to go into the hospital dawned on Sam and he understood the reluctance. "But she needs medical help" he pointed out.

"I know" Ben agreed. "I've called Dani and she's getting some things from the hospital and coming here."

"Well, what about the police?"

Ben looked up at him, but didn't reply.

"This needs to be reported to them" Sam explained.

"But this'll go to those two who are trying to fuck me up" Ben stated. "What good will come of going to them?"

Sam considered that for a moment. "Surely, if you report this to them, then they have to consider the fact that you can't have had anything to do with the other girls?"

"Or they can consider it as evidence of my guilt" Ben replied.

"This is different" Sam urged. "You know she went with Kenny and he must've had something to do with this. You can tell them that and, if nothing else, bring them back here to speak to Steph when she wakes up."

"I don't want them involved" Ben hissed, as the anger returned.

"You've got no choice" Sam confirmed.

Sitting back firmly, Ben bounced his head off the back of the settee a couple of times as he rubbed his hands over the top of his skull. "I know" he muttered. "This is all just so fucked up."

"Look" Sam stated. "I'll stay here while you go to the police. I'll wait for Dani to show up and I swear on my life that I'll make sure Steph's safe."

Ben looked at him, the reluctance obvious in his eyes, before finally letting out one, long sigh and rising to his feet. "Ok" he agreed.

Chapter 25

"Ben?" Steph called from the bedroom, her voice raspy and filled with confusion.

Leaping up from where he sat on the settee, Sam rushed to her and saw that she was struggling to push herself upright in the bed, wincing at the pain the movement caused.

"Here, let me help you" he said, moving over to the side of the bed.

"Sam?" she questioned, clearly surprised to see him. "Where's Ben?"

"He's gone to the police" Sam replied, as he helped her up and moved the pillows for her to lean back comfortably.

Her disorientation momentarily increased as she looked around, seemingly trying to understand why the last thing she remembered was being held by Ben and now Sam stood in front of her, in what appeared to be Ben's bedroom.

She looked up at Sam, her expression clearly indicating that she needed clarification, so Sam was quick to provide her with details.

"You were outside Ben's door when he got back from a ride this morning" he explained. "He brought you in, cleaned you up and he's called his doctor friend to come and take a look at you."

Looking down at the t-shirt she was wearing, her confusion was still very evident.

"Your clothes were ruined" he explained further, "so Ben dressed you in one of his t-shirts."

"Where is Ben?" she asked, again.

"He's gone to the police" Sam confirmed. "Do you remember what happened?"

Closing her eyes, Steph gave a slight shake of her head and, for a moment, Sam wondered whether she had any recollection at all. Eventually though, she started to talk and, the more she did, the easier she found it to recall.

"I went to a party with Kenny" she began. "He was a member of a motorcycle club, The Sons of Sorrow, and there were a lot of them there. I didn't want to go in at first, but he told me not to worry and I trusted him, so I went in."

Sam nodded encouragement, so Steph continued.

"He tried to get me to go into one of the back rooms" she said, again shaking her head as if she was trying to make the memory clearer, "but I didn't want that. He accepted it at first, but then he started to get angry and . . ."

Tears quickly began to fall from her eyes and Sam sat on the edge of the bed to hold her as she wept. Slowly, her anguish began to subside and she pulled away from him. Then, after taking a few seconds to compose herself, she continued to describe what she'd been through, further breaking Sam's heart as the full horror of the situation became all too apparent.

". . . and then all I heard was gunshots and, suddenly, people were running all over the place" she told him, as her tale came to its end. "I found a knife and managed to cut the ties on my wrists, then I grabbed what I could find of my clothes and just ran out of the place. One of the motorbikes had been left with the keys in the ignition, so I just jumped on and got away."

Shaking his head, Sam was struggling to comprehend the reality of the situation. "I didn't know you could ride" he said, ignoring the many questions he had, not wanting to draw her back into the nightmare.

"Yeah" she nodded. "I used to ride my dad's bike, before I moved here."

"Well, at least you got away" Sam pointed out, a little lost for anything else to say. "And when Ben gets back with the police, then you can tell them everything about Kenny."

"His name wasn't Kenny" Steph informed him, as her gaze became a little distant. "Just before he attacked me, he told me it was Ethan. I should've listened to Ben. He told me the man was lying to me and I just dismissed him completely."

Again, tears began to fall from her eyes. "I've really fucked everything up" she sobbed.

"No, of course you haven't" Sam replied. "You'll come through this."

"But what about Ben?" she asked. "I've treated him like shit. He doesn't deserve any of what I've done to him."

"And what exactly have you done to him?" Sam questioned.

Closing her eyes, Steph shook her head. "You know what I've done to him" she answered, solemnly.

"I know you've been confused" Sam confirmed. "But none of that's been of your own doing. First you had Rob fucking with your head and now this Ethan fella's been messing with you."

"But Ben tried to warn me about him."

"So?"

"So, I didn't listen to him. I didn't listen to the man who's always been there for me. I bet he hates me now, doesn't he? I wouldn't blame him if he does."

"Steph" Sam stated, drawing her attention to him. "Ben loves you and nothing you've done has changed that."

"I know he loved me" Steph replied.

"You don't know the half of it" Sam muttered, slightly unsure as to whether what he was about to do was right. "Ben loves you more than you could ever know. He always has done, right from the moment he met you."

Steph looked at him, slightly stunned by the comment.

"He's always asked me to keep quiet about it, to never mention it to you, but you mean the world to that man. Why'd you think he's never had a girlfriend in all of these years? It's not because he can't get one, it's because he's been searching for someone he wants more than you and, so far, no one's even come close."

"Well why hasn't he ever told me?" Steph asked, still a little dumbstruck by the revelation.

"He didn't think you'd want to hear it from him" Sam answered. "When he met you, he realised you needed a friend, so that's what he made sure he was. Then, when things got better for you, he worried that, if he told you, you'd question his intentions and it might damage what you had. That's why he never said anything and why he didn't go through with anything the night he came round to yours. In his words, he'd rather have you there as a friend, than not have you there at all."

As more tears fell, Steph shook her head. "I love him too" she whispered.

"Then you need to tell him that" Sam stated but, before he could say any more, a knock at the door echoed around the flat.

"That'll be Dani" he smiled warmly, as he rose from the bed.

Sitting in the same interview room as he had after being arrested, Ben fought desperately to keep himself calm as he stared across the table at Detective Crowther.

"So, what you're telling me" Crowther stated, "is that your friend, who's a girl but not your girlfriend, went out with someone called Kenny, whose surname you don't know, and that this Kenny bloke rides a motorcycle."

Ben nodded.

"You're also saying that this friend turned up at your flat this morning, carrying the same injuries as the girls found in the alleyway, and that, if we come with you now, she'll be able to tell us exactly who did this?"

Again, Ben nodded. "Exactly" he confirmed.

Turning to where Wishall sat next to him, Crowther raised his eyebrow as he spoke and seemed to emphasize the cynicism in his voice. "What do you think?" he asked.

Wishall shook his head. "It sounds a bit convenient to me" Wishall answered, glaring at Ben.

"I agree" Crowther nodded, now turning to also glare at Ben. "It does sound a little far-fetched and there's one thing that really bothers me. If your friend," he said, gesturing quote marks in the air with his fingers, "is as badly injured as you say, shouldn't she be in the hospital right now?"

Ben shook his head. "After what they did to the first girl in the hospital, I'm not leaving Steph to suffer the same fate."

"And what exactly did they do?" Crowther questioned.

"They murdered her, you know that" Ben stated.

Crowther acted as though he was surprised by the statement. "I thought she suffered a heart-attack?" he said.

"But the autopsy showed her to have a puncture wound in her foot" Ben pointed out, still fighting to contain both his anger and his hatred for the two men in front of him.

"And how could you possibly know that?" Wishall demanded.

"Why, Detective Wishall" Crowther smiled annoyingly, still with his gaze firmly fixed on Ben. "I would guess that the only way our friend here could know about the puncture wound, would be if he had some sort of supernatural insight into what happened to the poor girl. Either that, or maybe he knows more than he's let on?"

Letting out a loud sigh of frustration, Ben rubbed at his face. "Will you listen to me?" he implored. "Just come with me now and see for yourselves."

Before either detective had the chance to answer, Crowther's phone rang and he strode out of the room to answer the call, leaving Ben and Wishall sitting in silence. When he came back in a few minutes later, his attitude had noticeably changed.

"Well, Mr Trowman" he said, almost jovially, "I think we're done here, don't you?"

Ben just stared at him.

"Obviously, we'll take your concerns on board and look in to them as soon as possible" Crowther continued, holding the door open and gesturing that it was time for Ben to leave.

"What does that even mean?" Ben asked, remaining seated.

"It means" Crowther replied, "that maybe you should run home now and wait for us to contact you. I mean, you want to know how your friend's doing, don't you?"

Again, the man gestured quote-marks with his fingers as he uttered the word 'friend'.

"For fuck's sake!" Ben exclaimed, finally losing his control. "I'm giving you your fucking investigation on a plate and you're just sending me home with promises that you'll fucking look into it?"

"I think you need to watch yourself" Wishall pointed out.

"Or what?" Ben demanded, as the full force of his anger finally exploded. "You'll fucking arrest me? Well? Go on then! Fucking stick me in a cell and then go search my fucking flat!"

Crowther merely smiled at him. "We'll be in touch" he confirmed.

"Fucking Assholes!" Ben cried, slamming his fist on the table as he jumped up from his seat.

He strode over to Crowther and stood directly in front of him, his nose only a couple of centimetres from the man's face. "Will you do your fucking job?" he hissed.

"Thank you, Mr Trowman" Crowther smiled in reply. "You can go now."

Balling his hands into fists, Ben lost all control of himself. He reached up and grabbed Crowther by the lapel of his jacket and pushed him hard against the wall, causing Wishall to rush over and try pulling him away, but Ben was too strong and too incensed to be moved. "Why are you doing this?" he spat, more than asked. "Why are you bastards refusing to listen to me?"

At the sound of the commotion, three uniformed officers ran into the room and between them, they and

Wishall managed to subdue Ben. The officers looked to Crowther, who smiled broadly as he told them to escort Ben from the premises.

By the time he arrived home, Ben's anger had transformed into feelings of both panic and helplessness. Upstairs, in his flat, Steph was lying in his bed, battered and broken by a bunch of animals who, he had no doubt, had already taken the lives of two innocent women, yet they refused to listen to him. They refused to accept what he was saying and seemingly remained hell-bent on proving his guilt.

Maybe Dani could help, he wondered as he turned off his bike's engine and climbed off the machine, removing his helmet as he did. Maybe the voice of a doctor might add some weight to his statement? Once she'd seen the condition Steph had been left in, then she'd be able to confirm the injuries matched those of the previous victims and, maybe then, he'd be free to help her get through this, without the constant worry of what might be to come. Then again, he thought ruefully as he climbed the stairs, they'd probably still find some way of tying him to this, and maybe wrapping Dani into it all, just for good measure.

As he pushed open the door to the hallway, Ben turned towards his flat and his heart lurched when he saw that his front door was ajar. His mind began to race, trying to find some plausible reason for it being open but, when no explanation could be found, the cold sense of dread quickly became overwhelming.

Dropping his helmet, Ben rushed forward and practically threw the door open in his haste to get into the living room, where the air immediately escaped his lungs in a loud cry as his legs gave way and he dropped to his knees, staring straight ahead. His body began to shake uncontrollably as his mind tried desperately to process the sight that lay before him, to accept what he was seeing as being genuine and, all too quickly, reality smashed home.

He didn't need to see the cold, lifeless eyes that stared back at him to know that his friend was gone. Nor did he need to see the deep, crimson slit that viciously split the man's throat or the blood which pooled grotesquely across the floor.

Amidst the chaos in his head, a thought managed to find a foothold and Ben scrabbled to his feet and ran to his bedroom, where he found the bed to be empty.

"Steph" he cried out, as he ran to check the bathroom.

That too was empty and the racing of his heart increased as he checked the kitchen, despite knowing the gesture was futile. Shaking his head in a bid to clear his mind, he moved back to the living room, where he was confronted by Crowther and Wishall, who stood in the front doorway, each of them wearing broad grins.

"Well, well" Crowther smiled, glancing briefly back to Sam's corpse as he casually toyed with the handcuffs he had ready in his hand. "Let me guess? Your friend here, knowing what you've been up to, comes round in order to persuade you into turning yourself in. The confrontation is aggressive, quickly becoming violent, until you decide that this poor bastard needs to be disposed of. Having killed him, you realise you need to cover yourself, so you come to us with some bullshit story of a friend being attacked, asking us to come back with you to speak with her and then, when we get here and find this, I'm guessing you claim that whoever attacked your girlfriend, must've come back to finish the job?"

With his mind rapidly approaching collapse, Ben could only stand and stare at the man as he spoke.

Laughing, Wishall took the cuffs from Crowther and quickly strode to where Ben stood, helpless. "I probably don't have to tell you, Mr Trowman" he chuckled, as he secured Ben's hands behind his back, "but you're under arrest."

Chapter 26

For the first time in what seemed like an eternity, rain hammered the windscreen as Detective Steve Roberts parked up at the side of the road. He turned off the car's engine and unfastened his seatbelt before reaching into the well between the seats and pulling out his phone. Having searched through the directory he selected the desired number and then held the phone to his ear whilst the line connected.

"It's me" he muttered gruffly, once the call had been answered. "Tell the Sarge I've been held up on an enquiry and I'm running late."

He listened to the response.

"I don't give a shit" he answered, a little angrier than he intended. "Just tell him it's in relation to the Holtby case."

The voice delivered another question.

"I don't know" he said, glancing at his watch. "It's half eight now, so tell him I'll be there by ten."

Without waiting for any further response he ended the call, switched the phone to silent and slipped it into his pocket. He took a moment to look out of the rain-soaked side window, at the house in front of which he'd stopped, and wondered just what he was going to find in there today. Last week, the woman seemed ok, almost normal in her conversation and with clarity that belied the fragile state of her mind, but that was last week. This week, there was every chance she wouldn't know who he was, let alone be able to make any sense.

With a shake of his head, he rubbed the sleep from his eyes and let out a long, lingering sigh before reaching down into the passenger foot-well to pick up the bag of groceries he'd collected on his way there. He took a final, deep breath and then opened the car door, quickly stepping out into the rain and slamming it shut as he ran up the garden path. In his haste to get into shelter he fumbled the key in the lock, growing angrier as more and more water cascaded on to him from the broken guttering above until, finally, he managed to insert the key and open the door.

"Mum, it's me" he called out, as he pushed the door closed with the heel of his shoe and walked through to the kitchen.

"Mum?" he tried again, when there came no reply.

There was still no answer, causing him to curse inwardly as he set about putting the groceries away. With that done, he wandered through to the living room but found it to be empty, so he moved upstairs to the bedroom, where he saw his mother standing motionless at the window.

"Mum, are you ok?" he asked cautiously, whilst wondering how long she'd been there.

"They've taken him" she answered, without looking round.

"Taken who?" Roberts asked, stepping slowly towards her, so as not to startle her.

Suddenly turning to face him, the frustration was evident in her expression. "My Freddie" she exclaimed. "I woke up and he was gone."

Roberts fought back his own frustration. "Mum" he said, slowly and deliberately. "Dad passed away six years ago."

The woman shook her head vigorously. "No" she stated, pointing to the bed. "He was there when we went to sleep, he was drunk as usual, but when I woke up he was gone. They've taken him, I tell you."

"Who've taken him?"

Again, she shook her head. "They have" she insisted.

Rubbing his hands over his face, Roberts took a deep, long breath as he took another step closer to her. "Ok, Mum" he smiled. "I'll look in to that, but you need to get dressed first."

"You're one of them, aren't you?" she replied, backing away from him.

"Mum, it's me, your son" he answered.

"No!" she snapped. "You're one of them!"

"One of who?" he asked.

"The skulls!" she screamed, backing herself right into the corner.

Roberts stopped in his tracks. "What skulls?" he questioned.

"The crying skulls" she replied, hysterically. "You took the girl, you took my Freddie and now you've come for me!"

"I'm not a skull" he stated, struggling to maintain a level of calm in his voice.

"Show me!" she demanded. "Turn around!"

Desperate to combat her fear, Roberts slowly turned on the spot, holding his arms out as he moved but, before he'd completed the circle, a thought crept into his mind. She might be delusional, he realised, but maybe there was more to this than it just being a random tirade? She'd referred to crying skulls, asking him to prove he wasn't one of them by showing her his back, and that was something he'd come across before. In fact, it was something he'd spent the last few years trying to combat, despite the constant interference of Crowther and Wishall.

"What girl was taken?" he asked, once he was facing her again.

"That poor girl" she answered, pointing out of the window and along the road. "She went on his noisy machine and now she's gone."

That was all he really needed to hear, but following her gesture towards a house further down the street provided confirmation of his presumption. The house in question had been the home of the dead girl found in an alley, the girl Crowther and Wishall were investigating and the girl they so proudly had, what he'd suspected to be, an innocent man in custody for.

"Mum, I've got to go" he mumbled, momentarily forgetting her needs.

"Get out!" she snapped, proving there was nothing he could do for her right at that moment anyway.

Leaving the bedroom, he pulled out his phone and dialled the number for her health-visitor. Given the state she was in, that was probably for the best anyway, he argued to himself as he left the house.

As Ben walked out of the police station, he didn't notice the rain which continued to fall heavily, nor did he notice the man who appeared to be waiting for him.

"Mr Trowman?" the man asked, stepping forward and offering his hand in greeting.

Ben ignored the gesture.

"I'm Detective Roberts" the man continued, unperturbed by the lack of response. "It was me who arranged for your release. Can I give you a lift home? I'd like to talk to you about a few things."

A shrug was all Ben provided in reply.

Roberts led him to his car, which was parked in the bays at the front of the station, and quickly unlocked it so they could get in from the rain.

"So, where do you live?" Roberts asked, once they were ready to drive off.

Now Ben looked at him. "Why did you get me released?" he asked, somewhat abruptly.

"Because I stumbled across a witness who confirmed you weren't the one with the girl, the night she was murdered" Roberts answered, becoming abrupt himself.

"So, have you arrested the man who did it?" Ben asked, immediately.

Shaking his head, Roberts let out a small sigh. "No" he replied. "That's what I need to talk to you about. The witness wouldn't exactly be classed as being reliable, so I need to know what you know about what happened."

Ben considered that for a moment. "So, how did you manage to get me released?" he asked.

Roberts didn't answer straight away, taking a few seconds as though he was weighing up what information he was able to reveal. "Look" he finally said. "All I can tell you is that I've got concerns over a few things and I have a feeling I know who's involved in all this, so I checked the records and they confirmed you were in the interview room at the time of your friend's . . ."

His words drifted off as he realised what he was about to say, but Ben completed the sentence for him.

"My friend's death?" he stated, without any emotion.

Nodding, Roberts confirmed that.

"Where's Steph?" Ben asked, before Roberts could continue.

Roberts looked at him blankly. "Who?"

"Steph" Ben reiterated. "The girl who was in my flat when they murdered Sam."

As he spoke, the coldness in Ben's voice seemed to take Roberts by surprise and he hesitated before providing a response. "There was no girl" he eventually muttered, hesitantly.

Ben nodded. "How long did they have me in there?" he asked.

"Two days" Roberts answered.

Again, Ben nodded. "Can you take me to Steph's?"

Without saying anything further, Roberts started the engine and pulled away from the kerb.

Ben knew the house was empty, even before he hammered at the door. Unsurprisingly there was no reply, yet he continued to knock.

"Steph" he yelled out, futilely.

Roberts remained where he stood at the end of the path. "I don't think she's here" he pointed out, unhelpfully.

Ignoring him, Ben walked to the kitchen window and peered through the gap in the blind. Then he moved over to the living room window on the other side of the door but, as always, there was no way of seeing in through the drawn curtains.

He stepped back and looked up at the bedroom windows above. "Steph!" he yelled, cupping his hands either side of his mouth in a bid to increase the volume of his voice.

"She's not here" Roberts repeated.

Turning to face him, Ben shook his head. "I need to find her" he stated.

Looking at him, Roberts again felt some concern at the lack of any emotion in either the man's voice or demeanour. "Wait here" he commanded, before walking round to the neighbouring house and knocking authoritatively on the door.

As the door was opened, Roberts held up his badge and introduced himself. "When was the last time you saw the girl who lives next door?"

The elderly woman who'd answered his knock only stared at him for a few seconds, clearly taken aback by either the fact that a police officer was asking her a question, or the question itself.

"I'm not sure" she eventually stammered in reply. "I think it was a few days ago."

"Can you be more certain?" Roberts asked.

Giving a slow shake of her head, the woman thought about it and it seemed she wouldn't be able to clarify, until she saw Ben standing in the background.

"It was when he was here" she stated, pointing at Ben. "They had an argument on the street and there was another man here. I heard the noise and looked out of the window."

Roberts nodded. "Can you describe the other man?" he asked.

The woman shrugged. "Not really" she answered. "But he wore a leather jacket and rode a motorcycle. Is Steph in trouble?"

"No, she's fine" Roberts lied. "Thanks for your time."

Without giving the woman any chance to ask further questions, he turned and walked back to Ben.

"So, we know she hasn't been here" he confirmed, pointlessly.

"Take me to the hospital" Ben demanded.

"Let me handle this" Roberts stated, as they walked through the doors and approached the desk, where he again held up his badge, introduced himself and asked whether Stephanie Lewis had been either admitted or seen as a drop-in over the last two days.

The receptionist looked at him, glancing at Ben for a moment, before opening up the files on her computer. "No" she answered, after scrolling through the names. "We've not had anyone of that name."

"Any unknown females?" Roberts questioned.

"No, nothing" the receptionist confirmed.

"Can we speak to Doctor Danielle Draper?" Ben asked sternly, pushing his way in front of Roberts.

The woman hesitated, looking past Ben to Roberts, who nodded his approval.

"I'll page her" she agreed.

The two of them stepped away from the desk and Roberts looked at Ben. "Why do you want to speak to this Doctor?"

"Because I called her to come and look at Steph" Ben replied, staring only at the door to the waiting room. "I told her I didn't want Steph here, so maybe she's taken her somewhere else."

"You called her?" Roberts questioned. "So, why didn't you just call her when you came out of the station?"

Without replying, Ben reached into his pocket and pulled out his phone, which Wishall had taken great pleasure in destroying when they arrested him.

Roberts looked at the smashed screen. "What the hell?" he muttered.

Ben shrugged. "I guess they didn't want to allow me a phone call" he stated, without humour.

As Roberts opened his mouth to comment, the door opened and Dani walked in. She was clearly startled to see Ben and the hesitation was evident in her expression but, after taking a deep breath, she composed herself and walked over to them.

"What are you doing here, Ben?" she asked. "I thought you'd been arrested."

"He had been" Roberts quickly answered, understanding the concern in her eyes. "But new information has come to light and it appears Mr Trowman may not have been involved."

Dani looked at him, uncertainly.

"I'm Detective Roberts" he continued, once more offering his badge for inspection. "We're looking for a Stephanie Lewis and wondered whether you had any information on her."

After examining the badge, Dani shook her head. "No" she replied, turning to Ben. "What's going on? I was told that you'd murdered your friend."

"The people who attacked Steph and the two girls murdered Sam" Ben stated, coldly, "and Steph's missing. Was she there when you got to my flat?"

Again, Dani shook her head. "When you rang I was having a coffee with my friend, so it took me some time to come here and pick some things up. When I got to your flat it was cordoned off and the officer at the door told me you'd gone mad and killed your friend. I asked him about Steph and all he said was that no one else was in there."

Ben only nodded in response.

"Ben, are you ok?" Dani asked, now obviously worried by Ben's demeanour.

"I'm fine" Ben replied, the matter-of-fact tone in his voice only increasing Dani's worry.

"You don't sound it" Dani pointed out, reaching out to lay her hand on his arm.

Backing away from her, Ben turned towards the door. "Let's go" he ordered Roberts. "You're taking me to Sam's."

It was Karen's mother who answered the door, her expression mirroring the surprise shown by Dani, although it quickly turned to one of concern. Behind her, from deep within the flat, Penny's screams could be clearly heard and her narrowing of the gap in the door only emphasised her caution.

"What are you doing here?" she asked, harshly.

"I want to see Karen" Ben stated, with equal harshness in his voice.

"Well, she doesn't want to see you" her mother answered. "You've got some nerve showing up here."

Ben shook his head. "I didn't kill Sam."

Incredulity spread quickly across her face. "You expect me to believe that?" she asked, looking him up and down. "We were told exactly what happened and you deserve to burn in hell for what you've done."

Again, Ben shook his head. "I want to see Karen" he repeated.

The woman moved to close the door, but Ben quickly reached out to prevent it, requiring very little force to push it open and send her staggering backwards into the hallway.

"Karen" he called out, ignoring her mother's protest.

Penny's screams increased.

"Karen" Ben called again.

Roberts moved to position himself in between Ben and Karen's mother, holding up his badge as he again repeated his introductory line. The woman looked at him for a few seconds, before glancing at the badge.

"I have reason to believe that you've been given false information" he continued.

Karen's mother shook her head. "You think I'm going to believe that? How do I know that's even a real badge?"

"You can call the station" Roberts replied, warmly. "They'll confirm my identity."

"I don't care" the woman stated. "My Karen's been through enough over the last couple of days and she doesn't want to talk to you."

Opening his mouth to answer, Roberts quickly closed it again as Karen appeared in front of them. She stared only at Ben as she walked towards them and, once directly in front of him, she swung her hand round to connect viciously with his cheek.

"I trusted you" she whispered, as her tears fell freely.

Ben only stared back at her.

"Sam trusted you" she continued, slapping him again.

"I don't believe Mr Trowman killed your partner" Roberts interjected, realising that Ben wasn't about to defend himself.

Karen looked at him, shaking her head as she spoke. "On what grounds?"

"I can't go into detail" Roberts confirmed.

"Then why should I trust you?" Karen asked.

"Karen, I didn't kill him" Ben insisted, the wobble in his voice finally portraying the emotion that'd been so glaringly absent throughout the morning.

Looking back to him, Karen again shook her head. "They told me what happened" she sobbed. "They told me that you'd raped and killed those two poor girls."

Ben shook his head. "I didn't" he stated, somewhat lamely. "You know me. You know I wouldn't do that."

"Then why did they arrest you?" Karen cried.

"Because they want to pin all this on me" Ben replied.

Again, Karen shook her head in doubt. "But why you? What possible reason could they have?"

Now Ben looked at Roberts, who let out a long sigh before speaking. "I can't go into detail" he repeated.

More tears fell as Karen looked between them both and the uncertainty in her eyes increased as she backed away from Ben. "I don't know" she stammered. "I don't know what to believe any more."

"I think that's enough of this for now" Karen's mother stated, stepping protectively in front of her daughter. "You need to leave."

"Steph's missing" Ben exclaimed. "She was with Sam at my flat and, when I got there, she was gone."

The news seemed only to increase Karen's uncertainty. "What do you mean, she's missing?" she asked.

"They've taken her, I'm sure of it" Ben explained.

"Who've taken her?"

"The people who murdered Sam."

Covering her face with her hands, Karen broke down completely and, when she finally looked back at him, Ben saw the absolute confusion in her eyes. "Get out" she snapped, in between sobs.

Ben took a breath to speak but, before he could say anything, Karen turned and walked quickly back towards their living room. Her mother raised her hands to his chest and tried to push him back towards the front door.

"You need to go" she hissed.

Ben remained still against the force, so her mother pushed harder.

"I said go!" she yelled.

Roberts, realising no good would come of this, grabbed Ben by the arm and gently tugged him away. "Come on" he urged.

Reluctantly, after taking a moment to stare towards the living room, Ben backed away and, as they exited to the outside hallway, Karen's mother slammed the door in their faces.

"We'll sort this" Roberts confirmed, as he started walking towards the stairs. "What those two have done can be reversed."

No response came from Ben, so he turned to look at him and saw that he'd slumped to his knees in front of the door, with his head buried in his hands and his body shaking violently as he cried.

She was sitting on a chair in a small storage room, hidden deep within the confines of the club's headquarters, but the blindfold that'd been put in place at the flat prevented her from knowing that and the gag in her mouth stopped her from asking any questions. Her ankles were tied to the legs of the chair, her arms were secured tightly behind her back and she was still dressed only in the t-shirt Ben had used to replace her soiled clothing and the underwear he'd had the decency to leave in place.

Her body shook with fear, an abject terror that seemed to spread from the very core of her soul and she fought desperately to gain some semblance of understanding as to what was happening. Her mind pictured the sight of Sam's body hitting the floor, of the blood that gushed from his throat, and she thought of Ben getting home and finding his friend lying there.

More of her tears filled the already saturated blindfold before finding their way through the material and down her cheeks as she futilely struggled against her bonds. When she managed no movement, she allowed her head to drop forward as her heartache increased and her shoulders jerked violently under the force of her sobbing.

Muffled voices began to filter in through the silence and, at the sound of the door being opened, Steph lifted her head and tried to plead with whoever was there, but the gag was too tight for her to form any lucid words. She sensed someone approaching and, when she felt her bonds being checked, she froze as her blood ran cold.

"I don't see why we can't just kill her" one of the voices stated, seemingly right next to her ear.

"That's because you're thick as pig-shit" another voice, which she recognised as being Ethan, replied.

"Well, can't we at least have some more fun with her?" the unknown voice asked, as fingers were traced along her cheek and her head was turned, presumably to face the person speaking.

Involuntarily, Steph tried to plead once again, but she was silenced by a swift and painful slap across her face.

"Maybe later" Ethan answered, "but right now, we've got work to do."

"Ah, can't I just put that pretty mouth to use?" the unknown voice whined, running his fingers across her lips. "It'll only take a few minutes for me to pump my shit down her throat."

The question went unanswered as Ethan's phone rang.

"You're fuckin' shittin' me!" he exclaimed, after hearing what the caller had to say. "Jesus fuckin' Christ, you pricks are walking a fine fuckin' line! I'll fuckin' sort it out, shall I?"

"What is it?" the unknown voice asked.

"I swear that cunt's got some kind of guardian fuckin' angel" Ethan snapped in reply. "He's been fuckin' released by some piece of shit, too fuckin' nosey for his own good detective."

"What? How?"

"Crowther and Wishall fucked up royally" Ethan replied, angrily. "Go grab Jimmy, we're gonna put an end to this mother fucker."

Steph heard the door lock click into place as the two men left the room and a fresh wave of anguish flooded through her as she realised they could only have been talking about Ben.

The hammering on the door was incessant, beating its way through the drunken haze of Ben's mind, despite his determination to ignore it. Taking a final swig from the bottle in his hand, the second he'd opened in just over an hour, he threw it across the room and smiled as it smashed against the wood, bringing further knocking from the unwanted visitor.

"Fuck off!" he yelled, fumbling for another bottle.

Predictably, another knock came in response.

Closing his eyes, he tried to block out the intrusion but, as it continued, his anger quickly began to rise. He pushed himself upright on the settee and reached for another bottle from the table, unscrewing the cap and taking a long swig as he looked across at the door.

"Fuck off!" he repeated, louder this time.

The hammering continued, increasing in its aggression.

Shaking his head, Ben tried to stand up, immediately falling forward and sprawling across the table, dropping the bottle on the floor. Its contents spilled out on to the carpet as he again attempted to stand upright, momentarily succeeding until the room started to spin and he staggered forward, only finding balance when he was able to reach out and place a hand on the wall.

More knocking sounded from the door.

"I'm fuckin' coming" he slurred, whilst waiting for his vision to steady itself.

Using the wall to keep him on his feet, he moved slowly towards the door and it took several attempts for him to take a hold of the handle. Eventually, he managed to get a firm grasp and he opened the door, which was immediately forced from the other side, sending him staggering backwards until he landed heavily on the floor.

With his vision further blurred by the bang he'd taken to his head, Ben couldn't make out what was happening, but he felt hands roughly pick him up and drag him through the flat, towards the bathroom. He tried to talk, to challenge what was going on, but all that came out of his mouth was a torrent of vomit and, before he could gain any composure, he was being thrown into his bathtub.

"Fuckin' get off me!" he yelled, although the words were practically indecipherable.

"Hold him down" he heard, as his hands were pulled, extending his arms above his head.

A further wave of nausea flooded through him and he vomited again, choking when he was unable to move his head and clear his throat.

"Fuckin' disgusting!" he heard exclaimed, by someone who was out of his field of vision. "Get this done, quick."

"I'm fuckin' doin' it!" came another voice, from just above Ben's head.

With the alcohol acting as an anaesthetic, Ben didn't feel the blade of the knife as it sliced into his wrists and, already on the verge of unconsciousness, it took only a few moments for his eyes to close.

Dani hesitated as she reached out to knock on the door, wondering whether she should be doing this. Realistically, she hardly knew the guy, so turning up at his flat unannounced seemed to be somewhat inappropriate. Then again, she thought, the man had just lost his best friend and, from what was being said earlier, another of his friends was missing, so who else did he have?

With little in the way of confidence, she knocked on the wood of the door, automatically taking a step back in readiness for the answer, but none came. Maybe he wasn't here, she guessed. But where else would he be? She'd already been to the bar and they'd said he hadn't been seen. Maybe he was with someone else? Maybe he was with his friend's family? She decided to try one more time and then, when there was still no answer, she turned to walk away, figuring that, if he was with his friend's family, then it wasn't right to disturb them.

Before she took a step, something stopped her, a thought that seemed to grow rapidly from deep inside her mind. She didn't want to go, did she? For all she'd tried to tell herself that he was nothing more than someone she'd met at work, that was all just a smokescreen, wasn't it? The fact was that she hadn't stopped thinking about the guy since they'd first spoken in her office, she'd been enamoured by him and those feelings had only increased since then.

Realising there was no way she could just leave him to be by himself, she pulled out her phone and selected his number from the directory. Maybe he was with people who cared, she figured, whilst pressing the call button and raising the phone to her ear, but maybe he wasn't? Maybe he was alone and, right now, a friendly voice would be more than welcomed?

It took a moment for the call to connect and, when it did, it went straight to voicemail. She looked towards his front door as she hesitated in leaving a message, not knowing what to say.

"Hi, Ben, it's Dani" she mumbled, her heart racing a little. "I just, erm . . . I just wanted to see if you were ok after everything that happened. It probably sounds stupid, but I'm outside your flat and I'm guessing you're not here . . ."

Her words stumbled as a door opened along the corridor and she looked over in time to see an elderly woman walking out of her flat.

"Excuse me" she said, quickly cancelling the call. "I'm looking for Ben Trowman and I wondered if you'd seen him at all today?"

The woman looked at her for a few seconds, before shaking her head. "No, but I've heard him" she answered, a little angrily. "He was making a right racket, right while I was trying to watch my television programmes."

"When was that?" Dani questioned, as her concern increased.

"Oh, no more than ten minutes ago. I banged on the wall, but he didn't stop with the noise. He's normally so quiet, as well."

"What sort of noise was it?"

"I don't know" the woman shrugged. "It was lots of banging and crashing, like he was throwing the place around. And there was so much shouting . . ."

Cutting her off, Dani again banged on the door.

"Don't you start all that nonsense now, too" the woman scolded.

"Please" Dani implored. "I think he's in trouble. Do you have a spare key, or do you know if anyone else might?"

"I do" the woman answered.

"Then can you please let me in?" Dani urged.

Staring at her, the woman considered the request for a few seconds. "I don't know who you are" she eventually answered. "I don't think I should . . ."

Again, Dani cut her off. "Please just let me in" she snapped.

Slowly, the woman's expression began to mirror the concern Dani was showing. "Ok" she reluctantly agreed. "But I'm coming in with you. I'm not having a stranger walk around the man's home, all alone and whatnot."

With that, she went back inside her flat and emerged a moment later with the key. She unlocked the door and Dani quickly followed her in.

"Ben?" Dani called out uncertainly, looking at the broken glass on the floor and the empty bottles on the table.

When there was no answer his neighbour tried calling out his name, whilst Dani walked further into the living room, towards the open door to the bedroom. She saw the bed was empty so continued round to the kitchen and then, finding nothing in there, she moved on to the bathroom, where the note stuck to the door sent her stomach into a tailspin.

Ripping the paper down, she flung the door open and rushed in, screaming for his neighbour to call an ambulance.

Chapter 27

"They fuckin' saw us comin'!" Tommo exclaimed, after they'd practically stumbled in through the door. "I fuckin' told you it was the wrong call, but you wouldn't fuckin' listen!"

"Calm down" Billy ordered, although there was no stopping his friend's rage.

"And you!" Tommo continued, rounding on Ruckus, who stood at the side of the room, sporting an inane grin. "You're a fuckin' twisted son of a bitch! Where the fuck were you when it all kicked off?"

Ruckus merely continued to grin, raising Tommo's anger by several degrees.

"Will you fuckin' answer me?" Tommo hissed, striding across to stand immediately in front of the boy.

"You'd better back off outta my face" Ruckus muttered.

"Fuck you, you piece of shit!" Tommo hissed.

With seemingly the slightest of movement, Ruckus reached up and pushed Tommo away from him. After staggering backwards, Tommo regained his balance and rushed forward, but Ruckus was ready and timed the swing of his arm perfectly to plant his fist into Tommo's jaw, sending him sprawling to the side.

"You wanna try that again?" Ruckus chuckled, standing over the man.

Scrambling to his feet, Tommo initially appeared as though he wanted to accept the challenge, but thought better of it when he saw Ruckus reach to his belt and unsheathe the knife he always carried. Looking around the room, he took in the faces of the few remaining club members who'd survived the attack on the Minions, finishing up staring at Billy.

"Will you start actin' like our fuckin' President?" he urged.

"Yeah, Billy" Ruckus laughed. "Will you?"

Lost for words, Billy only stared back helplessly.

Shaking his head, Tommo removed his Cut and threw it across the room at him.

"Fuck you!" he exclaimed. "I'm not dealin' with this shit anymore!"

Still Billy struggled to reply, as Tommo turned and strode towards the door. Ruckus, seeing what was happening, rushed to get there first and held the door open to wave the man through.

"See ya 'round" he smiled, as Tommo walked past him.

"Go fuck yourself!" Tommo muttered.

As it had done so many times since Billy had left Tommo's house, the memory ended with the sound of the door being slammed shut and instantly started again, bringing with it the questions that seemed to tear at his soul. Why hadn't he spoken up? Why hadn't he shown the balls to stand up for his friend and retain control of his club?

His anger flared momentarily, causing his heart to race, and he stumbled as he walked, although he wasn't drunk.

He hadn't had any alcohol for days and, for the first time in years, his mind was free of the haze on which he'd been so reliant. The problem was that, no matter how clearly he could now think, he just couldn't find a way of hitting The Sons.

Maybe just a couple of beers would help him to work it out, he figured, as he walked into The Skinning Pit.

Chapter 28

"Dani" Emily whispered, gently nudging her friend awake.

Opening her eyes slowly, Dani looked confused for a few moments as her mind adjusted to the situation.

"Hi" was all she eventually said in reply, a tired smile creeping on to her lips.

"I've just come in and Jan said you were in here" Emily explained. "Have you been here all night?"

With a nod, Dani shifted in the chair and tossed the blanket she'd used to the floor as she nodded confirmation.

"Christ" Emily sighed, glancing over to where Ben lay peacefully asleep in the bed. "What happened?"

A shrug was all Dani gave in response.

"Jan said he'd tried to commit suicide?" Emily continued, with a slow shake of her head. "She said he'd slit his wrists?"

"Apparently so" Dani replied, although her lack of conviction was noted instantly by Emily.

"You don't think he did?" she asked.

Dani shrugged again. "I don't know" she answered.

Looking at the bandages on Ben's wrists, Emily again shook her head. "Well, who found him?"

"I did" Dani said. "When he came in here yesterday, he didn't seem himself and I was worried about him after everything he's been through, so I went to see him when I finished my shift. It's a long story, but his neighbour let me in and I found him lying in his bath."

"Christ" Emily sighed again. "Had he left a note or anything like that?"

"No" Dani stated, firmly.

Seemingly taken aback by her friend's sudden abruptness, Emily paused for a moment. "Then what do you think happened?" she asked. "I mean, like you say, he's been through a lot and it'd be understandable if it was too much for him to handle by himself."

"So you're determined to believe he did try to kill himself?" Dani snapped, now rising from her seat. "Is that what you're saying?"

"Whoa" Emily exclaimed. "I'm just saying that, whilst you've spoken to him a few times, you don't know him that well. You can't really say how he'd react to all of this. I mean, he's being investigated by the police for what happened to the two girls, which can't be without reason, and his best friend has been murdered, something for which, as I understand it, he's also being investigated. That's a lot for someone to deal with, especially if they're not completely innocent."

Dani's anger grew and she couldn't hide it from her voice. "You think he did it!"

"I'm not saying that" Emily replied curtly, now becoming angry herself. "But you don't know the guy and you don't know what he's capable of."

"I know he was in my office with me when the first girl was poisoned."

"That doesn't mean he couldn't have been involved."

"You've changed your tune" Dani pointed out. "It was only a couple of days ago that you were all for me getting involved with the man."

"That was before" Emily answered.

"Before what?"

"Before you found him lying in a pool of his own blood!"

As the argument reached its crescendo, Ben stirred in the bed, causing both of them to forget what they were about to say as they looked over to him. With a frustrated shake of her head, Dani pushed past Emily and moved quickly to be by his side as he fully awoke.

The blindfold meant the darkness was absolute, having become an all-consuming force in the face of which her mind was struggling to cope. For how long she'd been there, she had no idea. It could've been hours, days or even weeks. Even the simple understanding as to whether her eyes were open or closed had long since left her and whether she'd actually slept at some point was a complete mystery. The only thing she was sure of was that her head was lolling forward and that was only down to the pull she felt in the muscles at the back of her neck.

Moving tentatively in the chair, Steph tried to find a position in which she might receive some relief from the constant agony of the ties on her wrists, but they were too tight for that. Involuntarily, she let out a cry of pain as they seemed to cut further into her skin and a sob escaped her as her thoughts drifted, as they'd done so many times, back to Ben.

She pictured his face, the smile she now knew to mean so much more than she'd ever thought, and the warmth she'd always found when she looked into his eyes. She imagined the soft tones of his voice, especially when she'd been having a rough time, and she remembered how kind and caring he'd always been to her. Then her mind drifted to the way she'd treated him, the way she'd dismissed him without so much as a second thought, and the fact that she'd had no intention of calling him when they'd stood outside her house with Ethan watching on.

That was the last thing she would remember of him. Until she met whatever fate was coming to her at the hands of these monsters; that was the last contact she would know with a man who did nothing but love her and was now, based on the conversation she'd overheard, dead.

Racked with despair, her body jerked violently as fresh tears spilled into the blindfold and she welcomed the fresh pain in her wrists. She deserved it, she thought; she deserved to feel agony for her actions and whatever was in store for her now, she realised, it was an anguish she deserved to bear.

The sound of the door opening cut into her thoughts and, automatically, she lifted her head, although there was no way of knowing who was there. She felt hands on her cheek, the fingers running round to the back of her head, where they unfastened the gag in order to feed her.

Hungrily, she bit into the bread that was pushed against her lips, barely chewing before swallowing in her haste for nourishment. Then she gulped greedily at the glass of water that was offered to her, savouring the cooling feeling of the liquid as it went down her throat.

Quickly, the gag was replaced and the fingers returned to her cheek, checking it was tight enough to ensure it wouldn't be spat out at any time and then they traced a line down her chin. She flinched as they stroked down and briefly circled her throat, closing with just enough force to cause her discomfort, before they continued their journey.

As they slipped over the neck-line of the t-shirt and circled her breast, she tried desperately to block out what was happening, but a firm pull on her nipple brought her right back to the moment. She heard the assailant grunt as he cupped her, stroking his palm over her before squeezing hard on her flesh.

"Fuck" the man hissed, as a voice from outside the door shouted through for him to hurry up.

"You'll have to wait a bit longer for me" he whispered to her, giving a final squeeze before the hand left her body.

Roberts listened intently as Ben tried to recount the attack, pausing for long periods at a time as his memory faltered. Eventually though, he managed to paint a clear enough picture for the detective to understand both what had happened and the likely reason why.

"You were right to call me" he muttered, sitting back in his seat and glancing towards both Ben and Dani before studying the suicide note Dani had handed to him when he'd arrived. "There's no doubt about it, this has to have been designed to put an end to the investigation."

Neither Ben nor Dani replied.

"Have you told anyone about this?" he asked, briefly gesturing towards the note.

"No" Dani replied, with a slight shake of her head.

"What about the neighbour?" Roberts questioned.

Again, Dani shook her head. "I made sure it was down before she had the chance to follow me."

Roberts nodded his acknowledgement. "I think it's best you don't go back to your place" he stated, looking at Ben. "They probably won't attempt anything more there and there's a chance they don't even know you survived at the moment, but it's better to play on the safe side of this for now. Have you got anywhere else you can go?"

Ben thought about that for a moment, about the fact that he would normally have been able to stay with Steph or with Sam and Karen and he felt his heart lurch. "No" he confirmed, stubbornly fighting back the sudden emptiness that threatened to engulf him.

"You can stay at mine" Dani stated immediately, the quickness of her response bringing with it a slightly embarrassed smile.

Both Ben and Roberts looked at her, concern evident in their expressions.

"Seriously" she encouraged, a little more composedly this time. "You've nowhere else to stay and there's no reason anyone would look for you there."

Roberts displayed his approval of the plan, but Ben still held some trepidation in his eyes.

"I can't ask you to do that" he stated.

"You're not asking" Dani argued. "Besides, the only way you're going to be able to check out of here tonight is if I can keep an eye on you. Otherwise, you'll have to stay here."

"You can't stay here" Roberts pointed out. "If they got to the first girl in here, then they can damn sure get to you too and, once they find out you're still alive, it wouldn't surprise me if they tried to rectify that."

"Then it's settled" Dani exclaimed, now through a broad smile. "You're staying at mine and there'll be no arguing about it."

Despite knowing that he was fighting a losing battle Ben still wanted to protest, but he was prevented from saying anything more as Crowther and Wishall stormed in through the door, with Emily following closely behind.

"I told you to knock before coming in here" she berated, although her words were disregarded by the two detectives.

"This is our case" Crowther hissed, glaring at Roberts. "What the hell are you doing here?"

Roberts merely smiled in reply.

"I asked what you were doing in here!" Crowther demanded.

Standing to face him, Roberts continued to smile. "What's this got to do with your case?" he asked.

Crowther hesitated, grimacing as he considered the question. "He's our main suspect and he should still be in our custody" he eventually stated, clearly attempting to turn the conversation against Roberts.

"He was in your custody when Sam was killed" Roberts replied immediately, thoroughly enjoying the way Crowther was beginning to squirm. "So how does that make him a main suspect?"

"Well" Crowther rallied. "If he's so innocent, then why'd he try to kill himself?"

"Who said he tried to kill himself?" Roberts smiled.

Now visibly wilting, Crowther glanced round at Wishall and then back to Roberts. "What else would you call him slitting his wrists?" he practically mumbled.

"Isn't finding that answer the job of the investigating detectives?" Roberts questioned.

"Enough of this!" Emily snapped, stepping in between the two men. "This isn't the time or the place to have petty arguments. You all need to leave."

Both Crowther and Roberts looked at her.

"You're right" Roberts agreed, turning towards Ben. "I'm sorry for this" he smiled.

"Like I give a fuck" Ben replied, with a shrug of his shoulders.

Without waiting for any further comment from the men, Emily guided the three detectives towards the door. Crowther and Wishall walked through first and Roberts, pausing for just a moment, leaned towards Dani.

"Get him out of here" he whispered, before leaving the room. "With those two knowing he's still alive, it won't be long before other people are told about it."

Closing the door behind them, Emily shot a worried glance towards both Dani and Ben.

"What did he mean by that?" she asked.

"He doesn't think it's safe for me to stay here" Ben answered, candidly.

The worry in Emily's expression increased. "Why wouldn't it be safe for you here?"

Again, Ben shrugged.

"It's ok" Dani replied. "Ben's ok to leave anyway, so I've said he can stay at mine for a few days, whilst he gets himself sorted."

Grabbing Dani by the arm, Emily dragged her friend to the door and out into the corridor.

"What do you mean, he can stay at yours?" she asked, once she was sure no one was close enough to overhear. "Is that a good idea?"

"Why wouldn't it be?" Dani questioned.

"Look" Emily sighed, trying her best to display a warm smile. "I can see you like this guy, that much is obvious, but I just think there's a lot going on with him at the moment and letting him stay at yours is basically asking for you to become involved."

"I'm already involved" Dani pointed out. "I can't just leave him by himself now."

Emily shook her head. "He's not your responsibility and, whatever's going on, I don't want to see you become embroiled in anything that could hurt you."

"Of course I'm not going to get hurt" Dani smiled. "All I'm doing is letting him stay over for a couple of nights."

"Don't do it!" Emily exclaimed with genuine panic in her voice, as Dani turned to go back into the room.

"It'll be fine" Dani tried to reassure her.

Sarah placed the drink on the bar in front of him, although the gesture went unnoticed as he continued to stare straight ahead. Waving her hand in front of his face, she finally drew some reaction and Lee looked up at her.

"Why don't you go home?" she asked.

"What's the point?" he lamented.

Letting out a sigh, Sarah looked back at him for a few seconds before answering. "I don't really know" she admitted. "I just thought you could get your head down for a bit? You've hardly slept in days."

Lee shook his head. "I doubt it'll do any good. I just keep picturing him hanging there."

"Well that's bound to happen. You need to let the grief out before things get easier to deal with."

Sorrow's Requiem

"I'm not grieving!" Lee snapped. "I'm not sad that the man's dead, I'm fucked off that he's brought all this on us. Things were good, we were runnin' nice and smooth, until he decided he wanted more and brought everything down."

"But why does everything have to stop now?" she asked.

Staring at her, Lee once more shook his head but this time it was in a clear display of incredulity at the stupidity of the question.

"Fuck you" Sarah cursed. "I'm just trying to help."

Immediately, Lee realised what he'd done. "I'm sorry" he all but whispered. "I don't mean to take it out on you. I just can't believe it's all gone."

"Well, fuck you anyway" she replied, through a smile that demonstrated her understanding.

Returning the smile, Lee turned his attention to his drink as Alex approached the bar. Having noticed him walking across the room, Sarah had already set about pouring his usual beverage.

"Here you go" she smiled, placing the glass in front of him as he joined Lee at the bar.

"Well?" Lee asked, without looking at him. "How many are left?"

Taking a deep breath before answering, Alex released a long sigh. "Six" he replied. "And that's including you and me."

"Christ" Lee muttered.

"So, what now?" Alex questioned.

Lee shrugged. "I guess we go back to the clubhouse tomorrow and see if we can salvage anything."

"But what about the club?"

"What club?" Lee shrugged.

Alex looked at him for a few seconds, as though trying to figure out if he was serious. "You can't mean that" he eventually stated. "We've still got this place and none of the lads want out."

No reply came from Lee.

"Seriously" Alex continued. "We can start again. We'll find ourselves another clubhouse but, until then, we can stay here and there's no one who'll argue with you taking Michael's place."

Still no reply was forthcoming, so Alex just stared at Lee whilst he awaited an answer.

"We'll see" Lee eventually mumbled.

"You are fuckin' shittin' me!" Ethan exclaimed, pulling the phone away from his ear and looking at it for a few seconds before returning it to its original position. "Tell me you're shittin' me!"

He listened to the reply, before muttering a few more obscenities and putting the phone away.

"What is it?" Jimmy asked.

"He's fuckin' survived" Ethan replied, his tone clearly demonstrating his disbelief. "The mother fucker's still alive!"

"You're kidding?" Jimmy muttered, unnecessarily. "But he was pretty much dead when we left him. What the fuck happened?"

Ethan rubbed his eyes in frustration. "It seems we didn't wait long enough" he replied. "That bitch doctor turned up after we'd gone and found him. Crowther said that there'd been no mention of the suicide note either, so she must've binned it before anyone found it."

"Fuck!" Jimmy exclaimed. "So, where is he now?"

"He's at the hospital, but I don't think he'll be there for long and there's no way he'll go home. Crowther and Wishall are watching to see if he leaves but I'm fuckin' sick of that pair fuckin' things up. Get your ass over there and follow him when he leaves. I wanna know exactly where he goes."

"You want me to kill him now?"

"No. Just follow him. We still need him to take the fall and I've got an idea. Call me when you know where he's staying and don't take your eyes off the cunt."

Nodding, Jimmy hurried out of the room, leaving Ethan alone with Touchy.

"What about the bitch?" Touchy questioned. "Can we fuck her up yet?"

"Jesus Christ" Ethan exclaimed. "You need to pull your cock in and wake up. We still might need her, so don't you go fuckin' with her."

Touchy stared at him. "Ruckus 'ain't gonna like this."

"Ruckus don't need to know about this!" Ethan spat in reply. "I fuckin' mean it. Keep your fuckin' mouth shut and this'll all be sorted out. We don't need 'im fuckin' this up now."

Still, Touchy stared at him. "This 'ain't right, man" he muttered. "I 'ain't gonna keep 'im in the dark."

"Just give me this" Ethan urged. "Let me handle it and then you can do whatever the fuck you want to Steph when it's all over."

Chapter 29

They watched intently through the van's windscreen, as they had done for a couple of hours, waiting for the moment to arrive. Any conversation had long since died down, being replaced with boredom and frustration as time had drawn on, yet none of the men had the desire to voice the suggestion that there might be another way to do this, especially having seen the look in their Vice-President's eyes.

"You sure he's gonna be alone at some point?" Touchy asked, finally giving voice to the question that'd been burning on all their minds for some time. "Or are we gonna have to deal with that doctor bitch as well?"

Ethan continued to stare at the entrance to the building as he replied. "She'll be going out to work soon."

"Well, why don't we just take her out anyway? Even if we do manage to pin all this on the prick, you know she'll argue the guy's innocent and that'll just cause us more problems."

"More bodies won't make this any easier" Ethan pointed out, still without looking at him.

"But her body might add to the case against him. It must be known that he's staying there, so it wouldn't be hard to believe that he's killed her as well?"

Having remained silent for a while longer, Ethan finally provided a response. "We can handle the Doctor" he stated, making it clear that this would be the final word on the subject. "Nothing is to happen to her, do you understand?"

In truth, Touchy didn't understand, but he recognised the tone in the man's voice so he kept any further thoughts to himself and turned his attention back to the entrance of the building. Silence returned to the van and remained for a while longer, until they saw the door open and a woman walk out.

"Is that her?" he asked, sarcastically.

Ethan stared, craning his neck a little in order to get a better view. "I 'ain't sure" he answered. "I can't tell from here."

"Well how the fuck are we gonna know when she's gone if you don't know what the bitch looks like?" Touchy mumbled.

Leaning forward from where he sat in the back of the van, Jimmy took a look. "It 'ain't her" he answered.

"And how the fuck would you know?" Touchy hissed.

"I fuckin' followed them here, didn't I? What the fuck is your problem?" Jimmy replied.

"My problem is that this is all bullshit! We're fuckin' about, tryin' to set this guy up, and all that's happenin' is he's wormin' his way out of everythin' and leaving us lookin' like pricks. We should just fuckin' wipe him, the doctor and the bitch back at our place out and be done with it all!"

"Just fuckin' kill 'em? That's your fuckin' solution to all this?" Ethan questioned.

"It's always worked before!"

"And we've had brothers behind bars before!"

"So? That's all part of the life."

"Maybe twenty years ago" Ethan exclaimed. "But it's about fuckin' time we started thinking clearer. We do this right and none of us needs to go down."

"Ah, I get it" Touchy smiled, viciously. "You're fuckin' scared, 'ain't you?"

"You wanna step out of this van and see how scared I am?" Ethan replied.

"For fuck's sake" Jimmy sighed. "Will you two shut the fuck up? I dunno why you're fuckin' about like this and I don't fuckin' care but, if we're gonna do this, then havin' you two smackin' the shit out of each other 'ain't exactly gonna go unnoticed, is it?"

The two men glared at each other in silence for a few seconds, before Ethan nodded and turned his attention back to the apartment building. Touchy's stare lingered for a few seconds longer and he gave a shake of his head before he too turned to look out of the windscreen.

Ben looked up as Dani walked into the living room and noticed the slight surprise in her expression as she saw him sitting there, fully dressed and seemingly ready to leave.

"You're awake?" she exclaimed. "I thought you'd be dead to the world."

"I couldn't sleep" he replied.

"I told you to take the bed. I'd have been fine on the settee."

"I wasn't uncomfortable" he declared, rising to his feet.

Looking quizzically at him, Dani was still a little taken aback by the obvious change in his personality, by the bluntness that'd been so prevalent since he'd arrived at the hospital a couple of days before. "Where do you think you're going?" she questioned.

"You said you wanted to keep an eye on me overnight" he answered. "Well, you have, and now I'll go."

"And where exactly are you going to go?"

Ben shrugged. "I'll find somewhere."

"Or you'll stay here."

"No" Ben stated, firmly.

"Yes" Dani smiled, although her tone was equally as firm. "Now sit down and I'll make us some coffee."

Ignoring her, Ben moved towards the door, until she quickly blocked his path.

"I said sit down" she insisted, still maintaining the smile, although it was now faltering slightly.

"You have to go to work" he replied.

Dani shook her head. "I'm not going in today."

"Yes you are" he snapped.

"No, I'm not"

Staring at her, Ben stubbornly remained rooted to the spot. "Well that's up to you" he finally said. "I'm out of here."

"Please don't leave" she implored. "There's people out to get you and I don't want to see you hurt any more than you have been."

"Let them fucking come for me then" he hissed. "I don't give a fuck any more."

"But I do."

"Well that's fine" he replied. "But I don't need you to."

Helplessly, Dani watched as he moved around her and quickly walked through the door, without so much as a glance back to her as he pulled it shut behind him.

"What the fuck?" Jimmy exclaimed, as they saw Ben walk out of the entrance. "Why's he leavin'?"

"I don't give a fuck" Ethan replied, starting the engine and slowly pulling out from their parking space.

Cautiously, he rolled along the road, expecting Ben to notice their approach and readying himself to speed up if the man started to run, but there was no sign of him being aware of any danger as he continued to stroll nonchalantly along the pavement. Jimmy slid open the van's side door and the men in the back braced themselves as they drew near.

Gunning the engine, Ethan covered the last few yards at speed and screeched to a halt when they drew alongside. Finally turning to see what was happening, Ben stopped in his tracks and surprised them by merely watching on with an almost casual indifference as they jumped out and ran up to him. He put up no fight at all as they grabbed and pulled him into the back of the van.

Having been thrown from the van, Ben hit the ground hard and lay still as the men quickly surrounded him. He felt hands grab a firm hold of his arms and he didn't resist as he was dragged along the floor.

"We're takin' him in there?" he heard someone ask incredulously. "The place don't fuckin' look safe?"

"Stop bein' such a pussy!" came the response.

"I'm just sayin' . . ."

"Fuck off!"

Opening his eyes, Ben looked to where he was being taken and saw the burnt-out shell of a building. Ahead of him, he saw Ethan kick open the front door, which had previously been boarded up, and he closed his eyes again as he was pulled painfully over the step and into the wreckage."

"So, where are we doing this?" another voice questioned.

"More to the point, why the fuck are we doing this?"

"Jesus fuckin' Christ!" Ethan exclaimed. "Will you shut the fuck up? I've already told you, we're doin' this to give that pair of useless fucks something they can use. They find him here, link him to the pricks we wasted and then, even if they can't fight off the suggestion that it's all gang-related, they can at least point it to them and we're in the clear."

"And you think that'll work?"

"It's better than leaving a trail of fuckin' corpses!"

"Not from where I'm standin' it's not!"

"Will you two cut it the fuck out? Let's just get this shit done and get the fuck out of here. I swear this place is about to collapse."

At that, Ben tried to take another look at where they'd brought him, but he was dropped to the ground before he had the chance to see anything and a boot was driven painfully into his ribs.

"Here'll do" he heard muttered, as more blows were delivered.

The merciless beating continued and Ben remained silent as his pain increased until, finally, unconsciousness crept in.

"Who the hell is that?" Sarah exclaimed, as Lee and Alex struggled through the door carrying a prone body between them.

"That's what we're gonna find out" Lee answered, as they put the man down in a chair. "Get him tied up, I don't wanna take any chances."

Nodding, Alex set off to find something to secure him with and Lee walked over to the desk at which Sarah had been sat, doing the strip club's books.

"Make sure no one comes in here" he stated, without taking his eyes off the man.

"Why would anyone come in here?" Sarah asked, still stunned by their entrance.

"Just make sure they don't" Lee replied, bluntly.

If Sarah was angered by his tone she didn't show it, knowing better than to argue in a situation like this. A simple nod was the only gesture she gave as she stood up, although she hesitated before leaving the room.

"Who is that?" she asked again.

Lee didn't answer straight away and, for a second, it seemed he wouldn't.

"We found him bein' beaten senseless by a few members of The Sons at the clubhouse, but we managed to drive them off before they killed the bastard" he finally replied.

"But why would they do that to him? And why there?"

"I dunno" he shrugged, "but it's something we need to find out."

Hesitating again, Sarah clearly didn't want to ask her next question, yet she couldn't stop herself. "Do you think it's got something to do with what Michael was involved in?"

Another shrug came from Lee. "I dunno" he again answered. "I guess it could be."

"But why would they take him to our old clubhouse to do him over?"

Once more Lee shrugged but, this time, he didn't hazard any guess as Alex walked back into the office.

"I could only find this" he announced, holding up a roll of Duct Tape. "It'll do for now."

Looking over at Sarah, Lee made it abundantly clear that it was time for her to leave the room and she didn't argue as Alex set about securing the man in the chair. Once he was done and Sarah was gone, Lee walked over to the man and slapped him hard across the cheek, causing him to emit a groan but failing to wake him. He tried again, yet there was still no conscious response, and he was about to try for a third time when Alex stopped him.

"Use this" he suggested, handing him the glass of water Sarah had been drinking at the desk.

Nodding, Lee threw the liquid into the man's face and, finally, he showed some semblance of life. Slowly coming to his senses, he looked around the room and struggled against his binds as confusion painted itself clearly across his face, before the pain set in and he closed his eyes.

"Who are you?" Lee demanded.

The man didn't answer.

"I asked, who are you?" Lee tried again, more forcibly this time.

"Who the fuck are you?" the man hissed.

Stepping forward, Lee grabbed a hold of the man's jaw and turned his head up to face him. "You don't get to ask any questions" he stated. "Not when I just saved your ass. Now, I wanna know who the fuck you are and why the fuck The Sons were trying to kill you in what's left of our old clubhouse, so start fuckin' talkin'."

Now laughing, the man shook his head. "I didn't even know it was the fuckin' Sons who did that to me" he chuckled, "so you're shit outta luck if you think I'm gonna be able to give you anything."

"Well, who the fuck are you then?"

"I'm fuckin' no one" the man smiled, sardonically.

With a frustrated sigh, Lee looked to Alex for some suggestion as to what they should do next, but Alex merely shrugged his shoulders.

"Look" Lee muttered, as he turned his attention back to the man. "The Sons have wiped out pretty much all of my fuckin' club. They've burned down our clubhouse and killed some of my closest friends. We went back to see what we can salvage and we found you, bein' beaten shitless by the wankers. That tells me you've got somethin' to do with The Sons or you've got somethin' to do with what happened to us, either way, I need you to start talkin' and you 'ain't gettin' outta here until you do."

Despite his bonds, the man managed to shrug as he started to laugh.

"What's so fuckin' funny?" Lee snapped.

The man shook his head as he continued to laugh, so Lee stepped forward and delivered another slap, right to the bruising under the man's eye. The man flinched slightly, but seemed to immediately shrug off any pain the blow might have caused.

"Jesus fuckin' Christ!" Lee exclaimed.

"Start fuckin' talkin', you piece of shit!" Alex yelled.

"Fuck you" the man replied, as he calmly pulled his wrists apart, easily breaking the temporary bonds, and jumped up from the chair. "You wanna fuckin' stop me leaving, then you're welcome to fuckin' try."

Both Lee and Alex defensively jumped back and took in the size of the man as he towered before them.

"Whoa!" Alex mumbled, under his breath.

"Calm down" Lee urged. "There's no need for anything stupid to happen."

"Other than the fact you slapped me about?" the man asked. "You wanna go again?"

"I'm sorry" Lee replied. "Things are fucked up. I didn't know what to do."

The man stared at him for a few seconds. "Well, you can either get the fuck outta my way, or you can stand there and wait for me to beat the piss outta you both?" he suggested, stepping aggressively towards Lee, with his fists ready to swing.

"Please" Lee urged, backing away. "We're fucked up here and all I know is that you're somehow connected to the people who did this to us."

"You don't know the meaning of fucked up" the man replied, with a slow shake of his head.

"Then fuckin' explain it to us" Alex suggested.

Silence fell between them as the man seemed to consider the request for a few moments. "My name's Ben Trowman" he finally admitted, before going on to tell them about the situation he was in.

"Jesus" Lee exclaimed, once Ben had finished talking. "That's some fucked up shit."

Ben nodded.

"So, what the fuck are you gonna do now?" Lee asked.

"I dunno" Ben answered, with a shrug. "There's nothin' I can do."

"You could fight back?" Alex suggested, glancing at Lee. "That's what we need to do."

"Against a full club roster?" Lee stated. "That's fuckin' suicide."

"Well we can't just sit back an' fuckin' take it" Alex argued.

Lee shook his head. "There 'ain't no value in gettin' ourselves killed."

"Look" Alex sighed, clearly frustrated by the man's reticence. "They've ripped us apart and destroyed our home. Then we find this poor bastard being beaten shitless at the ruins, which tells me it 'ain't over. If we sit here an' do nothin', then I know we're gonna get fucked even more."

"I'm not gonna lead everyone to certain death" Lee replied, "and takin' them on is exactly that."

"Not if we do it right."

"But there's only six of us."

"Seven, if you count him" Alex pointed out, turning his attention to Ben. "What d'you think? You up for joining us on this?"

Taking a deep breath, Ben considered the question. "I dunno" he finally answered. "I just want this to be over."

"So, you're just gonna wait for 'em to finish fuckin' you up?" Alex asked. "And what about your girl? You just gonna let them do what they want with her?"

At the mention of Steph, Ben's mind began to race. "No" he exclaimed. "But what am I supposed to do? If I try to do anything they don't like, then they'll kill her."

"She's gonna be dead, whether you do anything or not" Alex stated, harshly.

Rubbing his eyes, Ben shook his head as he fought back his tears.

"It's obvious you're not in any position to think about this now" Lee smiled, happy to find a way to get Alex off the subject of retaliation. "Why don't you stay here for a bit, get yourself together and then you can decide what you wanna do?"

Ben didn't answer immediately, until a thought struck him. "What about Dani?" he suddenly exclaimed.

"Who?" Lee asked.

"The doctor" Ben clarified. "I stayed at her's and they took me from outside. If they know I survived but they don't know where I am, they might go after her."

"Get her to come here" Lee suggested. "We've got a couple of rooms for the girls to use when they stay over. You can have them for a couple of nights, until you've got your shit together."

"You sure?" Ben asked.

"Of course" Lee stated, pushing the office phone across the desk. "Give her a call."

Chapter 30

Of course, Billy had realised what was happening long before the Judge's gavel banged loudly and ominously. He'd seen it coming, the verdict that was so harshly delivered in front of the gallery's expectant crowd. It shouldn't have got that far, the proceedings should've been over a matter of hours after he'd been picked up, yet as the days had drawn on the glimmer of hope had all but faded and, by the time sentence was passed, the transparency of the plan was all too apparent and it was clear he'd been set up.

Both who had orchestrated his downfall and the reasons for it were also obvious and he'd spent every night of the last thirteen months lying in his cell dreaming of this moment, imagining his return to the place and the events that needed to play out. The only question was whether he'd have the chance to do what was required or whether his men had been poisoned to the point of no return, and the lack of either visitors during his incarceration or welcoming party upon his release painted a somewhat blackened picture in that respect.

Having handed the fare over to the driver, he stepped out of the taxi and stood for a moment, motionless, in front of the building. He could feel the low rumble of the music's baseline as it blared inside and he could see through the windows that the party was in full swing. For a very brief moment, he considered the possibility that the event was being held to celebrate his release, but those thoughts were soon pushed to the side as he realised just how unlikely that was; knowing the man he was about to face, the timing of it all was probably deliberate and intended to provide a very public backdrop in front of which this showdown was to happen.

With a deep breath, he stepped forward and pushed his way through the door, where he found himself standing amongst a host of unrecognised faces, despite all of the men wearing the Cut he'd been so proud of creating. Each of them stared at him as he pushed his way through, yet none of them questioned his appearance and no one raised any objection to the arrival of a stranger adorned with the club's colours.

Regardless of how recently they'd been enlisted, they should've prevented him access to the inner sanctum of the clubhouse until his identity had been established, yet they actively stood aside as he walked through, which could only mean that they'd been briefed on what was to happen that night. It could only mean that his arrival had been expected and that meant his target was waiting and ready to receive him, which was fine as far as he was concerned. One way or another, things were going to be resolved there and then, regardless of whether the outcome fell in his favour or not.

As he reached the centre of the main room, the music cut off and everyone stood still. Those closest to him began to shuffle back, creating a somewhat clichéd ring in the centre of which he remained stationary.

"Welcome back" announced Ruckus, breaking the uneasy silence as he stepped through the crowd in front of him.

Billy merely stared at him.

Glancing around, Ruckus smiled as he held his arms out. "I take it there's no need for any explanation?" he asked. "I mean, it must be pretty obvious what's happened, even to you?"

Still Billy stared silently, although he noted the President patch that now adorned the chest of his counterpart's Cut.

Now Billy nodded, slowly. "You think this is it?" he questioned. "You think I'm gonna hand it all over easily?"

"Oh, there's no handing over required" Ruckus replied. "You've got nothing to hand over."

"This is still my club" Billy stated.

Ruckus started laughing, which was gradually imitated by the rest of the watching crowd. "I think it's clear you're wrong about that" he chuckled. "So, why don't you just take off that Cut?"

Slowly, the laughter died down, being replaced by a tense silence as they awaited Billy's next move.

"Fuck you" Billy replied, reaching round to his back and pulling out the gun he'd obtained on his way there.

Levelling it directly at Ruckus' head, he braced himself for any reaction from the new members, but none was forthcoming.

"How fuckin' original" Ruckus chided. "Seriously? In thirteen months, this is the best plan you could come up with?"

"You set me up! Seeing your corpse hit the floor is the only plan I need."

Releasing a long sigh of pity, Ruckus started walking towards him. "Billy, Billy, Billy" he muttered. "Well go on then, if you're goin' to. Pull the fuckin' trigger."

As the words left his lips, the watching members all drew out their own weapons and trained them on the man in the centre of the circle. Billy tensed his finger as he glanced around and his arm dropped a little, before he steeled himself and raised it once more with fresh determination.

"I may not walk outta here alive" he announced, "but I'll die happy when I see a hole in your forehead."

"Well, pull the fuckin' trigger then" Ruckus repeated, drawing closer.

Despite dreaming of this moment for so long, Billy found himself struggling to go through with it.

"You really wanna follow this psycho?" he questioned, addressing the surrounding crowd.

None of the members flinched.

"You really trust this man not to hang you out to dry when he's finished with you?" he asked.

Again, there was no response.

"Fuckin' pathetic" Ruckus hissed, now standing directly in front of Billy and pushing the centre of his forehead on to the barrel of the gun.

Billy took a step back, but Ruckus followed and again pressed himself against the weapon.

"Do it!" Ruckus urged.

With a scream, Billy pulled back on the trigger but, as though he'd expected it, Ruckus had already moved by the time the hammer connected and the bullet fired harmlessly into the wall. With lightning movement, Ruckus turned and drove his fist into Billy's temple, buckling his legs and sending him slumping to the floor. He bent over him and pulled the gun from his hand as he pinned him down, before aiming it to the side of his head and firing it into the floor.

Instantly, Billy's hearing failed and he felt the blood pouring out of his ear before the pain registered in his mind. Too stunned and in too much agony to do anything else, he clutched at the side of his head and felt that his earlobe had been blown clean off. Ruckus stood up and gestured to a few of the men, who rushed forward and pulled the Cut from Billy's shoulders before he was dragged towards the door and thrown painfully out of the clubhouse.

Chapter 31

The August morning was brisk following the rain that'd fallen over the last couple of weeks, but the sun was just beginning to heat up the ground, causing a fine mist to rise gently from the grass. Accompanied by Dani, who'd refused to let him come alone, Ben watched from a distance as they lowered Sam's coffin into the ground and, as it disappeared from view, she reached out to hold his hand.

"It's not your fault" she whispered.

Ben didn't reply, but his grip tightened slightly. She glanced up at him, hoping rather than expecting to see tears falling from his eyes, but she was disappointed that there were none. He merely stared at the funeral party with no sign of emotion in his expression.

"You need to let it out" she said. "It's ok to be upset."

"I'm fine" he muttered, a little unconvincingly.

Slowly, the mourners began to filter away from the grave, leaving Karen and her parents to take a final few moments by the side of the man she'd loved. Eventually though, they too moved away and, as they walked, she looked up to where the two of them stood solemnly, pausing for a moment to stare at Ben.

"I'm sure she wouldn't have minded if you'd gone down to join them" Dani suggested, as Karen finally turned away. "She would probably have appreciated it."

Shaking his head, Ben released her hand. "No" he answered, sternly. "She didn't want me here."

"She can't have meant that?"

"She's convinced that I did this to him, she definitely meant it."

Unsure of what she could say, Karen didn't reply. Ben continued to look down, watching as the cars left the cemetery and, once they were gone, the two of them walked down to the grave. He grabbed a handful of dirt and stood at the side of the hole, looking down at the coffin.

"I miss you, dude" he whispered, choking up a little as tears finally began to roll down his cheeks. "I'm so sorry."

"This wasn't your fault" Dani stated again, as Ben tossed the dirt on to the lid of the coffin.

"I didn't kill him" Ben muttered, "but if I'd have got Steph to the hospital, instead of thinking I could look after her, then he wouldn't have been at my flat for them to kill him and they wouldn't have Steph now."

"But you did what you thought was right and, after what happened to the girl you found when she was in the hospital, I'd have done the same."

"Would you though?" he suddenly snapped, finally turning his attention from the grave to look at her. "It's like everything I've done since finding her has been the wrong fuckin' choice. It's like I'm on some kind of sick self-destruct and I'm fuckin' taking everyone else down with me."

A little stunned by both the outburst and the look of anger that'd appeared in his eyes, Dani took a step back.

"Well I'm fuckin' done with all this!" he continued, his rage increasing. "I'm fuckin' done with trying to do what's normal and what's right. It's time I started doing what needs to be done!"

With that, he turned and started to walk away, but Dani reached out to take a hold of his arm and pulled him back round to face her. "What are you talking about?" she asked.

"I'm gonna kill 'em" he stated, before looking again at the grave. "I promise you, Sam. The bastards are gonna pay."

With the doors firmly bolted, The Skinning Pit was closed to the public. Inside, the music was low-key, a track list of Sam's favourite tunes, and the only people in the bar were friends, family and a couple of the most regular customers. The drinks and food were being provided for free, the owner wanting to pay tribute to his barman, and he'd given assurance the place was to remain theirs for as long as they needed.

Karen sat in what had been always Sam's seat at their usual, after-work drinks table, accompanied by her parents and Andy, with Penny sleeping peacefully in her pushchair. The conversation was tentative, filled with condolences for the loss or reminiscences and anecdotes that painted a fond picture of Sam's unique tendencies and humour.

The banging on the door was ignored at first, presumed to be strangers looking for a drink but, as it continued and increased in intensity, they realised it needed to be answered. Rising from his chair, Andy rolled his eyes and walked over to the door. He undid the bolts and grasped the handle, but didn't have time to pull before it was forced open and he was sent staggering backwards as Ben strode in.

"Karen" Ben called out, searching the room for her.

"You shouldn't be here" Andy exclaimed, rushing forward in an attempt to prevent him from moving any further into the place.

"Get the fuck out of my way" Ben demanded, easily pushing Andy back as two of the men in the room ran over in support.

Together, the three of them tried to hold him back, but even their combined strength was no match for Ben's size or determination and he continued, barely hampered.

"Karen" he called out again, as he spotted her sitting at the side of the room.

One of the men, either through desperation or foolishness, took a swing at him, which Ben blocked easily, before returning the blow, collapsing the man's legs instantly and sending him crumpling to the floor.

"Enough of this!" Karen screamed, jumping up and running over to them. "Why are you doing this? Haven't you done enough already?"

Easily shrugging away what remained of the men's grip on him, Ben looked at her helplessly for a moment, until he found the words he was looking for. "I didn't kill Sam" he repeated.

Karen stared at him, the doubt clear in her expression.

"I know who did it" Ben continued. "It was a motorcycle club, The Sons of Sorrow. They killed Sam and they took Steph. They're trying to set me up for the rape of the two women and they tried to make it look as though I'd committed suicide."

With that he held up his hands, displaying the bandages that were still covering the wounds on his wrists.

"They left me for dead" he explained, "and, when I survived that, they tried to kill me and make it look as though a rival club were responsible."

Still Karen looked at him as though his story was incredible, but they were all stunned when a strange voice materialised from the bar.

"He's telling you the truth."

"Lobe?" Andy exclaimed, as all eyes turned to the man sitting on his usual stool at the bar. "Is that you talking?"

"My name's Billy" Lobe continued, ignoring everyone's disbelief. "And I was a founding member of The Sons."

Silence fell in the room, until Billy began to speak again. He told them of his role in the creation of the club and what he originally wanted it to be. He described the way in which he too had been set up to take a fall for Ruckus and how the man had forcibly taken control. He also revealed what had happened to Tommo and explained that he was looking for a way to both make up for his mistakes and to fight back against the man who'd destroyed his life.

"But I was told what happened by two detectives" Karen muttered, when he'd finished his tale.

"Crowther and Wishall?" Billy questioned, although it was clear he already knew the answer.

Karen nodded.

"Crowther's been in Ruckus' pocket for years" Billy confirmed. "You give that piece of shit enough money and he'll try to convince your mother that you're not her kid."

"But why would they have arrested Ben if he was innocent?"

"And why would they release me if I wasn't?" Ben immediately asked in response.

Again, the doubt played across Karen's eyes and she looked desperately towards her parents for some sort of answer.

"Karen" Ben pleaded. "Just give me the chance to tell you what happened and then, if you still want me to go, then I'll go."

"She wants you to go now" Andy muttered.

"Fuck off!" Ben replied, balling his fists in readiness for any physical reaction from the man, before looking back to Karen.

"Ok" she reluctantly agreed. "I'll listen."

They moved over to join her parents at the table, neither of whom made any attempt to hide their contempt for the man, and Ben started talking. He explained that he'd found Steph at his door and called Sam to come over, which Karen confirmed when her parents showed further scepticism. He then told them that it was Sam who'd persuaded him to go to the police and he talked about the way in which the two detectives had practically forced him out after Crowther had received a phone call. When he got to the part of his story in which he'd returned home to find Sam dead and Steph missing, he broke down and Karen immediately reached out to him, wrapping her arms around his shoulders and pulling him to her, in a way he'd never expected her to do again.

"I'm so sorry I ever doubted you" she whispered. "I needed someone to blame for what happened, but I didn't know who."

Slowly, Ben managed to pull himself together.

"Who was the girl you were with at the cemetery?" Karen asked.

"She's the doctor I called to help Steph."

"Well, why didn't you bring her here?"

Ben looked deeply into her eyes as he spoke. "Because I needed to be the one who convinced you that I'm innocent" he answered. "I needed to know that you believe me for what I'm telling you and not for what anyone else says."

"I do believe you" she nodded, without so much as a glance at her parents, who were still making noises of uncertainty from across the table. "So what happens now?"

"I'm gonna find them" Ben answered, bluntly, "and I'm gonna kill as many as I can before they take me down."

Whether it was the words he'd said or the tone in which he'd said them, a look of horror suddenly flooded across Karen's expression. "What?" she exclaimed. "What are you talking about?"

"They're not gonna stop until I'm either dead or in prison" Ben confirmed. "And I'm not gonna let them get away with this without paying some price."

"This can't be real" she replied, as her tears quickly began to fall. "You can't mean what you're saying?"

Only a nod was all Ben gave in reply.

"You won't get as far as even punchin' one of them without help" Billy interrupted, now rising from his stool and walking over to them. "They'll cut you down before you get close."

"I've survived what they've thrown at me so far" Ben stated.

"That's because they haven't started on you yet" Billy replied. "Once they see you as a threat, if you're by yourself, they'll take you out before you know it."

"So what am I supposed to do? Let the police take them down?"

"Don't be such a naive prick. You get the help you need and then you hit them."

"And where the fuck do I get that help from?"

"From me."

Her attention now flicking between the two of them, Karen's incredulity was apparent. "I can't believe I'm hearing this" she exclaimed. "Are you really being serious?"

Neither of the men answered.

"Ben" she continued, reaching out to grasp his hands. "This isn't like you. You're not like them."

"I've got no choice" Ben replied, before looking back to Billy and nodding his acceptance of the help. "So, how do we do this?"

Now openly panicking, Karen tightened her grip on his hands. "Don't do this" she begged. "I can't lose you now."

"If I don't" he answered, "then you'll lose me anyway."

Karen shook her head as he rose from his seat and pulled his hands away from her. "No" she insisted, also standing up.

"I've got no choice" he whispered, wrapping his arms around her and pulling her in tightly to his chest. "I love you Karen. Whatever happens, please don't ever forget that."

Before she could answer, he pulled away and turned to Billy. "Let's go" he stated.

Sitting at the clubhouse bar with Jimmy, Ethan shook his head as he stared over to where Touchy was in deep conversation with Ruckus.

"The piece of shit's goin' behind my back" he muttered.

"Huh?" Jimmy replied, turning to follow his gaze.

"Fuckin' Touchy" Ethan continued. "Look at 'im, over there. He's in Ruckus' ear like a fuckin' gnat and 'ain't gonna let up till he gets me fucked over."

"So, what you gonna do about it?" Jimmy asked.

"Nothin' yet" Ethan answered. "But in about thirty seconds, I'm gonna be called in for a friendly chat."

They watched for a few moments longer until, sure enough, the two men started walking towards the meeting room and Ruckus called across for Ethan to follow them.

"Fuckin' told ya!" Ethan exclaimed, as he jumped off the stool. "Son of a bitch!"

Still cursing, he followed them into the room and, whilst staring intently at Touchy, pushed the door closed behind him.

"Is what I'm hearin' right?" Ruckus asked.

"That depends what you're hearin', I guess" Ethan answered, still glaring at Touchy.

"I'm hearin' that, instead of finishin' off the doctor, you decided to play around with Ben and then you lost him to that fuckin' club I was told we'd wiped out?"

Ethan took a moment to consider his response. "Who the fuck was playin' around with anyone?" he eventually replied. "I was tryin' to make sure we got outta this clean instead of the usual, half-arsed bullshit we normally have to fend off."

"And what usual, half-arsed bullshit are you talkin' about?"

"I'm talkin' about the 'kill 'em and hope no one pins it on us' shit we've always done."

Immediately, in seemingly one, fluid movement, Ruckus pulled out his knife, pushed Ethan against the wall and pressed the blade firmly against his throat.

"Listen to me" he hissed. "Don't think for a second I won't kill you if you keep fuckin' about with all this. This is my fuckin' club and you need to remember that."

"Oh, I remember it" Ethan replied calmly, paying no heed to the blade. "An' I remember all our boys who've been locked up an' killed 'cause you were too fuckin' stupid to realise where you're goin' wrong."

Ruckus increased the pressure on Ethan's throat. "You wanna say that again?" he spat.

"I said you're too fuckin' stupid" Ethan hissed, his eyes wide with anger. "So fuckin' go on, give yourself another fuckin' body to bury."

As he pushed even harder, Ruckus glared into Ethan's eyes for a few seconds before, finally, he pulled away.

"You're treadin' a thin fuckin' line" he muttered. "You think bein' my son gives you some kinda special privilege to shit on anythin' I say or somethin'?"

"That 'ain't no fuckin' privilege" Ethan answered, with no trace of humour. "An' I 'ain't tryin' to shit on anythin' you say. I'm just tryin' to keep us fuckin' whole. I didn't create all this shit, but I'm sure as hell gonna make sure it don't kill us."

"Well you 'ain't exactly getting' anywhere with that" Ruckus replied, his voice still sharp with anger. "So now it's time to start listenin' to me."

Knowing better than to push his luck any further, Ethan didn't argue.

"I want that doctor bitch gone" Ruckus continued. "That fuckin' Club needs wipin' out an' that cunt you've got locked up needs to be buried."

With an exasperated sigh, Ethan shook his head. "More fuckin' dead bodies" he muttered. "That's your answer to all this?"

"No" Ruckus spat. "That's my word an', until you're sittin at the head of that fuckin' table, my word is the fuckin' law."

"We don't need any more corpses" Ethan argued. "Yeah, that club's gotta go, but the doctor's been handled an' she 'ain't a problem now."

"How the fuck 'ain't she a problem?"

"She 'ain't a problem because she's been linked to the murders of the two girls. She's been suspended from the hospital and, even if she's never actually convicted of anythin', the black mark'll stay on her record and her word means shit now."

"If she's breathin', then she's a fuckin' problem" Ruckus replied, shaking his head. "I want her gone an' I want it done today."

"Alright" Ethan reluctantly agreed, knowing there was no point in arguing. "But don't touch Steph, we still need her."

Ruckus stared at him, waiting for the explanation.

"We still need Ben to take the fall and we don't know where he is" Ethan pointed out. "If he's with that Club, then we can take him out at the same time as them and Crowther and Wishall can bury it as some kinda gang dispute. They can also close the files on the two girls with the suspect bein' dead. If he 'ain't with them though, then we need that bitch to hold over him until he confesses and, to do that, we need her to be able to talk."

After contemplating the argument for a few moments, Ruckus eventually nodded his head. "Fine" he mumbled. "But you need to get this finished, or I will."

"I'm in" Ben exclaimed, as he and Billy walked into the Strip Club's office.

"What?" Lee asked, looking up from where he sat at the desk.

"Retaliation" Ben explained. "Let's do this."

Somewhat surprised by both the announcement and the sudden entrance, Lee sat silent for a few seconds before he managed to pull himself together enough to reply. "Who's that?"

"This is Billy" Ben answered, after following his gaze towards the man who stood next to him. "He's gonna help us."

"Help us do what?"

"Finish The Sons."

Shaking his head, Lee let out a long sigh. "I've already told you, I'm not leading the men into a pointless suicide mission, so just let it go."

"I can't let it go" Ben stated. "If I do, then I might as well kill myself now, because I'm fucked if I don't."

Again, Lee's sigh was long and full of frustration. "Sit down" he ordered, pointing to the chair opposite him at the desk and to the spare one at the side of the room.

Grabbing the spare, the two men followed the command and, once they were seated, Lee began to talk.

"Look" he said. "I know Alex is keen on this, but he doesn't realise what he's going up against and how impossible it is to touch people like The Sons. Hell, they took us out without even breaking sweat and I know we're not the first club to feel that."

Now it was Ben's turn to shake his head. "Like Alex said" he pointed out. "They must've taken me to your old clubhouse for a reason, so sitting back and doing nothing now is just asking them to finish the job."

"So we stay vigilant" Lee replied. "We watch our backs and make sure we're not leaving ourselves open. We've already done that by stopping your corpse being left in our ruins."

"No, you've just made sure that their eyes are firmly on you. They know it was you who saved me from the kickin', you were wearing your patches when you did it. D'you think they'll let that go?"

"I'm not gonna go steaming in there, looking for trouble."

"But trouble's already found you" Billy stated, interrupting the conversation. "And it won't go away."

"And what would you know about it?" Lee asked, a little abruptly.

"A lot more than you think" Billy answered, pulling up his sleeve to show the club ink on his arm.

Lee immediately froze at the sight, allowing Billy to continue.

"The Sons of Sorrow were my club" he explained, "until Ruckus took it from me and left me a shell of a man. They took out my friend, the man who helped set the club up, and they'll come for me, eventually. The thing is, I'm not gonna sit back and take it like a pussy."

"I 'ain't a pussy" Lee exclaimed.

"You 'ain't shit!" Billy snapped. "I've seen pricks like you before, playin' at being a motorcycle club, without knowing the first fuckin' thing about it. You think it's all about looking cool in your Cuts, ridin' around and playin' at being the big men? Well, welcome to the life. Either grow some balls or dig yourself a hole, because they're comin' for ya and there 'ain't no stoppin' 'em when they wanna take you out."

"What about Dani?" Lee asked, trying to change tack as he turned to Ben.

"What about her?

"You think she's gonna be ok with you doin' this?"

"It doesn't matter whether she is or not, this is something we have to do."

Shaking his head once more, Lee was clearly struggling with the idea.

"If we don't do this, they're gonna fuck us up anyway and you know that" Ben continued. "We can either sit back and take it, or we can go down fighting. With Billy's help, we'll stand a chance at least."

"But we haven't got enough numbers" Lee argued.

"So I suggest you merge" Billy stated. "Join forces with another club who want to give The Sons something back."

"Oh, because they're easy to find, aren't they?"

"As it happens, yes" Billy confirmed. "The Sons took out Satan's Minions and they're struggling to recover."

"So, I just wander into their clubhouse and tell them to join us?"

"No. I go in there and bring their president in to talk with you. I know the guy and he'll listen to me. You're both fucked as individual clubs but, between you, you've got the makings of a force and, if you're willing to give some ground, then I think he'll be willing to consider a merger."

"And what if he isn't?"

"Then you'll at least need to get tooled up, if only to try and defend yourselves. What guns have you got?"

"None" Lee answered. "We're not that kind of club."

"Then you'll need to get some" Billy replied. "What funds have you got?"

"We've got the takings from this place, and not much else."

Billy considered that for a moment. "Well, we need some cash, quickly."

Now starting to accept what he was being told, Lee let out a resigned sigh and reached for his phone.

"What're you doing?" Ben asked.

"I'm sorting us some cash" Lee stated, before turning to Billy. "You go get your man" he agreed. "If he'll listen, then I'll talk to him, but I'm not makin' any promises."

Chapter 32

"How much are we getting' for these?" Billy asked, as he and Ben stood on lookout.

"It's hard to say" Lee answered, as he sprung the lock on the car's door. "It depends on demand, but it'll be enough."

"Enough for a couple of handguns and that's about it" Billy muttered. "How many more can we get today?"

"This is the last one we'll be able to do today, but my guy will let me know if there's any more."

Billy shook his head. "It 'ain't gonna be enough, but it'll have to do for now. How much do you trust this guy of yours?"

"Why?" Lee asked, as he reached under the car's dashboard to expose the ignition's wiring.

"Because, if he can guarantee there'll be more, then I can sort some kind of deal."

"There'll definitely be more" Lee assured him.

Nodding, Billy returned his attention to the rest of the car park, just as the door at the end opened and a couple walked through.

"Hold up" he urged, as he an Ben focussed on the open boot of the car they'd arrived in, making out they were loading it up as Lee and Alex ducked down between the rows of parked cars.

The couple didn't seem to pay them any heed as they made their way to a car that was parked further along the row and they didn't take any time in getting in and driving away, leaving the four of them to return to their task.

"How much longer is this gonna take?" Ben asked impatiently.

"It'll take as long as it needs to" Lee muttered in reply. "These alarm systems 'ain't a walk in the park, you know."

"Well, get a fuckin' move on" Ben hissed. "We've been here too long already."

"Shut the fuck up" Lee snapped.

"Both of you shut the fuck up" Billy interjected, turning to the car boot. "There's someone comin'."

Again, they took up their positions as a man walked towards them, but they could tell from his expression that he'd realised there was something going on.

"What the hell are you doing with my car?" the man exclaimed, rushing towards it.

Instinctively, Ben reached out as he passed and pulled him back, causing him to stumble and fall to the ground. The man lashed out from where he lay, but Ben was on him in an instant, pinning him to the floor as he drove his fist into the man's nose. In a rage, he connected with several more blows to the man's face, before Billy and Alex managed to pull him away.

Billy left Alex and Lee to try and calm Ben as he moved quickly to search the man for his wallet, which he found in the back pocket of his trousers. He pulled it out and opened it up, removing the driver's licence before he tossed the wallet on to the floor, next to the man.

"Listen" he said, moving in close to the man's face and holding the licence up where he could see it. "We know who you are and where you live, so if there's any sign that our descriptions have been given to the police, then we'll come for you. D'you understand?"

Despite his pain, the man nodded confirmation.

"Now" Billy continued. "We'll take the car and then you report it's missing to the police. You then claim on your insurance and they'll replace it for you, so everyone wins. There's no need to let principles get in the way of a good deal, is there?"

Again, the man demonstrated his understanding.

"That's a good boy" Billy muttered, as Lee managed to get the engine started. "Sorry for the inconvenience."

Having delivered the last of the stolen vehicles, the four of them were on their way back to the strip club and the atmosphere in the car was a little tense.

"What the fuck was all that?" Lee asked, without turning round to look at Ben.

"What the fuck was all what?" Ben questioned in reply.

"All that cowboy shit back there. What the fuck were you thinkin'?"

"We got the car, didn't we?"

"That's not the fuckin' point! If that guy decides to pass our descriptions on to the police, then we're looking at Assault and Battery on top of the theft charges, and that's a whole different world of shit."

"He's not gonna report us to the police, we've got his licence."

"That's no fuckin' guarantee."

"That's enough, boys" Billy interrupted. "It's done, so we've just gotta wait and see what happens."

With that, silence returned momentarily to the car.

"I'm sorry" Ben muttered. "I've never done this before and I panicked."

"You can say that again" Lee replied, his tone a little lighter than before. "But you've gotta keep yourself in check. It's things like that, that'll fuck us up."

"I'm sorry" Ben repeated.

"So, when do we get the money for all this?" Alex asked, happy to try and change the subject.

"We'll get it when . . ." Lee began, but he stopped his sentence short as he stared out of the windscreen. "Stop the car" he exclaimed.

Slamming on the brakes, Alex swerved to the kerb and all of them followed Lee's gaze to see a tower of smoke rising from behind the buildings ahead of them.

"That's not the club, is it?" he questioned, despite all of them knowing the answer.

No reply came from any of them, until Lee spoke up.

"We need to get over there" he urged.

"No" Billy snapped. "If The Sons have done this, they'll be waiting for anyone coming back. We'll go to a bar and check the news."

"But we need to know if anyone was in there" Lee replied.

"If there was, then the reporters will tell you" Billy pointed out. "Come on, let's go."

With that, Alex gunned the engine and quickly pulled away from the kerb. They drove away from the smoke and, a few streets later, pulled up outside one of the city's bars.

"Can you turn the TV on?" Billy asked the barman, as they rushed in. "Somethin's goin' on down the road."

Nodding, the barman flicked the switch on the set and they all stood at the end of the bar, their hearts racing as the news report unfolded.

"Thank fuck for that" Alex exclaimed, when it was announced there were no casualties. "But why wouldn't they make sure people were in there, like they did with the clubhouse?"

"They're trying to pull you out into the open" Billy stated, "make you easier targets."

"They really are looking to finish us, aren't they?" Lee muttered, before turning to Billy. "Set up the meeting" he stated. "I don't care what it takes, we need help."

Billy nodded his agreement.

"What about Dani?" Ben suddenly questioned, reaching into his pocket to pull out his phone.

"What d'you mean?" Lee asked. "They said no one was in there."

"But if she's at work, then she'll be going back there when she finishes. I need to warn her."

Again, Billy nodded agreement. "Go and pick her up" he suggested. "I'll go and sort out the meeting and you two round everyone up. We need to know whether we're still whole, or whether anyone's been taken down yet. We'll meet at Sarah's place, but make sure you're not followed there."

Moving away from them slightly, Ben dialled the number and waited for the call to be answered.

"What?" he exclaimed, once Dani had finished talking. "Stay there, I'm coming to pick you up."

When Dani opened the door, the redness in her eyes made it clear she'd been crying.

"Are you ok?" Ben asked, as he stepped into Emily's flat.

Shaking her head, she nearly burst into tears again, but she checked herself just in time. "No" she answered, frankly. "Those detectives have told the hospital that I've got something to do with the murder of the two girls and I've been suspended indefinitely."

"They know you're helping me" Ben stated, "so they're trying to damage you. They've got no evidence, so it'll only be a matter of time before the hospital realise their mistake."

"That won't matter" Dani muttered, still fighting to keep control of her emotions. "Whether there's any evidence or not, this is on my record now and I'm finished as a doctor. Ben, I've lost everything I've ever worked for."

Those last words were too much for her and tears started to spill from her eyes. Instinctively, Ben moved to try and comfort her, but she quickly backed away from him.

"I can't do this anymore" she sobbed. "The whole thing is ridiculous."

"I know" Ben agreed, "but we've gotta stay strong and we've gotta fight it. There's nothing else we can do."

"We can call Roberts" she argued. "We can report all of this to the police."

Taking a deep breath, Ben let out a long sigh. "There's nothing he or the police can do" he confirmed. "The Sons are too strong and have too many connections for them to be hurt like that."

"What's all this talk about hurting them?" Dani suddenly snapped. "Why do they need to be hurt? We're just normal people, living normal lives and the police should be there to protect us."

Again, Ben tried to comfort her but, again, she backed away.

"You keep talking as though you're one of them" she continued. "All that stuff about making them pay and killing them, that's not you. You shouldn't be involved in all this."

"I know" he agreed once more. "But I don't have a choice. If I sit back and do nothing, then they'll finish me and I'm worried they'll finish you too."

"But I haven't done anything wrong!"

With no idea of how to respond, Ben remained silent and allowed her emotions to pour out until, finally, she seemed to be calming a little.

"Look" he whispered, as gently as his own frayed emotions would allow. "There's a lot going on at the moment that we need to get our heads around. Come with me and we'll try to work out what we can do."

"I'm not going back to the strip club" she announced.

Taking another deep breath, Ben readied himself for her response to more bad news. "The strip club's gone" he told her. "The Sons have burned it down, just like they did to the Abyssus clubhouse."

"What?" she exclaimed, shaking her head in disbelief. "This can't be happening."

"No one was hurt" he stated, hoping to calm her a little. "But we can't go back there. We're all meeting at Lee's girlfriend's house. It should be safe there for the time being."

"I can't do this" Dani replied, almost breathlessly. "I'm sorry, but I'm not going with you. If I step away now, then I'll be safe and they won't hurt me anymore."

"Dani . . ." Ben began, but she cut him off before he could say anything else.

"No" she stated, firmly. "I'm walking away from all this. If they know I'm not involved, then they'll leave me alone and, maybe, I'll be able to get my life back."

With frustration getting the better of him, Ben suddenly lost his self-control. "You think I don't wanna walk away from all this?" he snapped. "You think I don't wanna just go back to the way things were, before I found that girl in the alley? My best friend has been killed, the woman I care most about in this world is missing and these bastards aren't gonna rest until I'm dead. Well, I can't walk away, so I've got two choices. I either stand up and fight, or I roll over and fuckin' die and, frankly, I 'ain't fuckin' ready for that yet."

Stunned by his outburst, Dani stared blankly at him for a few moments as a heavy silence fell between them. She eventually opened her mouth to speak, but the front door crashed open before any words could pass her lips and two masked men stormed in.

The sight of Ben standing there seemed to confuse them and they hesitated, just long enough for Ben to turn and face them.

Steph's dreams were erratic, partial visions that seemed to disappear as quickly as they'd arrived, until one image finally found a foothold in her mind. It was such a simple sight, yet it resonated in her subconscious as though it had been the most important moment of her life and, in a way only sleep can achieve, its realism was absolute.

A tear, that's all it was. A single tear, that'd fallen from Ben's eye whilst they stood in her kitchen. A tear that he'd wiped away quickly, apologising for how stupid he was being, but he couldn't have been any further away from the truth. The reality of the situation was that he should have allowed more to fall, he should have allowed his emotions to pour out and she would have willingly caught each and every one of them, but he hadn't ever really known that, had he?

Like a movie, playing in slow motion, the picture moved on and took her through the conversation that followed, the conversation in which she'd told him how much she loved him, without actually realising how true those words had been. Her mind recalled the way in which she'd leant back to check he was ok and the way in which the thought of kissing him had pushed itself to the very forefront of her desire. It was that moment at which the dream should have ended but, like all good night time recollections, this one continued, head-long, into the realm of fantasy.

Instead of Sam walking in and putting a stop to the proceedings, Steph's mind allowed an altogether different scenario to play out. In her visions now, Ben moved his head towards her and their lips met, sending sparks of pleasure coursing through every nerve-ending in her body as she succumbed fully to his embrace. She briefly saw where the kiss could have led, a lifetime of happiness alongside a man she loved with all of her heart but, suddenly, the dream became tainted with a harsh, cold reality that thrust her right back to where she was now, alone and scared with all hope gone.

Her thoughts pictured her sitting in a room, with Ethan standing in front of her. She was surrounded by blank faces that formed a ring in which she was at the centre and, when Ethan moved to the side, she saw Ben on his knees, with his hands tied firmly behind his back. As he looked over to her she tried to tell him how sorry she was, but no words could find their way out of her mouth and, when she tried to scream, she found her lips to be taped over.

Watching on, helplessly, she saw Ethan raise a gun to Ben's temple, before looking back at her as a sick and twisted grin spread widely across his lips. Again, she tried to call out, to scream at him to stop, but still no words came forth and, when she saw his finger tighten on the trigger, she watched as a single tear fell from Ben's eye.

The crack of the gunshot was so vivid, so real, that Steph jumped in her seat and awoke immediately. As her heart raced, she breathed as deeply as her gag would allow, but she stopped suddenly at the sound of the room's door being pushed open.

The sound of footsteps drawing closer filled her ears and she felt the gag being pulled roughly away. She opened her lips in readiness for the food that was expected, but she choked a little when it wasn't bread that was forced into her mouth.

"That prick 'ain't tellin' me what to do any more. The wait's over and you'd better suck it good, bitch" the man's voice commanded, as the cold steel of a gun barrel was pushed into the side of her head. "And if I feel any teeth, then you're fuckin' dead."

The meeting was going badly, slipping steadily from discussion to argument, and Billy was beginning to question how wise it'd been to suggest the merger. Having deliberately stood back from proceedings, he watched on as both Lee and Jason, the president of Satan's Minions, refused to budge from their individual standpoints, with each of them adamant that it should be the other's club that underwent the patch-over and changed their name.

"Jesus Christ!" he finally exclaimed, standing and striding over to the table. "Will you two pricks listen to yourselves? You're both bangin' on about one club joining the other, but the truth is that neither of you has got a fuckin' club to start with."

Both of the men stared at him, open-mouthed, for a moment.

"Lee" Billy continued, "you've got six men and fuck all else to speak of, other than a way of bringing in just enough cash to at least arm yourselves. Jason, you've got a clubhouse, a couple of experienced members and a few prospects who're pretty much pointless without any fuckin' guns. The fact is that neither of you is any good on your own an' neither of your club's names are worth shit any more, if they were ever worth anythin' in the first fuckin' place, so why don't you just fuckin' join up and start a new fuckin' club?"

"And I suppose you'll be the fuckin' president?" Jason asked, immediately.

Shaking his head, Billy let out a deep laugh. "You think I want any of that again?" he replied. "I'm too fuckin' old to be playing around with that shit nowadays. No, Lee will be the president and you're the vice-president, it's fuckin' simple."

"How the fuck does that work?" Jason snapped. "Why the fuck would I sit back and allow him control?"

"Because I fuckin' say so, that's why" Billy stated. "And if you want my fuckin' help with all this, then you'll agree to it. Besides, you've done nothin' but fuck up since you started tryin' to rebuild the Minions and it's about time you got some fresh blood on all this. Lee's got his head screwed on and that'll go a long fuckin' way in this business."

Jason opened his mouth to argue, but Billy didn't let him speak.

"Don't fuckin' think about it" he chuckled. "It's time for a vote."

With that, he looked around at the faces in the room and repeated his suggestion, clarifying the points about the new club and the leadership. As he finished, he called for a show of hands from all those in agreement, to which the majority responded.

"Well then" he smiled, banging his hand on the table as a makeshift gavel. "It's decided. Now you've just gotta think of a name and I'll sort out the Cuts."

Disgruntled, Jason sat back in his chair with his arms folded in a display of petulance that Billy chose to ignore when the sound of the doorbell rang out in the house. Sarah went to answer it and, when she came back in, she was followed by Ben and Dani.

"What the fuck's happened to you?" Billy asked, taking in Ben's dishevelled state as he walked through the living room and sat down heavily on the settee, staring nowhere other than straight ahead.

Ben didn't reply, he didn't even acknowledge the question as he continued to stare at nothing.

"They came for me" Dani replied, her voice shaking as she spoke. "I was at my friend's and they came for me there."

"Jesus" Billy muttered. "What happened?"

"Ben fought them off" Dani answered, taking a deep breath as she tried to steady herself. "But he killed one of them in the fight."

"What? How?"

"I don't know" Dani continued. "He punched him and the man fell. I think he caught his head on a drawer as he went down. The other man ran off."

"So where's the body now?"

"It's still at my friend's. Ben went into shock when it happened and I thought I'd better get him out of there."

Billy nodded vigorously. "You did the right thing" he smiled. "With all the shit that's being thrown at him at the moment, the last thing we want is to give Crowther and Wishall a chance to pick him up for good. You said you'd got a detective helping you?"

"Yeah, Detective Roberts."

"Well, give him a call. Let him know what's happened and see if he can get to it first. With it happening at your friend's, then it shouldn't be linked to the case against Ben and there's no reason for Crowther and Wishall to take over the investigation. You'll need to be quick about it though."

Dani nodded her understanding. "I'll need to call my friend, tell her not to go back there."

"Ok" Billy agreed. "But call Roberts first and, when you speak to your friend, don't tell her where you are. Someone has to have told The Sons you were there and, until we know who, you can't take any chances."

Again, Dani nodded.

"Look" Billy exclaimed, turning to Lee and Jason. "You see how close they're gettin'? You need to stop the bullshit and agree on this new club, otherwise none of you will last long."

Chapter 33

Ben sat silently, staring straight out of the Minions' clubhouse window, which was all he'd done since they'd relocated there a couple of days ago. The place was heavily fortified, a compound on the outskirts of the city, which resembled an Army base more than a motorcycle club's home. As she had done regularly since the move, Dani sat next to him, attempting everything she could think of to get him to talk, but there seemed to be nothing that would provoke a response. Still though, driven by a deep concern, she continued to try.

"They've finally come up with a name for the club" she muttered, casually. "The Angels of Nemesis."

He didn't even shrug.

"Lee came up with it last night" she continued. "He was going on about Nemesis being the Goddess of retribution and how the name seemed apt for what's going on. The rest of them thought it was a bit too clever but they went with it anyway, I guess mainly because none of them could be bothered to come up with something else. I like it though, it's got a good feel to it. The emblem's nice as well. It's going to be a skull with wings coming out of it, but the feathers of the wings morph into the tips of bullets. Billy's arranged for Cuts to be made for everyone and they're suggesting you should be sworn in without having to prospect or go through the normal probationary period."

Still, there was no response.

With a sigh, she reached out to take hold of his hand, a gesture that was neither acknowledged nor refused. "Look" she whispered. "I know you feel badly about what happened, but you didn't try to kill that man. He attacked you and you defended yourself, it couldn't have been predicted that he'd fall that way."

It was something she'd said to him several times, but either he wasn't listening or he didn't believe what she was saying. She considered repeating what Roberts had told her, that he'd been to the flat and could tell immediately from the way the body was lying that it was a simple accident, but he'd even said it directly to him and there'd been no change in his demeanour. The man was struggling with the guilt of it all and, along with everything that was going on, it was going to take time for him to come to terms with what had happened.

She looked up as Billy walked over to them.

"Still no change?" he asked, looking at Ben.

Dani shook her head.

"Well" he said, addressing Ben as he placed a pistol on the table in front of him. "This one's for you. You need to carry it with you, but make sure to conceal it and only use it if you've got no choice."

Briefly, Ben looked at the gun, but he didn't reach for it. He simply shrugged and turned back to the window.

"For fuck's sake, Ben" Billy snapped. "You're gonna need to get used to all this shit, if you're gonna do somethin' about what's happenin' to you. So the prick died? Big fuckin' deal. That's one less piece of shit we need to worry about."

Ben didn't respond, but a commotion from the clubhouse's main door caused all three of them to look over in time to see Lee, along with Alex and a couple of the prospect members, drag a man into the room. The man was tied up, his head covered with a sack, and they roughly threw him to the ground whilst one of the prospects grabbed a chair.

"What the fuck is this?" Billy questioned, leaving Dani and Ben at the table as he stormed across the room.

"He's a member of The Sons" Lee replied, as the man was pulled up into the chair and secured firmly. "We staked out their casino and grabbed this bastard when he left by himself. We need to know what they know and what they're plannin', so we brought him here to ask a few questions."

Shaking his head, Billy was clearly unhappy with the decision. "You stupid bastard" he exclaimed. "Even without taking that sack off him, I can tell you his name's Knuckle and you'll get shit all out of him. The man's a fuckin' moron and, even if he was told what they're plannin', the guy can barely remember his own fuckin' name."

For a second, Lee looked crestfallen, but he rallied quickly. "Well, fuck it" he replied. "We've got him here now, so we might as well try at least."

"Be my guest" Billy laughed, standing back as they removed the sack.

Suddenly free to see where he was, Knuckle also laughed. "You fuckin' cunts 'ain't got a fuckin' clue" he slurred, an impediment that was down to his natural state, rather than being caused by the consumption of either alcohol or narcotics.

"Shut the fuck up!" Alex snapped, driving his fist into the man's jaw.

"Well how the fuck am I gonna answer your fuckin' questions?" Knuckle chuckled in response, earning himself another smack.

In turns, Lee and Alex asked the man their questions, including demands to know Steph's location, but each one was met with nothing but laughter, despite the increased intensity of the blows. Eventually though, Dani had enough of what she was witnessing and rushed over to stop them beating him any further.

"This isn't right" she insisted, examining the cuts and bruises that now covered Knuckle's face. "He's clearly not going to tell you anything, so why are you carrying on with this?"

Both Lee and Alex stared at her, whilst Billy continued to laugh at their attempts.

"We need to get somethin' out of him" Alex argued.

"You'll get nothin' but a sore hand" Billy replied, sarcastically. "I fuckin' told you that."

"So, what the fuck do we do with him now?" Lee asked. "Try and trade him for Steph?"

Again, Billy's laughter filled the room. "Like they give a shit about him?" he smiled. "It's the fuckin' law of the jungle and, from where they're sittin', Steph's a lot more valuable to them than this pathetic piece of meat. If you offer him up as a trade, they're likely to shoot the fucker in the face right in front of you, just to prove a point."

"Then what the fuck do we do with him now?" Lee repeated but, before anyone could answer, Ben pushed past him and fired a bullet, point-blank, through Knuckle's skull.

"Problem solved" he muttered, staring only at the corpse in the chair.

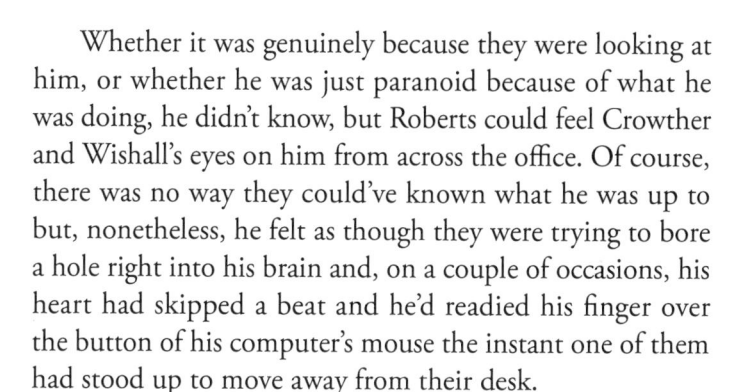

Whether it was genuinely because they were looking at him, or whether he was just paranoid because of what he was doing, he didn't know, but Roberts could feel Crowther and Wishall's eyes on him from across the office. Of course, there was no way they could've known what he was up to but, nonetheless, he felt as though they were trying to bore a hole right into his brain and, on a couple of occasions, his heart had skipped a beat and he'd readied his finger over the button of his computer's mouse the instant one of them had stood up to move away from their desk.

For a moment, he wondered whether this was what it was like for husbands who secretly browsed pornography websites whilst their wife was elsewhere in the house. Illicit viewing under the constant readiness to hide their tracks and pretend they were doing something innocent. It was ridiculous really but, if he was honest, there was a certain thrill to the whole thing that he enjoyed.

Having checked again that his colleagues weren't likely to catch him, he returned his attention to the computer screen and continued to scrutinise the file. It was the case involving the two girls who'd been found in the alley that he was reviewing, the case for which Ben was being accused and, according to what he was reading, he was surprised to find that the finger was also now being pointed towards Dani.

It was incredible, the way they'd pieced together the evidence in such a way that, if he was reading without any other knowledge of the situation, then he couldn't help but believe what was being alleged. What was more incredible though, was the amount of information that was missing.

For starters, there was no mention of any interviews carried out with Ben, despite the man being previously detained and having come here voluntarily to report what had happened to Steph. On top of that, the DNA evidence had miraculously yielded no results, which was surprising given that the girls had clearly been assaulted by numerous people, of which at least one was likely to have been recorded on the national database.

Shaking his head, he released a frustrated sigh and sat back in his chair. There was plenty of information from which he could raise concerns, but nothing that couldn't be passed off with the simplest of explanations. He realised that, if he was going to do anything to help Ben and Dani, then he wasn't going to find anything he could use here. He had no choice but to prove the link between the two detectives and the club, which was something he'd spent a long time both trying and failing to do.

Maybe there was another way to do this, he wondered; maybe he was going about this whole thing in the wrong manner? He was going to struggle to prove anything through their cases, they were too clever for that, but maybe he could find a way of raising enough doubt to question their integrity in the general sense? He'd managed to secure the investigation into Limpy's death for himself and, given the man's known affiliation with The Sons, could he find a way to demonstrate a link through that?

Switching off his computer, Roberts stood up from his desk and glanced over at Crowther and Wishall. They were still firmly engrossed in pretending to be detectives and hadn't seemed to notice his movement, so he took the chance to leave quickly and made his way over to the lifts, where he waited impatiently for one of them to arrive.

Eventually, the doors slid open and he stepped inside, firmly pressing the button for the car park as he did. Turning round, he breathed a sigh of relief as the doors began to close but, before they'd shut completely, a hand stopped them and forced them open once more.

"Where are you off to?" Crowther asked, as he and Wishall joined Roberts in the lift.

"Out" Roberts replied, bluntly.

"Out where?" Crowther questioned.

For a moment, Roberts wanted to provide him with an explicit suggestion as to what the man and his partner could do with themselves, but he fought against the urge and remained quiet.

"A lot of people might think he's actually got a lead on his case" Crowther continued, emphasising the word 'his' as he smiled conspiratorially at Wishall. "But we both know that isn't likely, don't we?"

"He's probably just going out to grab some lunch, the fat bastard" Wishall laughed.

"Or he's off to visit his retarded mother?" Crowther added.

Knowing they were trying to bait him, Roberts remained tight-lipped.

"Then again" Crowther suggested. "Maybe we've misjudged him? Maybe he's realised there's an obvious suspect in 'his' case and he's off to pick Mr Trowman up now?"

"Why would I be doing that?" Roberts asked, finally losing his battle to keep quiet.

"Because if you were any kind of decent detective" Crowther replied quickly, "then you'd already be aware that the word on the street is your new best friend, Mr Trowman, was the one who murdered the gang member you just happened to stumble across."

"Gang member?" Roberts questioned. "Surely you're aware that it was the man known as Limpy who was found?"

"Was that his name?" Crowther asked innocently, as the lift doors opened and he and Wishall followed Roberts into the car park.

Ignoring the two men, Roberts made his way directly to his car and opened the driver's door, which was immediately slammed shut by Crowther.

"You need to listen up" he hissed. "This case had better be solved in the right way, or you might just find yourself in deeper shit than you've ever come across before."

"That sentence doesn't even make sense" Roberts chuckled. "Do you want to try that again?"

"What do you mean, it doesn't make sense?"

Smiling broadly, Roberts shook his head. "I mean" he chuckled, "that surely you're the ones being told how the investigation should come out and, if it doesn't, then you two will be the first on The Sons' shit list? After all, that sort of stuff is what they pay you for, isn't it?"

All of them were used to the one, unoccupied seat at the end of the table, but the three additional empty spaces were causing no small amount of concern and the silence in the room spoke volumes.

"How the fuck has it all come to this?" Ruckus questioned, passing his gaze around everyone, but lingering longer on Ethan. "Since when do we let ourselves be hurt like this?"

The silence continued, until Ruckus spoke again.

"What the fuck happened?" he asked, staring at Jimmy.

"We didn't think he'd be there" Jimmy mumbled, acutely aware of the stares that were being aimed in his direction. "An' he was just too strong."

"There were fuckin' two of you" Touchy hissed. "How the fuck didn't you take him out?"

"He dropped Limpy before we knew what was goin' on."

"So you fuckin' ran?"

The question was spat, more than asked, and the tone of Touchy's voice positively dripped with derision.

"The guy's fuckin' massive!" Jimmy exclaimed. "I'd fuckin' see you stand your ground against 'im!"

"I wouldn't fuckin' crawl back here like a fuckin' pussy, that's for sure."

"Alright, that's enough!" Ruckus exclaimed, slamming his hand on the table. "Where we at with all this?"

As the club's Vice President, Ethan took a breath to speak, but Ruckus cut him off, indicating that he wanted Touchy to give the report.

"Well" Touchy began, flashing Ethan a disparaging glance across the table. "We lost Ray to the Minions and Limpy to Ben, Knuckle's missin' an' I'm guessin' he's gone the same way as them pair, but we've got Banjo back at the table. Ben and that doctor bitch are fuck knows where, Crowther an' Wishall have missed out on taking Limpy's case and they're nowhere near to pinnin' all this shit on Ben. Basically, the whole things fucked, but my freshly-sucked cock is appreciatin' the bitch we've got in the storage room."

"I told you to leave her alone!" Ethan hissed.

"An' I told you I 'ain't listenin' to you anymore" Touchy hissed back. "You fuckin' brought her here and you fuckin' fucked all this shit up, so don't try comin' the fuckin' boss with me now kid, you're fucked if you think you're still someone I give a shit about."

"Agreed" Ruckus stated, before Ethan had the chance to reply. "I told you to get this sorted an' you 'ain't done shit but bury us deeper. Take that fuckin' Vice President patch off an' give it to Touchy, unless anyone disagrees?"

His question, whilst open to everyone in the room, was clearly not something to be disputed and, predictably, all around the table kept their mouths shut whether they agreed or not.

"That's fuckin' settled then" Ruckus continued, without looking at Ethan.

Shaking his head, Ethan stood up and slipped his Cut from his shoulders. He pulled out his knife and cut the patch from the leather, which he then threw across the table.

"You can fuckin' 'ave it!" he hissed, as he sat back down.

"What the fuck are you doin'?" Ruckus asked, finally turning to look at him. "That 'ain't your fuckin' chair anymore."

"For fuck's sake" Ethan muttered, standing up again.

He walked round the table as Touchy took his seat, intending to take Touchy's old place, but Ruckus coughed as he reached Limpy's old chair.

"That'll do you" Ruckus grinned, nodding at the empty space at the far end of the table.

Again shaking his head, Ethan sat down heavily as Ruckus continued to talk.

"I'm fuckin' takin' this over" he announced. "I want the word out that we're to be told as soon as Ben and that Doctor are found, make sure all our associates are made aware of it and, when they're located, you let me know straight away, whatever time of the fuckin' day it is. As for the cunt in the closet, just fuckin' kill her now. I don't wanna hear about her again."

Touchy smiled broadly as the members around the table agreed, until Ethan piped up.

"I've already told you we can't fuckin' kill her yet" he stated, instantly drawing a scowl from Ruckus, but he continued, unperturbed. "You want Ben to confess to it all? You need her to be able to speak to him so, if you kill her now, you've lost the only leverage we've got and that guy's already proven that he's too dangerous to underestimate."

Ruckus, along with everyone else around the table, stared at him for a few moments, before he gave the briefest of nods. "Ok" he agreed, "but what's all this shit about leaving her alone? She's dead once we finish with her anyway so, Touchy, do whatever the fuck you want with her, just make sure she can still talk."

Smiling broadly, Touchy glared at Ethan as he replied. "Oh, I fuckin' will" he laughed.

Chapter 34

Sat in silence, Ben and Dani were the only customers in the coffee shop. The atmosphere between them had been tense from the moment he'd snapped yesterday, with Dani struggling to come to terms with what he'd done and Ben not making any attempt to explain his actions. Behind the counter, Albert watched them with deep concern in his eyes, although his worry had gone unnoticed amidst all the thoughts that were jostling for position in their respective minds.

The bell above the door sounded, drawing all their attention as Roberts walked in. He signalled to Albert that he didn't want a drink and made his way directly to the table.

"How're you two holding up?" he asked, as he joined them.

Ben merely shrugged, whilst Dani shook her head.

"Well" he continued, "the good news is that I've covered what happened at Emily's flat. It looks to be a simple case of break and entry that went sour, that's all. There's no leads on what actually happened, so the case will go unsolved and the victim had no family that I can find, so it'll be a state burial, unless someone comes forward and claims the body."

Still there was very little in the way of response and, looking at them, Roberts realised something was wrong.

"What's going on?" he questioned, uncertainly.

Dani glanced over at Ben. "Ask him" she mumbled.

Roberts followed her glance. "Well?"

"There's one less fucker to worry about" Ben answered, without any concern for the fact that Albert was well within ear-shot.

"What?" Roberts exclaimed.

Candidly, Ben provided an explanation as to what had happened at The Angels' new clubhouse, to which Roberts let out a long sigh.

"You're shitting me" he muttered. "Has this become some kind of game to you?"

"The body's been taken care of" Ben replied, bluntly. "So don't worry about it."

"Don't worry about it? Jesus, it's been hard enough helping you out as it is, and that's without you actively looking to get yourself arrested. By rights, I should be taking you in right now."

"Don't worry about it" Ben repeated.

"You could at least pretend I'm doing this by the book" Roberts exclaimed, glancing nervously across at Albert, who quickly looked away and acted as though he was busy. "You know? Pretend I'm actually an officer of the law and not announce things like this to the general public."

"Albert's fine" Ben stated, having noticed where Roberts was looking. "And there's no one else here to listen in."

Almost as though he was acknowledging the sensitive nature of the conversation, Albert left his position behind the counter and walked over to the door, which he bolted shut.

"What are you doing?" Ben asked, as Albert walked back towards them.

"It's dead in here" Albert replied, through an attempted smile. "So it's not worth staying open today. Don't you worry though, you three can stay here as long as you want and, if you need anything, just give me a shout. Let me know if you're done though, so I can lock the door behind you."

With that, he continued through to the back room, leaving them alone to keep talking.

"So, have you found anything out?" Ben asked, once privacy had been provided. "Is there anything you can use against those two pricks?"

"Crowther and Wishall?" Roberts replied. "There's plenty of shit in their file, but nothing I can use. The problem is that they know I'm looking into what they're doing and that's going to make it harder to catch them out."

"How the fuck do they know you're looking? I thought you were good at this under-cover shit?"

Ignoring Ben's tone, Roberts shook his head. "They've known my suspicions for a long time and bailing you out has hardly helped to keep it under wraps."

"So, what makes you think they're on to you?"

"The fact that Crowther had me pinned against my car yesterday was kind of a hint" Roberts stated, without any trace of humour. "And his subtle warning that I'd be in a world of shit if I don't arrest you pretty much confirmed it."

"Shit" Ben mumbled.

"Shit's right" Roberts agreed.

"What happens now, then?" Dani asked, realising the conversation was getting nowhere. "Where do we go from here?"

"Well, at the moment, there's not much we can do" Roberts answered. "You two need to keep your heads down while I see what I can do. And, for Christ's sake, stop killing people!"

"That's it?" Dani questioned, paying no attention to his last comment. "Keep our heads down?"

"Or you can give yourselves up" Ruckus stated, as he walked in from the back room.

Stunned, the three of them watched silently as four members of The Sons followed their president in and stood behind him as he casually sat down at their table.

"It's simple" he continued. "For all their faults, Crowther and Wishall have prepared a good case against you, all you need to do is confess to all the murders, which I'm guessin' will include Knuckle, and this'll all be over."

"And why the fuck would I do that?" Ben asked, showing no fear of the person sitting opposite him. "Why the fuck wouldn't I just kill you all right here, right now?"

Laughing, Ruckus shook his head. "You might be big" he replied, "but you really think you'll get that far if you take us on?"

In unison, The Sons reached into their Cuts and pulled out their guns.

"They'll shoot you all dead, the moment you move" Ruckus chuckled. "So good fuckin' luck with that."

Even in his current mental state, Ben realised trying anything would be futile, so he remained seated and continued to stare at Ruckus.

"As I was sayin', the deal is simple" Ruckus smiled. "You give yourself up and we release Steph, unharmed."

"How do I know she's still alive?" Ben asked.

"You don't" Ruckus answered. "So you'll just have to presume I'm tellin' you the truth."

"Well, how do I know you'll release her?"

"Fuck off!" Ruckus snapped. "I'm not playin' this game. The simple fact is that you know fuck all and it's gonna stay that way. Now, I realise it's a big decision, so I'm gonna give you a week to come to your senses. When that week's up though, if you 'ain't come forward with a confession, I'm gonna deliver Steph's head to you and put a bullet through all three of yours."

With that, he rose from his seat and led his men towards the back room.

"Oh" he muttered, stopping and turning to face them. "One other thing you should know is that my men are intendin' on having some seriously sick fun with the bitch while you decide and I'm not plannin' on stoppin' 'em. So, the longer you take, the more fucked she's gonna be. You never know, she might even enjoy it, even when it fuckin' hurts, judgin' by the way she's been so far."

Unable to contain himself, Ben jumped out of his seat, but both Dani and Roberts pulled him back down as Touchy turned and fired a bullet over his head.

"She's been screamin' out your name" he smiled, "and now I'm gonna make that bitch bleed, just for you."

"I've gotta do it" Ben lamented, shaking his head as he spoke.

He was sitting in the main room of The Angels' clubhouse, along with Billy, Lee, Roberts, Dani, Alex, Jason and several other members. The three of them had gone straight back there after their meeting with Ruckus and were busy discussing what they needed to do now.

"Don't be such a fuckin' idiot" Billy scolded. "You think they'll release her if you do? Even if she's still alive, she knows who's done this to her, so there's no way on this Earth that they'll let her loose to talk."

"I agree" Roberts pitched in. "They're just playing on your naivety and desperation. If she is still alive they'll . . ."

"She is still alive" Ben insisted angrily, cutting in on Roberts' sentence.

"You really believe that?" Roberts questioned.

"I have to" Ben stated. "Otherwise I might as well give up right now."

Silence fell in the room, until Lee spoke up.

"Well, you 'ain't givin' yourself up, that's for sure" he confirmed, looking at Ben, "and we're runnin' blind at the moment."

A general murmur of agreement rose up from everyone gathered there.

"So, where the hell do we go from here?" he continued, now turning to Billy. "You know these people. So d'you have any suggestions?"

"You said they came in through the back of the coffee shop, after the owner had locked the doors?" Billy asked, bringing a nod of confirmation from Roberts. "Well, they had to know you were there and the only way that could've happened, is if someone told them. Ruckus relies on havin' eyes on the street, so I'm guessin' the owners have been tied in."

"Albert and Mary?" Ben replied. "I can't believe they'd be involved."

"They're perfect candidates" Billy answered. "If the place was runnin' at a loss, then Ruckus would've seen that and I daresay you'll find they're now appearing to turn a tidy profit. That's what he does. He filters the club's money through a strugglin' business and puts the owners in a position where they have to do what he wants. It gives 'em a safe way to launder their cash and keeps him informed at the same time."

"The place is always empty" Dani agreed. "It's very possible."

"Then that's our way in" Billy announced, as he rose from his seat. "Roberts, you go and look into their books, find out what they've been turning in over the last year and you'll find the sinkin' ship has suddenly managed to right itself."

"And where are you goin'?" Jason asked.

"You two come with me" Billy commanded, pointing at a couple of the members, "I've got an idea."

With that, the meeting was over and, as they all filtered away, Roberts pulled Dani over to the side of the room. "How're you doing with all this?" he asked.

Dani shook her head. "I don't know whether I'm coming or going" she confessed.

"And how's Ben doing?"

Again, she shook her head but, this time, her eyes moistened a little. "He's lost it" she confirmed. "When he killed that man, just shot him in the head as though it didn't matter..."

Her voice tailed off mid-way through her sentence.

"Look" Roberts whispered, kindly. "What he did to that man was shocking and I know you're struggling to understand it, but he hadn't got a choice. It probably isn't much help, but you should know the man was evil and has killed a lot of innocent people in his time with The Sons. They couldn't let him go, or he would've gone straight back to the club and they would've wiped you all out in no time at all. That's who they are and, if you, Ben and the rest of this ragged bunch are to stand any chance of getting through this, then he's got to lower himself to their level. He's going to have to do things that no normal person would ever consider and it's going to change him. He needs someone like you to stand alongside him, no matter how difficult it becomes. That's the only way either of you are going to get through this."

Staring at him, it was apparent that Dani understood what he was saying, but that didn't make it easy for her to accept.

"I just want this to be over" she muttered, still fighting back the tears. "I just want to go back to my life."

"That's not going to happen" Roberts replied, bluntly but not unkindly. "I know it's hard to accept, but you've got to see that you can't go back to the life you had, not after what's happened and what you've seen. There are some big decisions ahead for you and for Ben, the only thing you can do, is make sure you know the reasons you've chosen them and go all in. There's no room for any half-measures, not if you want to come out of this alive."

Again, Dani stared at him, until she slowly gave a gentle nod. "I know" she reluctantly agreed.

In the relative solace of her dorm, to where she'd retired as soon as the meeting had reached its worrying conclusion, Roberts' words played continuously in Dani's head, rushing back and forth as she thought over everything that'd happened to them. She recalled the first time she'd met Ben, when he'd been so caring and warm in the hospital. She considered how much he'd lost, how quickly it'd been taken from him, and how cold he'd seemed when he pulled the trigger yesterday. That led her mind to her own situation, the way she'd ended up there in the first place, and how, without actually doing anything wrong, she'd found herself being ostracised from her job and forced out of her home.

It was hard to accept what was happening, with everything deteriorating so quickly in front of her eyes, almost as though she was stuck in someone else's nightmare and should be waking up soon, but that was the problem, wasn't it? She was very much awake and acutely aware of what was going on. Roberts had been right when he'd told her they had no control over the situation and that difficult decisions would need to be made. The question though, was whether she could bring herself to make them.

A commotion from the main room suddenly cut into her thoughts and she tried to block it out, but there was too much noise for that to be possible. Closing her eyes, she wondered what could be happening, a thought that brought nothing but more dread, and she decided it would be best to check, as her imagination would only heighten her concern.

The sight which greeted her when she walked into the main room left her stunned, knocking the wind completely out of her lungs as she instantly regretted her decision to investigate.

"What the hell is going on?" she demanded to know, staring intently at Albert and Mary, who were both sitting, scared witless, in the centre of the room.

"These two are gonna talk" Billy announced, without look away from the couple. "They're gonna tell us exactly how we can hit The Sons."

"But we don't know anything" Albert whined, looking imploringly towards Ben. "They don't tell us anything, we're just a way for them to launder their money, that's all."

Also looking at Ben, Dani wondered how he could be sitting there so impassively when two people he'd come to see as practically being family, were so obviously in trouble.

"So, when do they bring in the money?" Billy asked.

Albert glanced at Mary, who was now openly crying as she clung tightly to his arm, before shaking his head. "I'm sorry" he mumbled. "I can't say anything to you, or they'll hurt Mary."

"They're hurting Steph!" Ben suddenly snapped, striding over to Albert and leaning in close to his face. "You remember Steph, don't you? You remember the woman who was always kind and caring, even when things were going wrong for her? Well, she's currently in the hands of those vicious bastards and they're doing things to her that no woman, no person, should ever have to go through and, unless you start fuckin' talkin', I'm gonna start using your wife to demonstrate the shit they're doin' to her."

With that, he looked directly at Mary, who was now visibly shaking with fear.

"Ben!" Dani yelled, unable to contain herself any longer.

"Or maybe I'll just fuckin' kill her, right here" he continued, ignoring Dani's voice. "Then, like me, you'll have fuck all else to lose."

"Jesus Christ!" Lee exclaimed, stepping forward and pulling Ben away from the couple. "You need to calm the fuck down!"

Ben continued to stare angrily at both Albert and Mary.

"You see what's happenin'?" Billy asked, drawing Albert's attention. "You see what's goin' on? Someone you thought you trusted has reached the point where he won't hesitate to pull that fuckin' trigger and, honestly, I 'ain't gonna stop him if he does. Now, if you wanna get out of this intact, start fuckin' talkin'!"

Now shaking himself, Albert slowly nodded. "They dropped a bag of money off yesterday" he reluctantly admitted. "They said it wasn't to go through the books and we were to store it until they come and collect it in a couple of days."

"What's the money for?" Billy questioned.

"I don't know what this is for" Albert shrugged, "but last time they did this, they came back a few hours later with another bag that we were to store for them."

Billy nodded his understanding, but wanted to confirm things anyway. "What was in the bag?"

"They said not to open it" Albert stated.

Turning away from them for a moment, Billy seemed to be pondering something. "It'll have been drugs" he eventually announced. "They'll be storing them at your place for a few days, in order to check the bag's not bein' followed by anyone. You said they'll pick it up in a couple of days?"

Albert nodded.

"Then, when they do, you give me a call."

With his fear rising by the second, Albert couldn't find the words to either agree or disagree but, when Billy pulled out his gun and pushed it firmly into Mary's temple, he managed to indicate his willingness to abide by the request.

Chapter 35

Albert was agitated, fussing around and doing very little of any value as he tried to keep himself calm. Regularly, he glanced towards the back door, expecting it to open at any second whilst, in the corner, Ben, Billy, Lee and Dani waited patiently for the moment to arrive.

Of the four of them, only Dani showed any signs of nervousness as she shuffled uneasily from one foot to the other. She hadn't wanted to come along, especially given the reason she was there, but they'd insisted and left her with no choice. If things went badly, they'd said, then they'd need her to keep one of the men alive for long enough to talk, but they'd also insisted on her carrying a gun which, despite their assurances that it was simply for protection, only added to the uneasy feeling that weighed her down.

"Will you get a hold of yourself?" Billy commanded, staring fixedly at Albert.

"That's easy to say" Albert snapped.

"You managed it well enough when you were selling us out" Ben muttered harshly, bringing a cold glare from Billy.

"There's no need for that" he scolded. "Not today."

Ben shook his head, but kept his focus on Albert. "If anything happens to Steph" he hissed, but Billy cut him off.

"That's enough!" he snapped. "Jesus Christ! The man didn't fuckin' take her, did he? Yeah, he sold you out, but what choice d'ya think he had?"

"There's always a fuckin' choice."

"Is that why you're doing this?" Dani questioned. "Is that why you shot that man in the head?"

Ben turned to her, momentarily speechless.

"Is that why you're about to torture someone to the point at which you might need me to keep them alive?" she continued. "You're choosing to do this to these people?"

"I'm doing this because I have to" Ben replied, sternly.

"Exactly" Dani snapped. "So climb down off your high horse and give Albert a break. He could have chosen not to help us now, but I guess your threat to rape and kill Mary took that option away from him, didn't it?"

The room fell into a stunned silence as each of them exchanged awkward glances.

"This whole situation's fucked" Lee announced, in an attempt to break the tension. "None of us want to be here, but none of us has a choice. Let's just leave it at that, shall we? Fuckin' hell! We've got enough shit to worry about, without fuckin' about with all this 'you did this, you did that' bullshit."

"Fuckin' right" Billy agreed, as the others nodded their acceptance of the suggestion. "What time you expectin' 'em?"

Albert shrugged. "I never know" he answered. "It's normally a few hours after they pick up the money."

"So, what time did they pick up the cash?"

"It was just after I called you, about eight o'clock."

In unison, they glanced up at the clock on the wall and saw it was approaching half past eleven.

"So, where the fuck are they?" Lee questioned, to which the answer came in the form of the door being pushed open.

Immediately, Billy, Lee and Ben raised their guns and, as Jimmy walked in, he automatically reached for his own piece.

"Don't fuckin' bother!" Billy commanded, causing Jimmy to pause as he looked around the room. "Both of you, sit the fuck down and put the bag on the table."

The position of the open door meant that, from where she was standing, Dani could only see Jimmy but, as he obediently stumbled into the room, she couldn't hide her confusion when she saw who followed him in.

"Emily?" both her and Lee gasped.

"What the fuck are you doing here?" Emily snapped in response. "You stupid bitch, I told you not to get involved."

"Fuck that" Lee exclaimed, as Dani struggled for anything to say. "What the fuck are you doin' here?"

"You both know her?" Billy asked the two of them, as he gestured with his gun for Emily to take a seat next to Jimmy at the table.

Dani only continued to stare at her friend, whilst Lee shook his head in bewilderment.

"After the accident" he said, unconsciously reaching up to touch the scar on his still-shaven head, "she was my doctor in the hospital."

"And how is my favourite patient doing?" Emily sneered.

"A fuck of a lot better than you're about to be" Lee snapped.

"Now it makes sense" Billy muttered to himself, before looking at Dani. "I was tryin' to figure out how they knew Ben was at your place and how they knew where you went after the Strip Club was destroyed. I'm guessin' this is your friend?"

"Oh no" Emily answered with a grin, before Dani could speak. "I'm her best friend" she laughed, punctuating the air with her fingers.

Standing motionless, the conversation slowly worked its way into Dani's mind, although confusion was still painted firmly in her expression.

"But you didn't know Ben was there" she mumbled, shaking her head in disbelief. "So why did those two men come to your flat?"

Now it was Emily's turn to shake her head. "I told you not to get involved in all this" she repeated, "but you just had to keep helping Ben, didn't you? That's why I told them where you were and that's why they were supposed to kill you."

Even though the statement hadn't needed to be voiced, the words still stung Dani and she let out an involuntary gasp.

"You sent them there to kill me?" she questioned, somewhat morosely.

Emily shrugged. "You were a problem, so you needed to be handled."

"But you were my friend" Dani exclaimed. "I trusted you."

"You're so fucking naïve" Emily laughed.

"Alright!" Alex interjected. "This reunion shit 'ain't gettin' us anywhere."

His point was taken by both Ben and Lee, but Billy hadn't finished mulling over it all in his mind.

"I should've seen it" he muttered.

"Should've seen what?" Lee asked

"I just didn't think about it" Billy continued.

"Didn't think about what?" Lee snapped, becoming agitated.

"I didn't think about the fact that this bitch got herself placed into the hospital at Ruckus' request."

"How the fuck d'you know that?" Alex questioned, now sharing Lee's agitation.

"The Sons will always be my club" Billy replied. "I've always kept a close eye on what you're doin'."

Letting out a derisory snort, Emily chuckled. "It's not your club" she smiled. "And you know nothing about us, old man."

"Really?" Billy laughed. "So I don't know that Ethan's your brother?"

"Well done" Emily mocked, slowly clapping her hands together. "That's some truly outstanding insight you've given us there, seeing as Ruckus is our father."

"That's the thing" Billy continued, clearly enjoying the moment. "He isn't."

A stunned silence immediately filled the room, until Emily comprehensively shattered it.

"Fuck off" she hissed, all mockery now gone from her voice. "You're talking shit."

"Trust me" Billy smiled. "There's better shit I could lie about. Fuck, we don't even know your real name. I'd tell you to ask Crowther about it, seeing as he was the one who made it all possible, but you're not gonna see him again, so you're just gonna have to take my word for it."

"Take your word for it? Why the fuck am I going to do that?"

"Because I'm the only one here who knows the truth."

"No. You're the only one here who's claiming that what you're saying is the truth."

"I can't make you believe me" Billy sighed. "But I thought you should know what kinda man Ruckus is, before you choose to die for him."

"And, exactly, what kind of a man is he?"

"He's the kind of psycho" Billy began, "who, about twenty years ago, decided to walk into an innocent man's house and kill him, along with his wife, before coming back to the clubhouse with their kids in his car and claiming them as his own."

"You're lying!" Emily spat.

"Fair enough" Billy replied. "Tell me about your mother."

"You fucking bastard! You know my mother died when I was born."

"That's a fuckin' coincidence, ain't it?"

Doubt flickered momentarily in Emily's eyes, before it was replaced with burning anger.

Throughout all of this, Jimmy had sat silently listening but, as Emily floundered for a response, he finally added his voice to the conversation. "Why the fuck would he bring the kids back?"

"I dunno" Billy answered. "None of us did. To us, it wasn't something we'd ever have expected from a man who was willin' to kill anythin' that fuckin' moved but then, I guess, that's what makes him a psycho. There's no explanation for anythin' that sick bastard does."

"This is just a bunch of bullshit from a bitter, old man" Jimmy sneered. "You think this load of crap will get us to do what you want?"

Without taking his eyes off Emily, Billy stepped forward and smashed the handle of his gun into the side of Jimmy's face, knocking him out of his chair and sending him crashing to the floor. Immediately, Lee and Ben picked him up and sat him back down, before securing both his and Emily's hands behind their backs.

"I'm not relying on this to make you talk" Billy finally replied, as he once more stepped forward and again smashed his gun into Jimmy's face. "But, judging by the look in this bitch's eyes, I'm guessing she's having issues with doubt because, y'know, finding out your whole life is a worthless lie kinda does that to people."

"You're a drunk, twisted, bitter old man getting your kicks out of messing with my head" Emily hissed defiantly, resulting in Billy smashing the gun across Jimmy's face yet again.

"Keep talking" Billy dared her. "I'm fuckin' enjoyin' this and, every time you open your mouth and don't tell me what I wanna know, I get to smash your boyfriend's head in just a little bit more."

"Fuck you!" she spat, tears beginning to fall as Billy delivered another blow.

The process continued as Billy's questions were repeatedly ignored until, suddenly, Ben snapped and kicked Jimmy backwards in his chair, cracking the back of his head on the floor.

"You're a tough fucker" he hissed, leaning over the man. "But let's see just how tough your slut of a woman is."

With that, he dropped to his knee and pushed the gun into the underside of the chair, directly in line with Jimmy's anus. Pulling the trigger, he fired a bullet and then stood back, watching as the man's body twitch violently in the seat as Emily screamed.

"You see how agonising that is?" he asked, turning to Emily. "It's gonna take a long time for that piece of shit to die and every second is gonna hurt like he's never hurt before. You start talkin', and I'll put him out of his misery."

Unable to take her eyes off her boyfriend's pain, Emily wept openly. "You'll just kill me anyway" she sobbed. "So why would I tell you anything?"

"Killing you is a given" Ben replied. "The question is, do you wanna go quick, or do you want the same as him?"

Still, Emily didn't look at him. "Fuck you" she mumbled.

Slapping her across the face, Ben grabbed her chin and turned her head towards him, whilst Dani's voice could be heard in the background.

"You killed the girl in the hospital" she muttered. "You killed that poor, innocent girl."

Recognising the distress in her voice, they all turned to look at her and saw she was standing, shaking, with her gun pointing at Emily.

"Dani?" Ben implored. "What are you doing?"

"I trusted you" she continued, oblivious to his words. "You were supposed to be my friend."

"Dani" Ben tried, again.

"You've put us here. You've done this to us."

Slowly, Ben stood upright and took a step towards her. "Dani, please put the gun down."

"You're pure evil" she hissed. "You don't deserve to live."

"Dani!" Ben exclaimed, throwing himself forwards but, before he could reach her, she pulled the trigger.

As the click of the lock resonated around the room, Steph tensed up and fought to control her breathing. She heard the familiar sound of footsteps approaching and, when hands took a firm hold of her and lifted her out of the chair, she felt her skin crawl. Maybe she should put up some sort of fight, struggle against the inevitable but, through each time this had happened, she'd come to realise it only made the act more enjoyable for the sick bastards and depriving them of that pleasure was the closest she could ever hope to maintaining some kind of control.

Standing unsteadily, her legs weakened from sitting in the same position for too long, her t-shirt was pulled up and over her head before the hands worked their way down her body. She tried to close her mind to the feel of the man's touch, but the persistent pawing made the attempt futile and, when fingers pulled at her underwear, exposing her completely to the stranger, she couldn't prevent the sharp intake of breath that brought a satisfied grunt from the man.

Submissively, she allowed herself to be pushed down on to the cold, hard floor, where her knees were parted as the assailant took up his position between her legs. Turning her head away from the hot breath in her face, she braced herself as she heard the sound of a zip being unfastened and, after what seemed like an eternity, the sudden penetration brought a reactive gasp that she didn't want to provide.

Was this it, she questioned, as the man painfully thrust himself into her. Was this all her future was to hold? She'd long ago given up hope of being released, realising that her ability to identify Ethan meant she would forever be a danger to them and, through the snippets of conversation she'd overheard, it was clear that the vague dream of any rescue had never been more than a pathetic fantasy.

A loud groan signalled the end of the assault and, as she was lifted back into the chair with her clothing remaining discarded, her thoughts drifted inevitably to Ben and the fact that they'd surely killed him. Her tears moistened the already saturated blindfold as she was left alone once more and, for the first time in her life, she found herself hoping that there was a heaven. She prayed that her spirit would get there and she longed, desperately, for Ben to be waiting for her.

Ben sat silently at the Clubhouse bar, staring at the drink that remained, untouched, in front of him. He'd been there for a while, since they'd returned from the coffee shop, with an expression that made it abundantly clear he didn't want to be disturbed, which was something to which everyone had paid heed. Eventually though, Alex approached him.

"You actually gonna drink that?" he asked, keeping a safe distance between them.

No response came from Ben.

"You actually gonna talk?" Alex tried.

Still, there was no response.

"For fuck's sake" Alex snapped. "You've gotta pull yourself together. Dani needs you."

"Why?" Ben replied, finally looking at the man.

"Because she 'ain't said a word since she pulled that trigger."

"So, go and talk to her then."

"And what the fuck am I gonna say to her? I 'ain't ever killed anyone."

"Then get Billy or Jason to do it."

"But she needs you!"

"Why the fuck is it me who's gotta speak to her?"

Letting out a long sigh, Alex shook his head. "When you killed that man at Emily's flat" he stated, keeping his voice calm despite the anger he felt, "Dani sat with you and talked to you, desperate to help you deal with it."

Ben opened his mouth to reply, but Alex cut him off.

"I keep hearin' about how you're some kind of warm, compassionate, caring man, but all I'm seeing right now is a sack of shit who don't give a fuck about anyone else. A fuckin' psycho who won't think twice about shootin' a man up his ass."

Again, Ben opened his mouth to reply and Alex waited to hear what he had to say, but no words found their way out.

"She's done everything she could to help you" Alex pointed out. "She's lost her job, her home and now she's killed the person she thought was her best friend. It's time you started paying back what she's given you. Go and help her."

As Alex stood back and pointed towards the dormitories, Ben gave a shake of his head and jumped off the stool.

"Fine" he mumbled, before walking past the man and towards the corridor.

When he reached the dorm, he knocked on the door and wasn't surprised when there came no response.

"Dani?" he called out, knocking again.

This time there was a reply, although the voice was too quiet to hear what was said.

With a deep breath, he opened the door and leaned in. "Are you ok?" he asked, immediately realising the obtuse nature of the question.

Dani didn't answer straight away, continuing only to stare out of the window from where she sat in a chair. Eventually though, she gave an almost imperceptible shake of her head.

"Does it bother you?" she asked.

"Does what bother me?"

"How easily you've put an end to those lives?"

"They don't deserve to live" Ben answered, immediately.

Dani's reply came almost as quickly. "That's not what I asked."

Closing the door, Ben stepped into the room and took a seat on the edge of the bed, next to Dani's chair.

"Look" he began, keeping his voice calm as he spoke. "These people are nothing but vicious, violent killers who wouldn't think twice about doing the same to us."

"That's still not answering the question."

"I guess I don't understand the question, then" Ben replied, a little angrily.

"When I fired that gun" Dani muttered, almost to herself, "I knew exactly what I was doing. I looked at my friend, heard what she was saying, and all I wanted to do was put an end to her lies. I've dedicated my whole life to looking after people yet, as soon as I realised Emily was working against us, my first reaction was to kill her and now I'm sitting here, trying to feel sorry for what I've done, but I just can't find it in me to do that."

"You were reacting to the situation" Ben pointed out. "She tried to have you killed, she tried to have me killed and I'm sure she was involved with what happened to both of those two girls. She was also involved in what happened to Steph and Sam. The woman was evil and you shouldn't feel bad for what you've done."

"But what happens when this is all over?" Dani asked. "What happens when we're not dealing with these people anymore?"

"When we're not dealing with these people anymore, then there'll be no need for any of this."

"Do you really believe that? Do you really believe it'll be that simple?"

"Of course I do."

Finally, Dani looked at him, shaking her head as she spoke. "What you did to that man today, kicking him over and firing the bullet into him, that's not normal in any situation. It was like your mind went straight to the most pain you could put him in and you did it without any hesitation, as though it was nothing. Now you're sitting here and I'm looking into your eyes, but I see no sign of remorse, no regret for what you've done. It's like you don't care, which is almost how I feel about what I did to Emily."

"But none of them are worth caring about."

"Was the girl in the alley worth caring about?"

Ben stared at her, a little stunned by the question.

"When you found her" she continued, "you didn't think about who she was or what she might have done in her life to end up there. All you saw was someone in trouble and all you wanted to do was help. Do you really think you can be that person again? Do you really think that, having seen all of this, having been a part of this kind of life, you won't question whether anyone else is worth caring about?"

"I'm doing this because I care" Ben answered.

"I know" Dani agreed. "But what happens the next time someone hurts her? If someone threatens her in a bar, will you react the same way as you would've done before all of this, or will you find yourself going straight back to the violence?"

Hesitating, Ben struggled to find a response.

"I don't plan on letting this change me that much" he finally replied.

"Sometimes change happens, whether we like it or not" Dani stated.

A knock on the door interrupted their conversation, and Alex's head appeared. "We're sittin' down" he told them, "and Lee wants you there, Ben."

"What about me?" Dani asked.

Alex shook his head. "Sorry, Darlin', these are a man-only thing. Club rules."

Dani nodded, giving no sign as to whether she was offended by that or not.

"I'm coming" Ben confirmed, standing up and following him out of the room, giving a last, brief glance towards Dani, who'd returned to gazing out of the window.

"Is she ok?" Alex asked, as they walked.

"I dunno" Ben shrugged.

"It's all fucked" Alex continued. "The whole fuckin' thing's messed up."

"You got that right" Ben agreed, as they entered the clubhouse meeting room.

Already, the members were gathered around the table, including Roberts, who'd been invited by Billy, and, as the two of them took their seats, Lee began.

"So, here's the score" he announced, sweeping his gaze around the table. "We've got no clue as to where they're holding Steph and we've killed three of their members. We've also done away with Ruckus' daughter and, the way I see it, it won't be long before they discover she's missin'. When that happens, it won't take them much to figure out why and they're gonna be comin' for us, so we've gotta do somethin' big, fuckin' quick."

A general murmur rose around the room, until Jason spoke up. "Then we fuckin' hit 'em" he stated. "We go in hard and fuck 'em up."

"We do that" Billy replied, "and Steph's dead before we've fired a second shot."

"So?" Jason questioned, deliberately avoiding Ben's glare. "There's more at stake here than just her. She's probably dead already, anyway."

"She's still alive" Ben hissed.

"And how the fuck do you know that?"

"She's still alive" Billy stated, moving quickly to stop any row, "because Ruckus 'ain't stupid. He needs leverage against Ben and he's not gonna leave 'em with nothin'."

Jason stared at him, but Billy continued before he could say anything.

"Lee's right" he said. "We need to move fast and, so far, we've got nothin' from the members. If we're gonna hit 'em, then we need to make sure Steph's safe, before we go in."

"So, you got a plan or somethin'?" Jason asked.

"That's why I asked Detective Roberts to join us" Billy confirmed. "We go after Crowther and Wishall, and we do it tonight. They're both pussies and one of 'em will tell us what we need to know."

All eyes turned to Roberts, whose expression clearly displayed his surprise at the announcement.

"You can't do that" he stammered. "You can't go after detectives."

"You wanna tell me why?" Billy asked.

Roberts' surprise turned to incredulousness as he spoke. "You go after detectives, and you're gonna have the whole department looking for you. When that happens, I can't protect you."

"You don't need to" Billy replied. "All you have to do is put forward the shit you've dug up on 'em and let nature take its course."

"I haven't got enough evidence for that."

"But you've got enough to suggest they're involved in some shady shit. Just make sure some of that flies in the direction of The Sons."

Pensively, Robert's shook his head. "It's too risky" he stated.

"Let us worry about that" Billy smiled. "Just give us their addresses and start workin' on the evidence."

Still, Roberts' reluctance was obvious.

"Trust me" Billy urged.

Finally, Roberts' agreed.

"That's sorted, then" Lee announced, before the detective could change his mind. "Me, Ben and Billy will pay those two fuckers a visit tonight. Jason, you and Alex get us ready."

Both Jason and Alex nodded.

"Right" Lee continued. "Billy's got our new Cuts, which he's gonna pass out now. The Angels of Nemesis Motorcycle Club officially starts here."

With that, he banged the gavel and the meeting was brought to a conclusion. Billy moved around the table, handing each member their Cut and, when he got to Ben, he stopped.

"You've been voted in" he smiled, holding out the leather vest as the members started filing out of the room.

Ben looked at him, then looked at the Cut. He thought about his conversation with Dani, about her suggestion that there was no chance of returning to a normal life, and then he thought of Steph and what he wanted to happen when he found her.

"No thanks" he replied. "I just want to find Steph and go back to the way things were."

"You really think you can do that?" Lee asked, having seen the rejection and come over to join them.

"Why not?"

"Because the shit you've done and the shit you've seen doesn't tend to go away" Billy stated. "Trust me, I know."

"But this isn't me" Ben pointed out.

Both Billy and Lee looked at him.

"You could've fooled me" Billy told him. "You're a fuckin' natural."

"No, I'm not" Ben reiterated.

A few seconds of silence passed, before Lee spoke again.

"I 'ain't gonna force you" he said, "but you know that findin' Steph 'ain't gonna be the end, don't ya? There's gonna be a whole load of shit comin' later, and it 'ain't a good idea to deal with it by yourself."

"I can deal with it" Ben smiled.

Lee shook his head. "I'm just sayin'" he replied, "that this Cut's gonna be waiting for you, whenever you need it."

Ben nodded. "Thanks" was all he said.

Chapter 36

Wishall's house was well outside the city, amidst a quiet village in which money was clearly abundant, which was a fact that wasn't lost on the three men who sat, watching, in a parked car at the side of the road.

"Jesus Christ" Lee muttered. "How much cash does that fucker pick up?"

"He didn't get that on detective wages, that's for sure" Billy replied. "The mother-fucker's gotta be grabbin' a sweet taste on the side."

"Sweet? There's enough sugar there to make a bastard instantly diabetic" Lee joked.

"It won't deflect bullets" Ben pointed out. "And he 'ain't taking all that shit to hell with him."

"You got that right" Lee agreed. "Come on, let's get this done."

With a cursory glance along the street, they jumped out of the car and ran across the road, where they vaulted the low garden wall and dropped out of sight on the other side of it. The lights were on in the house and the car was on the drive, so they knew Wishall was home, but Lee crawled across the lawn to peek through the window.

"He's in there" he told them, as he made his way back. "And it looks like he's by himself."

"Could there be anyone in the kitchen, or anywhere else in the house?" Billy asked.

Lee shook his head. "Not by the looks of it. Roberts said he lives by himself, he's sat watching TV and there's only one plate on the coffee table in front of him."

"So, what's the plan?" Ben asked.

Billy glanced back at the house. "It don't look as though he's goin' anywhere tonight, so we've gotta get in there, I guess."

"But how the fuck do we do that?" Lee questioned. "We 'ain't got enough time to wait till that prick goes to bed and he'll hear us if we try to break in."

"I've got an idea" Billy replied, pulling out his phone.

The car raced along the street, picking up speed as it approached its destination. Slewing from its path, it mounted the kerb and glanced against a wall, smashing the bricks and spreading debris across the impeccable garden as it bounced back towards the centre of the road. The driver, a young man blindly following orders he didn't fully understand, had been braced for the impact and turned in his seat to watch the front door of the property until the resident stormed out to survey the damage, at which point he revved the engine and left tyre tracks on the asphalt in his haste to get away.

At the back of the house, Billy, Lee and Ben waited patiently, hidden away in the bushes. As the sound of the impact echoed in the night air, they sprinted across the lawn and flattened themselves against the wall. Billy looked in through the window of the door and, once he was sure the coast was clear, he used the handle of his pistol to shatter the glass and reached in to gain access to the house.

Without a word between them, they quickly moved in to the kitchen and positioned themselves along the wall, next to the doorway. Billy held up his gun, ready in case Wishall walked through, whilst both Lee and Ben braced themselves behind him.

A few minutes later, they heard Wishall come back into the house, talking on the phone.

"The car was unregistered" he stated. "I didn't get a look at the driver."

The three of them exchanged glances as they heard the front door being closed.

"It was no accident!" Wishall continued. "The driver waited for me to go out and then scarpered, so you'd best get the uniforms out there looking for him. I want him picked up tonight."

With that, Wishall cancelled the call and cursed under his breath as he walked back through to the living room. Billy signalled that it was time to move and, silently, they hurried through the doorway.

"What the hell?" Wishall exclaimed, reaching for his gun as they rushed in.

"There'll be no need for that" Billy stated, glancing at the pistol in Wishall's hand.

"I'd say there's every need for it" Wishall replied, aiming it at Billy.

"We just wanna talk" Billy continued.

"Bullshit!" Wishall hissed. "If that's all you wanted, then you wouldn't have set up that charade outside and you wouldn't have come in here with those things locked and loaded."

"What you gonna do?" Lee asked. "Shoot all three of us? You 'ain't that fuckin' quick, so you might as well give it up."

A wry grin spread across Wishall's lips. "Yeah" he replied. "But I'm guessing you don't want me dead yet, so what are you going to do if I pull the trigger?"

"I'll shoot you right between the fuckin' eyes" Lee snapped.

"Then do it" Wishall chuckled.

"Just tell us where they're holding Steph" Ben pleaded.

"Who?" Wishall laughed.

"You fuckin' know who."

Wishall shrugged. "Maybe you're right" he replied. "But if you are, do you seriously think I'm going to tell you anything?"

"You'd better, or I'll . . ." Ben began, but Wishall cut him off.

"Or you'll what?" he chided. "Take a look at yourself. Do you even know who you're up against? Or what they can do to you?"

Angrily, Ben took a step towards the man, but stopped as the gun was cocked and turned towards him.

"That's not a good move" Wishall smiled. "You want to see Steph again and, if you move another inch, I'm going to make this whole thing pointless."

"Just tell us where she is" Ben repeated.

Shaking his head, Wishall continued to smile. "And what do you think will happen to me if I do? You think The Sons' will forgive me?"

"What do you think we'll do to you, if you don't?" Billy asked.

"Ah, that's the point, isn't it?" Wishall replied. "I'm dead either way, so all I've got left is to decide whether I make this easy for you."

"Well?" Lee questioned. "Will you?"

Wishall merely looked at each of them, finally resting his gaze on Ben. "Good Luck" he laughed as, in one fluid movement, he raised his gun to his chin and fired a bullet through the back of his head.

"Fuck" Ben cried out, as Wishall's body hit the floor.

"Jesus Christ" Lee exclaimed.

"You've got that right" Billy agreed. "Come on, we've gotta get the fuck outta here."

Both he and Lee turned to make their way to the door, but Ben remained where he stood, rooted to the spot.

"Come on" Billy urged. "The neighbours will have heard that shot and they'll be on the phone to the police already."

"We're not gonna find her" Ben mumbled, still staring at the corpse.

"We'll worry about that later" Lee insisted.

Turning towards them, Ben's expression burned with an almost pure anger. "Crowther's our last chance" he hissed. "We can't fuck this up."

"And we won't" Billy replied, grabbing Ben by the arm and dragging him towards the door.

"You'd better get all of this" Touchy commanded, as the Prospective Member obediently held up the video camera and pressed record.

Outside the door, the music blared as The Sons' party continued at full swing.

"You hear that?" he asked, walking towards Steph. "If anyone actually gave a fuck about what happens to you, they wouldn't hear you anyway. So keep that in mind, if you think screamin' or shoutin' will do you any good."

With that, he removed her blindfold and, even though the light in the room was dim, she had to blink numerous times before her eyes adjusted. Once they had, she looked pleadingly towards the prospect.

"Don't look at him" Touchy insisted, grabbing her by the chin and turning her face towards him. "You don't take your fuckin' eyes off me, got it?"

Involuntarily, her pupils flicked over to the door, but they were quickly re-focussed when he spat in her face.

"I said, don't look at him" he hissed, before moving around her and untying her hands.

Grabbing her by the throat, he pulled her up to her feet and held her there until her legs were stable enough to support her without help. He then pushed her towards the camera and backed away.

"Strip" he demanded. "And make it look fuckin' sexy."

Staring at him, Steph remained motionless.

"Go on then" Touchy urged. "Strip like the slut you are."

Still, Steph didn't move.

"Maybe you're not gettin' this?" he exclaimed, stepping towards her and slapping her across the face.

Mumbling, Steph tried to respond, but the gag rendered her words incomprehensible. Laughing, Touchy pulled the gag away.

"I'm not going to do anything you say" she barely managed to whisper, her voice hoarse from lack of use.

"Really?" Touchy questioned, pushing the barrel of his gun into her temple. "If you don't do it, I'll pull this fuckin' trigger."

Smiling, Steph turned towards him. "Do it" she urged.

Slowly, a sick grin spread across his lips and he re-holstered his weapon. He took a firm hold of her neck and pulled a cigarette lighter out of his pocket, which he sparked into life and held between her thighs.

"Maybe I won't kill you just yet" he whispered, as the heat quickly began to burn and she struggled to get away from the flame. "But I will fuckin' hurt you."

As tears started to roll down her cheeks, she nodded her understanding and, when he pulled the lighter from her and backed away, she took a hold of the t-shirt's hem.

"That's it" he encouraged, as she lifted it up and over her head, leaving her standing, naked, in front of her audience. "Now, throw it away and get down on your knees."

Her shoulders jerked with each sob, but she followed his command. He instructed her to crawl towards the Prospect and, once she was in front of him, he told her to unzip his jeans.

"I don't want . . ." the Prospect began, but Touchy quickly cut him off.

"You'll let her do this" he insisted, "and you'll get every moment on that fuckin' camera, or you'll find yourself suckin' your own dick in the bin out back."

Knowing that any protest was futile, the Prospect closed his eyes as his jeans were undone.

"What the hell do you want?" Crowther demanded to know, as he opened the door and saw Roberts standing there.

"I need to talk to you" Roberts replied. "Can I come in?"

"It's half past three in the morning" Crowther snapped.

"I know" Roberts apologised. "But this can't wait."

Grudgingly, Crowther stepped back and opened the door fully. "Be quiet" he hissed. "Don't wake my son."

Nodding, Roberts walked into the flat, noticing that Crowther's gun was firmly in his grasp when he'd answered the door and that there didn't seem to be any intent for it to be put back into its holster.

"Were you expecting someone else?" he asked, as he was led towards the kitchen.

"Someone knocks on my door at this time of night" Crowther replied, "then it's wise to expect the worst."

"That makes sense" Roberts agreed, as he was offered a seat at the kitchen table. "Especially given what's happened tonight."

Taking a seat opposite him, Crowther looked a little confused. "What's happened?" he questioned.

Roberts feigned surprise. "You haven't been told?"

"Told what?"

"Damn" Roberts muttered. "I thought he'd called you."

"You thought who'd called me?"

"The Chief."

Crowther's confusion increased, so Roberts continued with a sigh.

"It's Wishall" he said. "He was found dead at his house a couple of hours ago."

Almost instantly, the blood drained from Crowther's cheeks.

"You're lying" he stated hesitantly, his grip tightening on his gun.

"I wish I was" Roberts replied, reaching in to his pocket and pulling out an envelope, which he slid across the table. "The neighbours heard a gunshot and this is the scene we found when we got there. It looks as though someone smashed into his garden wall to draw him out, broke into the house through the back and was waiting for him when he went back in."

Slowly, Crowther took the photographs from the envelope and studied each of them, finally letting go of his gun as he cursed under his breath. Roberts noticed his hands begin to shake increasingly as each image was examined until, suddenly, he threw them down and took a deep breath before speaking.

"Do you know who did this?" he asked.

Looking at him, Roberts shook his head. "That's why I'm here" he answered. "I think you do."

"Why the hell would I know?" Crowther snapped, defiantly.

With another shake of his head, it was Roberts' turn to take a deep breath. "Now's not the time to maintain that bullshit" he replied. "You and Wishall weren't exactly subtle when you gave me your friendly piece of advice. Now he's dead and, I suspect, they're going to come after you next."

"Who's they?" Crowther questioned, angrily.

"Come on" Roberts urged. "You think I don't know that you're involved with The Sons and that they want Ben Trowman to take the fall for the murders? I'm guessing the fact the man's still walking free has led to them deciding you're not worth keeping on the payroll."

Silence was all he received in response.

"Look" he continued. "I know we've had our differences, but I don't want to see you suffer the same fate as Wishall. You've got a wife and son to think of, so tell me what you know and let's take the bastards down."

"I don't know what the fuck you are talking about" Crowther hissed, reaching for his gun. "So get the fuck out of my home."

Defensively, Roberts raised his hands and backed away. "This is ridiculous" he sighed.

"Get the fuck out" Crowther repeated.

Letting out a long sigh, Roberts rose from his seat. "I just want to help" he insisted.

"You can help by getting the fuck out of here" Crowther snapped.

"Ok" Roberts agreed, as he allowed himself to be guided towards the front door.

At the end of the hallway, Roberts reached up to unlock the latch, but struggled to open it. "It's stuck" he muttered.

"Don't fuck around" Crowther replied. "Open the fucking door."

"I can't" Roberts stated, reaching up to try again. "The thing's stuck."

Angrily pushing past him, Crowther flicked the latch with ease but, before he could say anything, the door was forced open and Roberts, capitalising on the surprise, wrestled the gun from his grasp.

Lying helplessly on the floor, Steph gave up on her fight to hold back the tears as the agony of the assault seemed to burn through every fibre of her body. Only a few yards away from her head lay the belt that'd been used so viciously to first flay the skin from her back and then to choke her within seconds of unconsciousness.

Even though there was no way she could see the damage, she knew the moisture that soaked her skin was a mix of her own blood and the urine in which she'd been so callously doused and the bruising was rapidly becoming too painful to bear. She hadn't wanted to fight, to put up any sort of struggle, but her muscles had involuntarily contracted against the intrusion, which had only heightened the man's pleasure.

"Stand up" Touchy demanded, as he viciously delivered a kick to her stomach that instantly doubled her up and left her fighting for breath.

"I said, stand up!" he spat, when she failed to comply.

Slowly, she tried to move, but the lack of strength in her arms sent her crashing back to the ground, bringing with it a snigger of mockery.

"You still gettin' this?" Touchy sneered, aiming the question at the prospect who remained by the door. "This shit is internet gold. There's a shit-load of sick bastards out there, who'll pay top fuckin' money to watch this."

The prospect mumbled confirmation and, as Steph looked over to him, she saw that, whilst the camera was still fixed on her, he'd turned his head away from the abuse.

Having re-fastened his jeans, Touchy reached down and grabbed Steph by her hair, pulling her up and sitting her back on the chair, where he re-tied her arms behind her back.

"They'll fuckin' pay top money for the next instalment too" he hissed, as a sick grin spread across his face. "Oh yeah, that's right. Ruckus wants me to kill you, but fuck that. I'm havin' too much fun, so I think I'm gonna keep you."

Tied firmly in the chair, Crowther's head lolled forward as blood dripped from his broken nose, adding to the crimson pool that spread slowly across the kitchen floor. His left eye was already swollen from the beating they'd meted out and two of his teeth had been swallowed in the onslaught. His child's cries could be heard from the bedroom, where Roberts was keeping the man's family away from the horror, yet still he refused to talk.

After landing another punch, Billy lifted Crowther's chin and leaned in close. "This is ridiculous" he stated. "Just tell us where they're holdin' Steph."

Looking at him, Crowther tried to smile. "Fuck you" he replied, his words somewhat distorted by the blood that filled his mouth.

"Jesus Christ" Billy muttered, finally backing away from the detective. "It's no fuckin' good. It don't matter what we do to him, he 'ain't gonna tell us dick."

"Well, what the fuck are we gonna do?" Lee questioned. "We've gotta get somethin' outta this piece of shit."

They both looked at Ben, who'd remained quiet throughout all of this, only staring out of the penthouse flat's window at the street which lay fourteen storeys below. After seeing his anger flare at Wishall's house, they expected his manner to be the same here, but there was a worrying lack of emotion in his expression as he glanced towards Crowther.

"He's gonna talk" he muttered, as he finally moved away from the glass, striding past them and out of the kitchen, returning a few seconds later, dragging Crowther's wife by her hair with Roberts following closely behind, with their baby in his arms.

Paying no attention to the moans that emanated from Crowther, Ben located a sharp kitchen knife in one of the drawers and quickly sliced open the front of her nightie. He used the material to gag her and then positioned her, naked, in front of her husband.

"What the fuck are you doin'?" Billy asked, looking nervously in the direction of both Lee and Roberts.

Ignoring the question, Ben started to gently run the blade across the terrified woman's shaking body. "Tell me where they're holding Steph" he ordered, his words delivered slowly and deliberately.

"She's nothing to do with this" Billy insisted.

"Tell me where Steph is" Ben repeated, again ignoring the man.

"Ben!" Lee exclaimed, stepping towards him, but he stopped when Ben fixed him with an icy glare.

"Last chance" Ben hissed, looking back at Crowther. "Tell me where they're holding Steph."

"You think this bullshit's going to work?" Crowther smiled. "You think I don't know you're nothing but a rank amateur at all this? You don't have the bottle to . . ."

The sentence ended abruptly, as Ben shrugged and turned away from him. He grabbed the woman by the back of the neck and her muffled screams rang out as he cut into her chest.

It took only a couple of minutes for him to carry out his task and, when he'd finished, he stood to the side in order to clearly display the letters SOS that bled profusely from her skin.

"Tell me where Steph is" he asked calmly, as he again ran the blade down her stomach and pushed the tip of the knife between her legs.

Tears started to fall from Crowther's eyes and he cried out as he looked at his stricken wife.

"Fuck you!" he spat.

"Don't do this" Roberts urged, from where he stood in the doorway.

"I'm not doing this" Ben replied, without taking his eyes off the detective in the chair. "He is."

"I can't tell you anything" Crowther moaned.

Staring at him, Ben allowed him a few seconds to change his mind and, when there was no further comment, he shrugged and easily pulled the knife upwards, slicing deeply from her groin to her navel, where he pushed the blade firmly into her stomach.

As the last trace of life ebbed from her, he released his grasp and allowed the body to crumple to the floor at Crowther's feet. Without another word, he strode towards Roberts and took the baby from his arms, before returning to the chair and holding the child in front of his father.

"Tell me where the fuck they're holding Steph" he demanded, as he put the blade to the infant's throat.

"Jesus Christ" both Lee and Billy muttered, turning away from the sight.

Roberts stepped towards him, but stopped as Crowther began to talk.

"She's at their clubhouse" he sobbed. "They're holding her in a storage room at the back of the compound."

"And how many of them are there?" Ben asked, still holding the knife in place.

"I don't know" Crowther answered. "But if you're going to go in there, you'll need to get them away from the place first."

"How do we do that?"

"Take out their casino. They'll send reinforcements to defend it and that'll give you the chance to get in."

Handing the baby back to Roberts, Ben pulled out his gun and aimed it at the detective.

"Please don't hurt my son" Crowther begged.

"I promise you" Ben whispered. "He'll be looked after."

With a sigh, Crowther nodded his acceptance and closed his eyes as Ben pulled the trigger.

Chapter 37

Albert stopped what he was doing and looked towards the counter, where Mary was busy preparing for them to open, and a smile spread across his lips.

"What is it?" she asked, when she saw he was staring at her.

For a moment he didn't reply, as his mind drifted through thoughts of just how much he loved her and how desperately he wanted to keep her safe, but he pulled himself together as her expression became one of slight irritation.

"Why don't you have today off?" he suggested. "I can handle it here. Why don't you go and have your hair done, or meet up with the girls?"

The irritation took on a hint of perplexity. "What?" she questioned, uncertainly.

"I just thought you might like to relax today, that's all" he replied.

"I think you should worry more about getting them tables set up and opening the doors" she scolded, with a shake of her head, as she returned her attention to the cups and mugs on the counter.

Obediently, he continued taking the chairs from the tables and setting them on the floor as his thoughts and heart continued to race. Maybe he was just scaring himself, he wondered; maybe he was just presuming that today would have bad repercussions for them? Maybe things would be resolved and, like Ben and his friends had suggested, they wouldn't hear from The Sons again?

It was no good though. No matter how much he tried to convince himself there was nothing to worry about, the uneasy feeling in the pit of his stomach just wasn't willing to subside.

"Seriously" he stated, again stopping in his task and looking over at Mary. "Why don't you go and enjoy yourself today? I'll look after this place."

Now Mary stopped what she was doing and let out a long sigh of frustration. "Why don't you want me here?" she demanded.

"I just thought that . . ." he began.

"You've already said that" she snapped, cutting him short. "What's going on?"

With a deep breath, he walked towards the counter and tried to lead her round to one of the tables, but she stood firm.

"What's going on?" she repeated, sternly.

For the umpteenth time in the last twenty four hours, Albert found himself agonising over what he was about to do. He didn't want to tell her what Ben had done, or anything about what had happened in their back room the day before, but he realised she wasn't going to just take the day off without a reason and, honestly, he had nothing that might even come close to convincing her.

"Please sit down" he begged. "I have to tell you something."

"You can tell me here" she replied.

"Sit down!" he spat, instantly hating himself for it, but knowing he had no choice.

His tone stung her and she jumped in surprise, before allowing herself to be led towards one of the tables. When they were sat down, Albert took another deep breath and began to tell her everything.

As he spoke, the colour drained from her cheeks and, when he finished, she only looked blankly at him.

"That's why I don't want you here today" he whispered. "I don't think anything will happen, but I don't want to take the risk."

Mary only continued to stare until, eventually, she seemed to have reached a decision.

"Then we both go" she muttered. "We don't open the shop and we stay away until Ben has finished."

"We can't do that" Albert replied. "Ben needs us to act as though nothing happened and, if we close the shop, then they'll know something's wrong."

"We can put a sign up, saying that we're ill?"

Albert shook his head. "That'll be too suspicious" he answered. "We can't afford to do anything that might alert them. If we do, then they'll kill Steph."

"This is ridiculous" she sighed, before taking a breath to say something else, but she stopped herself and stood up.

"Are you going?" he asked, hopefully.

"No" she stated, as she turned and marched through to the back room.

The four young men staggered along the road, each of them fully decked out in smart shirts and trousers and all clearly suffering the effects of a long night spent drinking, which they were determined not to end on account of the sun rising in the sky. As they crossed the road, one of them tripped on the kerb and hit the pavement hard, causing the others to start laughing raucously.

"Fuck off, ya bastards!" he yelled, as his friends tried to pick him up and brush him off.

Further along the street, watching with a mixture of both contempt and mirth, Banjo stood next to Eddie. He didn't enjoy guarding the casino's door like an everyday bouncer but, seeing as he was still recovering from the bullet that nearly killed him, he knew it was the only thing he could get involved in for the time being. Soon though, he figured, he'd have proven he was back up to speed and be allowed back into the drugs business, where the real money was being made, instead of having to watch from the side-lines as his brothers earned big.

"Would you look at these wankers" he muttered.

"What d'ya reckon?" Eddie replied. "Stag party?"

Banjo shrugged. "Could be" he agreed, as the group approached. "Can we help you boys?"

One of the men, the one who'd hit the floor, practically fell into Banjo as he tried to come to a stop in front of him.

"We wanna come in" he slurred, breathing a vile blast of alcoholic air into Banjo's face.

"Come in where?" Banjo questioned, taking a step back from the stink.

The man nodded towards the door. "In there" he mumbled.

Flashing a glance towards Eddie, Banjo shook his head. "I dunno what you're on about" he replied. "There's nothin' in there but a bunch of old office furniture and a shit-load of dust."

"Then why you guardin' the place?" one of the other men asked.

"Who's guardin' anythin'?" Banjo smiled.

"What? You're just stood in the street for no reason?"

"We're stood in the street for none of your fuckin' business."

"Come on" the first man urged. "We know what's in there. Jimmy told us it'd be ok to come down here."

With raised eyebrows, Banjo looked questioningly at him. "You know Jimmy?"

The man nodded eagerly, reaching round to pull a wallet from his pack pocket. "Yeah, we met him tonight" he said, as he showed them the wedge of bank notes that were almost bursting out of the leather. "He said we just had to tell you that he'd said it was ok and you'd let us in."

"How, in the fuck, d'you know Jimmy?"

"We were out with him tonight, in the clubs."

"He was out in the clubs? By himself?"

"Nah, he had a woman with him. I think her name was Emma, or somethin' like that."

Banjo looked at Eddie and then back to the man, as he pulled out his phone.

"I'll check with him" he announced.

Immediately, the man reached out and grabbed his arm. "He went home a few hours ago" he told him. "The two of them were pretty wasted. You don't wanna be waking him up, do you?"

Hesitating, Banjo again looked at Eddie.

"They've got a lot of money" Eddie pointed out. "And they're fuckin' wasted."

"And it's all there to be spent" the man added, with an attempt to wink that, in his inebriated state, looked more like a nervous tic.

After a moment of thought, Banjo put his phone away and gave a nod. "Alright then" he agreed, stepping out of their path and gesturing to the door. "But the first sign of any shit from any one of you and I'm draggin' you all out by the fuckin' balls."

"Got ya" the man slurred, as he stumbled past and in through the door.

It wasn't unusual for the clubhouse to be quiet, especially at such an early hour, but the silence that filled the room was heavy, almost oppressive. There were a few people sat around in the main room, mainly girlfriends and wives of the club's members with a few of their children and a couple of Prospects, who were steadfastly keeping a vigilant eye on everyone.

From where she stood in the kitchen doorway, Sarah saw Dani sitting alone, staring out of the window. She'd been sat like that for a long time, not speaking or even acknowledging anyone, only occasionally checking over the medical supplies she'd been asked to bring, which was a request that, Sarah realised, could only be adding to her worries.

Grabbing two mugs of coffee, she left the kitchen and walked across the room.

"I figured you could use one of these" she announced, placing the drinks on the table as she sat down.

At the sound of her voice, Dani turned to face her and Sarah saw that she'd been crying.

"They'll be ok" she said, although the words felt hollow as she spoke them.

A half-smile told her that Dani appreciated the gesture, even if she did share the same doubt.

"Where's the baby?" Dani asked, clearly trying to compose herself as she took a sip of her drink.

"He's sleeping in one of the dorms. Jason's wife's watching him and trying to get a couple of hours sleep herself."

Dani nodded.

"Why don't you try to get some shut-eye?" Sarah suggested. "You look as though you're ready to drop."

"Even if I wanted to, there's no way I'd be able to sleep now" Dani admitted, looking around at the other people in the room. "I guess I'm not the only one?"

"I guess not" Sarah agreed.

"How often do you think they've been through this?" Dani asked, still looking at some of the wives and girlfriends.

"Oh, more than a few times" Sarah suggested. "It's part and parcel of the life. They're used to all this now."

"Do you think you'll get used to it?"

Sarah shrugged. "I'm kinda used to it already" she confessed. "Lee's always been involved in stuff that's not quite right."

"But he's not been involved in anything like this, has he?"

"No, but it's different for me."

Dani looked a little confused.

"I thought I'd lost him" Sarah explained. "When he hit that bus and ended up in a coma, I came to terms with the fact that he wasn't going to wake up. I accepted he'd gone and, when he did wake, it was like a second chance and this is all just borrowed time."

"But doesn't that make all this worse? Don't you want to make sure that chance doesn't disappear?"

"The second chance is a bonus" Sarah replied, a little bluntly. "What will be, will be."

A gentle nod was all Dani gave in reply, as her mind mulled over the comment.

"But why are you worrying about all this?" Sarah asked. "Ben turned down the Cut, didn't he? When this is over, you and him will be able to . . ."

"There is no me and him" Dani cut in.

Now it was Sarah's turn to look confused. "I'm sorry" she muttered. "I just thought that you two were together."

Dani shook her head. "No" she confirmed. "I don't think anyone will ever take Steph's place in his heart."

"But what if they don't get to Steph?" Sarah questioned. "What if they can't save her? He'll need someone to help him through all that."

Again, Dani shook her head. "If they don't save her," she replied, "then there's nothing that will save him."

"What do you mean?"

"When I first met him" Dani sighed, as a tear slowly rolled down her cheek, "he was special. He was the kindest, warmest man I've ever come across, but I've seen him do things that not even the nastiest of men would consider normal. When they got back here last night, he wouldn't even look at me and none of them would tell me what happened."

The tears started to cascade down her face and Sarah reached out to wipe them away. "Maybe they just want to protect you?" she guessed.

"Or maybe he's gone too far" Dani snapped, pulling away as a trace of anger crept into her grief. "Whatever happened last night, the Ben that came back wasn't the Ben I know."

Sarah looked at her, feeling somewhat helpless.

"Even if they find Steph," Dani continued, her voice breaking under the weight of the words, "I don't think he'll ever be the same."

Burying her head in her hands, Dani's misery reached its crescendo and Sarah quickly moved her chair round the table.

"Let it out" she whispered, pulling Dani into a hug. "And, whatever happens today, there's always a place here for you."

The shout was heard outside the building and Banjo looked instantly at Eddie, before they both turned and ran through the door. Inside, they saw one of the drunken men arguing with a croupier, yelling out that she was a cheat and throwing all the chips from the table as one of The Sons' Prospects grabbed him and pulled him away.

"You stay in here" Banjo yelled at Eddie, as the Prospect dragged the man out of the door, followed by his three friends. "And get that fuckin' table straight."

Out in the street, the Prospect had thrown the man to the kerb and, as the guy sprawled on the floor, he turned to confront the others. One of them threw a punch, which the Prospect easily dodged, landing a blow of his own that sent the guy to the ground, alongside his mate.

"I told you what'd happen if you fucked about" Banjo hissed, taking a swing and connecting easily with a third member of the group, as the fourth backed away.

"What about our money?" the man asked, as his friends picked themselves up.

"What fuckin' money?" Banjo smiled.

"The fuckin' money we exchanged for chips."

Banjo shrugged. "I dunno what you're talkin' about. As far as I can tell, you pricks 'ain't been in here and that's the way it's gonna stay. You got me?"

The man shook his head. "Fuck off!" he hissed. "We put a load of cash in there, we just want it back and we'll go."

"That 'ain't how this works" Banjo replied, calmly. "I suggest you start walkin' away now, while you still can."

"You fuckin' bastards!" the first man screamed, charging at the Prospect and sending them both crashing against the wall.

The two of them grappled, until the man was finally thrown off balance and, when the Prospect turned around, his eyes were wide as blood cascaded from the slit in his throat. He staggered a few steps towards Banjo, whose shock had briefly frozen him to the spot, before his legs gave way and he crumpled to the floor.

Reaching for his gun, Banjo's horror quickly turned to rage but, before he could pull it out, a pistol barrel was pushed on to the back of his head.

"Don't fuckin' move" Jason hissed, having snuck up from behind.

The rest of The Angels of Nemesis surrounded them, as Jason looked at the man who'd slit the Prospect's throat.

"What we got in there?" he asked.

"There's seven croupiers, all women" the man answered, perfectly lucidly, "and there's four members, all of 'em Prospects, watchin' over the floor. The office is up some stairs on the right of the room as you walk in and it don't look like anyone's in there."

Pushing the gun against the back of his head, Jason turned his attention back to Banjo.

"Anythin' else we should know?" he asked, although he knew the answer before it was muttered.

"Fuck off" came the predictable reply.

Jason again pushed at the back of the Banjo's head. "You're gonna take me in there" he told him. "We're gonna go up to the office and you're gonna call your brothers, tell 'em the place is under attack and make sure they bring reinforcements."

"And if I don't?"

The sound of the gun being cocked was all that came in response.

"You" Ethan commanded, as he stormed into the coffee shop and saw two customers sitting in the corner. "Get the fuck out of here, now!"

The couple stared at him, unmoving, until he pulled out a gun and pointed it in their direction.

"I said" he hissed. "Get the fuck out!"

With his gun staying firmly trained on them, he followed them to the door and slammed the lock into place when they'd gone, before turning on Albert, who stood, open-mouthed, at the counter.

"Is your wife here?" he asked.

Albert, his heart racing as abject terror gripped at his core, could only stare at the barrel of the gun. He wanted to say no, he wanted to keep his wife away from this but, before he could say anything, Mary walked through from the back room and stood silently next to her husband, taking his hand in hers and holding it tightly.

"Jimmy and Emily didn't come back to the clubhouse yesterday" Ethan announced.

Neither Albert nor Mary spoke, they only continued to look at him.

"Did they come here?" he questioned.

A nervous shake of his head was all Albert managed in response.

"No?" Ethan snapped. "You're sayin' they didn't come here? Well, can you tell me why not, given Emily called me while they were on their way?"

"Maybe something stopped them from getting here?" Albert suggested, his voice catching in his throat as he spoke.

Taking a deep breath, Ethan shook his head. "I don't think so" he muttered. "From the way you're shittin' yourselves, I'm guessin' they made it without any problems and somethin' happened whilst they were here."

Too scared to speak, Albert only stared back at him.

"Tell me what the fuck happened!" Ethan yelled, striding towards the counter, still with his gun raised.

"Nothing" Mary stammered. "They didn't come here."

"So they just disappeared, did they? They vanished into thin fuckin' air?"

Ethan's phone began to ring, so he pulled it out of his pocket and answered without lowering his gun.

"What?" he bellowed.

His expression changed as the voice on the other end of the phone spoke.

"What?" he questioned again.

This time, as the voice repeated what had been said, he began to shake his head.

"Who've you left there?"

Another pause whilst a response was given.

"Just the fuckin' Prospects? You fuckin' idiots!"

With that, he cancelled the call and re-focussed his attention on Albert and Mary.

"You're fuckin' lyin' to me" he stated.

Albert opened his mouth to speak but, before he could take a breath, Ethan fired a bullet into Mary's skull. He watched her body crumple and, when he looked back across the counter, a second shot quickly put an end to his life.

Chapter 38

"Is this gonna work?" Alex questioned, from the back of the van. "I mean, what if they don't go? What if they just stay put? We've got no chance against 'em all."

"It'll work" Billy reassured him. "The casino makes 'em too much money for 'em to just allow it to be taken out."

Though still unconvinced, Alex fell silent and the four of them continued to watch the gates of The Sons' compound. Occasionally, Lee checked his watch as his concern also grew.

"They should've been gone by now" he pointed out. "Or, at least, some of them should've gone to check on what was happenin'. Maybe Jason's fucked it up?"

Billy shook his head. "No" he insisted. "Jason's a lot of things, but he 'ain't a fuck up. He knows what he's doin' and he'll have the place locked down soon enough."

"But what if he doesn't?" Alex suggested. "We don't know what kind of security they've got at the place. For all we know, he's been grabbed and The Sons are in there, right now, killin' Steph an' waiting for us?"

Immediately realising the comment he'd made, Alex froze and all of them turned to look at Ben, who remained motionless, just staring at the compound's gates.

"Half their club have been taken out" Billy pointed out, keen to get the conversation past the possibility of failure. "Even if they've patched more in, they'll be short of reliable bodies and they won't send Prospects to defend a place that's so important to 'em. Even if they have got wind of Jason's attack, they'll have to send their key members and that'll leave 'em short when we go in."

"But why aren't they goin' yet?" Alex questioned, his nerves winning the battle over common sense.

"I'll give Jason a call" Lee stated, pulling out his phone.

Quickly reaching out to stop him, Billy shook his head. "We can't risk his phone ringin' and givin' him away. We've gotta trust him to do this."

With no more to be said, they continued to watch the compound in silence until, eventually, the gates swung open and a procession of motorcycles, led by Ruckus, were ridden out.

"I didn't see Ethan" Billy muttered, as the club rode away from the parked van.

"Maybe he's stayed in there?" Lee suggested.

Shaking his head, Billy disagreed. "I doubt it. They wouldn't leave their Vice President out of somethin' like this. Maybe he's already at the casino?"

"I'll find out" Ben stated, opening the door and stepping out. "Wait for my signal."

Before any of them had the chance to argue, he slammed the door shut and strode across the road towards the gates, which had now been closed. They watched, speechless, as he approached and there was a collective holding of breath when he hammered on them.

At first, in permanent darkness, the occasional noises she heard meant very little to Steph, other than the fact that they caused her to jump in surprise. Gradually though, she'd grown used to them and the only sounds that worried her were the click of the lock and the door being opened, for they meant that something was going to happen to her. Eventually, as the torment increased in both intensity and regularity, every sound had started to bring with it a sense of panic, every noise brought a heart-stopping moment in which she involuntarily braced herself for whatever torture was to be delivered next.

Somehow, it was worse when nothing happened, when she was left alone after the noise had stopped. That was when the absence of the expected physical abuse provided its own unique, mental barrage as she tried to calm herself. That was when her mind drifted to thoughts of what she may have to endure next, of what sick and twisted ideas were running through the heads of the depraved animals that held her, and it was in those moments that her own imagination proved to be nothing but another enemy.

How long could she continue to endure this? How long could her mind stay whole under this constant turmoil? Was she starting to lose the battle already? Was the weight of fear, pain and sorrow becoming too much to bear? Was there any reason she was even attempting to hold on to sanity? Knowing that death was her only end to all of this and even that was to be denied, she wondered whether allowing her mind to collapse in on itself might offer a last bastion of protection for her remaining days.

The sound of motorcycle engines filtered into the room, a large number of them, judging by the noise and the slight vibration of the floor, pulling her out of her thoughts as her body tensed automatically. She listened as they disappeared into the distance and, when silence once more returned, she bowed her head and let out a desolate groan.

The hatch in the gate slid open and a Prospect's face appeared in the hole.

"What?" he asked, gruffly.

"I'm here to see Ruckus" Ben replied.

"Who?" the Prospect questioned.

"Ruckus" Ben repeated. "Your club's president."

Blankly, the Prospect shook his head.

"Don't act like you don't know who I'm on about" Ben stated. "If Ruckus 'ain't here, then I wanna see Ethan."

Gradually, the Prospect's face took on a resigned expression. "They 'ain't here" he announced, "so why don't you just fuck off?"

His last words had barely left his lips when Ben raised his gun to the hatch and pulled the trigger, burying the bullet in the centre of the Prospect's face.

In the van, the three men watched the display in abject consternation.

"I guess that's the sign" Billy muttered, sardonically, as they jumped out on to the street.

Ben ran back to the van as the gates opened and he barely made it before other Prospects appeared and started firing.

"What the fuck was that?" Lee demanded, angrily, as they all took cover behind the vehicle.

Neither the question itself, nor the manner in which it'd been asked, seemed to register with Ben as he poked his head around and returned fire.

"Ethan's not there" he stated, as a matter of fact.

The shower of bullets from the compound had them pinned down, none of them able to get a clear enough shot in reply to cause any break in the salvo.

"What the fuck are we gonna do now?" Alex questioned.

"Follow me" Ben announced, jumping up and climbing quickly into the van's driver's seat.

The rest of them looked at each other as the engine started and, with the bullets shattering the windscreen, the van started to roll forward.

"Jesus Christ!" Alex hissed, as he, Billy and Lee tried to stay behind the moving vehicle whilst it edged closer to the gates. "The guy's fuckin' lost it!"

"Whether he has or not, it's the only way we're gonna get in there" Billy replied, as he returned fire.

Suddenly, without warning, the engine roared and the van shot forward, leaving the three of them standing in the middle of the street. Ben sped towards the gates and flew through them, momentarily drawing the Prospect's attention to him, allowing Billy and Lee to fire off three key shots that dropped their attackers to the floor.

"Jesus fuckin' Christ!" Alex repeated, as silence quickly fell.

They ran forward, to where the van had come to a stop in the centre of the compound, and pulled open the driver's door.

Billy grabbed hold of Ben as he practically fell out of the seat and he helped him to the ground as he tried to take stock of the man's injuries. He'd taken a bullet to the shoulder, one had grazed his neck and his face and arms were pockmarked with cuts from the shattered glass.

"A couple of them ran into the clubhouse" Ben muttered.

He tried to stand, but Billy forced him back down. "You've gotta rest for a minute" he told him.

Ben shook his head. "No" he hissed. "They'll kill Steph. We've gotta get in there."

Billy tried again to stop him from standing but, as he started to lose that battle, the sound of a motorcycle's engine filled the air and they looked up to see Ethan speeding into the compound.

It'd been the briefest of sounds, so quickly gone that it was questionable whether she'd actually heard it, but Steph was sure it'd been a gunshot. In the darkness, she listened intently for anything more and she flinched when a sudden cacophony of the same sound filled the air, followed by the roar of an engine.

Instantly, her mind was pulled back to the night of the party, when the same sounds had filtered in through the abuse to which she was being subjected and brought the proceedings to an abrupt and violent halt. She cried out as the memory, which she'd tried so hard to bury, forced itself back to the very forefront of her thoughts and, when the door burst open, she screamed her wish for them to just kill her, but the gag merely rendered her words impossible to comprehend.

"What the fuck are you doin'?" a voice yelled out.

"They're here for this bitch," came the reply, "so I'm gonna kill her."

"What the fuck are you talkin' about? How, the fuck, d'you know they're here for her?"

"Because that guy drivin' the fuckin' van is the guy the club have been after, I'm fuckin' sure of it."

"What?"

"He's the guy. Fuckin' whatshisname."

"Ben?"

"That's him!"

Steph's heart froze as the words filtered into her brain, instantly pushing its way through the painful images and atrocious memories. Suddenly, where all hope had been lost, a tiny spark of fight emerged in her soul and, as she heard the click of a gun being cocked next to her head, she tried to scream for the man to stop.

"Don't fuckin' do it, man" the first voice urged. "Ethan's on his way here and he'll fuckin' kill you if you do anythin' to her."

Again, Steph begged for the man to stop.

"He'll fuckin' kill us if they get to her" came the reply.

"If they get to her, then we'll be fuckin' dead anyway!"

Silence hung heavily as the response was awaited and, eventually, the click of the gun's hammer being disengaged brought a gasp from Steph.

"That's gotta be him" the first voice announced, at the sound of a motorcycle's engine. "We'd best get out there. There's only four of 'em and they can't have many bullets left to fire. We'll finish 'em off and then Ethan won't need this bitch anymore. She's his to fuckin' kill."

As Ethan rode in, both Lee and Alex fired at him, but he quickly turned and disappeared around the back of the building. They moved to give chase, but the clubhouse door opened and the two Prospects who'd hidden inside started shooting, sending them back into cover behind the van.

"What the fuck do we do now?" Alex exclaimed.

"We fuckin' calm down" Billy answered, as he tried to stem the bleeding from Ben's shoulder. "Running out there's only gonna get you killed."

"And sittin' here's gonna keep us safe, is it?" Alex snapped. "This is fucked!"

"Calm the fuck down!" Billy repeated.

Bullets started coming from the other side, where Ethan was taking cover behind the clubhouse.

"Fuck!" Alex yelled, as a shot nearly caught him.

"This is gonna be heard by someone" Lee pointed out. "They'll report it and it won't be long before this place is swarmin' with cops."

"Call Roberts" Billy suggested. "See if he can take control from that end and hold 'em off for a bit."

Nodding, Lee pulled out his phone as Ben tried again to stand up.

"Whoa" Billy muttered, as he was easily pushed to the side.

Now on his feet, Ben checked his gun and strode around the van, sending a hail of bullets towards the clubhouse door. One of the Prospects took a shot in the stomach, instantly crumpling him to the floor as the other scurried for cover, but Ben was relentless. As Ethan redirected his fire, Ben continued to stride towards the door, until one of the bullets connected with his thigh and sent him crashing to the ground. Seeing his opportunity, the second Prospect quickly aimed at Ben's head, giving Billy enough of a sight to put him down before he could get a shot off.

"Hold fire!" Ethan yelled, realising he was on his own.

Instantly, Billy, Lee and Alex sent a torrent of bullets towards his hiding place.

"I told you to hold fire!" Ethan screamed, tossing his gun out into the open. "I'm fuckin' unarmed."

"You're fuckin' dead!" Billy yelled back, again firing at the wall.

"If you want Steph, you'll let me take you to her" Ethan shouted. "That's the only way you're getting her."

Lowering his weapon, Billy let out a sigh, as Lee and Alex rushed over to where Ben lay on the ground. "Come out then" he instructed.

Tentatively, Ethan glanced around the corner and then stepped out with his hands raised. He walked slowly towards Billy, opening his mouth to speak as he approached, but Billy smashed him in the teeth with the butt of his gun, before the man could say anything. Grabbing him by the hair, Billy dragged the barely-conscious man towards the clubhouse doors.

"How's he doin'?" he asked, looking at Ben.

"I'm fine" Ben replied as, with Lee's help, he struggled to his feet.

Smiling, Billy glanced down at Ethan and then back to Ben. "I figured you'd wanna do this?"

Without a word, Ben limped forward and dropped to his knees next to Ethan, whose eyes were now wide with fear.

"This is for Sam" he muttered, as he drove his fist into the centre of Ethan's face.

"And these are for the girls" he continued, delivering two more blows.

Now choking on his own blood, Ethan tried to say something, but Ben cut him short as he pushed the barrel of his gun into the man's mouth.

"And this one's for Steph" he muttered, as he pulled the trigger.

The knowledge that Ben was there had given Steph a glimmer of hope, a prayer that this would all be over soon, but the bleak picture the men had painted stripped that from her almost immediately. When the second round of gunfire had echoed around the building, all she could picture was the man she loved being cut down and, as her hands were untied, there was no fight left in her. Free of her bonds, she remained seated with her head bowed as her blindfold was removed, yet she kept her eyes closed, not wanting to see what was about to happen.

"Steph" a voice whispered, gently.

It was a tone she hadn't been expecting, from a voice she didn't recognise and, slowly, she opened her eyes, blinking quickly to regain focus.

"Steph" she heard again, as she looked into the eyes of a man she'd never seen before.

Confused, she looked around the room, until her gaze rested on Ben, who was relying on the door-frame to keep him upright.

With a cry, tears flooded from her eyes and she jumped out of the chair. Her legs were unsteady, threatening to give way, but she fought against them and struggled across the room, until she fell into his arms. She pulled herself tightly against him as her emotions poured out and she savoured his embrace, determined to never let go, but there was something in the way he held her that didn't seem right.

Slowly, she pulled back and looked into his eyes, desperate to immerse herself in the warmth she hadn't believed she would ever experience again, but she recoiled when there was nothing there but a blank, icy stare. With horror, she looked at the blood that soaked his t-shirt, at the deep cuts on his face and at the bandages wrapped around his wrists. She tried to understand the image her eyes were taking in and, when he turned and silently walked out of the door, she immediately tried to follow.

"Let him go" Billy whispered, as he stopped her.

"Get off me" she yelled, as she tried to force her way past him. "Ben!"

Billy remained firm and held her tightly as he looked into her eyes. "Steph" he said, softly. "You need to let him go."

Still, Steph struggled against him, refusing to take her eyes off the doorway until, eventually, Billy managed to draw her focus on to him.

"You need to let him go" he repeated.

Steph looked at him, her eyes filled with confusion and panic. "I need him" she muttered, as more tears fell.

"I know" Billy smiled, "but he's not the man you knew."

The turmoil in her expression increased.

"To find you" he explained, "he's had to do things he never thought possible. He's had to embrace an evil that he won't be able to shake."

"What?" she finally mumbled, again glancing at the doorway.

"The man you love is gone. He's nothing but a shell of the man he was and he knows that, which is why he can't stay." Billy confirmed. "You have to let him go."

With her emotions overcoming her, Steph dropped to her knees and cried out. She continued to stare at the doorway until, with tears flooding down her cheeks, she buried her head in her hands.

"Ben" she sobbed.

Epilogue

MAY 2011

For all the time it'd been there, the bar had never been particularly busy on a Saturday night, not in comparison to other venues. Perhaps it was down to its location? Standing alone and proud amidst offices and small businesses, the place was well away from the central hub of nightlife. Then again, maybe its lack of popularity had more to do with the events that'd occurred nearly a year ago, when murder investigations and rumours of gang warfare had sullied its reputation to the point of driving custom away.

Realistically, it should have closed its doors, cutting losses on ever-decreasing profits, and it'd been on the verge of that, until one of the staff sold her house in order to buy it. Of course, people advised her against it, pointing out the financial folly of her plan, but a stubbornness that saw her now using the office as a makeshift bedroom had carried her through the dissenting voices.

As two men walked in, they stopped in the doorway and glanced around at the emptiness of the room. They engaged in a brief, muttered conversation, before seeming to decide that they'd give the place a try and approached the bar.

"Are you actually open?" one of the men asked, as the barmaid moved to take their order.

"Of course" the barmaid replied.

"It's just that," the man continued, again looking around at the few loyal regulars who sat in small, sparse pockets around the room, "I'd have expected more of a crowd on a Saturday night."

Ignoring the question, the barmaid asked them their order and set about preparing their drinks. When the glasses were placed on the bar, one of the men reached out to put the money in her hand, and was surprised when she immediately backed away from the gesture.

"Don't you want this?" the man chuckled.

The barmaid nodded. "Will you just put in on the bar?" she asked. "I'll take it from there."

Looking at her, the man seemed offended by the request. "Why don't you just take it from me?" he questioned.

With a quick shake of her head, the barmaid refused. "Please just place it on the bar."

"No" the man stated. "Just take it from me."

Continuing to shake her head, the barmaid looked at him but gave no reply.

"Take it" the man hissed.

"Just do what she wants" the man's friend suggested, having noticed the look of fear that flashed in the woman's eyes.

"No" the man snapped. "Why won't she take it from me? Am I dirty or something? Am I that bad she won't even touch my hand?"

"I'm sorry" the barmaid muttered. "It's not you. I just don't take money from anyone."

"Come on" the friend urged. "This is pointless, just do what she wants."

Reluctantly, the man did as she asked and, as the barmaid reached out to take the cash, he shook his head.

"You're not right in the head" he chided. "How the hell can you work behind a bar and refuse to take money from people's hands? If you ask me, I'll bet your manager isn't too impressed with this."

"I am the manager" the barmaid stated.

"Then no wonder there's no one in here" the man chuckled. "Jesus, how the hell do you survive? You can't be making any money."

"I don't keep it open to make money" she replied.

"Then why do it? It's got to be more trouble than it's worth?"

Looking past him, towards the doors, an unmistakeable sadness engulfed her expression. For a moment, it seemed as though she would break down as her eyes moistened, but she took a deep breath and only barely managed to compose herself.

"The Skinning Pit needs to be here" she stated bluntly, still staring at the doors.

The two men looked at each other, somewhat confused by the comment. "Why?" the man asked.

"Because, one day," Steph whispered, "someone who's lost will find his way home."

Acknowledgements

I'd like to thank each and every person who's had to suffer my endless spouting about "my book". Their patience, understanding and general ability to feign interest has always been appreciated and will never be forgotten. Of course, throughout it all, there have been certain individuals who have gone above and beyond in their support and, in no particular order, I would like to reserve special appreciation for the following:

Michelle Phillips, Vince Plater, Sheila Parkes, Andy Middleton, Lee Holman, Kim Hackett, Chris Parkes, Linda Taylor, Bethan Dodd, Donna Doran, Wendy Stanton and Alan Wilson.

Finally, I would like to take a moment to offer thanks to my uncle, Nick Jordan, without whom this novel may never have been completed. I hope I've lived up to your desire for me to achieve something special and that you continue to rest in peace. You'll never be forgotten and you'll never walk alone. Thank you.

Printed in Great Britain
by Amazon.co.uk, Ltd.,
Marston Gate.